A Sweeter Spot

by

Donna Simonetta

Rivers Bend Trilogy

A Sweeter Spot

Cover Art by *Debbie Taylor*

The Wild Rose Press, Inc.
PO Box 708
Adams Basin, NY 14410-0708
Visit us at www.thewildrosepress.com

Publishing History
First Champagne Rose Edition, 2017
Print ISBN 978-1-5092-1258-3
Digital ISBN 978-1-5092-1259-0

Rivers Bend Trilogy
Published in the United States of America

"Being cheated on is no fun.

It happened to me once. Up here," he tapped his forehead, "you know it's not your fault. But here," he tapped his chest over his heart, "you feel like it has to be your fault—like you could've done something to prevent it. But you couldn't have. It's all on him, Maggie. Not you."

She picked a dandelion, whose flower had turned into a puffball and blew on it, scattering the fluff to the wind. "Maybe. Maybe not. But thanks for the support."

She pushed to her feet and took a couple of steps toward the river. Jeff rose and followed.

How could he be so angry at a man he didn't even know? How could this Pierce jerk have slept around on a woman like Maggie? And the prick even made her doubt herself in the process. It was written all over her anguished face.

He stood behind her and gently kneaded her shoulders. He turned her to face him and cupped her face in his big hands.

"This Pierce guy is the biggest fool on earth to go to someone else when he had you at home, Maggie."

She blinked away tears, and he felt his heart constrict. Before he could think it through and decide it was a really bad idea, Jeff dipped his head and captured Magda's lips in a gentle kiss.

Dedication

As always to Leo,
my own Virginia gentleman.
~*~

Thanks to my brother-in-law, Robert,
another native Virginian,
for his help deciding
what kind of truck Jeff would drive.
~*~

And huge thanks to my editor, Melanie Billings,
who is a joy to work with,
and polishes my little pebbles into gems!

"Home, the spot of earth supremely blest. A dearer, sweeter spot than all the rest."

~Robert Montgomery

Chapter 1

A rest stop on the Jersey Turnpike was not in Magda Horvath's plans for tonight, but here she was. She held onto the leash and watched as her dog did her business on the grassy median. The garish orange lights of the Molly Pitcher made it feel like the middle of the day; although, it was well past sunset. She turned the wrist of her left hand to check the time on the watch that had been her dad's college graduation gift to her and smiled as she saw her bare ring finger. *Yup.* The Turnpike might not be where she thought she'd be tonight, but she was happy to be here, instead of the mausoleum of an apartment she'd shared with her ex until about an hour ago.

Once Petunia was done, she lifted the little rescue dog that she'd adopted last year and was rewarded with an adoring gaze from the pup's one eye. Petunia might not be even close to the breed standard for Shih Tzus, but Magda thought she was beautiful. Her fur was curly, so Magda kept it trimmed in a puppy cut. She pressed a kiss to the top of Petunia's velvety little head as she popped the dog in the crate in the back seat of her Mini Cooper.

Once settled in the front seat, she contemplated bringing a bag into the restroom to change out of the suit she'd worn to work, and then she decided she wanted to put more distance between Manhattan and herself, rather than taking the time to get comfortable. She reached over to the passenger seat to pull her cell phone out of her purse, tapped her best friend's number on her contact list, and put the phone on speaker as it rang.

"Hi, Maggie! What's up?"

"Hi, Bethanne. How are you feeling?"

"Fine. Well, as fine as I can be on bedrest, but if lying in this bed for five months is what I have to do for Cisco and our baby, then that's what I'll do. In case I haven't mentioned it five or six hundred times before, I really appreciate you rearranging your life to come down to cover the library for me while I'm out of commission."

Magda cleared her throat. "Yeah. About that. How would you like it if I came down to Virginia a little earlier than we'd planned?"

Bethanne gave a happy shriek. "I'd *love* it! And the people of Rivers Bend might throw a parade in your honor to have their library back in business. When can you be here?"

"According to my GPS—in about four hours with current traffic."

"What? What happened? Are you all right?"

She heard Bethanne's husband murmur in concern in the background, and Magda hastened to explain, "I'm fine, please don't fret—that can't be good for the baby."

"I'm calm. Both of you—stop fussing about me! I'm having a difficult pregnancy, not dying of consumption like Camille!" Bethanne's voice softened as she continued. "What happened, Maggie?"

"I quit M.I. and Pierce. Both without notice."

"Can you quit Mallory International, since your grandmother is Elizabeth Mallory? I thought you were in for a life of indentured servitude to her and that Pierce Allen was part of the bargain."

"It turns out that Pierce has been cheating on me with Taylor Brown. Apparently, I'm a cold fish, and the only reason he was with me was because Grandmommy dearest bought and paid for him."

"Oh, Maggie, I'm sorry. No, actually, I'm not at all sorry. He was a total jerkwad, so I can't even pretend to be sorry, and if it breaks you out of your grandmother's tentacles, all the better, in my opinion."

"I finally realized we had nothing in common, and I was going to break up with him anyway, this just moved things up a couple of weeks."

"How did you find out?"

"I was in the executive ladies room at M.I., bracing myself to tell my boss that I'd be taking a leave of absence to help a friend in Virginia. Luckily, the stalls there are bigger than the whole bathroom in the rancher where my dad and I lived, with actual doors on them, so Taylor and her friend didn't even realize I was there. Taylor didn't hold anything back. B.T.W., for a finishing-school kind of girl, she can be surprisingly crude. Bottom line—there's no doubt she's been sleeping with Pierce and that he's being paid by my grandmother to marry me."

"Wow. Harsh."

"It was a bit of a shocker, but nothing I shouldn't have realized before then."

"Give yourself a break, Maggie. With your dad's illness and passing, you've had a lot on your plate in the last couple of years."

Magda had loved her dad with all her heart. Since her mother died giving birth to her, it had always been her dad and her against the world. Elizabeth Mallory never approved of her parents' marriage, and when her daughter was gone, she ignored her granddaughter for several years. This was fine with Magda, since it meant she got to live a relatively normal life with her dad until high school, when her maternal grandmother came back into their lives insisting she go to the exclusive boarding school that the children of the Mallory family had attended for generations. Magda wanted to stay with her dad, but he'd insisted that he wanted her to have the opportunity to get the kind of education his salary at the helicopter plant wouldn't allow. She went to please him but never fit in with the Pierces and Taylors of that world.

She went on to college and library school, where she met Bethanne. When her dad fell ill, she'd wanted the best possible care for him, so when her grandmother slithered in like the serpent in Eden, Magda sacrificed herself and took her deal. She moved to Manhattan and took a job running the corporate libraries at M.I. In return, her grandmother arranged for the highest quality care available for the son-in-law she despised.

She swallowed hard at the painful memories, and replied, "That's true, but I still feel like an idiot. About all of it."

"You're not an idiot. You're a good person, who was in an untenable position. You did the best you could at the time. But, I'm glad you realized what Pierce was like before you actually married him. I wasn't looking forward to standing up at your wedding when the minister asked 'does anyone know why this couple can't be joined'…"

Her husband said something in the background, and Bethanne laughed. "Okay, maybe I was looking forward to it a little bit. Seeing the look on Pierce's snooty face would've been worth it, but I was worried about you."

Magda laughed. "It would've been the talk of Grandmother's social circle for years! But, worry no more; I'm on my way to Rivers Bend. After I quit M.I., I went back to the apartment, packed up my stuff, got Petunia, and left my ring with a note for Pierce. He's out of town on business, and I didn't want to wait until he got back to do it in person. A little chicken, on my part, but I couldn't face my grandmother or him just yet."

"You need to do what you need to do for yourself, for once in your life, Maggie. I think leaving tonight was a good idea."

"I know there was a cabin available for me in a couple of weeks, is there somewhere for me to stay before then, since I'm coming early?"

"Hold on, let me consult with Cisco."

Bethanne's husband, Francisco Cardoso, and his business partner, Jefferson Braden, had played in the NFL together. When they retired, they started a business together in Jeff's hometown—the Corporate Retreat at Rivers Bend. They said that Magda could stay in one of their guest cabins, when she came down to run the library during Bethanne's medical leave.

She heard a muffled conversation between Bethanne and Cisco, and then Bethanne came back on the line. "Cabin Five is actually available tonight. Cisco is going to go over and hide the key under the mat for you. Jeff is out of town, picking up his daughter from her grandparents' house, but we'll call him tomorrow to let him know you're there early."

"That's great, Bethanne! Thank you for everything. I don't know what I'd be doing right now if I didn't have you."

"Hey, what are besties for, right?"

Magda blinked back tears, her voice thick when she replied. "Right."

****

Jeff Braden tossed his daughter Sam's suitcase into the trunk of the car and ruffled her honey blonde hair with easy affection.

"Ready to head home, Peanut?"

Sam smiled and her awkward eleven-year-old appearance transformed for an instant, giving Jeff a glimpse of the beautiful woman she'd be one day. Man, he wasn't looking forward to the time when the boys realized his little girl was a beauty. Of course, being a former NFL player wouldn't hurt when it came time to subtly let the boys who came sniffing around Sam know that he was a force to be reckoned with—a six-four, two hundred and twenty pounds of muscle father from hell.

Sam closed her lips over her braces self-consciously under her father's gaze. "What? Do I look weird? Why are you staring at me like that?"

Jeff smiled, and little lines crinkled at the corner of his gray eyes. "I was just thinking about how beautiful you are."

"Dad!" Her embarrassment turned the word into two syllables. She turned red and rolled her eyes as she got into the car but couldn't completely hide her pleasure at his words.

Jeff looked back at the tidy brick Colonial where Sam's maternal grandparents lived and shook his head. He knew they were distant and none too fond of him, but couldn't they tear themselves away from their daily cocktail hour long enough to see off their only grandchild? He remembered when he brought Sam down here the week before. His mother, sisters, brother, and Sam's cousins all turned out to say goodbye. They all stood on the front porch and waved until the car was out of sight, but this set of grandparents wouldn't even cut into martini time long enough to wave out the front window. He ran one of his hands through his perpetually messy brown hair and got into the car.

"Thanks for coming to get me a week early," Sam said.

Jeff rested his right arm on the back of the seat and turned to look out the rear window as he backed out of the driveway.

"No problem. I've missed you, Peanut; I'm happy to have you home. The place always seems empty when you're away." He winked at her as he turned to face forward to drive away from his former in-laws' house. "At first it's pleasantly peaceful and quiet, but after about ten minutes, I miss all your ruckus."

They drove along in silence for a few minutes before Jeff asked as casually as he could, when the curiosity and worry were about to kill him, "Want to tell your old man why you wanted to come home early?"

Sam shrugged and looked out of the passenger window. "I was homesick, I guess. I missed Grandma Joyce and her horses, and going riding with Uncle

Jason and my cousins."

"Fair enough." Jeff eased the car from the on-ramp into the highway traffic. "I just wanted to make sure everything was okay. Y'know, that your grandparents treated you right."

Sam twisted her mouth as she thought before answering. "They weren't mean to me or anything, but I didn't feel like they wanted me there. Grandmother Evelyn kept telling me how much more beautiful my mother was when she was my age. Mom was Little Miss Fayetteville or something."

Jeff gripped the wheel so tightly he feared it would break apart in his hands, and he ground his molars together. He tried to keep the anger out of his voice. "Your mom was a looker, but you're every bit as pretty. Plus, you're smart, funny, and kind. You're one of the best people I've ever known, Samantha Jane Braden."

Sam turned her head toward him. He glanced at her for a second and could see gratitude and disbelief at war in her teary, sapphire blue eyes, that looked so much like her mother's, in spite of whatever line of bull that her grandparents were sending her way. Sam blinked rapidly to try to stem the tears and turned to look out the window. She cleared her throat. "Thanks, Daddy. You're not so bad yourself."

Jeff laughed. "High praise indeed. Seriously, Peanut, I don't tell you nearly often enough, but you're one in a million. I'm the luckiest guy in the world to have you as my daughter."

He heard Sam sniffle, and she turned her head to try to hide her tears from him. He turned up the car radio to help her keep her dignity.

After a few minutes, she asked, "Where's your

truck? Why are you driving Bethanne's car?"

"Francisco asked me to take it. Since Bethanne might be laid up until the baby gets here, she won't be using it, and cars need to be driven to keep running efficiently. Plus, I thought it would be more comfortable for you than my old truck."

Sam shook her head in disbelief. "Gosh. The baby isn't due for months. I can't imagine having to stay in bed so long."

"No, my little live nerve end, I don't reckon you could. But Cisco and Bethanne have been waiting a long time to have a baby. They'll do whatever it takes to make sure everything is okay. We'll just have to be sure to visit her lots to keep from going stir crazy."

"I'll go to see her every day until I go back to school."

"That'll be nice for Bethanne. And by the time you head back to school in September, her friend, Magda, should be here to run the library for her until Bethanne's back on her feet."

"She must be a good friend—that's really nice to do."

"It is," Jeff agreed. "She'll be down in two weeks. Cisco and I thought she could stay in Cabin Five."

Jeff and Sam lived with their housekeeper, Mrs. Wilson, in the renovated plantation house that was the center of the Retreat. Francisco and Bethanne lived in a cottage on the grounds but were in the process of building a bigger place for their growing family. The Retreat had a scattering of cabins for guests to stay in, as well as some hotel style rooms in a wing of Jeff's sprawling house.

"I wonder what she's like. I hope she's nice."

"If she's friends with Bethanne, she must be a good person. And I hear she has a dog," Jeff said.

Sam's eyes grew wide and she grinned. She'd been angling for a puppy for almost a year. Jeff figured he'd break down soon and get her one, even though he knew he'd end up doing most of the work.

Sam bounced in her seat. "A dog? Really? It'll be so much fun to have a dog around! I can help her with it. Then you'll see just how responsible I would be with a pet."

Jeff smiled at his daughter, with his heart in his kind eyes. "It's gonna be great having you home, Peanut."

His words and the obvious sincerity behind them seemed to cheer her up—or maybe it was just the hope that he was weakening about getting a puppy. Either way it warmed his heart when she forgot her hated braces and flashed a bright smile his way. "Thanks, Daddy. I missed you, too."

Chapter 2

Almost home. Jeff sighed with satisfaction as he turned off Route 15 onto the country road that wended its way to Rivers Bend, Virginia. The cool breeze from the air conditioner blew on his face, and he had the radio tuned to his favorite country music station but with the volume turned down low, so as not to disturb Sam. When she'd fallen asleep a hundred or so miles back, he needed the music to help keep him awake while he drove.

He yawned and realized Bethanne's car still had that new car smell. Cisco and she had bought it right before they found out she was finally pregnant. His friends had been trying for years to have a baby to no avail. Everyone was overjoyed when Bethanne announced she was expecting. But then last week the baby decided he wanted to see the world almost five months early, and now the doctors had her on bed rest, possibly for the rest of her term.

A quick glance at the odometer told him he'd put more miles on the sedan in this one trip than Bethanne had in the short time she'd been able to drive it. Oh well. When the littlest member of the Cardoso family got here, and Jeff squelched any fear that the baby would arrive in any way other than on time and healthy, this car would get a workout.

As a single parent, Jeff felt as though he was

always chauffeuring Sam somewhere: school, horseback riding, friends' houses, the mall. Not that he regretted a minute of his time—Sam was a gift for which he was always grateful.

His attention drifted briefly off the road to look at his daughter, who was curled up in the passenger seat. Wrapped up in the blanket he brought for her, she'd wedged the pillow he'd supplied between her head and the window. He watched her sleep for a second, the way he used to when she was a baby, and then turned his eyes forward to watch the road.

From the very first time he'd seen her on the ultrasound screen, his daughter had been the most precious thing in his life. He knew lots of guys wouldn't have been happy to find out their girlfriend was pregnant in their senior year of college. Especially a guy like him, who'd just been signed in the draft to play tight end for an NFL team after graduation.

And he had to be honest; when Crystal first told him she was pregnant, it threw him for a loop, but family had always been the center of his world, and he couldn't be sorry about the new life they'd made. He *did* wonder how exactly they'd made said new life when Crystal was on the pill, but those were the days before he realized how devious and manipulative she could be to get what she wanted. A truth about their only child that Crystal's parents never acknowledged.

He grasped the steering wheel a little tighter and frowned as he remembered what his daughter told him earlier. He didn't understand why Crystal's parents couldn't just love Sam. Yes, their daughter was dead—killed in a car crash when Sam was only a baby—but they still had their granddaughter. And, no, he hadn't raised her to be a pageant girl like her mama had been, but Sam was so many things Crystal hadn't been. His daughter was open, honest, loving, loyal, and sharp as a tack. Instead of appreciating all those things about Sam, her maternal grandparents denigrated them. It was like they resented the little girl for living, when their daughter hadn't.

Well, he would never make Sam visit them again if she didn't want to go. She had plenty of family here in Rivers Bend to love her. He put on the turn signal out of habit, even though there wasn't another vehicle around for miles, and turned into the long, wooded drive to their home. He wondered if Sam would wake up when they stopped, and if she didn't, if he should wake her or just carry her to her room like he had when she was younger.

As his headlights swept through the woods, he was surprised to see them reflect off a parked car at one of the guest cabins with a view of the Potomac River. He slowed to a stop as he peered through the windshield into the night. There was a square yellow light visible through the trees. Huh—there was a light on in Cabin Five. No one was supposed to be in it tonight. There was a group staying at the main house, which was set to leave tomorrow. And then the Civil War re-enactors, who were staying at the Retreat rather than roughing it in the fields while they recreated the Skirmish of Rivers Bend, weren't due to arrive until Friday afternoon.

"What the hell?" he muttered.

Sam stirred beside him. "Are we home?" She blinked and peered through the windshield. "Why are we stopped? What's up, Daddy?"

"Don't know, Peanut. It looks like there's someone

in Cabin Five, but no one is scheduled to be there until day after tomorrow."

She covered her mouth as she said through a jaw-breaking yawn, "Francisco would know what's going on."

He glanced down at the clock illuminated on the dashboard. "It's almost midnight. I don't want to call and wake up Bethanne."

Sam sat up straighter and said with excitement, "Let's go investigate."

He smiled. His daughter had been on a serious Nancy Drew reading binge of late, and she seemed eager to do a little sleuthing of her own.

"We don't know who's there, Peanut. No way I'm taking you into that kind of situation in the middle of the night. I'll drop you at the house, and you can go in and get ready for bed while I head back here to check things out."

He put the car back in gear and pulled forward as he spoke.

His daughter shook her head vigorously. "I've been sleeping for hours. I feel wide-awake. I'll go with you. You might need my help."

Jeff grinned at his peanut of a daughter, thought of the athlete's build he retained even after his retirement from pro ball, and wondered how the little spitfire thought she'd be able to protect him.

They got out of the car and met at the trunk. He grasped his daughter by her shoulders and gently steered her to the welcoming lights on the verandah-style porch, which stretched the considerable length of the two-story plantation house.

"I'll be just fine, Peanut. I'm sure it's nothing.

Maybe someone decided they'd rather stay in a cabin than at the main house, and Cisco changed their room assignment. No need for both of us to go. You head on in, and I'll be back before you know it."

Sam folded her arms across the daisy printed on the front of her pink T-shirt and set her stubborn jaw, a trait his mother insisted she inherited from him. Jeff didn't want her coming with him. It was unlikely to be anything dangerous, but he didn't know who was in the cabin or why they were there, and he was damned if he'd expose his child to even the most remote hint of danger. Even if she did fancy herself a pint-sized girl detective like her fictional idol.

"Go inside, Sam. I'm not going to ask you again."

"Fine," she huffed. "But you have to come and tell me what's going on when you get home."

"Deal. As long as you're not asleep." He grinned and shook her tiny hand to seal their deal, and watched her go inside before he turned to lope down the path.

****

Magda put a bowl of water on the red-and-white checkerboard floor of the cabin that was to be her home for the next few months. Petunia lapped up the cool water eagerly. The noise of her tongue splashing the water around and the persistent buzz of crickets, or cicadas, or some other kind of bug she knew nothing about—she felt like such a city girl here in the woods!—were the only sounds to break the silence of the night. She thought she heard a car on the main drive a little while ago. It must have been a guest returning to the Retreat after a night on the town. Although, from what she saw when she got to Rivers Bend tonight, the town rolled up its sidewalks after dark. The only place open was a 24-hour gas station and minimart, where she stopped to top off her gas tank and buy a soda.

She took a sip of her drink as she looked around. It was rustic and cozy. The cabin was a traditional log one, so the interior walls were the same timber that made up the exterior ones. Aside from the cheery linoleum squares in the miniature kitchen, the floors were wide pine planks. The furniture in the living room was made of solid wood and had a rough-hewn appearance. The red cushions, and red-and-white checked pillows on the sofa and chairs looked overstuffed and comfortable. Magda longed to sink into one of them and rest her eyes, but she still had to unload her car.

With a weary sigh, she took another sip of her diet cola. Petunia finally stopped slurping up the water. That little dog had to be part camel. She lifted her head from the water bowl and minced over to Magda with a cheery wave of her tail. She gazed up at her mistress. Water dripped from her whiskers, and her liquid brown eye was worshipful.

"Who's the best dog in the world? You are, Miss Petunia."

The Shih Tzu's compact body wriggled as she wagged before she moseyed over to her hot pink and black leopard print dog bed, which Magda already placed next to the fireplace in the living room.

Magda had been so excited to see an honest-to-goodness wood-burning fireplace in the cabin; although, it was too hot tonight to enjoy it. Gracious, it was after midnight and the air was still sultry! Oh well. It was Virginia in August; she supposed heat and humidity were to be expected.

She walked to the thermostat next to the fireplace to lower the temperature on the air conditioner and thanked God for the modern conveniences in the cabin. She noticed the two framed and autographed football jerseys, which flanked the fireplace. One had the name Cardoso on it, and belonged to her friend Bethanne's husband. She met the handsome Brazilian when he came to visit Bethanne at graduate school. He'd been a soccer player in his native land but came to the states for university and was snapped up as a kicker for his college football team. He went on to play in the NFL, and that was what led him to Bethanne. Her brother's best friend played ball for the same team. He brought Francisco home to Rivers Bend once, and the rest was history. Magda remembered Bethanne telling her it was love at first sight. The way Bethanne described the feeling when she met Francisco was one of the myriad reasons Magda knew she wasn't in love with Pierce. Her grandmother had thrust them together, and she'd been lost and lonely after her father's death, so she allowed it to happen.

She looked at the jersey in the frame on the other side of the fireplace. It had the name Braden on it, and it belonged to the man who introduced Bethanne to her husband. On the phone tonight, Bethanne said Jeff Braden was out of town doing something for his daughter, and she'd probably meet him in the next couple of days. Since they'd all be living together on the grounds of the Retreat, Magda hoped he'd be as nice as Francisco.

She froze with the straw in her mouth as she heard a sound from outside that was most definitely not crickets. It sounded like the crunch of gravel, as if someone were coming up the path to her cabin. Unless they had mutant crickets here, the likes of which were usually only seen in movies on the Syfy channel, a person was approaching her cabin. It had to be her imagination. Who could be coming here at this hour? But when Petunia lifted her head and growled low in her throat, Magda knew it wasn't her imagination.

She might not be a country girl, but she didn't think anyone with good intentions would be walking through the woods at this hour of the night. She placed the Styrofoam cup on the mantel over the fireplace. Her heart pounded and wide-eyed, she searched the room for some sort of weapon to fend off irradiated crickets, or a human intruder, which was actually the more frightening option to Magda.

Wouldn't it be just her luck to live in New York City for months, and never even have her purse snatched, only to be murdered here in Middle-Of-Nowhere Virginia?

Her eyes lit on the wrought iron set of fireplace tools, and she saw a potential weapon. She grasped the handle of the one closest to her and whipped around to face the front door. She saw a huge shadow and heard steps clump up the two stairs that led to the entrance. She braced herself and tried to wield the fireplace tool in the most menacing manner possible as Petunia jumped out of her bed and barked frantically.

Chapter 3

As Jeff approached the cabin, he noticed a white Mini Cooper parked out front. He looked into the car and saw it was jammed with suitcases and what appeared to be a crate for a mini-sized dog. He twisted his head to try to see the license plate in the ambient light, which came through the door of the cabin. New York plates. The cute little car packed with designer luggage and a crate for what was probably a matching designer dog, didn't seem to be the ride of choice for a desperado on the lam.

Who one earth could be in the cabin, and how did they even know it was buried here deep in the woods near the river? He shrugged and climbed up the cabin steps to the small porch with its two Adirondack chairs and table between them. At his approach, the sharp yapping of a small dog joined the symphony of chirping crickets. He paused at the screen door and rapped on the wooden frame with his knuckles. The dog's barking increased in volume and intensity.

"Hello," he called out over the racket. "Who's here?"

He peered into the door and saw a petite woman, clutching a fireplace tool. A tiny dog stood bravely in front of her and barked as if it were a pit bull, instead of the kind of dog that wore a little barrette on its head. The woman certainly didn't look like a desperado. She was dressed in an expensive-looking white silk blouse and a pale pink linen skirt. He glanced around the room and saw the matching suit jacket draped over the ladder-back of one the kitchen chairs. A pair of pink do-me pumps were discarded on the floor next to it. She wouldn't look so tiny with those babies on her feet. But why was he even thinking about her sexy footwear? She wasn't a potential hook-up, she was a trespasser—and one who looked ready to do him harm.

Her voice sounded frightened and a little squeaky when she answered him. "The better question is who are you?"

He pulled the screen door open and said as he stepped over the threshold, "I'm the owner of this cabin, which is supposed to be empty tonight. So, I see your 'who are you,' and I raise you a 'what are you doing on my property?'"

The dog's barking now alternated with a growl that seemed too deep to be coming from such a little pooch.

She thrust the fireplace tool at him with menace. "Don't come any closer. I know the owner, Francisco Cardoso, and you're not him."

Jeff held up his hands in the classic "I'm harmless and unarmed" gesture. "No. I'm not Francisco. I'm his business partner, Jefferson Braden. How do you know Francisco?"

The woman narrowed her eyes, which he happened to notice were the exact same color blue as cornflowers. "I happen to know Jeff is out of town with his daughter tonight. So try again, bub."

Bub? Were they in a movie from the 1940s? He didn't know why this woman managed to both attract and amuse him, but he really needed her to put down the fireplace tool.

"We just got home and saw the lights on in here. I came over to investigate."

She furrowed her brow, and bit her lush bottom lip, like maybe she was thinking about believing him, but then her fear seemed to win out and she tightened her grip on the fireplace tool.

"I can show you my driver's license." He lowered one arm to reach for the wallet in his back pocket. He flipped it open to his driver's license, and tossed it gently to her. When it landed on the floor at her feet, the dog sniffed it with suspicion.

The woman bent slightly at the knees to look at it. Her lips formed an 'O'.

"You *are* Jeff Braden. I'm so sorry! Bethanne told me you'd be away tonight, and she'd let you know tomorrow morning that I came in early. Hush, Petunia."

Jeff assumed the last words were intended for the dog and not for him, especially as they made the barking cease.

A wide smile creased his face. "You must be Bethanne's friend, Maggie. Welcome to Rivers Bend. Is it okay for me to put my arms down now, or do you intend to sweep me into submission?"

****

Magda looked down at the tool she brandished like a weapon, and realized she'd snatched up the little broom for brushing out the fireplace, and not the more fearsome poker she thought she wielded.

"Well, darn," she said with disgust as she put it back in the stand with the other tools. "Some weapon I chose. Lucky for me you turned out to be a friend and not a foe."

Jeff cocked his head, as he considered the broom. "I don't know. If you whomped somebody on the head with the non-broom end, the wrought iron would do some serious damage. So you are Bethanne's friend, Maggie, right?"

An errant curl had escaped her grandmother-approved French Twist, and she tucked it behind her ear. She smiled and said, "I am. I'm Magda Horvath. Bethanne and her family are the only ones who call me Maggie. That's how I know you are who you say you are. Even without the photo I.D." She picked up the wallet and tossed it to him. He caught it one-handed and tucked it into the rear pocket of his shorts.

"Sorry. Do you prefer being called Magda?"

She rolled her eyes. "As long as you don't call me Elizabeth, or any of its corresponding nicknames, I don't really care."

"Okay," he drew out the word. "I don't know why I would ever call you Elizabeth, but since it means that much to you, I'll be sure I don't. How about I go with Maggie? You look like a Maggie to me."

He squatted and held out his hand to the dog. "Who's this little cutie?"

Maggie readied herself to intervene in case Petunia snapped, as she sometimes did with strange men. "Oh! Don't do that. She doesn't like…" She abruptly stopped talking as Petunia walked to Jeff, sniffed his hand, and wagged.

Jeff seemed to realize the wagging was an invitation to pet her, and he scratched Petunia behind her ears. The little dog wagged so hard that Maggie was afraid her back end was going to break off, and her one eye was closed in bliss. As Magda watched her dog bask in Jeff's attention, she had no doubt he could use those big hands to bring any woman to a state of bliss.

When he smiled up at her, his eyes crinkled, and Maggie could swear her heart stopped for a moment. He wasn't handsome in the way Pierce was—all delicate bone structure and whippet thin. Combined with his baby-fine blond hair, Pierce was almost pretty. Jeff was all man. Tall and muscular with his messy brown hair that looked in serious need of a cut. He wore a sloppy T-shirt and olive colored cargo shorts, but the baggy clothes did nothing to hide the hard body underneath. His nose was just a little too big and a tad crooked, as though it had been broken. His tan skin stretched across strong cheekbones, but it wasn't the kind of orange tan you got in a booth. It was the tan of a man who spent a lot of time outdoors. But it was those gray eyes, with the little laugh lines around them that really drew her to him. They were full of intelligence and kindness—now that he knew she wasn't a trespasser.

"She doesn't like what?"

Magda shook her head in amazement, "Men. She'd been abused before I got her, and she doesn't usually like men."

He grinned as the dog rolled on her back to reveal her belly for rubbing. He obliged, and winked at Magda. "Maybe she's just been around the wrong men."

Her and me both. Magda felt her knees go weak at his playful expression. Cold fish, indeed! Watching this man pet her dog had her hot enough to melt the zipper on her skirt. Pierce could take his opinion of her steaminess factor and stick it where the sun don't shine, because her physical reaction to Jeff made Magda think any problems they'd had in the bedroom were definitely *not* because she was a cold fish.

She started when she realized the object of her lustful observations was speaking to her.

He stood as he spoke and smiled at Magda. "So what do you think? What do you want to do?"

She blinked owlishly. What did she want to do? Jump his bones, that's what, but that couldn't possibly be what he was talking about, unless he was a mind reader. And even then, this man was totally out of her league. She wasn't the kind of woman that men like Jeff Braden looked at twice.

"Do? About what?" She finally managed to ask.

"About the cabin?" He still smiled, but he drew his brows together and looked confused by her response.

She blushed and stammered out what she feared was a lame excuse for her inattention. "I'm sorry. I totally zoned out there. It's been a long day. What did you say about the cabin? Francisco told me it was okay for me to stay here. He even left the key under the mat for me."

His eyes softened. "I know how you feel. I've been driving all day, too, and I'm beat. What I said was Francisco didn't realize someone has reserved the cabin for the weekend. They're checking in on Friday." He looked at the bulky, rubber dive watch on his wrist, "Which is officially tomorrow, since it's one o'clock. We've got some Civil War re-enactors staying at the Retreat this weekend, and one of them called my cell today to ask for another cabin. I haven't had the chance to tell Cisco yet. You can stay here tonight, but you'd have to move tomorrow anyway, so I thought you might want to stay at the main house tonight, too. Rather than unpacking your car here and then having to pack up again tomorrow. My daughter and I have a guest room, and you and Petunia are welcome to it."

"I'd hate to impose on you. Maybe I should stay here tonight, and then stay with Bethanne and Francisco for the rest of the weekend."

"Your call, but their place is tiny. You'd be riding the sofa, and Sam and I have a bed for you. We really don't mind at all."

She narrowed her big eyes. "Are you sure? Especially since I have a dog?"

He grinned. "The dog will actually be a major selling point for my daughter."

"Well if you're sure..." she said with uncertainty.

"I'm sure."

He bent and scooped up Petunia. "We could take your car back now, and I'll park it in the garage for you." He winked conspiratorially. "With Johnny Reb about to overrun the place this weekend, I can't be responsible for your safety if they see those New York license plates."

She smiled, and dipped into a curtsey. "I hope Billy Yank would come to my rescue in that situation."

Jeff held his hand over his heart and pretended to stagger back, "Cute as a bug, and smart as a whip. Where have you been all my life, darlin'?"

She felt her cheeks grow hot at his words and just knew she was blushing. She busied herself emptying Petunia's water bowl in the kitchen sink. She'd never been skilled at this sort of flirtation, and her time with Pierce had done a serious number on her self-confidence. She tried to sound light when she replied,

"Oh, I've been around. Just ask Bethanne."

"I'll be asking her about you, and where she's been hiding you all these years. Don't doubt it for a minute."

****

As Magda started her car, she glanced out of the corner of her eyes at Jeff in the passenger seat. She smothered a smile at the sight of his tall frame folded into her little car, with Petunia cradled in his arms. The dog rested her cheek on his bicep and gazed out the window into the night. Magda couldn't believe the canine hussy.

"What are you smiling about?" Jeff asked.

"Petunia. I can't get over how she's taken to you. Every time Pierce and she were in the same room, she'd growl and the fur would stand up on her back."

"Maybe she was trying to tell you something about this Pierce guy," Jeff suggested. "My family owns a horse farm, so I grew up with animals, and in my experience, dogs are excellent judges of character."

"And since she adores you, Petunia *must* be a good gauge, huh?" Magda teased.

"Interpret her actions how you like, but I'm thinking she's highly intuitive." Jeff chuckled as Petunia rubbed her face against his arm in a contented manner.

Lucky dog. Magda thought she'd probably be doing the same thing if she were in Petunia's position.

"So," he asked with studied casualness, "who's Pierce?"

Magda pursed her lips and took a deep breath. "My ex-fiancé."

"I'm guessing Petunia was right about him. Y'know, since he's an '*ex*' fiancé?"

26

"She sure was," she replied without even looking his way.

"We all make mistakes. Lord knows I've made more than my share. How long has he been an 'ex'?"

Magda looked at the clock on the dashboard as they pulled up the circular drive in front of the main house. "A little over eight hours."

Jeff turned as much as he could, given the way he was wedged into the small seat. "Wow! So, does that have anything to do with why you're here two weeks early?"

Magda turned off the ignition and unbuckled her seat belt. She didn't look at Jeff, "As a matter of fact, yes. I didn't think there was much reason for me to hang around in New York."

Since Petunia was nestled in the crook of his right arm, Jeff reached for the door handle with his left. "Well, New York's loss is Rivers Bend's gain."

****

The apartment was silent as a tomb when Pierce stepped through the front door. Magda must be sleeping. If she were awake there would be music blasting or the television would be on. And that little one-eyed rat she called a dog would be growling at him as if he were a cat burglar. He shuddered with distaste. Honestly, he only kicked it that one time, and the vile creature never forgot.

He went straight to the master bedroom and stopped short when he found it empty, with the bed neatly made. He looked around in confusion.

"Magda?" His imperious voice echoed through the empty apartment.

Where could she be? Not out with friends, that's

for sure. Pierce had followed Elizabeth Mallory's orders to the letter, and he had isolated Magda from any old friends she had left in Connecticut.

Puzzled, he wandered back to the entryway. The light from the crystal chandelier glinted off something on the hall table. He frowned as he picked up Magda's diamond engagement ring and turned it in his long, thin fingers. His hand stilled as he read the note, which he found under the ring.

He felt frozen in place. Except for his heart, which was racing like it was in the Grand Prix at Monte Carlo. "No, no, no. You can't leave me. Your grandmother will cut off her payments to me. And I so need her financial assistance."

His pale blue eyes opened wide as a thought occurred to him. "Oh, God. Will I lose my job at M.I.?"

The ring clattered on the table as it fell from his fingers. He picked up the note and clutched it in both hands as he read it aloud again to the empty apartment. It was certainly a brief missive, considering it turned his world upside down.

"We've made a mistake…blah, blah, blah….end things now before we make a bigger one by getting married…prattle, prattle…gone to help a friend…blather, blather…signed Magda."

He took a deep breath and exhaled through tight lips. *Friend? What friend? Here in the city?* The little bitch gave no indication where she was going, and he really needed to know, so he could find her and persuade her to take him back. Preferably, before her grandmother learned she was gone.

He crumpled the note and threw it across the hall with force. "Sorry, Magda darling, but I owe too much money to too many unpleasant people to let you go. I will find you, and you will marry me, if it's the last thing you do."

He smiled as he warmed to the thought. "And all the better for me if it is. I'd inherit your lovely trust fund, and I wouldn't have to share my bed with you. Yes. Indeed. The last thing you do. Certainly something to think about."

****

Jeff peeked into his daughter's room. He smiled, stepped back, and closed the door with a gentle snick. The munchkin was out like a light. So much for her protestations about being wide-awake when she tried to wheedle him into taking her to the cabin.

He'd taken a couple of steps when the bathroom door popped open, and a little blonde whirlwind hustled out and straight into him. He chuckled, and put his hands on Magda's shoulders. He could feel the warmth of her skin through the thin nightshirt she wore.

"Whoa there," he whispered. "Where's the fire?"

"Sorry," she murmured back. "I needed to get ready for bed, but I didn't want to leave Petunia alone for too long. I was afraid she'd bark and wake up your daughter."

Jeff looked her up and down before he released her shoulders with reluctance. Her blonde hair was out of the severe hairdo from earlier, and riotous curls tumbled to her shoulders. Her face was scrubbed and devoid of make-up, but she looked fresh and adorable to him. Two adjectives that didn't apply to any woman he'd ever dated. He laughed when his perusal got to her sleepwear.

"Love the nightshirt," he whispered.

It had a cartoon of a woman behind a counter handing a stack of books to a man, and the words *Librarians Do It For Free* were printed above it.

His smile was devilish. "Good to know."

She blushed and brushed past him into the guest room. Petunia was on her dog bed next to the charming four-poster bed, which was covered with his grandmother's antique quilt. Her tail thumped on her cushioned bed when she saw Magda.

Magda tossed the carrying case for her toiletries into her suitcase, which sat open on a folding tapestry luggage stand at the foot of her bed.

Jeff leaned one broad shoulder against the doorframe and fought the smile he felt tugging at the corners of his lips. Maggie amused him, but he didn't want her to think he was laughing at her.

She tugged at the bottom of the nightshirt in a vain attempt to cover up what Jeff thought were one very fine set of legs and said, "Bethanne gave it to me. She bought it at a conference last year."

He nodded and dragged his eyes to her face. "Ah. The swinging librarian's conference she went to. I remember that."

He paused and jerked his head to the right. "My room's at the end of the hall in case you need anything." He raised one eyebrow and drawled, "Anything at all."

Her jaw dropped and she shook her head. "It's a novelty nightshirt, big guy. You shouldn't take it too literally."

He shrugged and said without shame, "A man's got to try, right?"

He straightened up and flashed a smile. "I'll say

goodnight, then. Help yourself to breakfast in the morning. Just go down the back stairs we came up tonight, to our private kitchen, and grab whatever you'd like."

She returned his smile, and the sight of her white teeth and dimples made his heart stutter.

"Thanks, Jeff. I really appreciate you letting me stay here. It's so nice of you."

He took a deep breath and called quietly over his shoulder as he walked down the hall to his room, "Oh, the pleasure is all mine, Maggie."

Chapter 4

Private investigator, Bernie Felder, shifted his weight on Elizabeth Mallory's fragile antique chair. He was just an average-sized man, but he always felt like a behemoth on his client's fussy furniture. Her apartment was one of Manhattan's finest addresses, and he thought it looked more like a museum than a home, but they always did their business here, since the cases he worked on for her personally were highly confidential.

He glanced at the panoramic view of Central Park outside the windows, and wished—not for the first time—that he could tell Mrs. Mallory to take her work and shove it.

He heard the door open and turned to see Mrs. Mallory's male secretary come out of her office. If possible, Ned Bellingham was an even bigger elitist than his employer. His upper lip curled as he took in Bernie's brown sports coat and khaki slacks. Bernie felt his temper rise at the obvious assessment; although, he didn't really care what this man thought of him. As a detective, he needed to blend in with the crowd a lot of the time, and a custom-made suit like Mallory's lackey wore wouldn't cut it in his world.

"Mrs. Mallory will see you now."

Bernie rose, shot his cuffs, and picked up his briefcase from where it rested against the delicately curved leg of his chair.

He grinned at the secretary. "Thanks, Jeeves."

If the other man could shoot lasers from his eyes, Bernie knew he'd be a pile of ashes on the floor, but he knew too many Mallory family secrets to be treated to more blatant disrespect.

He entered Elizabeth Mallory's office. The large French provincial table she used as a desk was positioned in front of a pair of windows that offered the same multi-million dollar view of the Park. The table was set on a slightly elevated platform, so that Mrs. Mallory could always look down on her visitors, both literally and figuratively.

The lady herself was deceptively soft looking, with fluffy white hair in an elegant coiffure and a pale blue suit over a white blouse with a Belgian lace collar. Her gimlet stare told the real story, though. Perched high at her desk, her icy blue eyes regarded him over her aristocratic nose, and she put Bernie in mind of a bird of prey.

He sat across from her and pulled his laptop out of the briefcase. "Morning, Mrs. M. How are you this fine day?"

She pursed her already tight lips. "Fine day, Mr. Felder? Really? Only if you can tell me you've located my granddaughter, Elizabeth."

Bernie knew enough about her grandchild to know she preferred to be called by her first name, Magda, but her grandmother insisted on everyone in her employ using the girl's middle name, Elizabeth.

So of course, he had to needle her. "I found Magda. No worries."

She frowned. "And where is *Elizabeth*?" She put pointed emphasis on the name.

Bernie always felt sorry for the poor kid. He'd never met her, but Mrs. Mallory had him do surveillance on her many times. She seemed like a nice, down-to-earth girl, and he secretly applauded her guts for standing up to her grandmother time and time again.

He called up his notes on the computer and cleared his throat. "After you called me yesterday afternoon, I began to trace her through her debit card activity. She stopped for gas and dinner on the Jersey Turnpike heading south last evening."

Mrs. Mallory's one raised eyebrow registered as much surprise as she'd ever deem appropriate to show. "She's traveling south? Not north?"

He shook his head. "No ma'am. Definitely south. The next place she used her card was in some Podunk town in Virginia—Rivers Bend. That was last night at around 11:30."

"And after that, where did she go?"

He shrugged, but drew his bushy brows together. "Nowhere. She seems to have stopped in Rivers Bend."

"Perhaps she stopped there for the night. Did she use her card at a hotel?"

"No. And I did a little research on Rivers Bend. There is no hotel there—not even a dive motel. Only a place called The Retreat at Rivers Bend. It's a corporate retreat facility, which specializes in team-building activities in an outdoor environment. You know the kind of thing—an Alpine Tower, hiking, horseback riding. Looks like a pretty nice spread right on the Potomac River. It's run by two former NFL players."

At Mrs. Mallory's blank, unblinking stare he clarified. "Professional football players."

She sniffed in disgust. "Elizabeth certainly

wouldn't be there."

"Are you sure? Maybe she had a professional obligation to honor at The Retreat?"

"In case you missed the point of this assignment, Mr. Felder, my granddaughter quit her job at M.I. yesterday. She no longer *has* any professional obligations."

"Maybe she's there for personal reasons, then. The owners are both good-looking guys. I did a little digging on them—Francisco Cardoso is married, but Jeff Braden is single. Maybe, she left Mr. Allen for him?"

Mrs. Mallory allowed a small smile, and even that looked like it pained her.

"A professional athlete who's an innkeeper now? I don't think Elizabeth would leave an Allen for some nobody from nowhere."

Elizabeth wouldn't, but Magda might. Bernie smiled to himself at the thought.

"Precisely what is there in this situation to amuse you, Mr. Felder?"

He schooled his expression. "Jefferson Braden was always very popular with the female fans. As a matter of fact, he's my wife's celebrity free pass."

Mrs. Mallory arched one elegantly-shaped eyebrow. "I beg your pardon?"

Bernie couldn't resist poking a little at his oh-so-proper employer. "Aw, c'mon, Mrs. M., you know what I mean. If the missus ever had the opportunity to hit the sheets with a celebrity of her choice, she's got a free pass to do it. Jeff Braden's her pick." He poked his thumb at his chest. "Mine's Angelina Jolie."

Mrs. Mallory didn't deign to reply, but her gaze

was so frigid, it occurred to Bernie that she might be the one-woman answer to global warming. If she went to the North Pole, one look like the one she was giving him right now and she'd re-freeze the melting polar ice caps.

When Bernie didn't speak or squirm under her glare, Mrs. Mallory finally spoke. Her upper-crust accent was even more pronounced than usual.

"Yes. How frightfully interesting. So you believe my granddaughter is staying in this town in Virginia?"

Bernie nodded. "Rivers Bend. Yep. It looks that way."

"I would like to know why. How soon can you get there?"

"I could have someone there this afternoon."

Mrs. Mallory shook her head. "Not someone. You. This is a very delicate matter; I don't trust anyone but you to handle it."

Bernie took a deep breath as he worked out the schedule in his head. "Okay. I'll need to reassign the other cases I'm working on right now."

Mrs. Mallory raised one shoulder and said with disinterest, "That's not my concern."

"No, it's not. I was just thinking out loud. If you want me, personally, I can't be there before the weekend."

"Tomorrow is Friday. Be there by then," she insisted imperiously.

Bernie realized he was getting too old for this bullshit. He exhaled and conceded. "Fine. Tomorrow. But it's not going to be cheap."

"Money is not a problem. Just get there tomorrow and observe what Elizabeth is doing. Do not approach her, and keep me informed. In order to best determine how to get her back here, I need to know what she's doing. I also don't want word of her childish actions to get out, so as always, Mr. Felder, I'm relying on your discretion."

"That's what you pay me the big bucks for, Mrs. M. I'll be in touch."

****

Magda sat on the back steps by the kitchen door. She cupped a dark blue stoneware mug in her hands and laughed as she watched Jeff's daughter, Sam, try to teach Petunia to fetch.

"I don't think Shih Tzus are able to grasp the basic concept of fetch. Since Petunia is certain she's the queen of all she surveys, she doesn't understand why *you* don't bring the ball to *her*," she called out.

Petunia sat and looked pointedly from the ball to Sam. Her tail swished through the grass as it wagged.

Sam sighed. "You might be right."

"They were bred to be ornamental, so she lacks the hunting instincts of a retriever."

Petunia rose and sashayed up the steps to Magda, who stroked her wide back. "But you sure are a good friend, aren't you, girl?"

Sam smiled and flopped on the next step down. She twisted at the waist and reached up to scratch behind Petunia's ears. "And she's awful cute."

Magda returned her smile. "You're a very kind girl. Petunia won't win any beauty contests, but I love her, so she's gorgeous to me."

Sam's lips turned down. "I won't win any beauty contests either."

Magda opened her eyes wide. "What are you

talking about? You're lovely."

Sam shrugged and looked across the backyard toward the barn. It was obvious to Magda that the child was avoiding looking at her, and she knew they were talking about more than her dog, but she didn't know what it was.

"Do you want to be in beauty contests, Sam?"

The girl shook her head so hard that her ponytail hit her shoulders as it swung back and forth. "No, I *so* really don't. But my mother was in pageants and my grandmother…." Her voice trailed off.

Magda put her mug down on the stone porch and reached out to tweak Sam's ponytail. "And your grandmother?"

Sam bit her bottom lip. "She said I'd never be as pretty as my mother, so it's just as well I don't want to enter any pageants."

Magda felt pity and anger intermingled but fought to keep both off her face. She scooted down a step and put her arm around the child whose lips quivered as she put up a valiant effort not to cry.

"I didn't know your mother, but I think you're beautiful."

Sam gave a watery laugh. "Yeah, but you think Petunia is beautiful."

Magda chuckled. "True, but that's because inner beauty is more important in the long run. You're lucky—you've got beauty inside and out."

"You sound like my dad."

Magda squeezed Sam's shoulder before she removed her arm. She picked her mug up and took a sip of coffee, to buy some time to think before she replied.

Finally she said, "I know what it's like to be a

disappointment to your grandmother. It hurts. I tried to be the person my grandmother wanted me to be, but it didn't work. Take it from me; you've got to be true to yourself. From what I've seen of you, you're a great kid, so maybe your grandmother will realize it. And if she doesn't, that's her loss."

She paused and then added, "Of course, I was twenty-eight by the time I learned that particular lesson."

Sam turned her head to look at her with open curiosity. "How long ago was that?"

Magda laughed shortly. "Yesterday."

They sat in silence for a few moments before Magda said, "One thing that really helped me was knowing my dad was always in my corner."

Interest sparked in Sam's eyes. "Bethanne told me your mom died when you were a baby. Like me."

Magda smiled sadly and nodded. "Yep. It sucks, huh?"

Sam bobbed her head. "Sure does."

"But I was lucky to have a great dad who stepped up to the plate and took care of me; seems like you are, too."

Sam nodded and leaned her elbows back on the top step as they sat in companionable silence. The distant roar of a truck's motor grew louder as it approached and broke the stillness of the morning.

Sam sat up and grinned. "I bet that's Uncle Jason! He's bringing horses over from the farm for the guests to take on a trail ride this morning."

****

Jeff was in the barn, getting the tack ready for this morning's trail ride. He heard the rumble of his brother's horse trailer, the slam of the truck door and his daughter's excited squeal.

He strolled to the barn door and leaned one shoulder against it. He crossed his arms across his chest and smiled as he watched Sam run to her uncle. When she got close, she launched herself at him, and Jason laughed as he caught her and twirled her around.

Jeff glanced at the house and saw Magda sitting on the back steps, her faithful dog by her side. He was pleased to see she'd left her hair down today instead of in that tight twisty do it was in when she arrived. He didn't think she had a lick of make-up on her face, and her T-shirt, cutoff shorts, and flip-flops were a far cry from the chic suit she wore the night before, but as she laughed at his daughter's joyful display, he'd never seen a prettier sight.

Magda put down her mug and tucked Petunia under her arm before she walked over to Jason and Sam.

He pushed off the barn door and approached the group. He saw a slow, easy grin cross his brother's face as he watched Magda approach, and quickened his pace. His little brother was a notorious flirt, and he saw the masculine appreciation on Jason's face as he looked over their cute new guest.

"Hey Sam," Jason asked his niece. "Who's your pretty friend? Is she a guest at the Retreat?"

Sam giggled. "This is Magda. She's staying with Dad and me this weekend."

Jason's eyebrows shot up. "Really?"

Jeff called out as he approached, "Yes. Really. Maggie is Bethanne's friend. She was able to get away early to come and look after the library, but we won't have a cabin for her until Monday."

****

Magda balanced the dog under one arm and held out her free hand. "Hi. I'm Magda Horvath."

Jason took her hand, but instead of shaking it, he held it between his two big hands. His steely eyes held a hint of sensual promise. Magda blushed and held her dog up to divert his attention from her. "And this is Petunia."

Jason took the hint and let up on the flirtatious stare. He shook Petunia's paw. "It's very nice to meet you, Petunia. I'm Jason Braden."

Magda felt the dog's tail thump against her side. What a little flirt Rivers Bend was turning her previously prickly pooch into, but she couldn't blame the dog—the Braden brothers were two fine looking male specimens.

She stepped out of the way as Jeff, Jason, and Sam began to unload the horses from the trailer. While they were occupied with their task, she had ample opportunity to watch them.

Jason was more classically handsome, with his straight nose and full lips. His light brown hair looked perfect, but there was something about Jeff that called to her. He was dressed casually, in a navy blue T-shirt and jeans, but the way the sleeves pulled tight against his brawny arms gave her a little shiver of pleasure. His hair looked as messy this morning as it had the night before, so she guessed that was its natural state, and the lines around his eyes and mouth when he smiled clearly labeled him the older brother.

So why did handsome Jason's smooth flirtation leave her cold, while normal conversation with Jeff made her hotter than this August day in Virginia?

She started when she realized Jeff noticed her staring at them as the two men led the horses into the barn. A frown creased Jeff's brow as he looked at her and muttered something to his brother. What on earth was that all about?

****

"Don't you have enough women, Romeo? Leave this one alone," Jeff said in a low voice, so Maggie and Sam wouldn't hear him.

He glanced over his shoulder and saw Maggie as she watched his daughter unload another horse from the trailer.

Jason's eyes twinkled, and his grin was pure mischief. "Why, Big Brother, are you staking a claim on this woman?"

"No!" Jeff snapped. "She's here to do a favor for Bethanne, and I just think she should be spared the patented Jason Braden charm assault. If you hurt her and drive her out of town, Bethanne will be stuck with no one to run the library."

"Maybe she doesn't want to be spared. Lots of women are dying for a taste of my charm."

Jeff rolled his eyes. "Spare *me* then. Please, spare me."

He heard the clop of hooves and looked over his shoulder to see his daughter approach with a pretty chestnut filly. He muttered so she wouldn't hear him, "Just leave Maggie alone, all right?"

Jason laughed, and clicked his heels together and snapped a salute. "Sir! Yes, sir! Although, I don't believe for a second that you want me to leave the cutest girl to hit Rivers Bend in years alone for

Bethanne's sake. Admit it or not, brother, you're staking a claim."

"Maggie!" A deep voice with a heavy Brazilian accent boomed from the yard. "Thank you so much for coming to help *minha esposa*. Bethanne can't wait to see you."

Jeff followed the voice and saw Magda enveloped in a bear hug by his business partner.

"Cisco, you're going to crush the poor woman," Jeff called out.

Francisco eased up on the clinch, and both Magda and he turned toward the barn, where Jeff, Jason, and Sam all watched with smiles on their faces.

Francisco kept one arm around Magda's shoulders, and her face was wreathed in smiles, which brought out those deep dimples in her cheeks. Damn, his little brother was right—she was the cutest woman to hit Rivers Bend in years.

Francisco released Magda and held his arms open. "And Sam, too! Welcome home. What a great day this is for us to have two such lovely ladies here." He hugged the girl with only slightly less muscle than Magda had been subjected to.

"Hey Cisco, Jason brought the horses for the trail ride. I'll take that group if you'll handle the people who opted to go on the hike instead."

"Will do, partner," the jovial Francisco agreed, his teeth white against the golden tan shade of his skin.

"I'll leave all of you to your work. If someone will just tell me the way, I think I'll run over to see Bethanne now," Magda said.

"I'll take you," Sam volunteered. "I wanted to see her this morning, too."

"Great." Magda smiled at Sam. "I'll bring my coffee mug inside and get Petunia's leash. Then, I'll be ready to go."

"I'll carry Petunia for you," Sam offered, without even attempting to disguise her eagerness.

Magda handed her the dog, and bent to pick up her mug from the step. The denim cutoffs cupped her round bottom.

Standing between Jeff and Cisco, Jason whistled between his teeth as the kitchen door closed behind Magda and Sam.

He said with appreciation, "That is one woman who looks as good going as she does coming."

On either side of him, Jeff and Cisco each punched Jason in the arm.

"Ow! What the hell is with you two?"

Cisco eyed Jeff with suspicion. He jerked his head at him, which caused a lock of his silky black hair to fall into one of his eyes. He brushed it back with impatience. "I don't know what's with Jeff, but Maggie is like a sister to Bethanne, which means to me, too. I'll kick the ass of any man who messes with her. And you, *meu amigo*, are a famous messer of women."

Jason threw up his hands in frustration. "Why is everyone saying that to me?"

"Because it's true?" Jeff suggested with false solicitation in his voice.

"It's not true. I don't 'mess' with women—I'm always very upfront about my lack of interest in commitment," Jason defended himself with dignity.

"Just take your open lack of commitment down the road to the next willing victim. I told you—Maggie's off limits."

"Yeah." Francisco nodded in agreement, and then stared at Jeff through narrowed eyes. "Why are you being so protective of her? You better not mess with her either."

Jason shoved Cisco's shoulder. "Now you're onto something. This time you're picking on the right Braden brother. Jeff's staking a claim on little Magda. Not me."

Cisco's dark eyes narrowed. "Really?"

Jeff sighed in exasperation. "I just met the woman last night. I'm not staking any claim. Would you drop it already, Jase?"

His brother shook his head. "Sorry, bro, but no I won't drop it. You're acting mighty peculiar about her."

Cisco nodded in agreement. "This is not your usual m.o., *meu amigo*. You usually find your women outside Rivers Bend when you need to scratch an itch."

"That's to protect Sam," Jeff bristled. "I don't want her to get attached to a woman who's not going to be around for the long haul. It would hurt her too much when we broke up. She's got enough abandonment issues with her mom dying when she was just a baby."

"And that's without her knowing all the facts about the accident. If she knew the whole story…"

Jeff interrupted Jason with a curt, "She won't ever know the whole story. Not if I can help it. It would hurt her too much."

Both men bobbed their heads in agreement. They'd both been there for Jeff after the accident, and remembered how much it hurt Jeff at the time, and knew it would be worse for the young girl who idealized her late mother.

He cleared his throat before he went on, "So, back

off about Magda and me."

His daughter threw open the kitchen door and bounced down the steps to the three men. Magda followed at a more sedate pace; Petunia pranced at her side on the end of a hot pink leash.

"Dad, guess what! Magda knows how to ride."

Magda smiled. "The high school I went to had equestrian courses. It seemed like a good way to get my phys ed credits without being forced to play field hockey." She shuddered and continued with an impish grin, "I've never been very sporty. But it's been years since I've been on a horse."

"Ladybug is a nice quiet mare. Jason can leave her here for the weekend, and we can go for a ride. A sedate ride." He smiled and crossed his heart. "I promise. Even if you haven't been in the saddle in a long time, we'll go easy."

Jason and Cisco exchanged raised eyebrows, which neither Sam nor Magda noticed. Sam, because she's squatted down to pet Petunia, and Magda because she only had eyes for Jeff.

"I'd like that. It sounds like fun."

"Maybe we can go later this afternoon. After this group checks out, but before the re-enactors get here."

"Good idea, because a bunch of twenty-first century guys running around with Civil War weaponry doesn't sound conducive to the sedate ride you promised," Magda joked.

Her dimples made another appearance, and Jeff felt his heart stutter in an unfamiliar way.

"So, it's a date then," he said and then swallowed hard. "Um. I mean an appointment."

"Right. An appointment." She nodded, but her

smile faded. "Ready to show me the way to Bethanne's house, Sam?"

"Ready!" The girl jumped up and chattered happily as she led Magda and Petunia to a path through the trees behind the barn.

The three men watched them go. Once they were out of earshot, Jason burst out laughing. "A date-slash-appointment, huh? Man, you are so lame." He pounded his brother on the back and walked into the barn, his shoulders shaking with laughter.

Cisco's smile was kind. "Maggie's a good woman, but she's just getting out of a bad relationship, and she's still dealing with her father's death. Go carefully, *meu amigo*."

"I don't know what I can say to convince you there's nothing going on." Jeff ticked off his reasons on his fingers. "She's not my type. I just met her. Sam knows her."

Cisco shook his head once, his expression skeptical. "Those excuses might work if I hadn't just seen the sparks fly between you two. It was like the July 4th fireworks show all over again."

Jeff's mouth was a tight line. He spoke between his teeth, "I repeat. I just met her. I don't even know her."

Francisco shrugged. "Time doesn't matter. You were there when I met Bethanne."

The tension fell away from Jeff's face, and he laughed. "I remember. One look and you froze like a tree. Your jaw was hanging down to your feet. You looked like such a goober; it's amazing she ever agreed to go out with you."

Cisco smiled at the good-natured ribbing. "I don't know why she did, but it was the luckiest moment of my life. My point is this, Jeff—one look. That's all it took. Remember that day—one look at Bethanne, and I was lost. And, so, *meu amigo*, are you."

Chapter 5

"I don't think I'll be getting my dog back from Sam." Magda smiled as the child's laughter, and her dog's happy yipping drifted into the bedroom in Bethanne's cottage, where she sat on the bed next to her best friend.

Magda had kicked off her sandals and sat with her back propped up by pillows. A tall woman, thin except for her mid-pregnancy belly lay on her side beside Magda, a pillow between her legs. Her long reddish-brown hair was pulled back in a loose ponytail.

She laughed. "Doesn't sound that way. They're having a blast together. Why on earth did you say that dog is skittish? She seems really friendly and affectionate."

"Yeah—*here*. In New York she wouldn't let anyone but me near her."

"If by anyone you mean Pierce and your grandmother, that's just an indication of Petunia's excellent judgment, not skittishness."

"I know," Magda slumped her shoulders. "I feel so stupid, Bethanne. How did I get so sucked into that world? I swore I would never be a part of it."

Bethanne reached over to squeeze her friend's hand. "Don't be so hard on yourself. You'd just lost your father, and you were looking for someone to fill the void."

Magda sighed. "But did I ever pick the wrong person."

Bethanne wrinkled her freckled nose in distaste. "From what you've told me today, *you* didn't pick him. Your grandmother did. And, as usual, she didn't have your best interests at heart."

"She knew just how to play me. Without my dad, I had no family left but her. I was so desperate for connection, for a home, that I fell right into her clutches. And I was all set to walk down the aisle with the man of her choice in front of a select group of five hundred of her closest friends."

"At least you found out what was happening before you married Pierce. Even after you called last week to say you could come and help me out because you were breaking things off with him, I was afraid he would pull you back in. I was holding my breath and keeping my fingers, toes—everything—crossed until you got here. I was so relieved to get your call last night; I finally let myself believe that you were leaving him."

"Oh, I was leaving him, believe me. This info just made it easier. Pierce is not a nice man. He hid his true colors until he thought I was well and truly ensnared—his mistake was in not knowing who I am. He believed I was the lonely, needy woman I was when we met right before my dad died, but that's not who I really am."

"No way! You're one of the strongest people I know. He just caught you at a low point in your life and manipulated the situation to his benefit. Once he got you in his life, then he isolated you from your friends. Classic abuser behavior."

"Oh, he never hit me. Even at my most depressed, I

wouldn't have put up with that."

"There are other kinds of abuse besides physical, and that's what I mean. He tried to get you completely under his control. I can't tell you how many times I'd call your apartment, and he'd claim you weren't home and swear he'd give you my message. Just out of curiosity, how many of my messages did you get?"

Magda's eyes flashed in anger. "None. He gave me none. I'm so sorry, Bethanne. I had no idea."

"I even had my brother call for me. I thought if he didn't know it was me, you might get the message."

Magda shook her head and said through gritted teeth, "Nope. No messages from Ty, either. That son of a bitch! I thought you were just busy with your life here and had moved on from our friendship. It was so upsetting to me that I even talked to Pierce about it."

"Did you just growl?" Bethanne asked with a laugh in her voice.

"Maybe." Magda clutched a pillow to her chest and turned her head to look at her friend. "But enough about me and my colossally effed up life. How are you feeling? Aren't you sore from lying in this position?"

"A little," Bethanne acknowledged with a grimace. "But it's the best position from a blood flow point of view. At least that's what my doctor claims. There are moments when I suspect he's the reincarnation of the Marquis de Sade, and the whole blood flow thing is just a bunch of hooey designed to see how long he can trick me into lying this way."

"I'm sorry, sweetie. You're such an active person, this must be torture for you." Magda commiserated.

Bethanne waved her hand dismissively. "I can sit up the way you are a little bit every day. And I can get up to use the bathroom and take a quickie shower—although Francisco hovers over me like a mother hen the whole time I'm in there. Shower time with him used to be sexy time, but I guess that's a thing of the past. But all things considered, it could be worse. While I was in the hospital week before last, my roommate had to lie flat on her back, with her head lower than her feet."

"Yikes! By comparison, this isn't that bad."

"No, it's not. And at the end of it, Francisco and I get a beautiful baby."

"Right." Magda nodded briskly. "Eyes on the prize. And you'll have sexy shower time again someday. Like, in eighteen years, when your child goes off to college. It's a lucky baby to be coming to a family so filled with love."

"Speaking of which, we'd like you to be part of the baby's family, too, Maggie. We'd be honored if you'd be his godmother."

At the request, Magda felt truly happy for the first time in months. She bounced a little on the bed. "Really? You want me to be the godmother? I'd be thrilled to be his godmother!"

She shifted to gently hug her friend, but Bethanne's Dr. de Sade-approved position on her side made it awkward, and they both laughed.

"Who's the godfather?"

"Jeff. He's Cisco's best friend, and he's so great with kids."

"He does seem like a wonderful dad, but is he ever a flirt."

"Jeff. A flirt?" Bethanne cocked her head. "Don't you mean Jason? He's the playboy in the Braden clan."

Magda chuckled and inclined her head in agreement. "I met him this morning, and he's a flirt, too, but I really meant Jeff. He's been coming onto me from the second he realized I wasn't a burglar."

Bethanne laughed. "Sorry about the misunderstanding last night. We thought we'd talk to Jeff about you arriving early before he saw you. But did we ever laugh when we got Jeff's voicemail—did you really threaten him with a fireplace broom?"

Magda straightened her spine and defended herself with great dignity. "I thought it was the poker." She saw the humor in the situation and chuckled as she added, "Good thing he wasn't a crazed serial killer. I don't think sweeping at him would've been an effective weapon."

"Well, you must have swept him off his feet because Jeff is not a flirty kind of guy."

Magda rolled her eyes. "Men like Jeff Braden don't get swept off their feet by women like me."

"Women like you? What are you talking about? You're great."

"I'm okay. But I'm short and not exactly thin." She tugged at her wild corkscrew curls. "And my hair is totally out of control. Sam told me her mom was a beauty queen. If that's his type, I'm not it."

Bethanne laboriously adjusted her position so she was sitting up on her pillows with her long legs stretched out in front of her. She rested a protective hand on her baby bump.

"You're petite, not short. Curvy, not overweight. And I would happily trade my stick-straight hair for your curls. Plus, if what you're saying about him flirting with you is true, you're the first woman he's been interested in here in Rivers Bend since he moved back."

Bethanne lowered her voice and glanced to the closed window, where Sam's muffled laughter wafted into the room over the soft hum of the air conditioner. "And between you and me, his marriage was in trouble when his wife died, so I don't really think the pageant queen is his type. But Sam doesn't know anything about her parents' troubles, so mum's the word."

"I'd never say anything to her."

Bethanne smiled. "I know. Confiding in you is as safe as the bank; otherwise, I wouldn't have said anything. But if you're letting misguided insecurity keep you from responding to Jeff, I wanted to make sure you understood where he's coming from."

They sat in companionable silence for a few moments, and watched the girl and dog frolic together on the lawn outside the window.

"So, is Jeff *your* type?" Bethanne asked with studied casualness, never taking her eyes from the window.

Magda jerked her head to look at her friend. "What? No. Why? Maybe."

Bethanne smiled as she took a deep breath and glanced at Magda before looking back out the window. "Which one is it? No, or maybe? Or possibly, is it that dark horse contender—which my money is on—yes?"

"Fine." Magda huffed. "Yes. It's yes, okay. The man makes me feel like I'm made of molten lava. Happy now?"

Bethanne smiled beatifically and rubbed her belly. "Yep. I am. Molten lava, huh? That's a good thing."

Magda shrugged. "I guess." She pulled her legs up

and tucked them up as she turned her whole body to sit facing Bethanne. "But I just broke up with my fiancé yesterday. Granted, Pierce might be the worst fiancé in the history of fiancé-dom, but I'm a hussy for feeling the lava for someone else so fast. And Jeff is so far out of my league it's not even funny. Pursuing anything with him right now seems like a really bad idea."

"Opening up to someone is always a risk, no matter when you do it. You did with Pierce—"

"And look where that got me."

"If you would've let me finish, I was about to say, and you got smacked down. But Jeff isn't Pierce. He's one of the good ones. Think of him as the anti-Pierce."

"I know. You, Cisco, and Ty wouldn't have been friends with him for so long if he weren't a nice guy. I've just never felt this instant attraction before. And it's not just physical," she flapped her hands as she searched for a way to explain it. "We just sort of click. On all levels. And it scares me. A lot."

Bethanne reached over to still her hands and then continued to hold them as she said, "I know, Maggie. It's scary stuff. Just remember you don't have to rush into anything with Jeff. Take your time—get to know each other—you can be friends first and see where it goes."

They heard the front door open and Petunia's claws clicked on the wood floors. Sam's voice called out in exasperation as she followed the dog into the bedroom.

"You're right, Magda. Petunia is *never* going to fetch."

The dog managed to look so pleased with herself that they all laughed. Even Sam.

Magda gave Bethanne's hand a final squeeze and

uncurled her legs.

"I better head back to the main house and change. I'm going horseback riding with a friend this afternoon."

Bethanne winked at her. "Have fun."

Sam was unaware of any emotional undercurrents between the two women. "Yeah. Have a nice ride. We'll have to go for one sometime."

Magda smiled. "I'd like that. Hey, would you mind watching Petunia for me while your dad and I are riding this afternoon?"

"Mind?" Sam squeaked. "Are you kidding? I'd love to!"

****

Elizabeth Mallory sat at her imposing desk and watched as her assistant, Ned, escorted Pierce into her home office. Like her meeting with Bernie Felder, this was one she preferred to have away from M.I. If possible, she wanted her granddaughter back in New York with a minimum of gossip about her flight.

Pierce had an unhealthy pallor and his pale blue eyes looked too bright. She cocked her head as she observed him and wondered if he was high on something. Mr. Felder's investigation of Pierce revealed he over-indulged in liquor and illegal drugs. And gambling. And women. None too discreetly, either. She assumed the infidelity was what drove her granddaughter away.

Perhaps she'd been wrong to manipulate their engagement. Pierce was weak, yes, but that made him easy to control. Her granddaughter seemed to still have some ridiculous middle-class notions about romance and marriage. Fairy tale endings were just that—fairy tales. Not real life—at least not in the circles in which Mallorys moved. The girl needed to be disabused of her childish ideas. Pierce was an excellent match, and her granddaughter should be grateful he was willing to overlook her dubious lineage on her father's side to marry her.

"Good morning, Mrs. Mallory," Pierce's voice sounded strained. "How are you today?"

"How do you think I am, young man?"

He gulped, and she was pleased by his fear. *The fool.* Had he intended to come here today and pretend nothing was wrong?

She kept her gaze trained on him, like a bird of prey on the field mouse it had picked for its dinner, but spoke to her assistant. "Ned, you may leave us now. This is a family matter."

Ned bowed slightly. "Certainly ma'am."

He backed out of the door as if he were leaving a royal chamber, and pulled the door shut with a soft click.

Pierce fidgeted with his silk necktie under Mrs. Mallory's continued unblinking stare. He cleared his throat.

"You wanted to see me?"

"That would be overstating the matter. I don't actually *want* to see you, but needs must. Please, sit down."

Pierce sat in the chair opposite her and licked his lips. His gaze darted around the room as he tried to look at anything but her.

She sighed. He was a handsome boy but such a fearful imbecile. She'd make this meeting as brief as possible. If he weren't an Allen, she wouldn't make her granddaughter marry him. But she'd dreamed of an alliance between their families since her own daughter was an infant. She pressed her lips together. But instead of marrying Pierce's father, her daughter had chosen a Hungarian-American factory worker. History would not repeat itself in this generation. Elizabeth would marry this idiot, but first they had to find her and get her back.

"My granddaughter. Where is she?"

He held out his hands, palms up. "I don't know. She left me this note with her engagement ring."

He fumbled in the inside pocket of his suit coat, pulled out a crumpled piece of paper, and handed it to Mrs. Mallory.

She propped a small pair of reading glasses on her nose as she smoothed the note and read it. Upon completion of the brief missive, she lifted her gaze above their wire frames to pin Pierce with her stare. "She's gone out of town to help a friend. *What* friend? I thought you'd separated her from any friends not of my choosing."

He rubbed his hands on his thighs in an effort to dry his sweaty palms. "I did."

She arched one eyebrow, and Pierce wilted. Such a weakling. One look and he crumbled. It made him so easy to manipulate. Why didn't her granddaughter see what a gift she gave her in this man? A husband this easy to control was a wonderful thing in Elizabeth Mallory's mind.

He cleared his throat. "At least I thought I had. Obviously not."

"Obviously. I have my personal investigator trying to locate her. Do you know anything at all that would help him?"

He stared over her shoulder out the window as he racked his brain. He shook his head. "No. I'm sorry, but I don't."

She straightened an already perfectly arranged pile of papers on her desk and said with deceptive gentleness, "It is in *your* best interest to find her. Quickly and quietly. As you know, she cannot access her trust fund for two more years. While she worked at M.I. and was engaged to you, I allowed you both access to funds. I've frozen that account, and it will remain frozen until she's back, and your ring is on her finger again."

He gripped the carved arms of his chair until his knuckles were white. "You can't do that to me."

The corners of her mouth turned up. "Oh, but I can, and I have. My investigator has unearthed some rather unsavory aspects to your character. I'm aware of how desperately you need the money I supply. The frozen account is a little added incentive to find her and win her back as quickly as possible."

His head jerked in a nod, as he rose. "I'll be going then, so I can start looking for her right away."

She called after him as he walked away, and her words stopped him in his tracks. "One more thing, Pierce. I am a woman of the world, and I understand a man's needs. I was raised to look the other way when Mr. Mallory sought to fulfill them away from the marital bed. My granddaughter was not. Your involvement with Taylor Brown is at an end. She is not to know your engagement is broken, or that we don't know where your fiancée is. Once you're married, if you can learn to be discreet..." She shrugged, before continuing, "Then you may do as you like, but until we have my granddaughter back in the fold, your extracurricular activities are over. You may practice the art of discretion, now, by keeping this dilemma between us. I will not have any gossip about my family. If any arises, I will know the source, and you will be sorry you crossed me."

****

Jeff's horse plodded along the trail, behind Magda on Ladybug. He could tell his horse was chomping at the bit to go faster, but when the trail narrowed, and they had to ride single-file, he decided to let Magda set the pace. She chose slow—really slow. He took a deep breath of the pine-scented air and took in his surroundings.

He was actually enjoying the leisurely pace. It was a good ten degrees cooler here in the woods, always a treat on a late summer day in Virginia. Some light broke through the dense foliage, and it dappled through the leaves in a beautiful way. It was quiet, aside from the dull clop of the hooves on the packed dirt path and the cheery sound of songbirds. He felt at peace, and it was nice to share it with someone. He felt odd around Magda—both all keyed up and a bone-deep calm at the same time.

An added benefit to letting her take the lead was the superior view he now enjoyed. Magda's curvy shape filled out jeans nicely. Her T-shirt had ridden up a bit at her waist and revealed a line of pale skin on her lower back. He wondered if her skin was as soft as it looked. He felt a purely male satisfaction at the way her waist nipped in before the curve of her hips gave way to her round bottom bouncing a little on the saddle. The white V-neck T-shirt she wore had a very nice view from the front, too; although, he could not see it at the moment.

She might be petite, but she had a perfect hourglass figure. A pocket Venus, his father would've called her. He smiled at the thought. It had been fourteen years since an unexpected heart attack took him in the prime of his life, and sometimes, Jeff missed him as much as he did when it first happened.

The path opened up to a small field of grass and wildflowers, which overlooked the Potomac River. He heard Magda's gasp of pleasure and urged his horse forward to pull up alongside her.

She turned in her saddle to smile at him, "Wow! What an amazing view. And it's so unexpected. We were riding along in the woods, and it felt like we were in a green tunnel. And then all of a sudden…"

She gathered the reins in one hand and gestured toward the vista in front of them with the other. "Everything opens up and the sky is back, and there's this amazing river view."

"It's one of my favorite rides." He pointed to the opposite bank. "That's Maryland over there."

Her eyes grew dreamy and distant. "I've been thinking about the Civil War this afternoon."

He bobbed his head. "It's the re-enactors coming this weekend; it always puts me in a historical mindset."

"Probably," she agreed. "It's so peaceful now; it's hard to believe that so much bloodshed and violent death happened here."

She gestured with her head to a small ranch-style house visible on the Maryland side of the river. "And Maryland wasn't a Confederate state. Those people would have been your enemy. It's incomprehensible."

"Brother against brother. This border saw its fair share of that situation during the war." He smiled at her. "But these are depressing thoughts for such a pretty summer day. Want to get off and stretch your legs a bit before we head back?"

She nodded with a rueful grin. "I'd like a break. I'm pretty out of shape. I'm afraid I'll be walking like John Wayne when I get off Ladybug."

Jeff laughed and forced himself to squelch any and all thoughts of more carnal ways to cause her to have to walk like John Wayne. He swung one long leg around and dismounted.

Magda followed suit, and he hurried around the head of his horse to help her down. He put his hands around her waist to steady her and she was such an itty-bitty thing, damned if they didn't almost span it. He saw goose pimples rise on her flesh at the skin-to-skin contact in spite of the heat of the day, and he knew he wasn't alone—she was feeling the same magnetic pull that he was.

She looked up and over her shoulder at him. Her eyes looked as confused as he felt. "Thanks. I'm good now."

"Right." He smiled and released his hold on her. He looped their reins over a low-hanging tree branch. "These two are well trained. They won't go anywhere without us, but just in case."

She stretched her arms over her head and turned her face to the sky. "Mmm. Yesterday my life was all turmoil, and today, I'm here. I feel so calm—so right. Thanks for bringing me to this lovely spot."

"Anytime." Jeff's voice was a little rough as he

watched her breasts strain against her T-shirt as she stretched. She dropped her arms.

"You're lucky to live here. To be a part of this land."

"I am. I never really fit in anywhere else I've lived. My roots are here. My family."

"It's your home." Her voice sounded wistful.

He dropped to the ground and leaned back on his elbows, his mile-long legs stretched out in front of him. Magda assumed the same position at his side. One of the horses nickered softly behind them, and the river glistened in the sunlight as it flowed in front of them.

"Where's your home, Maggie?"

She shrugged. "Nowhere. I'm from Connecticut originally. Stratford. But my dad died last year, and I sold our house there when I moved to New York to live with Pierce. Now I guess I'm just a drifter."

"No siblings?"

"My mom died when I was born and my dad never remarried, so it's just me. How about you? Any other siblings besides Jason?"

"Two sisters—Heather and Deidre."

"Four of you? That's a big family by today's standards."

"Yep. Deidre's the oldest; she's married to Hank Anderson. They've got twins—a boy and a girl—who just turned seventeen. Then, there's me, and then Heather. You'll meet her when we get back. She works at the Retreat, managing guest relations. Jason's the baby of the family."

"And he helps your mom run the horse farm?"

"Yeah. Jase and Hank both do. Deidre owns the Nosh Pit; it's a little bakery café kind of place on Main

Street. You'll have to go there for lunch sometime when you're working at the library."

"It's nice for Sam to have cousins nearby."

"It is. Although the gap between seventeen and eleven is a chasm. There's just four years between Heather and me. Now that we're adults, it seems like nothing, but when we were kids it put us in different orbits."

He glanced at her with curiosity. "Don't you have any family left?"

She frowned. "Just my grandmother. She's my mother's mother, but I'm coming to realize she's never going to be the grandmother of my daydreams, and that my life might be better without her in it."

"Not your typical granny, I guess?"

"Not even a little bit," Magda scoffed. "My grandmother is Elizabeth Mallory."

His jaw dropped. "*The* Elizabeth Mallory? Of Mallory International?"

She nodded, her lush lips pulled tight. "The one and only."

He furrowed his brow. "Wait a minute. I remember when your dad died. Ty, Bethanne, and Cisco went up for the funeral. Ty told me he worked in the plant of a big defense contractor up north. Building helicopters."

The clouds cleared from her eyes, and a soft smile tilted up her lips. "That's right. He worked his way up to being a shop foreman."

"So if your mom was a Mallory, they must have had a real star-crossed lovers thing going on, huh?"

"Sort of. No stars crossed with them—they were made for each other—but my grandmother wasn't at all pleased with their relationship."

"How would a regular guy even meet Elizabeth Mallory's daughter?"

She chuckled. "My mom went to Yale. One night she went to a concert at a club in New Haven. My dad was there that night with his buddies. One look at each other across a crowded, smoky club, and it was love at first sight."

"That's the second time today someone mentioned love at first sight to me. I'm not sure I believe in it. Lust at first sight—that I've experienced. But love? I don't know."

She smiled and looked out at the river. "I'm a believer. I have my parents as an example. And Bethanne and Francisco. But I don't have any firsthand experience of it either."

"Not even with Pierce?"

The calm left her face at his question. At the sight of her frown and sad eyes, he felt bad for spoiling the mellow mood of the afternoon. "Sorry for asking. It's none of my business."

"It's fine. I just feel like a world-class idiot for falling for his line of bull. I should've seen through his pretense to the real him."

"Been there, done that," Jeff drawled.

"Really? You don't seem like the sort of person who'd be easy to fool. I have the feeling under all that laid back good-old boy charm, you're one of the sharpest people I've ever met."

"Thank you." He chuckled. "I think. There *was* a compliment buried in there somewhere, wasn't there?"

She tossed back her head and laughed. It sounded as pretty to Jeff as the music of birds in the woods around them. "There was supposed to be. I meant that I think you're very smart."

"I'd like to think I'm pretty savvy about people, but when you give your trust to someone, if they really want to deceive you, it makes it easy for them to do it. That's what makes a relationship scary. It really exposes all your weaknesses and leaves you open to serious hurt."

"It's mainly my pride that's hurt. I guess that means I wasn't that emotionally invested in Pierce."

Jeff plucked absently at a long piece of grass next to him. He wasn't one to pry into someone else's business. If Maggie wanted to talk, then she would without his poking and prodding at her open wounds.

After a long moment of silence, Magda said, "He cheated on me. Among other, even worse things that I don't want to talk about."

"Being cheated on is no fun. It happened to me once. Up here," he tapped his forehead, "you know it's not your fault. But here," he tapped his chest over his heart, "you feel like it has to be your fault—like you could've done something to prevent it. But you couldn't have. It's all on him, Maggie. Not you."

She picked a dandelion, whose flower had turned into a puffball, and blew on it, scattering the fluff to the wind. "Maybe. Maybe not. But thanks for the support."

She pushed to her feet and took a couple of steps toward the river. Jeff rose and followed.

How could he be so angry at a man he didn't even know? How could this Pierce jerk have slept around on a woman like Maggie? And the prick even made her doubt herself in the process. It was written all over her anguished face.

He stood behind her and gently kneaded her

shoulders. He turned her to face him and cupped her face in his big hands.

"This Pierce guy is the biggest fool on earth to go to someone else when he had you at home, Maggie."

She blinked away tears, and he felt his heart constrict. Before he could think it through and decide it was a really bad idea, Jeff dipped his head and captured Magda's lips in a gentle kiss.

Chapter 6

The kiss started sweet, but when Magda stood on her toes to twine her arms around his neck and weave her fingers into his hair, Jeff caught fire and turned up the heat. Her curvy little body pressed against his and drove him wild.

He swept his tongue into her mouth and wedged his thigh between her denim-clad legs, which lifted her higher to accommodate for their height difference, but based on the needy little moan she just made, Jeff guessed the pressure on the seam of her jeans felt pretty good to her, too. He pressed more firmly and was rewarded with a louder moan as she gripped his hair tighter.

He lowered his hands from her face to cup the round bottom, which had been driving him crazy while he followed her on the trail ride. He used his leverage to press her even closer to him. He heard a low groan and realized it came from his throat.

This woman set him on fire like none he'd ever known before. And they were still fully clothed and just kissing—if they ever got naked together, Jeff feared he'd spontaneously combust.

He felt her tongue stroke against his as she tried to wriggle impossibly closer to him. He felt her soft breasts, with their hard points, press into his chest, and knew his own hardness was snug against her belly.

God, he wanted this woman. Right here. Right now. But then what? She would be living on the grounds of his home for the next few months. They couldn't just scratch this mutual itch and then go their separate ways. They'd see each other every day, and damned if he didn't want to keep seeing her, but she'd be seeing *Sam* every day, too. He didn't want his daughter to get used to a woman in their lives, in their family, one who'd be gone by springtime.

His heart hammered against his chest as he pulled away from her with a reluctance that surprised him. In spite of all his very good arguments against getting involved with Magda, he still wanted her. In his bed— yes—but also in his life, and that scared the living hell out of him.

"Whoa, Maggie. I think we need to slow it down."

Her eyes were wide, and he noticed they were almost the same shade of blue as the Bachelor's Buttons that grew wild in the grass around them. She lifted the back of her left hand and pressed it to her mouth. Her breathing was every bit as ragged as his own, which made him glad—he'd hate to be the only one feeling this wild passion.

"Right. Slow down. Good idea," she murmured in a disoriented manner.

He felt the need to explain things to her. He never had a problem walking away from the women he occasionally dallied with, but she was vulnerable from Pierce's betrayal, and Jeff didn't want her to think she wasn't desirable.

"It's just that I don't get involved with women my daughter knows. After her mother died, I promised myself I wouldn't introduce Sam to a woman I was with until I was certain she'd be a permanent part of our lives."

Magda gulped and nodded. "That's very kind of you. I understand. I wouldn't want to do anything that had the potential to hurt Sam. She's a great kid, and I really like her already."

"Thanks for understanding. I shouldn't have started something I couldn't see through."

She grimaced. "That's okay—stopping is a good idea for me, too. After the Pierce debacle, I'm not really trusting my own judgment right now. I don't want to jump into another relationship until I get my head on straight again. And, in spite of what you must think of me after that display, I don't engage in meaningless sex."

"I don't think any less of you. What just happened was amazing, but we're agreed; it wouldn't be sensible to let it happen again. So…friends?"

She smiled. "Friends. I'd like that."

Jeff turned and took a couple of steps away from her. He stopped and ran a distracted hand through his already tousled hair. He turned back to Magda.

"For the record, whatever problems you and Pierce might have had in the bedroom are all on him."

"What?" She gasped.

"When we were talking, I got the impression you blamed yourself for his cheating. Believe me, darlin' Maggie, it had nothing to do with you. If I were any hotter right now, I'd have to jump in the river to cool off before we rode home."

Her wide gaze dropped to his crotch, and she saw the proof of his words straining against his fly.

"Oh my," she whispered.

At her admiring gaze, Jeff felt himself grow impossibly harder.

"God, Maggie. Unless you want to wait while I take that cold dip, stop looking at me like that."

She dragged her gaze to his face. "Sorry. It's just…" She fluttered her hand in the general direction of his zipper. "*I* did that?"

A slow, easy smile spread across his face. "You most certainly did. Trust me, Maggie—you could do *that* to a dead monk. So, if Pierce felt the need to look elsewhere, it was his problem. Not yours."

****

Early that evening, Jeff walked through the empty lobby of the Retreat. He jiggled the handle of the front door to double check that his sister Heather had locked it when she left for the day. The public part of the house was more formally decorated than the part of the house he shared with Sam. He stepped behind the mahogany check-in desk and opened the door to their living quarters.

He locked that door behind him and walked down the hall to the living room at the front of the house. A smile played at the corner of his mouth as he went in— he really loved this room. Heather helped decorate it, and it was both comfortable and attractive. He didn't know what he would have done without his little sister's help in the years since Sam's mother died.

He paused in the doorway and looked at the fireplace opposite him, lovingly restored in the renovation. Above the mantel hung a framed photograph of his family on his mother's horse farm. The professional photographer they used had captured the closeness their family shared, as well as their love of the land. They were all dressed in jeans and white button-down shirts, and posed on hay bales in one of the fields. The white nineteenth century farmhouse where he was raised stood in the background.

A turquoise love seat with plump brown pillows was positioned in front of the fireplace. On either end sat two matching armchairs and instead of a coffee table, an oversized brown hassock was centered between the seats and the fireplace, so on a winter night people could gather around the fire, prop their feet up and relax.

To his right were French doors, which led to the front porch, and to his left was his current destination—a soft leather sectional sofa, the color of dark chocolate, aimed at a huge flat-screen television set mounted on the wall. Behind it was a sofa table, every square inch of which was covered with framed photos of family and friends.

But the prime seat he was headed for was already occupied. Magda sat on the chaise portion of the sectional with her legs stretched out in front of her. She hadn't heard him enter the room, and he took a moment to observe her.

He smiled and cocked his head to one side. She had changed after their ride into lime green and hot pink plaid shorts and a pink T-shirt. The shorts lived up to their name and revealed a long expanse of leg. For such a short woman, her legs were long and pale, like they didn't get to see the sun too often, but they looked as silky soft as the rest of her skin.

She had one of the turquoise pillows on her lap and one of those impossibly thin laptop computers balanced there. She stared at the screen, her big eyes were round and her mouth hung open, as if she was surprised by something she read on the screen.

"Everything okay, Maggie?"

She jumped and the laptop rocked on the pillow. She clutched it to keep it from falling, and turned her head to look at him.

"Oh! Jeff. I didn't hear you come in."

He grinned and walked over to the sofa. "I'm stealthy. Shockingly so for a man of my size."

He plopped down next to her and pointed at her computer. "Bad news? You were looking kind of shell-shocked when I got here."

She shook her head and the blonde corkscrew curls bounced. "Not bad news for me, per se; although, Pierce won't be happy. I didn't think my grandmother could still shock me, but somehow she manages to keep redefining family in a way that amazes me."

"What did she do?"

At her hesitation, Jeff held up one of his large, work-calloused hands. "Forget I asked. It's none of my business."

She swatted his hand down, and he wondered if his new "friend" felt the same electrical charge at the brief contact that he did. By the way she pulled her hand back, as if she'd received a shock, he guessed that she was feeling it, too.

"It's not that, I just don't know where to start." She took a deep breath. "My grandmother really hated my father. Not him so much as the *idea* of him. She thought he was beneath my mother. She wanted Mom to marry Pierce's father. She couldn't get past it when my mother chose someone else."

He frowned. "When that didn't work, she waited

twenty-some years and expected you and Pierce to get married? That's kind of…" he paused to search for the right word to describe the situation and landed on one of his mother's favorites, "Unsavory."

Magda laughed. "That's a very genteel, southern way of describing it. Unsavory. I think Grandmother thought of it as 'if at first you don't succeed, try, try again.'"

"Now that her matchmaking has failed in two generations do you think she'll give up?"

Magda shook her head, and those sexy curls swung again and released the vanilla scent of her shampoo. "Grandmother give up on her dream to unite the Mallory and Allen dynasties? No. She won't give up. She *never* gives up."

Her usually cheerful voice sounded defeated. "As a matter of fact, I can't believe I haven't heard from her yet," she pointed to her cell phone next to the glass of iced tea on the coffee table in front of them. "I've had fourteen voice mail messages from Pierce, and now that I've checked my email I know why. I had an email from my bank notifying me that a joint account my grandmother set up for Pierce and me when we got engaged, has been frozen."

He winced. "Ouch. So instead of reaching out to you personally, trying to make sure you're all right after quitting your job and dumping the slime ball fiancé who disrespected you, she just cut off your funds? That's cold. What kind of grandmother wouldn't be climbing the walls with worry until she knew you were safe and well?"

She sighed. "My kind of grandmother." She lifted her chin and smiled. "But her plan to make me come crawling back by cutting off this account is going to backfire on her."

He grinned at her spunk. "Oh yeah? How come?"

"A lifetime of seeing the way she treated my father and me made me a little leery of her friendly overtures after he died."

"Sensible," Jeff nodded his approval.

"I never touched the money in this account, but Pierce did. A lot. I don't know what he's going to do now."

Jeff's head flopped back on the sofa. He felt sympathy for Magda that he suspected the proud woman would hate if he showed any sign of it. He forced his expression to be neutral, but it didn't stop the feeling inside. The poor little thing. Did no one in her life love her just for who she was? Her grandmother wanted her as a pawn in some archaic matrimonial power play, and her former fiancé wanted her back so he'd have access to her family's money. He glanced at the portrait-sized photo of the Braden clan over the fireplace, and thought about the unconditional love in his family. It made his heart twist in his chest for Magda.

"That's why you're getting so many calls from loser Pierce. He wants his gravy train back home." He couldn't quite keep the anger out of his voice, but better anger than anything Maggie could perceive as pity.

"That's what I'm thinking."

"Tell me, amazingly smart woman, how did you manage to never touch the money you were clever enough to know would come with lots of strings?"

She blushed at his praise, and smiled as she peeked at him through her long lashes. "I put all the money from the sale of my dad's house and his estate into an account as a sort of a safety net. I grew up living on a budget, so it should easily last me until I get a permanent job after I'm done helping Bethanne with the library here. Even if I can't find any work, it should last until I turn thirty, and the trust I inherited from my mother comes to me."

"How long is that?"

"Two years. I know Pierce could hardly wait for me to turn thirty, but frankly, I don't know what I'll do with the money."

"I felt that way about the obscene amount of dough I was paid to play football. I used some of it to buy and renovate this property so Cisco and I could start our business. I've got money set aside for Sam, and in case of a rainy day." He shrugged and continued, "With the rest, I figure there's always a lot of good to be done with it."

"Like donating to worthy charities?"

He hung his head and could feel his face heat up. He didn't like to blow his own horn by drawing attention to what he did with his money, but it seemed like Magda was in a similar position—or would be in two years—of having more money than her simple lifestyle required, and the urge to do some good with it.

"Or starting your own worthy charity. I have foundations for inner-city youth in Portland, D.C., and Baltimore. We set up rec centers with mentors in their neighborhoods, and give kids a chance to get off the streets and succeed in school and sports."

"That's wonderful! Why do you look so embarrassed? You should be really proud."

He shrugged. "I'm not a braggart. My folks didn't

raise me that way, and I don't do it for attention. That's why I try to keep my foundation from becoming some sort of tribute to me. Although, my involvement does help bring in donations, so I'm not able to stay as behind the scenes as I'd like."

Before she could answer, Magda's cell phone rang on the coffee table. The ringtone was "Your Cheatin' Heart".

Jeff raised an eyebrow and chuckled. "Pierce, I presume?"

Now it was her turn to look sheepish. "Yeah. Childish of me, huh?"

****

Jeff flashed the grin that melted her heart as well as her panties, and leaned forward to pick up the phone.

Magda gasped as she stretched to take the phone from him. He easily held her off with his left arm, while he answered the phone with his right.

"Maggie's phone. How may I help you?"

"Jeff! Hang up!" She hissed the words between her teeth.

"No. I'm sorry." His smile turned devilish and his voice was laden with innuendo. "She can't come to the phone right now. She's most delightfully indisposed. May I give her a message from you when we're done? In two or three days?"

She could hear Pierce's angry voice squawk through the tiny speaker as Jeff winced and held the phone away from his ear. She couldn't help but smile.

When Jeff spoke again, his voice was all southern charm. "Her fiancé, you say? Well now, I find that mighty hard to believe, seeing as Maggie is spending the weekend with me."

He paused as the unpleasant squawking resumed and nodded. "Yes. This is Magda Horvath's phone. Maggie's just my little pet name for her."

The voice on the line got shriller, and Jeff winked at Magda.

"I'm sorry, friend. I can tell you've got lots you want to say, but you're keeping me from Maggie right now. And she looks mighty fine, all freshly showered and stretched out on a chaise lounge. I'll tell her you called. Eventually."

He rolled his eyes and pulled the phone as far from his ear as his arm could reach, as the angry voice reached fever pitch. He pulled the phone back and interrupted Pierce's tirade. "You've left a lot of messages for her already. Maybe you should take the hint. She doesn't want to talk to you. When she does, Maggie will call you. Until then, I strongly suggest you leave her alone. Are we clear?"

He touched the screen to end the call and tossed the phone back on the table.

"Maggie. Maggie. Maggie. What did you see in that man? The only words I can think of to describe him are not suitable for a lady's ears."

She bit her bottom lip and sighed. "I'm trying to chalk it up to temporary insanity and move on with my life."

He nodded his approval. "Sounds like a plan. Let me know if he keeps bothering you. It would be my pleasure to put him in his place."

A sense of heaviness weighted down her chest. "I'm sure he'll keep calling. He's not making the moving on part of my plan easy."

"For the short term, we can turn off your phone.

For the long term, you could get a new number."

"Good idea." She leaned forward, snagged the phone, and turned it off with a flourish.

He grinned. "And also for short term distraction, Sam's at a sleepover tonight, and I was getting ready to make popcorn, drink a beer or two, and watch a movie. You in?"

She swung her legs down, and clicked on her keyboard to shut down her laptop. "I wouldn't want to intrude on your alone time. I'll go up to my room."

He placed his hand on her arm to stop her from running out. She felt the simple contact shoot through her body like lightning and ignite all her fun places.

"Don't be silly. Friends hang out like this all the time, and that's what we agreed to be, right? Friends?"

Magda had never had this kind of out of control chemistry with a friend before in her life, but she fixed a smile on her face and said, "Friends. Right. That's what we are. Need any help making the popcorn, pal?"

****

"Hello? Hello?" Pierce shrieked into the phone. When no one responded, he disconnected, and threw the phone across the room. It landed with a clatter on the marble floor, and skittered until it hit the wall and broke into pieces.

Great. How was he going to replace it? With Magda gone, Elizabeth Mallory had frozen his access to their joint account. He shouldn't have let his temper get the best of him. Maybe if he went to the store where he bought the phone, with enough high-handed attitude, he could convince them it was defective and replace it at no charge.

Damn it all to hell! Where was Magda? And who

was the man who'd answered her phone? He sounded like an extra on *The Dukes of Hazzard*. Had Magda really sunk so low that she was getting it on with some redneck?

How could she have met the yokel? Pierce and her grandmother had controlled all her activities since she moved in with him. He had to be someone from her past, but Magda had never lived outside of the northeast, and this clown had a southern-fried accent.

He walked to the desk where he kept his paperwork, and scrambled through the papers to find an old phone bill. Magda had to have been in touch with this guy before she ran off—she wasn't the sort of woman to meet a man and leap right into a sexual relationship. God knows she kept Pierce waiting long enough—not that the wait was worth it, in his opinion.

He tossed papers to the floor in his quest to find an old cell phone bill. Frigging woman had taken everything of hers from the apartment. It was like she never lived here.

In frustration, Pierce used his arm to sweep everything off the desk. He sank down into the chair at the desk, and pounded his fist on the desktop. He had to think. There had to be some sort of connection to the man Magda ran away with—or ran away *to*. Was she down south somewhere, or holed up in a hotel in Manhattan? There was no way to know. The huckleberry said she was on a chaise—could they be in Miami, or the Caribbean? Hell—they could be anywhere, and he had no fucking clue what to do, or where to look for her.

He had to figure something out. People—and most decidedly *not nice* people—had loaned him money, and they wanted payment. Without Elizabeth Mallory's funds he had no way to pay them back. His grandfather convinced his father to wash his hands of Pierce financially years ago, so Allen family funds were out. And the only way to get Mallory money was to get Magda back with his ring on her finger.

Personally, he would be just as happy to let her go, but he couldn't afford to. He had a serious attachment to his kneecaps, and they were currently in jeopardy if he couldn't pay back the money he owed.

"Sorry, Magda. I know you don't want me any more than I want you, but I need to find you, and marry you. ASAP."

****

As the credits rolled and the heavy metal soundtrack reverberated through the family room, Magda smothered a yawn and nestled her head into the soft pillow behind her back.

Jeff grinned, and raised his voice a bit to be heard over the music. "I know it's not like those movies they make of Jane Austen novels that women all seem to love, but Sam was out, and this movie is rated R, so it seemed like a good time to see it. Next time, we'll watch a chick-flick, I swear."

Magda thought back to the action film they'd just watched, with its graphic violence and even more graphic sex. The violence made her screw her eyes shut until Jeff told her it was safe to open them, and the sex scenes, with a walking, talking, kissing sexual fantasy come to life sitting a Shih Tzu length away from her on the sofa, made her squirm.

She wasn't sure exactly *what* Jeff and she were to each other, but it wasn't friends—at least not just friends. Magda did like him a lot, but there was also an undercurrent of sexual tension humming between them like a high-voltage wire.

She couldn't just erase the memory of the best kiss of her life this afternoon. It made her want to do so much more, but Jeff and she both had very sound intellectual reasons for not getting romantically entangled with each other.

Mmm…entangled….maybe in some silk sheets, Magda shook her head briskly to dispel the image. Her mind grasped the soundness of the "just friends" thing, but her heart and body were having a little trouble getting on board with the program.

"I didn't expect the movie to put you to sleep, though; it was non-stop explosions toward the end."

"It wasn't the movie; it was really exciting. I was up a lot later than usual last night, and yesterday was a stressful day." She fought back another yawn. "I probably should make it an early night."

With one hand, Jeff reached down to pet Petunia's head, resting in his lap. He used his other hand to aim the remote at the television. In the sudden silence, Petunia's snoring reverberated in the quiet room.

Jeff chuckled. "For a little dog she certainly sounds like a big, old steam engine."

Magda stroked her dog's rear leg, which was propped up on her thigh. "It's the short snout—she can't help it."

"No. Of course you can't. Can you, girl?" Jeff cooed, as he ran his hand from the top of Petunia's head down her side.

Magda's eyes locked on the movement, and her heart rate sped up a little bit. Jealous of a dog? This had to be a new low for womankind.

"She's got to take one last trip outside before bed, but she's out like a light."

"I'll take her," Jeff offered without hesitation.

Magda flapped her hand at him dismissively. "I couldn't ask you to do that."

"You didn't ask. I volunteered. I wouldn't mind a little fresh air before hitting the sack."

"If you're sure…" Magda sounded hopeful, but doubtful. She hated that last trip outside when she was all comfy and sleepy, and couldn't imagine it wouldn't be an inconvenience for Jeff.

"I am." Jeff lifted his feet off the coffee table, where they'd been propped up during the movie and stretched. It made his loose T-shirt rise up a little and revealed a glimpse of his washboard abs. Yep. Magda's suspicions were right. The baggy clothes he favored were hiding a world-class body.

He picked Petunia up, and tucked her under his arm.

He smiled. "She feels like a little, furry football tucked in there."

Magda laughed. "In case my little, furry football does number two, I have plastic bags tied to her leash. It's hanging from a coat hook next to the kitchen door."

Jeff winced and squinted his eyes. "Ouch. Pooper-scooper duty. Footballs don't poop, but if I could handle Sam's stinky diapers when she was a baby, I can handle this situation."

Magda nodded as she swung her legs off the chaise and stood. "I used to babysit when I was a teenager, and I can say without question—doggie poop pick-up is better than diaper duty."

She bent over the coffee table and picked up the popcorn bowl, which now just held the unpopped kernels, re-solidified butter, and salt. With her other hand she grabbed their empty beer bottles between her fingers. They clanked together as she walked to the kitchen. "Fair is fair. While you take Petunia out, I'll take care of cleaning up in here."

Jeff bobbed his head with approval; he was raised in a family of hard workers, who would pitch right in when help was needed, so it was a trait he respected when he saw it in others.

"Thanks, Maggie, I appreciate it. We make a good team."

He stopped short as he realized that was how Francisco had once described his marriage to Bethanne, and he didn't want Magda to read too much into his words. Even if he kind of meant them.

He added in a rush, "Of friends. A team of friends—that's what I meant we were."

Magda shot him a puzzled glance over her shoulder as she led the way down the hall to the kitchen. "Okaaay…a team of friends."

****

Jeff shook his head at her retreating back and muttered, "A team of friends. Could I be more of a dork?"

In response, Petunia gave her tail a sleepy wag before she yawned and planted a sloppy kiss on his hand.

He chuckled. "Well at least you don't hold the stupid 'team of friends' comment against me, Miss Petunia."

He continued to the kitchen and saw Magda at the

sink, beneath a window that looked out over the backyard.

She put the bottles and bowl in the sink and went to the back door, where she pulled a plastic bag off the leash and held it out to Jeff with a flourish and a bow. "Your poop-removal tool, sir."

Jeff returned her bow as he took it. "Why thank you kindly, ma'am." He grinned. "Maybe I should tie it around my arm like the knights used to do with their ladies' favors."

Magda tossed back her head and laughed. Like her dog's bark, it was surprisingly deep and husky, from such a little bit of a thing.

"I guess you really aren't just another dumb jock. How do you know about jousting?"

He bristled with mock defensiveness. "Hey, I could still be a dumb jock *and* know about jousting. It's a real sport, you know. Why, just across the river in Maryland, jousting is the state sport."

Her jaw dropped. "Jousting is Maryland's state sport? No way!"

"Way."

"So that's how you know about it? From all the Marylanders jousting on the weekends?"

"Naw. It *is* the official state sport there, but I can't actually say I've ever seen anyone joust. When we were kids, Heather and Bethanne used to make Ty and I play 'Jousting Tournament' with them. Don't ever let those two talk you into going to a Renaissance faire, it's not pretty."

When she laughed her deep, throaty laugh again, the sound almost brought him to his knees with desire, and he realized anew that this "just friends" thing was going to take some work.

"And you guys went along with it? It sounds a little girly for two big, bad football players."

"The start of the game was kind of girly," he conceded. "Heather and Bethanne would pick a champion, and tie their favor—usually an old rag from the barn—around his arm. But then..." A slow grin spread across his face "...Ty and I would try to knock each other off a fence with sticks. It got kind of brutal."

She caught her breath from laughing and gasped out, "I'm surprised you weren't on horseback. You did grow up on a horse farm, and it is the traditional jousting method."

He opened his eyes wide with horror. "We would never have used my parents' horses that way. We might have spooked them, and if they got hurt we would've been in a world of trouble. Us kids getting hurt was just sort of expected."

He put Petunia on the ground while they talked, and she danced anxiously at the door, her little nails tapping out a staccato beat on the tile floor. They both turned their heads to look at her.

"My lady awaits." Jeff clicked his sneaker-clad heels together and threw open the back door. Petunia rushed out into the dark night. He flipped a switch by the door, and the backyard was bathed in a soft, yellow light from the fixtures on either side of the door.

"Back in a bit," he said as he followed the dog and shut the screen door behind him with a clatter.

Petunia appeared to want to sniff every square inch of turf before she decided on a spot to do her business. As he trailed after her meandering path, movement from the kitchen window caught his eye.

Illuminated by the bright kitchen light, he watched as Magda rinsed their bottles, and washed the popcorn bowl. It was nice, seeing her in there working, while he was outside with the dog. It made the big, old house seem more like a home. He was shocked by the sharp pang of longing he felt in his gut. He wasn't one to dream of a cozy, domestic life with a wife. Crystal, Sam's mother, had done a fine job of putting that notion out of his head years ago.

But seeing Magda's cheerful face at his kitchen window, it looked like she might be singing to herself as she scrubbed. It filled him with a yearning for it to be his life, so strong it felt like an actual physical ache.

He looked down to see Petunia squat to do her business a few feet away. He scrubbed his face with a hand as he walked to pick it up with the bag. These feelings wouldn't do at all. They'd agreed to be friends. So, why did this little bit of a woman, and her even littler bit of a one-eyed dog, make him wish he'd never agreed to such a dang fool thing?

Chapter 7

Friday night found Bernie Felder in Rivers Bend. He was surrounded by Civil War re-enactors, which worked to his advantage. If he'd come here on a regular weekend, he would've stuck out like a sore thumb in a little burg like this one. But tonight, the little pizza joint where he'd just finished his dinner was packed with middle-aged men from out of town, so he fit right in.

He sat alone at a small, round table that held an empty pizza tray, a glass of root beer, and his laptop computer. He leaned back in the frou-frou, little chair that would be more at home in an ice cream parlor than a pizza joint. He crumpled his paper napkin and tossed it on the empty tray.

Bernie rubbed his belly with appreciation—who would've guessed a backwater town like Rivers Bend would have decent pizza? He was seated near the counter where you placed your order with a burly older man, who was clad in black-and-white checked chef's pants. Salt-and-pepper chest hair peeped out of the V-neck of his white T-shirt. Behind him, three younger versions of the man bustled around in the kitchen to fill the orders of the mob of out-of-towners that crowded the small restaurant. Bernie understood just enough Italian to know that the older man was the owner and namesake of Vinnie's Pizzeria, and the three younger guys were his son and two nephews.

Bernie inhaled the aroma of oregano, tomato sauce, and the pleasant, yeasty scent of freshly baked bread and pizza dough. He would eat at Vinnie's even if it weren't the only place open in Rivers Bend after five o'clock—which it was. Used to the hustle and bustle of New York City, Bernie thought this town seemed like a graveyard.

He looked past the other tables and ignored the men at them arguing about 150-year-old battle strategies, out to the Main Street. Yes—*the* Main Street. The one and only main drag through the center of town. Rivers Bend was pretty, in a quaint, rural way, if you liked that sort of thing. The merchants all had planters on the sidewalk outside their businesses. The one in front of Vinnie's was a riot of red geraniums, greenery, and white wave petunias, which flowed over the sides of the terracotta pot. In case you missed the red, white, and green message, a small Italian flag was stuck in the center of the pot, next to its American counterpart.

Directly across the street was the library, housed in a small, brick building. Bernie had tried to visit it earlier, as the library was usually a good place to get the lowdown on a small town, but there was a printed sign on the door that read:

Closed Temporarily
You're in our thoughts and prayers, Bethanne!

Tacked up next to it was a piece of paper with the handwritten message on it:

Opening Monday!

Next to the library was a similar one-story brick building that housed the Rivers Bend Sheriff's Office, a place Bernie speculated did not see much activity. A few other shops; a restaurant even tinier than Vinnie's, which served breakfast and lunch; a couple of doctors' offices and one lawyer's office; an old-fashioned service station that doubled as a little market; and that was it. Nowheresville—at least to a man who lived in Brooklyn.

In the middle of Main Street, there was a gap in the buildings, which revealed a Town Green placed on overview of the town's namesake, a large bend in the majestic Potomac River. A gazebo sat in the middle of the Green, and signs were posted all over town that there would be music and fireworks there on Labor Day, which was coming up the next weekend.

Yeah. It was a pretty little spot. More like a movie set than a real town to a born-and-bred city boy like Bernie, but he wouldn't mind bringing the missus here for a weekend sometime. If there was somewhere to stay, which there wasn't. Bernie had to get a room in nearby Leesburg, not at all convenient for his current assignment. As far as Bernie was concerned, Rivers Bend was missing two key elements for his comfort and wellbeing: a Ramada and Magda Horvath.

He'd seen no sign of his quarry as he walked around town this afternoon and heard no mention of her in any of the conversations he eavesdropped on either. Of course, there were more visitors than locals in the town this afternoon, but Magda didn't seem to be here for the Skirmish at Rivers Bend reenactment, not that he really thought she was. It made about as much sense as any other reason he could come up with for a young woman like Magda to suddenly sever all ties and travel to this little town on the Virginia-Maryland border.

Yet, that is just what she seemed to have done. There was no further activity on her debit or credit cards, so she had to be in Rivers Bend somewhere. Maybe she was staying with friends or at that corporate retreat outside of town. A lot of the re-enactors mentioned they were staying there this weekend, so they sometimes took people as guests without being part of a corporate retreat. He needed to do a little re-con on the place. Boy, would his wife ever be jealous if he got to meet Jeff Braden while he was here! He knew he should be worried that she had been the victim of foul-play, but his well-honed instincts told him that she was on the run of her own volition, so he'd keep looking.

The little bell attached to the door jangled merrily, and as if he'd been summoned magically by Bernie's thoughts, in strolled Jefferson Braden, larger than life. At least, he looked that way compared to all the warrior wannabes who filled the pizza joint. Braden was the only man in the place who looked like he could be a real warrior. Not that he looked mean, Bernie mused— not at all. Braden's face was open, kind, and intelligent, not the face of a man who'd use his superior size and strength as a weapon unless, Bernie suspected, he was provoked.

Vinnie's chubby face was wreathed in smiles as he bellowed in heavily accented English, "Jeff! So good to see you! I wasn't sure if you'd be in for your regular Friday night dinner since your *bambina* is away."

Jeff grinned in return and stuck his hand over the glass counter display filled with pizza for sale by the slice, antipasti, and pasta dishes. Vinnie grasped the proffered hand and shook it vigorously.

"Mr. Mancini, do you think I could stay away from your pizza on a Friday night?"

When he got his hand back from Vinnie, Jeff waved to the three young men in the kitchen. "Hey guys, how's it going?"

They all smiled broadly as they returned Jeff's greeting and quizzed him on what he thought of the Redskins' chances in the upcoming football season. Jeff answered their questions patiently, but not so patiently as to be patronizing. If you didn't know he used to play pro ball, you'd think he was just a local guy discussing the home team. Based on the hero-worship on the faces of the younger Mancinis, it couldn't be easy for Braden to keep as down to earth as he seemed to be—he was clearly a favored son here in Rivers Bend.

Bernie realized the conversation had turned back to personal matters and focused his attention on it, without giving the impression he was doing anything but finishing up his root beer and digesting his dinner while he surfed the net on his laptop. It was a skill he'd perfected in his years as a P.I.

"Actually, Samantha came home early, and there's a slumber party in full swing at my house as we speak, so I need more than my usual pizza order tonight."

The little bell on the door jingled again, and a nice-looking fellow in a business suit entered with an easy smile. He looked familiar to Bernie, but lots of guys looked like this one. He was in his mid-thirties with reddish-brown hair and hazel eyes. The newcomer was tall and lanky, with attractive enough features, but nothing really stood out about him. In Bernie's professional experience people watching, this guy had lawyer written all over him—something about the suit, the oversized briefcase, and the confident way he carried himself.

"Jeff!" The man called out, as he wended his way through the small, but crowded restaurant. "I thought I saw your truck out front."

Jeff turned, and pleasure lit up his face. "Hey Ty! I didn't think you'd be around this weekend. I figured you'd be down in D.C. with that hotshot lobbyist you've been seeing."

A shadow chased across Ty's eyes, and his wide grin faltered. "Nope. I'm thinking I'm going to end things with him. We're like the 'city mouse' and the 'country mouse'. He hates to come up here to 'the sticks.'" He made air quotes as he spat out the last word. "And I'm not happy in the city. Nice place to visit, but I wouldn't want to live there. We're going nowhere, and I'm getting too old to stick in a relationship I know is a dead end."

Jeff clapped his friend on the back. "I'm sorry, man, but truth be told, I was never that crazy about him."

Ty's jaw dropped. "Really? You never gave any sign that you didn't like him."

Jeff shrugged his broad shoulders. "If you liked him and he made you happy, I decided to keep my mouth shut. Not my place to say anything, I just felt like he looked down on all of us Rivers Benders."

Ty looked sheepish. "He didn't do a very good job of hiding it, did he?"

The corners of Jeff's mouth quirked up as he shook his head. "Not really—no. You know Ethan who works down at the gas station?"

"The kid who took your niece to his prom last spring?"

"That's the one—he actually called him 'Gomer.'

Y'know, like Gomer Pyle? I guess he thought we were all such dumb hicks we wouldn't get the joke. Or the insult, I'm not really sure which one he intended his crack to be."

Ty scuffed his Italian loafer angrily on the black-and-white checked floor. "Ethan? He's such a good kid. He just left for Virginia Tech on a full academic scholarship; he's not some dumb yokel! Okay, that's the last straw—dump city for him, baby. I was pissed that he didn't understand why I would want to stick close to Bethanne this weekend. I mean, she was just released from the hospital, and if anything happened to my kid sister and my soon-to-be nephew while I was away, I'd never forgive myself."

Ty and Bethanne? Something pricked at Bernie's memory about those names in connection to Magda Horvath, but he couldn't remember what it was. Maybe he was getting too old for the fieldwork—he should start thinking about switching to a managerial role in his firm and leave this crap to the young staffers.

"Speaking of Bethanne," Ty said, "I hear Maggie got here early to help her out with the library."

Bernie observed the barest hesitation before Jeff answered. "Yep. She's staying with Sam and me this weekend. Since the Retreat is booked solid with re-enactors, we didn't have a free room or cabin for her."

"I heard about that, too." Ty winked. "We *are* in Rivers Bend after all—no gossip is too small to be shared here. Maggie's a great girl, don't you think?"

Another hesitation on Braden's part—interesting. Bernie didn't know what it meant, but unless he was more over the hill than he thought, his instincts told him there was something between this Maggie and Jeff.

"She's very nice and a good friend to drop everything to come here and help Bethanne."

Drop everything? Wait—could Maggie be Magda?

Jeff continued over Bernie's thoughts, "Speaking of Maggie, I better order and get back home—I left her there with a houseful of eleven-year-old girls."

Ty shuddered. "You'd better hurry then; if you leave Maggie with the girls for too long, she might catch the 'Bieber Fever.'"

Jeff chuckled. "Certainly a possibility, as they were all singing along with one of his songs when I left to get dinner."

Ty raised his eyebrows. "*All* of them? Even Maggie?"

Jeff's chuckle turned into a full-blown laugh. "No, Maggie wasn't singing. As a matter of fact, she looked a little like Alice did when she was at the Mad Hatter's tea party. Her 'hurry back' when I left was particularly heartfelt."

Ty roared with laughter. "Thanks, man, I was feeling really bummed, and I needed that laugh."

"Breakups are always hard, but you made the right decision. Tell you what—why don't you come back and have dinner with us. Then, you can see Maggie."

"Sounds good, thanks. I wasn't looking forward to a lonely meal at home. I was thinking about barging in on Francisco and Bethanne, but this sounds like fun."

Jeff placed an order with Vinnie for two large cheese pizzas and a large half Mega-Meat and half eggplant pizza.

Vinnie glowered. "You goin' vegetarian on me? You two been ordering the same thing since you were in high school—and it's never been no 'eggplant' before! You always get a large Mega-Meat."

Jeff smiled. "Trust me, I'm still a carnivore through and through. The eggplant's for my houseguest; she's the lady who's going to be watching the library for Bethanne."

Vinnie beamed. "It will be good to have the library open again. Tell you what, I'll give you your regular large Mega-Meat, and a small eggplant pie—on the house—for the lady. As a 'thank-you' for helping out the town and getting our library running again."

"That's mighty nice of you, Vinnie. I'll let her know."

The two men stepped away from the counter to await their order. Fortunately for Bernie, it brought them even closer to him and made his eavesdropping all the easier.

Ty looked around and seeing no one he knew nearby, he said to Jeff in low tones, "Call it best-friend's intuition, but there's something up with you and Maggie—I can tell by the way you're acting when you talk about her. Spill."

Jeff rolled his neck to loosen the tension, and Bernie winced at the audible crack it caused; something had this man stressed, and there was nothing like a woman to do that to a guy. Bernie guessed Ty was right.

Finally, Jeff answered, "Maggie and me? Nothing *to* spill about us. Sorry."

Ty took a deep breath and raised an eyebrow skeptically. "Try again, buddy. It's me you're talking to here, and I'm not falling for this 'nothing' bullshit. You get this look when you talk about her—kind of dreamy. It reminded me of something, but I can't place what it is. So take your phony 'nothing to spill' up the road and try to sell it there, 'cause I ain't buying it. Spill."

Ty put his briefcase on the floor next to him and loosened his necktie. He smiled expectantly at Jeff, in spite of his friend's glare.

Finally, Jeff huffed. "I kissed her. There. Are you happy now? I kissed Maggie, and it was mind-blowing—earth-shaking..."

Ty grinned and gestured with his hand for Jeff to continue. "Earth-shaking, huh? Cool. I never pictured you two together, but now I can see it would be a good match. So you kissed her and...?"

Jeff dropped his eyes. "And we decided to be friends. Nothing more."

Ty ran his hands through his previously impeccably styled hair and shook his head. "Why the hell would you decide to do something half-assed like that? 'Mind-blowing,' 'earth-shaking' kisses don't come along every day, and on top of that fact, she's a great girl—smart, funny, loyal, pretty." He smacked Jeff in the chest with the back of his hand. "What's the matter with you?"

Jeff frowned, and smacked Ty back. "Nothing's the matter with me. Maggie's terrific—yes—no argument here, but she's also staying in the house with my daughter, and you know how I feel about girlfriends getting involved with Sam. On top of that, she just broke things off with her fiancé—she's not ready for anything more."

"Yeah, well, said fiancé was a total dipshit rich boy. I don't think she needs to waste any time mourning the loss of his sorry ass."

"So...you knew him?" Jeff asked with open

curiosity.

"I saw him at Tom Horvath's funeral. He swooped in on Maggie like an Armani-clad vulture. All solicitous words, but I didn't trust him."

Bernie mentally slapped himself on the forehead. Now he remembered why the names Bethanne and Ty rang a bell. Bethanne had shared an apartment with Magda when the two women were in library school together. He saw her at the funeral with her brother—the man talking to Jeff right now. No wonder Ty looked familiar. So Magda had to be the Maggie who was staying with Jeff Braden this weekend; the woman who shared some major chemistry with her host, based on his comments about their kiss.

God, he was slipping! He should've made the connection before. While he was internally beating himself up, the two men had moved to the counter to pick up their order.

"Thanks again, Mr. M." Jeff grinned as he balanced the hot pizza boxes in his arms. The beaming pizza man cartoon on the lids looked frighteningly like Vinnie himself.

"I'll be sure to tell Maggie her pizza was on you. I'm sure you'll see her in here when she starts working across the street."

"She is welcome here anytime," Vinnie bellowed with genial sincerity as the bell rang when Ty held the door open for Jeff and his delicious-smelling cargo.

Bernie stood and stretched. He picked up the aluminum pizza tray and brought it back to the counter.

"Thank you, sir. You didn't have to do that—we would've cleared your table," Vinnie said.

Bernie smiled and tried to look sheepish. "No

problem. I have to admit that I wanted an excuse to talk to you and ask you about the guy who just left. Was that Jefferson Braden? Used to play ball for the Portland Pintos?"

Vinnie's barrel-chest swelled with pride. "That's him! Greatest tight end to ever play the game."

"That he was." Bernie smiled and leaned forward to say confidentially, "My wife's not going to believe it when I tell her I saw him; she always had kind of a thing for him. It was the only way I could get her to watch football with me on Sundays. Bet a guy like him is a real ladies' man, huh?"

Vinnie shook his head vigorously. "Not Jeff. He lost his wife about ten years ago, and a lot of the ladies around here have tried their best with him, but no go. He's more concerned with raising his daughter—a real gentleman. I'm proud to know him."

Bernie handed his bill with a twenty-dollar bill across the counter. "Thanks for everything. That was the best pizza I've ever had south of the Mason-Dixon line. I'll be back!"

"You're welcome here anytime, sir. Enjoy the battle this weekend."

Vinnie thought he was a re-enactor. Good. It bought him a few days here in town. He sat back down and opened his laptop.

This whole job went against the grain for him. Magda Horvath was a good kid, and Pierce Allen was a first class schmuck. She deserved better. And she deserved better than that cold fish of a grandmother she was saddled with, too.

Here in Rivers Bend, she had friends who appreciated her for who she was, not for the size of her trust fund, and it seemed like she had a shot at love with Jeff Braden. That's why Bernie had wanted to confirm with the pizza man that Jeff wasn't some kind of love 'em and leave 'em sort of guy, and Vinnie's comments had verified his opinion that Jeff was worth a thousand Pierce Allens.

He might not look like Cupid in his pizza-smeared T-shirt and jeans, but he was about to give the chubby little imp a hand.

It was only a matter of time before Elizabeth Mallory found her granddaughter, but he could buy Magda a little time to be with Jeff to see where things between them could go before the old bitch stormed into Rivers Bend, like Hurricane Katrina did in New Orleans.

He opened his email and with a deep breath began to type a message to his biggest client. Maybe he was being a romantic old fool, but retirement was starting to look good anyway, and the wife was on him all the time about moving to Boca. So, even if what he was about to do blew his career out of the water, it would be okay. And he'd like Magda to break away from her grandmother's tentacles.

Mrs. Mallory,

I'm in Rivers Bend, but I haven't seen your granddaughter here. I'm going to expand my search area. Will notify you when I have something more to report.

—B.F.

He paused a moment to gird his loins and then clicked "send" with conviction. He was doing the right thing. Elizabeth Mallory's reign of terror over her sweet granddaughter needed to end, and if he could help move

things along then it was his responsibility to do so—
damn the consequences.

As the computer made the whooshing sound it did
to indicate an outgoing email, Bernie exhaled loudly
and thought—there goes your "Celebrity Free Pass,"
Jeff Braden. You better not blow it—don't make my
sacrifice be in vain. Please take advantage of this time
with her to win Magda's heart, and get her away from
her grandmother, that worm Pierce Allen, and her
miserable life in New York.

Chapter 8

The slumber party was still in full swing in the family room. Pop music blared, and the chatter of high-pitched voices and frequent bursts of giggling could be heard over the tunes.

But the adults had taken possession of the kitchen. The empty pizza boxes sat on the light-colored granite counter of the island, while Magda, Ty, and Jeff sat at a table in the corner of the room. It was surrounded by windows that let in bright light during the day, but at the moment only showed the reflection of the cheery kitchen against the dark of a country night outside. Booth style seating was built-in beneath the windows on two sides of the table, and the other two sides had ladder-back chairs, painted white to match the cabinets.

They'd moved on from pizza to dessert, so a plate of Mrs. Wilson's homemade cherry, chocolate chip cookies sat in the middle of the table, and each of them had a stoneware mug of tea. Jeff's housekeeper's cookies tasted like ambrosia; Magda couldn't remember the last time she'd been treated to homemade baked goods.

Magda held her mug cupped in both hands as she laughed. The two men were laughing so hard they could only make wheezing sounds as their shoulders shook.

Magda spoke through her own laughter, "I can't believe you guys streaked at a girls' softball game!"

With some effort, Jeff stopped his wheeze-laughing long enough to admit, "Not the brightest decision of our high school careers."

Ty pulled himself together and picked up his mug to take a sip, but Jeff's words brought the laughter back, and he almost did a spit-take before he slammed the mug on the table. "Don't blame me—I wanted to streak the boys' lacrosse game."

Jeff nodded as he munched on a cookie and then said, "He was outvoted on that idea."

Magda reached for another cookie and said in amused surprise, "Outvoted? I thought it was just the two of you—how many of you streaked?"

Jeff leaned against the back of his chair and looked at the tin ceiling as he pursed his lips and thought. "Eight—no—*nine* of us. Most of the starting offense of the football team. It was the off season and we needed something to keep us from getting too bored."

Ty appeared to remember something, and it started him laughing again. "Looking back on it, the best part is that one of the 'Notorious Nine' was Dan Monroe."

Jeff threw back his head and roared with laughter. "Oh man, that's right." He shook his head as he continued to chuckle. "Dan Monroe. Good stuff."

Magda wrinkled her brow and looked back and forth between the two chortling men. "What's so funny about this Dan Monroe streaking with you? C'mon guys—let a girl in on the joke."

Jeff took a deep breath in an attempt to control his bubbling laughter. "Dan is now the respected sheriff of the fine town of Rivers Bend."

Ty wiped his eyes and gulped down the last of his tea. "Sometimes, when he's testifying on a case in court, looking all official in his uniform and so serious, I get a flashback to that day and—man—is it hard not to laugh. He can always tell when it happens—the man is uncanny—that instinct is probably why he's so good at his job. Anyway, he gets so pissed and glares at me fit to beat the band. Our fine sheriff doesn't like to be reminded of his misspent youth."

Jeff's eyes crinkled as he grinned. "And I'm sure *your* client would be thrilled to know that back in the day, his attorney got nekkid and ran through a softball game with the arresting officer."

As a fresh round of laughter threatened to overtake her companions, Magda looked up at the clock on the buttery yellow wall and slid down the booth. As she rose, she shook her head and smiled, "You guys are a riot! I wish I'd grown up here with you; my high school experience wasn't nearly so much fun."

Ty pressed his lips together and intoned, "But you're younger than us, so you would've been in Bethanne and Heather's class, and frankly, they weren't nearly so much fun as we were."

As she walked to put her mug in the sink, Jeff asked, "Where you headed—do you want to get back to the family room in time for pedicures?"

She smiled and rolled her eyes at him. "Yeah. That's where I'm going—I'm feeling a little Katy Perry withdrawal."

She patted her hand lightly on her thigh, and at the sound Petunia trotted out from under the table where she'd been having a snooze while her humans yucked it up.

"It's time for Petunia's last trip outside, and then these two girls are going to head up to bed."

An especially loud shriek erupted from the family room, as a song came on that the girls apparently loved, since they all began to sing along somewhat tunelessly. All three adults looked in the direction of the noise.

Magda smiled. "Although, the clearly incorrectly named 'slumber' party is still in full swing, us older girls need our beauty rest."

Jeff pushed his chair back from the table, and the wooden legs made a squeaking sound as they grated against the tile floor. He sighed, and his shoulders slumped. "Which reminds me, it's about time to start herding them upstairs. Not that any actual slumber will happen tonight, a dad has to go through the motions. They might be awake and giggling all night, but darn it, they'll be doing it in their sleeping bags in Sam's bedroom."

He grinned ruefully at Magda. "I just hope they don't keep you up all night."

She bent over to pick up Petunia, and with her free hand, she tugged a plastic bag off the leash on the coat hook next to the door. As she turned the doorknob, she smiled at Jeff. "No worries about me. That dreadful high school experience I mentioned—it was at a boarding school, so I learned how to sleep through anything." She paused, half in and half out of the back door as she pondered. "Possibly, it was the only useful thing I acquired there." With that, she stepped all the way outside and shut the door behind her with a soft click.

Jeff stood for a moment and watched her go, while a half-smile played around his lips.

Ty pushed his chair back and stood up; he carried his mug to the sink—all the while looking at his friend with a furrowed brow. "See—there's that look on your face again. It reminds me of something, but I can't figure out what it is. It's driving me crazy; it's like having a word on the tip of your tongue—it's there, it's just slightly out of reach."

"I'm not sure I *want* to know what I remind you of when I look at Maggie; call me psychic, but I have the distinct feeling it won't be a compliment."

"Probably not," Ty conceded with a nod.

Jeff looked down the hall to the source of the noise and squared his broad shoulders. "This is not going to be pretty; why do kids never want to go to bed and adults can't wait to get in there at night?"

Ty inclined his head toward the back stairs. "We can do fun things in bed that kids know nothing about. For instance, you would be sprinting up those stairs faster than when you streaked at the softball game if a certain hot little blonde we know was waiting for you in your bed with her Marilyn Monroe curves…"

Jeff fixed Ty with a stare. "Dude, what the hell?"

Ty smirked. "I'm gay—not blind. She doesn't do it for me, but anyone could see that Maggie's a cutie and that you have the hots for her."

"Whatever," Jeff huffed in exasperation. "I've got a room full of girls to round up, and they're all hopped up on soda and sugary snacks. Are you going to help me, or are you just going to stand around and make wiseass observations all night?"

"Nice attempt to change the subject, but we'll get back to it later. In the meantime, I'll help you," Ty rolled his shoulders like a boxer waiting for the bell. "Okay. Let's go."

Jeff smiled as they walked down the hall toward

the loud music and even louder shrieking and giggling.

As they got closer, they heard Sam's friend Hadley call out over the babble, "Sam, it's your turn—truth or dare?"

"Truth," Sam replied without hesitation.

"Does it bug you that your dad is crushing on Ms. Horvath?"

Jeff and Ty both stopped in their tracks to await Sam's response.

"My dad likes Magda? What? No way—they're just friends."

Jeff started to nod in agreement in an I-told-you-so kind of way at Ty, but a shrill burst of laughter greeted his daughter's response. Jeff's eyes grew wide as he swung his head from the partially closed door to the family room to meet Ty's gaze.

Ty shrugged and mouthed, "They're right."

Jeff rolled his eyes and punched his friend in the arm.

"Grow up, Sam, he looooves her," Hadley teased. "My mom has been throwing herself at your dad ever since she dumped husband number four, and he acts like he doesn't even notice her. But the soppy look on his face when he looks at Miz Horvath…"

Sounds of girlish agreement from the other partygoers interrupted her worldly assessment of the Jeff-Magda situation.

"You guys all see it?" Sam asked in amazement.

Her friends all answered as one with an exasperated, "Yes!"

"I haven't noticed anything—how does he look at her?" She asked with curiosity, but not seeming at all displeased, which surprised her father.

"Like the Grinch," Hadley replied to a flurry of giggles.

"The Grinch? All crabby you mean? That doesn't sound like love to me," Sam replied regretfully, which surprised Jeff even further. They had such a close father-daughter bond; he had always assumed Sam wouldn't want to share him with another female.

"Not the *crabby* Grinch at the beginning of the cartoon; I mean the dreamy way he looks at the end—when his heart grows three sizes."

Ty smothered a laugh. He whispered to Jeff, "That's it! The Grinch—that's what you've been reminding me of lately."

Jeff glared at him, but Sam's reply stopped his angry retort.

"Dad and Magda. Huh. I hadn't thought about it, but that might not be too bad. I mean she's fun and nice—and she's got a cool dog."

The girls all murmured in agreement.

"Stepmom-wise, you could do a lot worse than Ms. Horvath. Trust me—I'm an expert on stepparents, between my mom and dad, I've had five," Hadley intoned in a way that was too world-weary for her tender years.

Jeff felt bad for the kid; her mother was a piece of work. He'd never met the father, who'd been the first of Hadley's mother's four husbands and who now lived in Richmond with his third wife.

As the girl's words sank in, he shoved Ty back to the kitchen. He shut the swinging door behind them and hurried to peer out the back door, to make sure Magda was still out there. Yep, the dog was taking her sweet time, and Magda was sitting on an Adirondack chair under a big magnolia tree as she watched her dog sniff around the backyard. It looked like he had a few minutes to talk to Ty in private before she came back inside. He turned and leaned his back against the door.

"Explain this whole Grinch thing to me," he commanded.

Ty was laughing so hard, he had to lean one arm on the island for support and held the other over his stomach.

"I'm actually sore from laughing—what a great night! I haven't had this much fun for a long time; thanks for asking me over here for dinner."

Jeff crossed his arms. With his scowl and the muscles of his chest clearly outlined through his snug Under Armour T-shirt, he knew he looked pretty intimidating; even if his usual baggy cargo shorts and bare feet took a little away from the tough guy image he was trying to project.

Clearly, their lifetime of friendship had rendered Ty immune to his attempt at intimidation.

Ty held up one hand and wheezed. "Stop it, man, you're killing me!"

"Pull yourself together, Ty, we don't have much time before Maggie comes back in—explain this Grinch bullshit to me."

With a couple of gasping breaths, Ty composed himself. He stood up straight and nodded. "Okay, okay, I'm good now." He inhaled deeply and continued. "You have to remember the end of the Grinch—when he's stolen all of their stuff and he's waiting to hear the Whos cry, but instead they all clasp hands and sing?"

"Yeah, I remember it; what I don't understand is what the hell it has to do with Magda and me."

"Well, his heart grows, and he gets this dippy look on his face—like this…" Ty relaxed his shoulders and plastered a dreamy smile on his face, while he made his eyes soft and wide.

Jeff kept his arms across his chest and shook his head once. "Still not seeing the connection to me, Ty."

"It's *exactly* the way you look at Maggie."

Jeff dropped his arms and clenched his jaw. "It is not."

"Sorry, buddy, but it is. Can Hadley Diemer and I both be wrong?"

****

Magda stood in the morning sun with Jeff to see off the last slumber party guest, firmly planted at Jeff's side, where he'd kept her since Hadley's notorious mother had shown up to get her daughter. All the parents had come inside to pick up their daughters in person. Curiosity about Magda was one reason, as news of her arrival, and the library's reopening had spread like wildfire through the small community. However, it was clear that some of the mothers had come in to flirt with Jeff. Hadley's mother was just the most blatant in her pursuit.

Magda was pretty sure it was Jeff's presence on the porch that put a little extra twitch in the woman's narrow hips and an extra bounce to her improbably bountiful breasts, as she walked to her Mercedes sports car. She tossed Hadley's overnight bag in the trunk and flashed a coquettish smile over her shoulder at Jeff, who might have actually shuddered a little; although, his smile never faltered.

"What a piece of work that woman is," he said out of the corner of his mouth.

Magda took in Gloria Peterson's painted on white Capri pants, her little kitten heels, and the lilac silk top with the ruffles covering the front of it. The sun caught in her black hair, and she saw a glint of blue in it, like a raven's wing. The woman shaded her midnight blue eyes by putting an elegant hand to her forehead as she watched Hadley, Sam, and Petunia run out of the barn, where the girls had gone to see the two horses Jason had left behind yesterday.

"She does come on kind of strong, but she's really beautiful," Magda replied truthfully.

Jeff shrugged. "I guess she is, but my terror at the notion of becoming husband number five probably colors my opinion of her appeal."

Magda opened her eyes wide. "*Four* husbands?"

"Yep."

"Wow! Poor Hadley."

They watched the two girls hug goodbye before Hadley climbed into her mother's shiny, red car. Gloria waggled her fingers at Jeff, and the look in her eyes was so steamy it could remove wallpaper. It drove Jeff to put his arm around Magda and jerk her to his side. Gloria sighed visibly, and slid behind the wheel.

"I know. I feel sorry for the kid. She's one of the reasons I don't bring women around Sam; I've seen Hadley get attached to stepparent after stepparent—her dad's on wife number three, so she gets no stability there either, and I know I could never do that to my Sam."

He smiled at his daughter as she stood squinting in a patch of bright sunlight, holding Petunia in one arm and waving at the departing car with the other.

"I understand," Magda tapped at his hand on her

shoulder. "But this little display is going to have everyone in Rivers Bend thinking we're a couple."

Jeff pulled his arm away, and his cheeks reddened a little. "Sorry about that, but our friends and family will know the truth." A wicked grin replaced his previously sheepish expression. "And if it would get Gloria off my ass—both literally and figuratively—I'd pretend I was dating Lucretia Borgia."

Magda sneaked a peek at his tight buns. "I *thought* I saw her grab your ass!"

He rubbed his right butt cheek. "At least it was just my ass this time."

Magda's jaw dropped, but Sam's approach put an end to any further questions on what precisely the woman had grabbed the last time.

She saw a speculative gleam in Sam's eyes as she looked at them standing together on the porch, and Jeff and she both took a step away from each other.

"Thanks, Daddy! The party was awesome!"

Jeff hoisted himself up on the porch railing and swung his bare feet. "I heard y'all giggling into the wee hours. I was going to ask if you wanted to drive down to Tysons Corner to do some back-to-school shopping today, but you're probably too worn out."

Sam must not have seen the twinkle in Jeff's eyes that Magda did as the girl said breathlessly, "I'm not too tired to go shopping. I'm *never* too tired to shop!"

Jeff chuckled. "You're such an easy mark, Peanut."

Sam swatted at her father. "Dad, you are *so* not funny."

Jeff grinned unabashed. "I don't know—I think I'm a regular Henny Youngman."

Sam wrinkled her brow. "Who?"

"George Carlin?" Jeff offered.

Sam shook her head. "Try someone from the twenty-first century, Dad."

"Cruel, cruel child—teasing an old man about his age. I'm tempted to stay home today."

He chuckled at Sam's wide-eyed horror. "See—you *are* an easy mark—it's so easy to get you going. Don't worry, we're still going shopping. Besides, Maggie needs a new phone, so she can come along if she wants."

****

Pierce was sprawled in his rumpled, 1000-thread count sheets, clearly nude beneath them. He watched Taylor in her matching scarlet strapless bra and panties, as she picked up her wrinkled red dress from where they had tossed it on the floor the night before. She shook it out before she shimmied back into it.

She smiled like a cat with a bowl of cream at his lustful expression, and Pierce knew she had him just where she wanted him—at her mercy.

"So, we're agreed. There's no way we're letting Elizabeth Mallory dictate our sex life. We'll have to be more discreet, but we're going to keep right on seeing each other."

Pierce frowned and squirmed a little under her narrow-eyed stare at his hesitation. He wasn't at all sure that standing up to Mrs. Mallory was a good idea, but Taylor was the brains of their operation. Speaking of which, maybe she'd have an idea about how to track down his runaway fiancée/meal ticket.

"If we could just find Magda, everything could go back to the way it was. Do you have any thoughts on how to do it?"

Taylor's eyes flashed with anger at his question. "Why do we want things back the way they were? Am I not woman enough for you?"

Pierce watched hungrily as she ran her hands down the red silk dress that clung to her body. He licked his lips.

"You're more than enough woman for any man, but I need Magda for financial reasons. She's my golden ticket back into the Mallory family vaults, not to mention my job at M.I. And my father has implied that marriage to her will get me back in the Allen family fold."

"It's not a very good deal for me; I'm relegated to being your mistress when it's obvious I'm more suited to being a wife to the Allen heir than Magda Horvath ever could be."

Pierce held up his hands in a conciliatory gesture. "All very true, but for the short term I need Magda to find my way back into the family fold. Once I'm back in with my family, I won't need Magda anymore. She'll become expendable."

With a resigned sigh, she said, "Fine. I'll help you find Magda. As long as you realize I'm the one you'll be with in the end."

Pierce sat up and smiled. "Of course you will be; I knew I could count on you, Tay-Tay. So, what's our first step?"

She tapped a perfectly-manicured nail on her chin. "I'll need time to think; I haven't given a lot of thought to *keeping* Magda in our lives before. It's a total change of direction for me."

She sat gracefully on the edge of the bed as she thought over the possibilities. "I do have one preliminary idea. You could set up an online news alert for her name."

Pierce furrowed his brow. "What on earth do you mean?"

Taylor rolled her eyes, and said with exaggerated patience, "Really, darling, you need to join the rest of us in the 21st century. It's a way to be notified via email any time her name is mentioned online in a news story. It's a long shot, but it's a start. She *is* heir to the Mallory fortune, so she'd have to be in the hinterlands, for it not to be news. Anyway, it's a start, and I'll begin to think seriously about how to find her."

Pierce held up his long index finger in warning. "To find her with the least possible fuss. We don't want to drag too many people into it; discretion is a non-negotiable requirement for Mrs. Mallory. And I can't afford to pay a detective until my account is released."

"Understood. We'll figure something out, Pierce, never fear. The sooner Magda is back in our lives, the sooner she can be out of it again."

Chapter 9

Magda watched Sam scramble up into the back seat of Jeff's huge, black truck. From her petite perspective, it loomed large in front of her, and she had no clue how to get into it and still retain some dignity. Sometimes, it really sucked to be short.

With a sigh of resignation, she bent her knees and prepared to launch herself into the cab. With no warning, she felt strong hands at her waist and she was lifted off the ground. She squeaked in surprise and looked over her shoulder, while Sam giggled in the truck.

"Jeff! You scared me—I didn't hear you coming. How can such a freakishly large man be so stealthy?"

"It's my ninja training—helps me to close silently in upon my prey."

She let herself relax and leaned back against Jeff's broad chest. She could feel his body heat through his polo shirt, and it managed to be both a comforting warmth and an inferno-starter at the same time.

Just.

Friends.

Magda repeated what was fast becoming her internal mantra, as her body's liquid response to his display of strength belied the words in her mind. She decided to crack a joke to try to diffuse the electric response of her body to his touch.

"Do you intend to carry me all the way to the mall?"

She felt the rumble of his chuckle against her back, and his breath tickled her ear as he whispered, "If I decide to carry you off, Maggie darlin,' it won't be to any damn mall—it will be to my bedroom."

At her sharp intake of breath, he raised his voice, so Sam could hear him. "I'm just helping you into the truck; you looked like you were winding up to do a major Olympic long jump into it. Thought I could give you a lift and maybe avoid an injury."

He carried her the last steps to the truck and then deftly turned her and deposited her on the passenger seat.

She swung her legs in and buckled up, as Jeff jogged around the hood and hopped effortlessly behind the wheel.

"This big, shiny, black behemoth is not just a truck," she declared. "It's so intimidating looking. Let's face it—if the Spanish Armada sailed up the Potomac, they would want this monster to be their land transport. It would strike fear in all the villagers."

Sam giggled in the back seat, and Jeff fought a smile, in order to maintain his innocent expression.

"I don't know what you're talking about. Sometimes I need to haul horse trailers, or my fishing boat, so I need a good, sturdy dually for towing."

Magda smiled at him. "Very practical. And the gleaming black paint job and the shiny silver grill—they have nothing to do with presenting a macho appearance?"

Jeff took his eyes briefly off the road to flash her a look full of wounded innocence. "Of course it doesn't! I don't need my truck to show the world how macho I am."

"Then why couldn't we get that cheery yellow pickup truck that I liked?" Sam piped in from the back.

Jeff looked at his daughter in the rear view mirror and raised his eyebrows. "Another county heard from," he observed with a wry smile. "Fine. You girls have got me; I like the big, black Darth Vader look of this truck. Happy now?"

"Yes!" Maggie and Sam chirped in unison, before dissolving into laughter.

****

Jeff sat in a chair outside of the dressing room at Nordstrom. Another man sat in a chair beside him and held his wife's purse in his lap. The two men exchanged a grim smile of camaraderie, and Jeff went back to surfing the web on his phone.

He raised his head to watch as Magda entered the Juniors department. This connection between them was like nothing he'd ever felt before—it was like there was a live wire flowing between them. He hadn't decided yet if it scared the shit out of him, or if it filled him with a sense of peace like he'd never known. Right now, it felt like a little bit of both.

He watched as she made her way through the racks of clothes and mannequins dressed in trendy teen fashions. Her eyes never left his, and she smiled bashfully as she approached.

"Hey," Jeff said with what he feared was a soppy grin.

"Hey, yourself."

Jeff rose and stuck his phone in his pocket. "How'd it go at the Apple store?"

"Good." She nodded; although, her smile vanished and her eyes looked guarded. "I got a new phone with a different number; I even treated myself to an upgrade to the newer model."

"What's wrong then?" Jeff asked with concern.

"I'm just a little angry—or hurt." She paused as she considered and then shook her head. "Nope. It's not hurt. I'm pissed."

"About your new phone? I don't understand."

"My new phone is great—it's not that—I thought I'd call Pierce before I got my old number disconnected. I don't want him to have my new one, but I felt as though he deserved the chance to try and explain his actions."

Jeff cocked his head. "Very fair of you—more fair than most people would be given the circumstances. What did he have to say for himself?"

"I didn't actually talk to him. The woman he's been cheating on me with answered the phone and told me he was in the shower. She even had the nerve to complain that I had woken her up!"

Jeff whistled low between his teeth. "So all those messages about wanting you back—"

"Had more to do with wanting access to my grandmother's money again, than wanting me back in his life. He's perfectly happy with Taylor—which is fine—I don't want him, it just makes me feel so stupid and angry with myself!"

Jeff reached out to tuck a stray curl behind her ear, and she briefly leaned her cheek against his hand for comfort, the way a kitten might. The low thrum of electricity between them flared to life, even at that slight contact.

****

Magda jerked her head away from Jeff's touch. There was such a spark between them; she was surprised smoke wasn't rising off the top of her head. She shouldn't—*wouldn't*—turn to Jeff for comfort. That type of behavior is what got her into this situation in the first place. Grief-stricken at her beloved father's death, she turned to Pierce to fill the void in her life. Well, this time she'd fill it by herself. She needed to figure out what she wanted to do, and where she wanted to do it, without depending on a man.

Jeff was clearly a better man than Pierce, and maybe someday...but she couldn't let her mind go there. She needed to help Bethanne and use her time here in Virginia to take a good, long look at her life and decide what she wanted to with it.

Jeff dropped his hand at her clear withdrawal and an elegant, middle-aged saleswoman beamed at them from the dressing room door. "Oh good, your wife's back." She called over her shoulder to Sam, "Your mother's here—I'll send her in."

Jeff and Magda exchanged a panicky look, and both took deep breaths to correct the saleswoman when they heard Sam's voice, a little shaky but loud and clear. "Thank you, ma'am."

Magda gave Jeff a quizzical look, and he shrugged in response and looked as confused as she felt.

Oblivious to their emotions, the saleswoman gestured for her to come in and smiled. "You look way too young to be her mom. You're just going to love the outfits your daughter chose, she looks simply darling in them..."

Magda followed in the woman's chattering wake

and saw Sam standing in the entrance to a changing room, biting her lower lip nervously.

"You're so lucky to have your mother's pretty blonde hair, I have to pay a fortune for mine." The saleswoman smiled and patted her hair before sweeping back out into the store.

Sam's eyes were like saucers, and her voice was a little squeaky as she brushed at the cute, floral dress she wore.

"How does this look on me?"

Magda smiled and stepped around her into the dressing room. "It looks really nice."

"Not too girly?"

"It's a little girly—but cute. You could wear it on the first day of school. My dad always insisted a girl needed a pretty, new dress for the start of a new school year."

She stood behind Sam and nipped the waist in a little, where it drooped a little due to Sam's straight, coltish figure. She tilted her head as she looked at their reflection in the mirror. "We might need to take it in a little, but I can help you with that. I bet Bethanne will let us use her sewing machine."

Sam smiled so broadly that the fluorescent lights in the ceiling glinted off her braces. "Thanks, Magda. It's great having you here."

Magda smiled gently and rested her hands on Sam's shoulders as they continued to look at their reflection in the full-length mirror on the wall in front of them. Sam was so tall already that they were about the same height. Magda didn't really see how the saleswoman had mistaken her for Sam's mother—yes, they were both blonde haired and blue eyed, but their resemblance ended there. Sam was all long legs, with stick-straight hair that was more the color of honey than her own lighter shade, and she wished she had Sam's lean build.

She didn't want to ruin Sam's good mood, but she had to ask, "Want to tell me why you didn't tell the saleswoman that I'm not your mom?"

Sam's smile faltered. "It just felt good to have her think we were a normal family."

Magda smoothed the girl's hair. "One thing I've learned as I've gotten older is that there is no such thing as a 'normal' family. Each one is weird in its own way."

"I guess." Sam sighed. "But there's no one else in my school whose mother is dead. Lots of the kids have parents who are divorced, and I know that's hard, too, but they've still got both of their parents, even if they don't all live in the same house. I feel like a freak sometimes, y'know?"

"I do know. It was the same way for me when I was growing up."

"So, you understand then? I didn't mean to lie. It just felt so good to have someone think you, Dad, and I were all a family—that for once, I could be like other girls and have my mom come into the dressing room to help me pick out my school clothes."

Magda pursed her lips as she considered the matter; hopefully, Jeff would understand when she explained the situation to him.

"I guess there's no harm, as long as *you* know we're not a family—your dad and I are just friends."

"I know. The other girls last night were trying to tell me that Dad *liked you* liked you, but I told them you were friends." She lowered her eyes. "But if I had to have a stepmom—I'd like her to be just like you."

Magda felt a flock of butterflies take up residence in her stomach at the notion of Jeff *liking* liking her, but she took a deep breath to get them under control. She didn't think it was in her best interest to pursue a romantic relationship with Jeff. Hadn't she just decided that she needed to learn to stand on her own two feet? And now those traitorous butterflies were trying to pull her back in; it also didn't escape her notice that Sam's words indicated Jeff's fears about the repercussions of a relationship between them weren't unfounded. Sam was already getting attached to her after just a few days, but she could relate to how Sam felt about today. Her dad always used to take her shopping and wait outside the dressing room, just like Jeff was doing now. While she appreciated her dad's sacrifice, it wasn't the same as going shopping with your mom the way all the other girls did.

Sam's eyes were anxious. "Are you going to tell the saleslady the truth?"

The girl's voice sounded so small and worried, it tugged at Magda's heartstrings.

She shrugged and said with a half-smile, "I don't think we need to; we'll probably never see her again." She squeezed Sam's shoulder. "But I just want to be sure we're clear—I'm not going to be your stepmother. Your father and I are just friends." She felt like a broken record with the "just friends" talk, but she didn't want to lead on a child who clearly longed for a traditional family.

Sam sighed. "I know. I'm not a little kid; I understand the way things are, and I just wanted to pretend for a little while. And I really didn't want the saleslady to give me the pity face, y'know?"

Magda nodded. "I hated the pity face. Okay, as long as you're clear on how things stand with your dad and me, we can let her think what she wants."

Sam threw her thin arms around Magda and squeezed with all her might. "Thank you, thank you, thank you! You're the best!"

Magda hugged her back, but worried anew that this sort of bond with his daughter was just what Jeff didn't want to happen.

****

Bernie slouched on a bench in the mall outside the entrance to Nordstrom, where he'd been since Magda went in to meet Braden and his kid a little while ago. He munched on a soft pretzel as he waited for them to come out. Not the most nutritious lunch in the world, but typical of what he had to eat while on a stakeout; his colon would probably send him a thank-you note if he did retire after this case.

He heard a low buzz and felt his cell phone vibrate in his pants pocket. He held the pretzel in his left hand and fumbled for the phone with his right. He looked at the caller on the screen and cursed under his breath before he answered.

"Hello, Mrs. Mallory. What's up?"

Without any polite greeting or preamble, Elizabeth Mallory began to speak. Her voice was so frigid, the phone almost felt cold in his hand. "Do you have the means to track my granddaughter through her mobile phone activity?"

Damn, but the old woman was quick. It had been barely thirty minutes since he overheard Magda leave a message for her grandmother. He forced his voice to sound easy; although, he'd never withheld vital information from a client before, and it made him a little shaky. Technically, he supposed he wasn't *hiding* information so much as delaying when he shared it with Old Woman Mallory in order to buy some time for Magda.

"Sure, I do. There hadn't been any activity on it as of this morning."

"Check again, Mr. Felder, I received a message from her twenty-eight minutes ago. She called to spare me worry about her well-being." A delicate snort followed that statement, as if it were ridiculous to assume she would be worried in the way a non-glacial grandmother would be. "But she didn't reveal where she was."

Bernie had actually overheard Magda's end of the conversation and knew she said more than the old lady told him. The girl had guts—he'd seen powerful men cower when faced with Elizabeth Mallory's wrath, but Magda told her off good and proper. She said she wanted her grandmother to know she was fine but was so angry at her manipulation and interference in her life that she needed time and space to cool off before she could speak to her.

"Sure thing, Mrs. M. I'll check it out and get back to you with her location when she called you."

"Fine." Mrs. Mallory disconnected with no further conversation.

Bernie took another bite of his pretzel and smiled. Magda was smart not to call from Rivers Bend. She certainly knew her grandmother's M.O. and that Mrs. M. would be able to trace her through her phone. She made the calls to Mrs. M. and that snake Pierce Allen here at the mall and then promptly got a new phone and number.

Her savvy in calling from Tysons Corner would help him to help her. He took his last bite of pretzel, crumbled the paper napkin, and tossed it in the waste bin next to him. He opened the email on his cell phone and pecked out a message to Mrs. Mallory with his thumbs.

I've got a location for your granddaughter. She made the call from the Washington D.C. area. Seems she was only stopping in Rivers Bend on her way south. I'll move my operation to Washington and be in touch from there.

He smiled in satisfaction as he tapped the send button. Not a lie, precisely, his operation was currently outside D.C., but it would be moving back to Rivers Bend when Braden and Magda finished shopping.

****

Jeff and Magda sat across from each other in the booth of a noisy family restaurant in Leesburg, where they stopped for a late lunch/early dinner on their way home from the mall.

Jeff leaned his head to watch his daughter's progress to the ladies room and spoke as soon as she was out of earshot. "Want to tell me what the hell was going on in the store?"

Magda took a sip of her strawberry lemonade to try to buy some time. She'd been dreading this conversation with Jeff.

"Um…what do you mean?"

"You know what I mean," he grumbled. "Why did the two of you let the saleswoman think we were a family? This is *just* why I don't bring the women I date home to Sam."

Magda bristled under his accusing glare, but the waitress arrived with their appetizer and cut off her angry retort. The teenage server put the platter of southwestern egg rolls between them on the table with three small plates and a pile of paper napkins.

She raised her bored voice above the pulsing eighties pop music, which blared out of the speakers in the ceiling, "Can I get y'all anything else right now?"

Magda smiled at her, grateful for the interruption, which had kept her from responding in anger to Jeff. She didn't want to fight with the man—she wanted to go to bed with him, and since that wasn't in the cards, she wanted to be friends with him.

"No thank you, we're all set for now."

The waitress nodded and lifted the empty tray to bustle back to the open kitchen at the rear of the restaurant.

"Well? I'm waiting for an answer," Jeff drummed his fingers on the table.

Great. It looked like the interruption hadn't cooled his temper any. Magda understood his fears for his daughter but couldn't help feeling a little insulted that he thought she'd use Sam to get close to him. She took a breath and launched in to her explanation, "In the dressing room, Sam told me she wanted to feel normal—just a girl shopping for school with her mom—and I remembered feeling that way when I was a kid, so I played along."

He slammed a hand on the table and the little stack of plates rattled. "See! It's just what I was afraid of— she's building up this fantasy about you." He gestured angrily between them. "About *us* and you're going to be gone in a few months and…"

Magda held up her hands to stop him. "Hold on. Let me ask you something—do you like being pitied?"

He leaned against the back of the red vinyl booth and blinked at the unexpected question. "Of course not—no one does."

She nodded. "You're right—no one likes to be pitied. It's an awful feeling, but when you're a little girl who's lost her mother, you're on the receiving end of *a lot* of pity, especially when you're in a situation like today, something you'd normally do with your mom. The saleswoman jumped to the conclusion I was her mother, and for once Sam didn't feel that pity. And I decided to let it slide when she told me because I remember feeling the same way when I was a kid, and it sucked eggs!"

****

Jeff could hear the pain in Maggie's voice at the memory, and her eyes glistened with unshed tears. He could feel his anger dissipate at the sight. He reached across the table, and his big hand engulfed her smaller one; he felt the zip that he always felt at even the most casual contact with this woman, but fought to suppress it. After all, this was just the type of complication he wanted to avoid and how much worse would it be if they gave in to their mutual desire? It would be hard for him to give her up at the end of her time in Rivers Bend, and Sam would be heartbroken.

She flashed him a brave little smile. "Sorry about the waterworks, talking to Sam brought back all those feelings from my childhood. I want you to know I made it clear to her that you and I are just friends and she understands—she just wanted one day without a stranger's pity."

Jeff saw his daughter hurrying to the table and pulled his hand back quickly, before she could see them holding hands and misinterpret it. "Here she comes."

Magda blinked a couple of times to clear her eyes and managed to look passably composed by the time Sam got back to their booth.

"Yum! The eggrolls are here; they smell great! You guys didn't have to wait for me."

The girl slid into the booth next to Magda, who distributed the little plates and put an eggroll half on each of them. For a moment, Jeff let himself experience his daughter's fantasy—that the three of them were a family on an outing together. It felt damned good. Too good for any sort of comfort.

Chapter 10

Magda met Mayor Davis at the library bright and early on Monday morning, in order to give herself some time to get the lay of the land before she opened. If the cheerful, rubicund little man kept talking, she'd miss that opportunity. Unfortunately, he exhibited a native Virginian's inclination to chat and seemed disinclined to leave. They made it as far as the small vestibule by the front door and Magda's eyes popped at the sight of the overflowing bin beneath the library's after-hours book return slot. The mayor followed her gaze and observed with the sort of pride he might if they were on a fishing boat, and Magda had just landed a trophy sailfish. "Quite a catch there."

With a grunt, the older man bent to help her pick up the books that had fallen on the floor. Young and old—these Virginia men were nothing if not chivalrous.

"It sure is." She stooped to pick up more books. "The people of Rivers Bend are very conscientious about returning their library books."

"We've got good folks here." The mayor puffed his barrel chest out with pride. "I guess I should be getting on my way and let you get to work."

He handed her an old-fashioned key and a notecard with the alarm code printed on it in neat handwriting that she recognized as Bethanne's.

"Call me if you need anything, y'hear?" He

beamed at her.

She returned his smile. "I will. Thank you for coming in early to open the library for me."

"You're very welcome. Thank *you* for coming here on such short notice to help our Bethanne. The town is in your debt."

With a courtly bow and a cheery wave, the mayor opened the door and toddled down the steps.

Magda left the door open and stood with her hands on her hips as she looked at the book return. She'd better find some book carts and get these books checked in; if the good people of Rivers Bend cared enough to return them on time, she'd do her part to keep the books circulating.

Her eyes caught on the community bulletin board on the wall opposite the front door and realized that some of the flyers were out of date, since Bethanne had to stop working without notice. All the ones about the re-enactment could come down now that it was over. The town seemed sleepier with the participants gone, but it had been quite a sight to see Main Street overrun with people in period garb over the weekend. She'd seen bedraggled soldiers from both sides of the conflict, and women dressed as camp followers and belles in hoop skirts.

She crumpled the flyer she'd taken off the board and tossed it into a recycling bin a few feet away.

"Two points!"

The man's voice caused her to jump. She turned to the door to see an attractive man in a tan sheriff's uniform. In his hands was a cardboard container, which held two paper coffee cups with *The Nosh Pit* printed on them and a mouth-watering blueberry muffin in the center.

"Sorry, miss, I didn't mean to startle you. Thought you'd have heard me coming up the stairs. I'm your new neighbor—professionally speaking, anyway—the sheriff's office is right next door, so I thought I'd stop off with a welcome to the neighborhood coffee and muffin."

"That's so thoughtful, c'mon in," Magda bent over to pluck some books out of his path.

"I'm Dan Monroe." He placed the tray on the circulation desk and pulled one of the cups out of the tray. He flashed her a grin. "This one's mine."

Magda stuck out her hand. "I'm Magda Horvath; it's nice to meet you, Sheriff."

She tried. She really did, but she couldn't keep the amusement from bubbling in her voice as she beheld the infamous "Streaking Sheriff." Based on the three participants she'd met so far, the girls' softball team had been treated to a mighty fine view the day of the football team's streaking incident.

The Streaking Sheriff had skin the color of a well-creamed cup of coffee and eyes like liquid dark chocolate. All these food analogies had her thinking she shouldn't have skipped breakfast this morning in her effort to get here early. She suppressed a giggle as she lifted the lid off her coffee and inhaled the delicious aroma of the freshly brewed beverage, before peeling open the little creamer and adding it to the cup.

"Someone told you about the softball game, didn't they?" He grumbled.

Magda stirred her coffee with the little wooden stirrer and batted her eyes in what she hoped passed for an innocent manner. She took a breath to answer and the sheriff held up his hand to stop her reply.

"You're staying out at Braden's place, and you're friends with Ty's sister, so it had to be one of them. Which one spilled the beans—it was Ty, wasn't it? When I see Harris, I'm going to kick his..." He caught himself before he revealed what part of Ty's anatomy he wanted to kick.

To hide her grin, Magda took a sip of her coffee and then said, "To be fair—they both told me about it."

He scowled and took a swig of his own black coffee. "It was one disastrous decision fifteen years ago. You'd think we could put it to rest already, instead of blabbing about it to our newest, prettiest resident right away."

Magda felt her cheeks heat a little at his gentle flirtation. In New York, she had felt invisible, but here in Rivers Bend she was the belle of the ball. Man, if she could package the charm of the men in this town, she could make a fortune to rival her grandmothers.

"I thought it was a cute story, and I find myself a little envious of the girls' softball team—so don't fret, Sheriff Monroe."

"Dan. Please call me Dan."

"Okay, Dan, since this muffin is as big as my head, do you want to stick around and share it with me?"

His smile was regretful. "I'd love to, but I've got to head next door and relieve my deputy. Maybe we could go to lunch instead?"

She hesitated and then mentally kicked herself, she had no reason to turn down lunch with a good-looking man. Certainly not because his handshake didn't cause the kind of electric charge that Jeff's did. They were just friends, right? At least that's what she spent most of yesterday trying to convince Bethanne.

Her smile was bright. "Sure. Lunch sounds good."

His smile softened his face, which could look a little stern, she'd observed in their brief acquaintance. "Great. I'll be back at noon."

As he went out the front door, Magda heard him greet someone, and a young woman's voice answer him. Her first patron. She felt her heart skip a beat. Magda always wanted to work in a public library, and it looked like it was show time. She really wanted to do a good job—both for Bethanne and for herself—so she hoped she didn't blow it.

In strolled a teenaged girl, in a yellow sundress and flat sandals. She was tall and athletic looking—and clearly part Braden. Okay—breathe—it wasn't a patron, but instead the part-time assistant Bethanne told her about, Jeff's niece Caitlin Anderson.

She smiled in relief as she really needed help in the library today. "Hi! You must be Caitlin. I'm Magda, and I'm so happy to see you."

The girl smiled in a polite way, but wrinkled her lightly freckled nose in confusion. "Nice to meet you, but how did you know who I am?"

"You look a lot like your Aunt Heather must have at your age."

The girl beamed. "Gosh! Thanks—Aunt Heather's a hottie!" She looked at the overflowing book cart. "How about I get started on checking those in, and you can do whatever it is Bethanne does in her office?" She gestured to the glass box of an office, behind the circulation desk.

"That would be great, thanks." Magda picked up the tray with her muffin and coffee. "Bethanne told me yesterday that there would be a mountain of bills and paperwork for me, since she had to leave without notice."

Caitlin nodded her head toward the mug. "Did you meet my mom at the Nosh Pit when you were there this morning?"

"No, actually Sheriff Monroe got this in for me."

Caitlin's face fell. "Oh. I thought you and Uncle Jeff…"

She stopped mid-sentence, and Maggie realized her eyes had grown wide and her mouth was in the shape of an "O."

"You thought your Uncle Jeff and I…" Magda waved her free hand to prompt Caitlin to finish her sentence.

The girl's fair complexion flushed. "It's just that my cousin Sam seemed hopeful that you two might—y'know…" She paused before blurting out, "That you and Uncle Jeff might be hooking up. And Mrs. Peterson told everyone at the Nosh Pit at lunch on Saturday that you were living with him. I'm sorry. Wow, listen to me ramble on about stuff that is totally none of my business. Shutting up now!" Caitlin lowered her gaze and grabbed an empty book cart. "Here's me—working—not prying into my new boss's life in any way."

Magda chuckled. "Caitlin, it's fine, I was just surprised; I guess I'm not used to living in a small town, and your Uncle Jeff and I are just friends. I stayed with Sam and him—in their guest room—over the weekend because the Retreat was booked solid. I'm moving into a cabin today."

Caitlin didn't seem convinced but put a big smile

on her face. "Right. Just friends." She rolled the cart to the overnight drop box, and Magda heard the steady thump of the books as Caitlin transferred them to the cart.

Magda shook her head as she went into the small office and put her breakfast tray on top of a pile of unopened mail on the desk. She absently tore off a bit of muffin and munched it while she thought about Caitlin's transparent disbelief.

"But we *are* just friends," she murmured to herself. "Does the whole town think we're an item?" And if so—what was the point of not taking their mutual attraction to the next level?

She swallowed the muffin with a gulp and looked at the mess on Bethanne's desk; she had her work cut out for her here. There was no time to worry about the small town gossip concerning Jeff and her. She shook her head as she skimmed around the corner of the gunmetal gray desk and plopped in the chair.

Whoever rhapsodized about the simplicity of country life was blowing some serious smoke. The people of Rivers Bend seemed to know more about her after a few days than anyone in her building in Manhattan did after months; she couldn't think of a single neighbor there who would even notice she had moved, but people that she didn't even know here were speculating about her living arrangements with Jeff.

She grabbed an envelope and sliced the flap with a letter opener. She better get her mind on work and get some of these bills paid before the lunch crowd at the Nosh Pit stopped talking about her imaginary love life and started talking about their town library being hounded by bill collectors.

****

The hum of conversation in the Nosh Pit ceased abruptly when Magda and Sheriff Monroe entered the small restaurant for lunch. The little bell on the door sounded like Big Ben booming in the sudden silence.

"Holy moly," she whispered to the Sheriff as a roomful of friendly, interested faces turned their way. "I feel like Julia Roberts arriving at the Academy Awards."

Dan chuckled as he put his hand under her elbow to guide her to the counter. "You are a major person of interest here in Rivers Bend—they wouldn't be nearly so interested in Ms. Roberts."

She looked around as they made their way past the tables to the counter of the café. She smiled nervously and ran her sweaty palms on her linen pants, which were creased beyond hope even in the high humidity of this August day. With all the attention on her, she wished she looked a little less hot and rumpled.

Conversations resumed; although, she now knew enough about Rivers Bend to be pretty sure all the talk was about her.

The woman in the apron with the Nosh Pit logo printed on it stuck her hand over the counter. "I'm Deidre Anderson—Jeff's sister—it's nice to meet you. Sorry about that, in a small town, the new blood is always the most interesting."

Like the rest of her family, Deidre was tall but more comfortably rounded than her sister or daughter. Her short hair was a darker shade of brown than her sibling's, but her eyes were the same shade of gray as Jeff's.

"You're Caitlin's mom—your daughter has been a

137

godsend to me today at the library. I'm Magda Horvath." She grinned and shook Deidre's hand.

Deidre laughed. "After that entrance, did you think I didn't know who you were? Seriously, though, I'm glad Caitlin's been a help to you—she's a hard worker."

"She sure is—I would've been lost without her this morning."

Deidre looked pointedly at Dan's hand, still holding Magda's elbow. "So do y'all need a table for two?"

"Yep," Dan answered for them, with a grin splitting his face.

"There's one in the corner you might want to grab, so what can I get for you?"

Magda looked at the chalkboard behind the counter and ordered the chicken salad sandwich; Dan asked for Virginia ham and cheddar.

Deidre smiled. "Great. I'll bring those to your table in a minute. Is sweet tea okay?"

"You bet," Dan responded with alacrity.

"Um…unsweetened for me," Magda replied apologetically. She knew sweet tea was the beverage of choice in this area, but she'd tried it over the weekend, and it was a little too sweet for the uninitiated.

Dan inclined his head toward the free table. "We better get that before someone else does."

They'd gotten about halfway to the table, when an older lady with her white hair looking like it was fresh from a weekly shampoo and set at the beauty parlor, stopped them with a loud voice that would be right at home braying "tally-ho" on a fox hunt.

"Sheriff Monroe, aren't you going to introduce me

to your lunch companion?"

He stopped and hung his head, managing to look more like a schoolboy in trouble with the teacher than the lawman he was.

"I'm sorry, ma'am, this is Miss Magda Horvath. Magda, this is Mrs. Anne Warren."

"Nice to meet you Mrs. Warren," Magda said politely.

The woman inclined her head like an empress receiving her due homage. "I've heard a lot about you. I must say, I'm surprised to see you here with the Sheriff. I thought you were keeping company with Joyce Braden's oldest boy."

Her loud voice cut through the room and silence once again descended, as everyone seemed to hold their breath while they waited for her answer.

She swallowed hard, feeling shy in front of the rapt audience and Mrs. Warren's stare. She cleared her throat and said, "No, ma'am, Jeff and I are just friends."

The woman snorted. "Not what I've been hearing, but if you say so."

Magda really had no idea how to respond to that, and was rescued by Deidre popping up beside them with their plates. "C'mon, y'all, your sandwiches are ready, let's get you that table before someone else comes in and nabs it."

The sheriff ducked his head at Mrs. Warren. "Enjoy your lunch, ma'am."

Magda smiled at the older lady before Dan and Deidre hustled her away.

"I'll just run back and get your teas," Deidre announced loudly before whispering when she bent down to deposit their lunches. "Sorry about the inquisition; Mrs. Warren is kind of the Queen Bee around these parts. She thinks she can say whatever she wants to whomever she wants."

As Deidre bustled away, Magda put salt and pepper on her sandwich and said conversationally to Dan, "You know, I was invisible in Manhattan."

Dan grinned wolfishly as he picked up his hearty sandwich with both hands. "I find that very hard to believe."

****

Magda twisted her head to look at the clock on the wall behind the circulation desk, so she didn't see anyone come in. It was a surprise when she heard Caitlin call from the periodicals rack, where she'd been putting the new magazines in their protective binders.

"Hiya, Uncle Jeff!"

"Hey, Caitlin," he answered, and Magda could hear the warm smile in his voice. She swiveled on the tall chair to face Jeff; she was surprised to see him with her dog in his arms.

Magda's face lit up, and she scooted around the circulation desk to pet her wagging dog and was rewarded with a sloppy, doggy kiss on the face.

"Did you come to visit me at work, Petunia?" She raised a quizzical eyebrow at Jeff. "I thought Sam was watching her today?"

"She got invited to the movies and dinner with some friends, so Miz Petunia has been my assistant for the afternoon."

Caitlin rushed over to pet the dog. "What a sweetheart! Sam told me all about her at Sunday dinner yesterday."

"Jeff, I'm so sorry you got stuck taking care of

her," Magda said.

His slow smile made her breath catch in her throat, as usual.

"No problem. She hung out in my office while I made some phone calls and did some paperwork. Then, we went for a ride in the golf cart to look over the property—make sure the re-enactors didn't tear things up too bad—and I have to tell you, she loved the golf cart."

Magda smiled. "I bet she did. She is a dog who loves her bye-byes in the car—or golf cart, evidently."

"You look whooped, how was *your* day?"

Before she could answer, Caitlin piped up. "Poor thing got waylaid by Mrs. Warren when Sheriff Monroe took her to the Nosh Pit for lunch. She accused Magda of two-timing you."

Jeff frowned. "You had a lunch date with Dan? Well, that's fine. I mean we're just friends, right?"

Magda found herself explaining to him, "It was just a friendly lunch—not really a date, but y'know, you and I *are* just friends, so…"

Caitlin went back to work as she scoffed with the level of sarcasm only a teenager could achieve. "Just friends—riiight—keep telling yourselves that and maybe someday you'll find someone who'll believe you."

"Caitlin," Jeff said her name as a warning.

Magda shook her head at him and said, "It's closing time, Caitlin; you can finish up the magazines tomorrow. Why don't you head on home. Thank you for all your help today; I couldn't have done it without you."

Caitlin walked over and reached behind the

circulation desk for her purse. "It was actually good to be back at work; I need the money to buy clothes for school." She gave Petunia a final scratch behind the ears. "See you in morning, Magda. Bye, Uncle Jeff."

"Have a good night, kiddo," he replied with a smile.

The girl ran out the door, and Magda sighed. "Oh to have the energy of a seventeen-year-old. I'm seriously dragging."

"Long day?"

She nodded. "It was, but it felt so good to be working in a public library; it's the type of work I've always wanted to do. The corporate library gig at M.I. wasn't my thing at all, so I'm tired, but it's a good kind of tired."

"Cisco and I had all your stuff moved to Cabin Five today, so at least you don't have to worry about doing that after work."

"Thanks, that's great! I appreciate it. I need to get to the grocery store on my way home, then. I guess."

"You're 'too pooped to pop', as my grandmother used to say. Why don't you just head home tonight? You can take a dip, and I'll grill us up some burgers."

"Take a dip? Where—in the river?" She squeaked.

"No, city girl, *not* in the river. In the Retreat's swimming pool. We don't have any guests coming until tomorrow, so we'll have the pool and barbecue area to ourselves."

She sighed deeply. "A cool swim sounds heavenly and so does dinner cooked by someone other than me— I'm in."

She heard a throat being cleared and looked around Jeff to see the Streaking Sheriff in the door, with his hat in his hands.

"Hi, Jeff. Don't think I've ever seen you in the library before."

"Hey Dan, I could say the same to you."

"Hi Dan! Thanks again for lunch—oh—and the coffee and muffin this morning."

Jeff raised his eyebrows at his old friend. "Breakfast *and* lunch. Aren't you a regular Welcome Wagon? You can take the night off, Dan, I've got dinner covered."

Dan pointed at the Shih Tzu still snuggled in Jeff's arms. "So you got yourself a dog, huh Braden? I would've figured you more for a hound man, but whatever floats your boat."

Magda patted Petunia's head. "She's my dog. Jeff was just watching her for me today."

Dan recovered quickly and strolled over to pet Petunia, who wagged her tail and batted her eye at the newcomer like the shameless flirt she'd become since they left New York. "Well, aren't you just the sweetest little thing? Just like your mamma." He put his hat on and smiled widely at Magda. "See you tomorrow, Magda."

"Good night, Dan. Thank you for making me feel so welcome here today."

She waited until the door closed behind him and then asked, "Are you sure that was enough? Or do you want to pee around the circulation desk, too? Just to really mark your territory and get the message across to any other men?"

Chapter 11

"See! I told you she loved riding in the golf cart." Jeff grinned at Magda as they puttered along in the cart. His mirrored sunglasses obscured his eyes, but she could see his smile lines around the edges of the frames.

How did Jeff manage to ooze masculinity out of every pore, even while in a T-shirt and floral board shorts, driving a golf cart with one hand, while he held a Shih Tzu in place on his lap with the other?

Petunia lifted her face into the wind, her pink tongue hanging out, and an expression of doggy ecstasy on her windswept face. Magda realized she'd be just as ecstatic to be taking a ride on Jeff's lap—in or out of the golf cart. She pushed her big round sunglasses up on her nose and sighed as she looked away from the temptation of Jeff in a bathing suit.

This whole "just friends" thing was working a little less for her every day.

They rounded a curve on the golf cart path and came out of the cool shade of the woods into the bright sunlight of the hot, humid summer evening, and the pool area appeared before them. It was an Olympic-sized pool, with wide steps leading down into the water that looked cool, sparkling, and oh-so-tempting. Magda still wasn't used to the August weather south of the Mason-Dixon line.

There was a hot tub attached to the pool, which didn't hold much appeal on such a toasty evening, but it might be nice come the fall. At the shallow end of the pool, there was a one-story pool house, whose architecture mimicked the main house. Masses of multi-colored roses climbed on trellises attached to it, and Magda could smell their spicy perfume as it wafted on the warm breeze.

The pool was perched on a crest overlooking the Potomac River below on one side and forest on the other. There was a giant built-in barbecue and wet bar on the river side of the shallow end between the pool and the pool house, with umbrella tables around it. On the opposite side of the pool were lounge chairs placed so the loungers had a view of both the river and the pool.

Jeff stopped the golf cart with a lurch and put Petunia on the ground before unfolding his own long frame from the distinctly non-giant-sized cart.

"This is it. What do you think—not bad, huh?" He stood with his hands on his narrow hips and looked around at this piece of his little kingdom.

"It's beautiful!" Magda enthused as she hopped out of the cart. She wore a sheer, gauzy, white cover-up, which revealed glimpses of the red tankini she wore beneath it. She spun around to see everything, and Petunia ran over and yipped happily as if they were playing a game.

"Cisco and I thought this was the perfect spot for it. It's away from everything else, so it feels secluded."

She stopped her spin so that she was facing him and beamed as she threw her arms out to the river. "And you can't beat the view!"

Even with his sunglasses shielding his eyes, Magda could feel his stare never waver from her when he responded huskily. "No. You really can't beat this view."

She felt her face get as red as her bathing suit and changed the subject. "So, are you ready for a swim?"

The only hope she had of keeping up this "just friends" charade was to keep her responses light and ignore the innuendo in his words and actions.

It must have worked, because he cleared his throat and said, "Right. Swimming. You go ahead in, and I'll get the grill fired up before I join you. It needs some time to heat up before we can cook."

Unlike her—Magda couldn't believe how this man could rev her engine! She was all fired up and ready to cook just from a look. Confused by her out-of-character response to Jeff, she watched as he hoisted a blue and white cooler, which contained their dinner fixings, from the back of the golf cart and carried it to the barbecue area. The weight of the full cooler made the strong muscles of his back bunch in the most interesting ways, and Magda couldn't tear her eyes away to save her soul.

He called over his shoulder as he walked, "I stuck some sodas and beers in here—do you want anything?"

She licked her lips and took a deep breath. Oh yeah. She wanted something all right—him! But that didn't appear to be on tonight's menu, so she replied, "A beer sounds great."

He bent over to open the cooler and the sight of his bathing suit pulled across his tight buns almost made her moan out loud. He stood up and popped the tops off two bottles of beer and they moved toward each other as if drawn by a powerful magnet.

Jeff held out one of the bottles. When she took one, he clinked his bottle against it and toasted. "Here's to friends enjoying a swim and dinner together."

"To friends," she responded with false cheer, when what she really wanted to say was *screw this friends noise—I want you!*

She took a sip of beer and put the bottle of amber liquid down on a nearby table. She smiled gamely and pulled her cover-up over her head. Magda felt the top of her bathing suit pull up to reveal more belly than she was comfortable showing as she shimmied the gauzy fabric over her head. She got the cover-up off, but it had knocked her sunglasses askew, so she took those off too and tossed both items on the table with her beer.

She was surprised to still feel the weight of Jeff's gaze upon her. She turned to look at him, and watched as he took a long draw on his beer, while his gaze wandered from her face down. The trip took a little break at her breasts, and then continued down to the band of skin exposed by her suit pulling up. She yanked the stretchy fabric down and squirmed self-consciously under his continued stare.

He pulled his Ray-Bans off and tossed them on the table by hers. He pulled his phone of out a pocket of his suit and chucked it on the table, too. The fact that it made it without hitting the deck amazed Magda, as his attention was focused solely on her.

His expression was fierce as he growled. "You know, Maggie, I *really* don't want to be your friend."

His words stung, but Magda wasn't really surprised—she told Bethanne men like Jeff Braden didn't want women like her. But, his actions told a different story, and she'd been starting to hope that in time they might be able to have something between them.

"You don't?" To her embarrassment, her voice squeaked, so she cleared her throat and continued in a lower voice, "What *do* you want?"

"This," Jeff said before grasping her upper arms and jerking her to him. He pulled her into a tight embrace, lowered his head, and slanted his mouth over hers to capture her lips in a hard kiss.

****

"Sam, you don't *really* think your dad—Mr. Big Time Football Star—agreed to watch a Shih Tzu this afternoon to help you, do you?" Hadley asked through her laughter. She fell back on the queen-sized canopy bed in her palatial bedroom, where the girls had gathered after going to the movies.

Sam shrugged. "Sure. Why else would he do it?"

Their friend Madison shook her head. "Don't ask me—Hadley's the expert on boys."

"C'mon y'all—grow up! He did it to score points with Ms. Horvath."

"What! No way, Had. He did it because it's the last week of summer vacation, and I wanted to hang out with you and Mad."

"Had n' Mad" were an unlikely pair of best friends. Hadley was old beyond her years, and Madison was known to be the sweetest girl in their grade, but the two were inseparable and had taken to including Sam in their outings.

Hadley sighed. "No, he didn't, at least not entirely. This way he gets to help you *and* see Ms. Horvath when she gets home from the library. Plus, he looks like a hero to her, too, since she's so crazy about that dog."

"Why would he care about being Ms. Magda's hero?" Mad asked innocently, as she hugged one of the mountain of stuffed animals on the bed to her chest.

"Did no one listen to me on Saturday? Because he loooves her."

"I don't know, Had. I talked to Magda about it when we were shopping on Saturday, and she told me they're just friends."

Hadley rolled her eyes and tossed a stuffed bunny at Sam. "Because she doesn't want you to freak."

Sam wrinkled her nose in confusion as she stroked the pink bunny she caught with the ease of a natural athlete. "Why would I freak about them dating? I like her a lot."

"She *is* pretty cool," Hadley inclined her head to concede the point. "But once your dad and her are an item, everything will change. It won't just be you and your dad anymore. She'll be there with you *all* the time."

Madison gave Sam an encouraging smile. She was the only one of the three to still have both parents alive and happily married to each other. "Is that such a bad thing, Had? It'll be nice for Sam to have a woman around. You had a great time on Saturday, didn't you, Sam? And she's agreed to help you hem the pants you bought, and take in that dress for you…"

Hadley interrupted with a loud smacking smoochy sound. "She's trying to kiss up to Sam; trust me, I've seen it happen before. They're always your BFF until you get in between your father and her and then…" She made a slashing motion across her throat.

"It doesn't have to be that way," Sam said confidently, but she wilted under Hadley's stare and patronizing head shake. "Does it?"

"It's always happened with my stepmothers. The worst is when they have another kid. Once my father's current wife had her baby, it was like I didn't exist to them anymore."

"I can't see my dad and Magda doing that to me," Sam said staunchly, but all she'd ever known was her dad's complete attention, and the thought of sharing it with someone else was a little unsettling—even someone as nice as Magda.

Uncertainty made her heart thump and her voice shaky as she said, "Besides, they're just friends, right?"

****

As Magda felt the sparks between them burst into a forest fire of passion, she realized this "friends" thing *so* wasn't working for Jeff and her. That was her last rational thought, before she heard Jeff's low groan of desire—more like a growl, really—and her brain pulled over and let her body take the wheel.

She twined her arms up and around Jeff's neck and ran her fingers into his thick, brown hair, and tugged gently. At her signs of acceptance, Jeff deepened their kiss. She felt his hands running up and down her back, which was bared in her halter-style bathing suit top. His touch managed to be both strong and gentle at the same time.

With a needy moan, she pressed her soft curves into his impossibly hard body. He probably wasn't as ripped as he'd been when he was a professional athlete, but riding and hiking kept his body in great condition, and he felt like he was made of granite. He rotated his hips against her and she felt a rush of liquid desire. Oh yeah. The granite thing was true for his *whole* body.

One of his hands moved up to her hair and wrapped her corkscrew curls around it; he tilted her head, and she felt his lips move off of hers to trail kisses to her throat. When he placed wet kisses up to her ear and nipped at her earlobe, a moan of pure desire snuck past her lips.

Playing it cool no longer seemed to be an option. If she got any hotter, she'd burst into flames. She could even smell the smoke. She frowned and sniffed as Jeff continued his sensual assault on her neck. Hold on. She really *could* smell smoke. Her eyes shot open and she craned her neck to peek over Jeff's shoulder.

"Oh my God, Jeff! Fire! Fire!"

"I know baby, I feel it, too," Jeff murmured into her ear as he nuzzled the delicate flesh beneath it

She pounded her small hands on his broad shoulders. "No—I mean a real fire—on the grill!"

Jeff reluctantly tore his lips from her skin and turned his head to look over his shoulder, and dropped her like the proverbial hot potato.

There were flames dancing in the grill. He rushed over and flicked the lid down to cut off the oxygen supply to the fire and then turned the knob to switch off the propane.

He mopped his forehead with his hand and then ran it through his perpetually messy hair, managing to rumple it even further.

"Good thing you realized that was happening, Maggie. Some old grease must have caught fire. I'll have to give the grill a thorough cleaning."

Maggie's heart raced; although, she attributed it more to his kisses than the fire. What the hell were they doing? Friends didn't make out while half-naked in bathing suits—at least not any friends she'd ever had before.

"Maybe it was a sign."

Jeff tilted his head and frowned. "A sign of what?"

"A sign that says 'friends don't stick their tongues down each other's throats.'" She softened the words with a sheepish grin and received one from Jeff in return.

"True. Okay, maybe a time-out is in order. Let me deal with the grill, and you can hop in the pool and cool off some."

Magda felt her heart drop to her feet, which was ridiculous because she was the one who suggested they put on the brakes, so why was she so disappointed? Cooling off sounded like a good idea. Always one for thinking things over—she'd been accused of over thinking everything—she needed the time to mull over what had just happened.

****

Jeff turned his back on temptation as he set to fussing with the grill. After a moment, he heard a thump on the deck as Magda kicked off her sandals and then her bare feet padding to the steps into the pool. He heard the water slosh as she walked down the steps and then a little splash as she began to swim.

He glanced over his shoulder and saw her craning her neck to keep her head out of the water as she doggy-paddled. *Hmm...is swimming the only thing she likes to do doggy style? Don't go there*—he shook his head briskly to dispel the tantalizing image in his head and raked his hands through his hair, before putting them on his hips and exhaling a puff of air. He really needed to get his mind out of the bedroom where

Magda was concerned, especially if they had any chance of making this just friends bullshit work.

He must be losing his touch; he thought he'd made his position crystal clear. Just friends—bad. Hot sex—good. But she'd taken the first opportunity to pull away from him.

Jeff grabbed the wire brush and pulled up the lid of the now-extinguished grill, and scrubbed the racks with more vigor than was strictly necessary. He knew she was still paddling around in the pool, because he heard the water lapping gently against the tiled sides.

There was no way he'd misinterpreted her reaction to their little make-out session. She was burning as white-hot as he was; he snuck another look at her and grinned. Her skin had been so overheated when he was caressing her a few minutes ago, he half expected to see steam rising off the water around her. No—he didn't misinterpret a damn thing—their attraction was 100% mutual, so he just needed to figure out a way to get what they both wanted, without ignoring their very valid reasons for not getting involved. He threw the brush on the brick barbecue. Damned if he knew how, though.

He turned the grill back on and waited a minute to be sure it didn't ignite again. Man, if only it was as easy to figure out what to do with Magda, as it was to fix the grill. Maybe a swim would help clear his mind, he always found brisk physical activity a great outlet to relieve stress and get his brain in order. Unfortunately, his first choice of brisk physical activity was off the table right now, so he'd swim a few laps instead.

****

Magda reached the end of the pool; the cool water

Donna Simonetta

felt soothing against her overheated skin. She turned back to the shallow end and froze in place at the sight before her. Jeff was peeling off his T-shirt—and man-oh-man—the term Greek god didn't do the man justice. Under his baggy shirt were broad shoulders, rock-hard abs, and a narrow waist that tapered into sexy hips, upon which sat his low-slung board shorts.

"Whoa." She breathed before kicking off the wall and paddling back toward the shallow end.

He strode across the pool deck, and when he got to the deep end, he dove into the water. The splash made her bob a bit. She turned her head and saw Jeff slicing through the water like a knife. He passed her, turned around, and swam back toward her again. By the time she paddled to the steps and sat on the middle one, Jeff had made it to the opposite end, turned and was on his way back again.

He stood when he reached her and shook his head like a dog after a swim. She felt her mouth go dry as water sluiced over the hard ridges of his stomach.

Jeff sat down next to her, but one step lower, and took a deep breath before he said, "I know we agreed to just be friends, but that's not working out so well—y'know, since we kiss the stuffing out of each other every chance we get."

She laughed and splashed a little water his way. "You're right. We really need to stop doing that."

His laugh lines eased as his face grew serious. "Do we? Have to stop, I mean. Maybe if we put our heads together, we can figure something out." His eyes locked on to hers, and his voice was low and rough when he continued, "Because I really, really don't want to stop kissing the stuffing out of you. And every time we kiss,

154

it leaves me wanting more."

Magda licked her dry lips and watched his gaze follow the movement hungrily. "I don't want to stop either, Jeff, trust me, I *really* don't. And I know you're nothing like Pierce. Even if I doubt my own instincts after falling for his line of bull, you have the Best Friend Seal of Approval—Bethanne's always told me what a great guy you are. But it doesn't change the fact that I'll be leaving Rivers Bend in a few months and your roots are here."

He nodded. "True. But you don't have any concrete plans yet, do you?"

"No, but I learned something today working at the library. I loved it—really, truly loved it! Don't get me wrong, it was a lot of work, and I'm beat tonight, but it was the type of library work I've always wanted to do. Corporate library work never did it for me, but this...this was right. I could feel it."

Jeff's face brightened. "That's great, Maggie! To find meaningful work you love to do—that's huge! But why does that have to impact us?"

"With this economy, public library budgets are being slashed, and jobs are hard to come by, so when Bethanne is ready to come back to work, I'll have to go wherever I can find a job, and I don't know where I'll end up living."

"There's no reason to assume you'll have to move across the whole country. I say we jump off that bridge when we come to it," Jeff suggested with a casual shrug of his muscular shoulders.

"I didn't mean that to be long-term pressure, it's just that..."

Jeff smiled and reached up to grasp one of her wet

hands with his. "You don't do casual sex—I know—I don't want casual with you, either. And I didn't mean to sound flip, I just meant that we could see where things go between us now, before we start worrying about the future."

He gently rubbed her knuckles with his thumb; she'd never realized before that knuckles could be an erogenous zone. Before her mind clouded over completely, she remembered the most important reason of all for their potentially ill-fated "just friends" decision.

"But there's still Sam to think about."

His thumb stilled; she hadn't meant to bring an abrupt end to the knuckle lovin', but if they were going to find a solution, then all their concerns needed to be addressed.

"Wow." He exhaled. "Thank you for thinking about my daughter. You're a really nice person, so I hope you understand that Sam's always my top consideration."

"Of course she is. That's one of the things I like most about you—what a great dad you are to her. You never have to worry that I won't understand."

He smiled his relief and resumed knuckle rubbing. "Thanks, Maggie. So what do we do here? We both clearly want more than friendship, but…"

Magda took a deep breath and blinked rapidly before shifting her gaze away from Jeff's face to a random point somewhere in the deep end of the pool. She girded her loins, licked her lips and stuttered, "I was thinking…um…we could…you know…"

He raised his eyebrows and grinned. "I *don't* know, Maggie, but a verb might help."

A nervous laugh escaped with a whoosh of air. "Right. A verb. I've heard good things about them. Okay. I was thinking maybe we could be friends with benefits. Sam already knows we're friends, and she's okay with it, so we'd just have to be careful about enjoying the—uh—benefits when she's not around, so that she doesn't get her hopes up about us being together for the long haul."

Magda swallowed hard and waited for Jeff's response. She'd never been so forward with a man before and was terrified about getting shot down.

Jeff slid his hand up to clasp her wrist and then without warning he pulled her through the water to his side. The movement caused little waves in the pool and matching little flutters in Magda's stomach. When she got close enough, he snaked one arm around her waist under water and ran his fingers over the small band of exposed flesh between the top and bottom of her bathing suit. Magda gasped softly at the contact and looked up at him through her lashes; Jeff had a wide grin on his face.

"Darlin', that's the best idea I've heard in a long time. Maybe ever."

Relief flooded through her—it didn't look like Jeff was going to reject her unprecedented advance. He pulled her up onto his lap and what she felt there confirmed her opinion. Nope. Definitely no rejection here.

He held her in place and said in a low voice, "And since Sam's out with her friends tonight, I'm thinking we can start exploring that benefits package right now."

He slid his hand under her suit and stroked her lower back. She shivered and squirmed on his lap as she felt *his* impressive benefits package jerk underneath her bottom.

"Sounds like a plan," she said with a sigh.

His eyes crinkled as he chuckled and brought his other hand up to cup her face. Her eyes drifted shut as she leaned into his strong hand. She felt it slip around under her hair to the nape of her neck.

The hand at the base of her spine pulled her forward so they were even closer together, and he brought his lips to hers. He whispered against them, "You're so beautiful, Maggie."

Before she could disagree, he pressed his lips more firmly to hers; he gently ran his tongue across her bottom lip, and she gladly opened to him.

Jeff used the buoyancy of the water to assist him in turning them on the step, so his back was against the wall and his legs were stretched out with Magda lying on top of him, all without ever breaking the contact at their mouths.

With the feel of his hard body beneath her soft one, the scent of the grill mingling with that of the roses and honeysuckle that grew against the pool house, Magda felt as close to heaven as she ever had before. She rubbed her breasts against him and reveled in the sensation of his crisp chest hair abrading the tender flesh revealed by the deep vee of the halter-top of her suit. She moaned into his mouth, and he answered with a groan of his own, as he lifted his hips to press his erection into her highly aroused center.

The sounds of the river rushing, the hum of cicadas, and the gentle lapping of the pool water were joined by the loud ring of Jeff's phone, as it vibrated on the table where he'd tossed it with his sunglasses.

He broke their kiss. "Shit—that's Sam's ringtone. I've got to get it. I'm sorry."

Magda floated off of him and tried to keep the disappointment from her voice, since she understood a parent couldn't ignore a phone call from a child, no matter how hot and sweaty the activities it was interrupting were. "Of course you do. No problem."

****

Jeff rose and splashed out of the pool. His wet feet slapped on the deck as he jogged to his phone, and he felt uncomfortably aware of the erection tenting his loose bathing suit and thanked God he wasn't a Speedo man.

He snatched the phone off the table, to answer before it went to voice mail. "Hey, Peanut. Are you ready for me to pick you up already?"

"I'm home now. Madison's mother wanted her home for dinner, so we didn't eat out after all. They dropped me off a little while ago. Where are you?" There was a hint of accusation in the question.

"I'm sorry I wasn't there when you got home, Peanut, but I wasn't expecting you for a couple of hours yet."

"Aunt Heather saw you drive off in a golf cart with a cooler. What are you doing?"

Nope. The accusation wasn't in his imagination. What bee had gotten into his girl's bonnet?

"I'm at the pool with Maggie. We're going for a swim and then I'm grilling up some burgers. Why don't you put on your suit and head over to join us? There's plenty of food for all of us."

"I wouldn't want to intrude." Sam's voice sounded stiff and formal.

"What are you talking about, kiddo? I didn't think you were going to be home for dinner, or I would've waited for you. Quit dawdling and head on over. The grill's almost ready."

He looked at Maggie standing in the shallow end of the pool, sipping her beer and regarding him with an expression that was equal parts desire, confusion, and disappointment. *Right there with you darlin'.*

"If you're sure you want me, I'll be over in a few. Is Petunia there, too?"

The eagerness back in her voice made her sound more like his best girl. "Yep. Miss Petunia is here, too. See you soon."

He heard his sister's voice in the background, then Sam said, "Aunt Heather said she'll drive me over in a golf cart—she wants to talk to you."

Jeff gulped. He was fairly certain his baby sister had plenty to say to him, and he didn't want to hear any of it.

"Great," he said with false cheer.

He disconnected and smiled apologetically at Magda. "Sorry, but our time alone is about to be cut short. Sam and my sister Heather are on their way here to join us for dinner."

While he wasn't looking forward to facing his sister, maybe this interruption was for the best. Magda was a special woman—hell, she'd put his daughter's best interests above her own just now, and women like that were few and far between in his experience. She deserved more than this friends-with-benefits situation. Unfortunately, right now he couldn't think of another option for them, but that didn't mean he couldn't show her how special he thought she was when they were alone.

An interim solution for that problem reached, he frowned as he thought about his sister's imminent arrival. He walked back down the steps into the pool and sank down until he was submerged up to his shoulders.

"Is something wrong?" Magda asked with concern.

His grin was rueful. "I was dodging Heather today, and now she's on her way here to talk to me. See, Cisco and I did something I don't think she's going to be happy about, and I was hoping to avoid her until she had a chance to cool down and be less inclined to holler at me."

Magda tread water in the deep end; the tips of her hair floated in the water around her and made her look like a mermaid. "What did you do?"

"We hired a buddy of ours from the Pintos organization to be the CEO for us here at the Retreat and use his contacts to help drum up new business. He lost his job when a new GM took over the team and brought in his own people. With this economy, Cisco and I are looking for ways to grow the business, but both our plates are already full without taking that on, too. Mick can take over a lot of the day-to-day management and sales work."

Magda wrinkled her brow. "Why would that make Heather mad? It sounds like a good solution—unless she wanted the job."

Jeff shook his head before he pushed off to paddle out to tread water by Magda. "No, that's not the problem. She just hates him. I don't know why—he's a stand-up guy."

"How does she know him, too? Did they used to go

out or something?"

"God no! Heather lived with me when I played for the Pintos. She'd just graduated high school when Sam's mother died, and she put off going to college to come help me with Sam." His eyes grew soft. "I don't know what I would've done without her. I'll owe her forever for everything she did for us; that's why I'm sorry I've done something to upset her now. She helped so much with the baby, and was the biggest Pintos supporter around. She became everyone's kid sister— we used to joke that she was our team mascot. She got along great with everyone—except Mick."

"And Mick is the guy you've hired?"

"Yep," he said shortly as he continued to tread water.

Magda thought over the situation. "Well, if he's doing sales, he'll have to be on the road some; maybe Heather and he won't have to spend too much time together."

He raised one hand out of the water with wet fingers crossed. "Here's hoping. Speaking of spending time together, I'm sorry I invited them to join us. Sam sounded funny on the phone—she seemed put out that I wasn't home when she got there, but she was early. I wasn't expecting to hear from her for a couple of hours, and then I thought I'd have to go get her at Hadley's house. So it's not really fair of her to be mad at me about it. It's not like her."

Magda cocked her head. "She might have been scared when you weren't where she thought you'd be. When I was a kid, I was always worried that my dad would go away—the way I thought my mom had."

"Maybe, but if that's the case, I really don't want

her to know that we're involved. It seems like it might be too much for her right now. Maybe when she's a little older she'd understand." He waggled his eyebrows at her. "So for now, I think we need to keep our 'benefits package' a private matter."

Magda blushed and tried to paddle past him. "Maybe that was a stupid idea. I won't hold you to it, if you want to change your mind."

He wrapped an arm around her middle and pulled her through the water, until her lush little body, all wet and slippery, was pressed against him. "No way, Maggie. A deal's a deal. We just won't be sealing our deal tonight, the way I'd hoped."

He rested his forehead against hers. "Besides, a lady like you deserves a little wooing."

She swallowed hard. "Wooing? What kind of wooing? I don't think I've ever been wooed before."

He turned his head to the buzz of a golf cart's motor, signaling Heather and Sam's arrival. He kissed the tip of her slightly turned-up nose before separating from her and idly backstroking away. "Well, now, I'm a little rusty, but back in the day I gave good woo, so brace yourself darlin', you're about to be wooed good and proper."

Chapter 12

Pierce slouched in his seat at the conference table and twirled his Montblanc pen between his fingers. He felt the weight of someone's stare upon him and looked up to see Mrs. Mallory's gimlet gaze boring into him. He straightened in his chair and glanced across the table to Taylor, who didn't seem to even be aware that he was in the room, but then he felt one of her stiletto-clad feet toy with the hem of his pant leg. He smiled in a self-satisfied manner until he turned his attention back to the topic under discussion.

One of the obsequious toadies with whom Elizabeth Mallory surrounded herself asked, "Will your granddaughter be joining us today?"

Elizabeth answered with such confidence that even Pierce almost believed her, and he knew the truth. "No, I'm afraid not; the dear child is out of town. One of her friends needed her, and you know what a soft heart my Elizabeth has."

More like a soft head, was Pierce's unkind thought, as he went back to twirling his pen. Magda was willing to throw away a fortune and become a card-carrying member of the middle class, but he'd be damned if he let her drag him down, too.

Luckily for him, Magda was a more honest person than he was, and she'd left the few pieces of jewelry he'd given to her behind when she left. He'd already hocked them to pay small installments to both his dealer and his bookie, but they were pressuring him for more, so he was in dire need of Magda back in his life.

Elizabeth Mallory smiled at him, with what he knew to be false benevolence. "Hopefully she'll be home very soon; poor Pierce looks like he's wasting away without her."

She rose from the table and nodded to all those assembled there. "That will be all for today."

She swept out of the room, to the sound of chairs being pushed back and papers rustling, as everyone except Taylor and Pierce gathered their things and rushed after the great lady for one more chance to curry her favor.

Taylor scrunched down in her chair and used the position to run her foot farther up Pierce's pant leg, which he jiggled at a frantic pace.

"Why so jittery?" She purred.

"If you must know," Pierce's eyes darted around and he lowered his voice, "my dealer has cut me off."

Taylor looked at her blood-red fingernails with indifference. "Is that all?"

"All? Isn't that enough? Just because I owe him some money, he's abandoned me!"

She glanced up from her manicure inspection with a wry smile. "*Some* money? Darling, he wouldn't cut you off unless you owed him a considerable sum. I'm not your naïve little Magda, so don't try to fool me."

Pierce tapped a staccato beat on the table with his pen. "Fine. You're right; I owe him a considerable amount. So what's a little more? I need a fix, so I can focus on my plans to find Magda, and then everything will be fine."

Taylor huffed in frustration. "I'm so tired of hearing about you getting your precious Magda back."

Pierce scowled. "I'm so sorry that my dilemma is boring you, Taylor."

"No need for sarcasm, darling—not to the woman who is going to help solve your immediate problem."

His hand and leg both stilled. "You can solve my problem with my dealer? Do you have money you can loan me? I swear, I'll pay you back as soon as—"

"As soon as Magda's back in your tender care. I know, I know," Taylor interrupted in the bored voice of a woman who'd heard this song before. "No—I have no intention of loaning money to you. I don't have much to spare," she waved her hand from the top of her head down to her feet. "All of this beauty and elegance is not inexpensive to maintain. And quite frankly, you're a bad investment."

"Then what can you do to help?" Pierce sneered.

"I know a dealer in Brooklyn, who won't know what a deadbeat you are, so I'm sure he'll be willing to extend some credit."

"Taylor, you're wonderful! Can you arrange a meeting today?"

Her smile was feline. "Of course."

Pierce licked his lips and relaxed in his chair. After a moment, he asked with studied casualness, "Do you know if he has the means to supply things other than drugs?"

A frown marred Taylor's flawless countenance as she asked with suspicion, "Like what?"

Pierce jogged his papers on the conference table and avoided her narrow-eyed gaze. "Oh, you know, things like guns?"

Taylor's eyes bulged, and she hurriedly pushed her chair back from the table and jumped to her feet. "I don't want to know anything about *guns*!" She continued emphatically, "I'll provide an introduction and then you're on your own. I'm going to pretend you never asked me that question."

Pierce's oily smile gave him the appearance of a crocodile. "That's probably for the best. You just make the connection for me, and I'll take care of everything else."

****

Magda crouched in the stacks with a duster, which she ran over the books on the bottom shelf. The air conditioner made the library a cool haven, even on this scorching summer day. She took a deep breath and reveled in the familiar aroma of a library—a combination of paper, dust, and mustiness made her feel at home. The dust motes floated lazily in the air around her as she swished the duster back and forth.

Caitlin wasn't due to come in to work until the afternoon, so she'd been alone here all morning. Well, not really alone, a steady stream of Rivers Benders had been through the library today—some to check out books and some to check out her. She smiled at the thought as she stood to run the duster over the top shelf of the next section of books.

She turned her head when she heard the familiar creak of the front door—and here comes someone else now. Would this one want a book, or to use a computer, or just to meet the new girl in town? It didn't much matter to Magda—she enjoyed all the patrons. She discovered that she loved being part of the fabric of this small town, and its residents' curiosity about her filled her with an unaccustomed sense of warmth and belonging.

She swatted at the dust on her wide-legged navy slacks as she walked out of the stacks to see who was here. A bright smile was on her face as she emerged with a cheery, "Hello!"

"Hello, Ms. Magda," said a giant arrangement of roses and lilies.

At least that's what it looked like, but Magda was sure a person had to lurk behind the massive display. A fresh-faced young man peeked around them with a crooked grin. She recognized him as the landscape architecture student from Virginia Tech, who worked at the Retreat on the grounds crew during his summer vacation.

"Hi, Bill. What've you got there?" she asked with a warm smile. She stuck the duster on a shelf behind the circulation desk.

"Jeff asked me to deliver these to you. They're from the gardens at the Retreat."

Magda raised a dusty hand to her throat. "Oh, they're lovely!" She reached out to take the vase.

Bill put it on the counter instead and warned, "Be careful of the lilies, with your nice white blouse. If you brush against the stamen, it can leave a nasty stain."

She looked down and smiled ruefully at her already dusty outfit. "Thanks for your concern, but I'm not sure I can get more dirt on these clothes."

She put her face down to the arrangement and shut her eyes as she breathed in their intoxicating, spicy scent. She heard paper rustling and looked up to see Bill shuffling through three envelopes, all the while juggling a red and white gift bag with matching tissue paper blooming out of it.

He frowned in concentration. "Jeff gave me strict instructions about which envelope goes with what." His face lightened, he smiled, and stuck out a square envelope with the Retreat's logo printed in the return address area. Her name was printed in neat, block letters on the front. "This one goes with the flowers."

She took it from him with a puzzled smile and used her finger to open the flap. Her eyes grew soft as she read the note written in Jeff's boxy print.

Maggie,

I saw these flowers in the garden, when I was taking a group to the Alpine Tower, and they made me think of you. Like you, they look lovely, almost fragile, but are much stronger than they appear. In fact, they're able to withstand the sudden, summer storms, which are so common here. Just like you'll be able to weather the sudden storm in your life right now and emerge as vibrant and beautiful as these roses and lilies.

Jeff

Her eyes misted over, and she blinked rapidly to clear them before she looked up at Bill, who held out the festive gift bag and another note.

"Oh my," she murmured.

"This one's next," he said.

She opened the second envelope and read the note, which was printed in the same square, neat hand.

These presents are for Petunia and you, in the hopes I can turn the two new ladies in my life into Pintos fans.

Magda took the bag from Bill and put it on the counter next to the flowers. She dug through the tissue and pulled out a leash and collar set, with the Portland

Pintos logo on them. They were white, with a pattern of a running wild Pinto printed on it in red.

"Petunia's going to look might pretty in that set," Bill observed with a grin. "Red is definitely her color."

Magda chuckled as she pulled the last item out of the bag, a Pintos jersey with Jeff's name and number on it.

She shook it out and held it up in front of her. She struck a pose and asked with a grin, "What do you think—is it me?"

Bill chuckled. "You and Petunia will match, but beware this is Redskins country. Although, folks will probably cut you a break since it's Jeff's jersey."

She smiled as she folded it carefully and put it back in the bag.

Bill held out a third envelope. "This is the last one, so I'm going to head back to work now."

She took the envelope and smiled at him in gratitude. "Thanks for delivering all this—it was a fun break in the day for me."

He called over his shoulder with a laugh, "It was a fun break for me, too—way easier than weeding and mulching."

She tapped the envelope against her palm and wondered what it could possibly contain. She sat in the tall chair behind the circulation desk and opened it. She bit her bottom lip as she read.

Maggie,

I think it's about time we had an actual date, even if we're the only ones who know we're on one. (Well, except for Bill now!) Would you do me the honor of accompanying me to the Labor Day concert and fireworks on the Town Green this Saturday night? Call

me with your answer—I'll be waiting.
Jeff

She leaned back in the chair and swung it gently to and fro, a dreamy smile on her face, as she reached for the telephone.

****

Jeff closed his office door on the babble of voices in the hall, as the guests passed by on their way to the conference room for their afternoon meeting.

Cisco had already flopped in a chair and was rolling his neck in an effort to alleviate tension. "Tell me the truth, Jeff, was that the worst Alpine Tower experience we've ever had?"

Jeff took a deep breath and then puffed out his cheeks as he exhaled and sat in the big leather seat behind his desk. "They certainly couldn't seem to grasp the concept of teamwork. Maybe it was too much to hope for from a firm of personal injury and divorce attorneys."

Cisco shook his head. "I thought that one woman was going to push the older fellow off to get him out of her way."

Jeff chuckled. "Yeah, until she came to her senses and realized he's a senior partner. Shoving him off would definitely have taken her off the fast track to making partner."

Cisco smiled and stretched out his legs; the two men were dressed in similar outfits—red polo shirts with the Retreat's logo on them in white, khaki shorts and hiking boots. "Speaking of maiming—I hear that Heather sliced you a new asshole last night."

Jeff shook his head. "You mean 'ripped', not 'sliced,' but you have the general idea, and yes—she did."

Cisco whistled softly. "An angry woman can be a frightening thing. I managed to dodge her all day yesterday. Today, I haven't been able to, but she's moved on to giving me the ice treatment."

Jeff nodded in agreement. "The real deep-freeze, I think my toes have frostbite, but she'll calm down." He frowned as uncertainty swept over him. "Right? It's not possible for her to stay mad at us about hiring Mick forever, is it?"

Cisco shrugged. "She's your sister, *meu amigo*, you tell me. Why does she hate him so much, anyway? They both get along so well with everyone but each other."

"No idea. We'll just have to keep them apart as much as possible, a devilish glint lit in his eyes. "Or we can lock them in a room together until they fight it out."

Cisco threw back his head and laughed. "No, no, no. I don't want Mick's murder on my conscience. And there's no doubt in my mind that Heather would be the victor in their death match. At least he'll be on the road sometimes, doing sales work for us, so they won't have to see each other all the time."

"That's what Maggie said, too."

Cisco narrowed his eyes and scowled. "Remember my warning about Maggie—do not mess with her or you answer to me. Best friend or not."

Jeff held up his hands. "Back down, *el Diablo*, I remember, but it doesn't matter because I'm not going to hurt her."

"You may not *mean* to hurt her, but you could. And what about your—"

Jeff's cell phone buzzed and cut Cisco off mid-sentence. He pulled it out of his pocket and smiled when he looked at the number on the screen. "I've been waiting for this call."

Cisco stood and motioned with two fingers from his dark eyes to Jeff's light ones, in the classic "I'll be watching you" warning before he strode out of the room.

Jeff waited until the door shut behind his friend before he answered. "Hello, Maggie."

"Hi," her sweet voice sounded shy. "I wanted to call to thank you for all the thoughtful presents and say that I'd like to go to the concert on the Green with you this weekend, but I have to be home before the fireworks. They scare Petunia so much that she gets sick. I have a doggy downer for her to take, but I want to be home with her to try to keep her calm."

Jeff's clenched jaw relaxed at her answer. "That's no problem; we can leave after the band, but before the fireworks. They set them off over the river, so we can see them from your porch anyway, if it doesn't scare the pooch too much."

"Thanks for understanding. I know I seem like a mother hen, but she's been through so much trauma. I try to make her life with me as comfortable as possible."

"I don't think it makes you seem like a mother hen. I think it shows what a kind soul you are." He felt a grin spread across his face. "So—how do you like the wooing so far?"

He heard her deep-throated chuckle and the smile in her voice as she replied, "I've got to say—it doesn't suck."

****

Bernie sat at the desk of his typical chain hotel room and powered up his computer. He couldn't put it off any longer. As a matter of fact, he couldn't help but be insulted that Mrs. M. believed it had taken him this long to find Magda. After all, she employed him because he was the best in the business, and this job was a total cakewalk.

With a few keystrokes he called up his email. Maybe he was a coward to tell her this way, rather than calling her, but he didn't feel like talking to her tonight. He hoped this way would buy Magda another night of peace. It was after business hours, so he was hoping her assistant had gone home for the night, and he knew she never checked her own email.

He took a swig of the soda he'd bought from the vending machine in the hallway and began to type.

"Sorry kid," he muttered. "I'm afraid this email is going to bring the wrath of 'Typhoon Elizabeth' into Rivers Bend, and I know you've been happy here. I did everything I could to stall her, but now it's up to you to stand up to her. You can do it—your mother did."

****

"Where did Petunia get the Pintos collar?" Sam asked with suspicion as she looked at the dog ensconced on the floral cushions of the seat set into the bay window of Bethanne and Cisco's bedroom.

"Your dad," Magda mumbled around a mouthful of pins.

She knelt on the carpet next to the footstool where Sam stood in a pair of her new pants. Magda pulled a pin from her mouth and used it on the hem of the pants. She pulled the rest out and stuck them back in the strawberry-shaped pincushion, and set it on the hassock of an overstuffed chair next to her. The floral upholstery matched the cushions where Petunia was perched like a queen.

There was not much of Cisco's macho presence in the cottage's master bedroom. It looked like Laura Ashley exploded in here, but it was a look suited to the cottage and was a cozy, welcoming space.

Her mouth now free of pins, Magda sat back on her heels and smiled up at Sam. "He thought if Petunia and I were going to live on the grounds of the Retreat, we needed to show some Pintos love. Petunia got the collar and leash, and I got a jersey."

"Whose jersey?" Sam asked through tight lips.

Her tone caused Magda to hesitate a fraction of a second before she replied, "Your dad's."

She decided to ignore the icy silence that news brought and stood and stretched. "Okay. I need to press the hems, and then I'll be ready to sew. Take those off and add them to the pile."

Bethanne called from the bed, where she lounged on her side. "The ironing board is by the washer and dryer in the mudroom off the kitchen."

Magda gathered the pinned pants carefully in her arms. "Got it. I'll be back in a bit."

"Cisco threw in a load of laundry before he left, could you toss it in the dryer for him?"

"No problem. And I'll bring back some of the lemonade I brought over for all of us, when I'm done pressing the hems."

"Thanks, Maggie. You're a doll," Bethanne said with a smile at her friend's departing back.

****

The smile faded as she looked over at Sam, who

had pulled her shorts back on, and now stood with a frown on her face and her arms crossed tight against her chest.

"What's wrong, Sam?" Bethanne asked softly. She heard the slam of the dryer door and the thumping of the machine as it began to tumble and knew Magda wouldn't be able to hear much over it.

"Wrong? What makes you think something's wrong?" Sam asked in a brittle voice.

"Oh, I don't know—the fact that you're coiled tighter than a trampoline spring?" Bethanne suggested with a kind smile. "I thought you liked Maggie?"

The child slumped on the window seat and pulled a willing Petunia into her lap to pet. She shrugged with feigned indifference. "She's all right."

"She's my best friend, and she dropped everything to come here to help me out, so I'd have to say she's a darned sight better than 'all right.'"

Sam looked down at the dog to avoid Bethanne's searching gaze.

Bethanne frowned at the normally sunny child's uncharacteristic sullenness. "And she's been nothing but nice to you since she got here. Tonight, for example, she has to be wiped out. I know she's working long hours at the library, but instead of going home and taking a bubble bath, she came here to help you get your school clothes ready."

Sam pouted and fixed Bethanne with a narrow-eyed stare. "Maybe she has her reasons for being nice to me. Did you ever think of that?"

Bethanne's eyes opened wide at the outburst and for about the millionth time that day cursed her bedridden state; she saw the hurt behind Sam's harsh words and longed to go to her and draw the child she loved like a niece into her arms to comfort her. "Oh, Sam, sweetie, Maggie's not that kind of person!"

Sam took a deep breath, and tears shimmered in her eyes. "Dad likes her, y'know. *Likes her* likes her."

"I think maybe he does—is that a problem for you, sweetie-pie? I thought it would be nice for you to have Maggie in your lives that way."

Sam bit her lip and swatted at a tear that escaped her eyes and was making its way down her cheek. "I thought so, too—at first—but then Hadley told me how her dad ignores her now that his new wife has a baby. And I'd hate that, Bethanne." She sniffed loudly. "My dad's all I have. You can't understand what it's like."

Bethanne's face softened, and she patted the bed next to her. Sam rose and put Petunia back down on the window seat. She crawled up next to Bethanne and cuddled up to her like a kitten.

Bethanne pressed a kiss to the top of the child's head. "You're right, Sam. I can't understand. I still have both my parents—they may be retired and living in Hilton Head now, but they're just a car ride or a phone call away. But, you know who does know just what it's like? Maggie. That's why I know she would *never* use you in such a hurtful way. Trust me on this one. Maggie is being nice to you because she likes *you*. Period."

She chuckled and stroked Sam's corn silk hair as she continued, "Besides, if he already *likes her* likes her, she doesn't need to kiss up to you, now does she?"

Sam's face lit up as she sat up and beamed at Bethanne. "That's true!"

Bethanne wrinkled her freckled nose. "Not to be

harsh or anything, but I'd take Hadley's views on family with a grain of salt. She's not coming from the best point of reference. Her parents are…" her voice trailed off as she searched for a kid-friendly description of Hadley's family's soap opera life.

Sam giggled and spared her the trouble. "They are something else, aren't they?"

They heard the ice dispenser clanking cubes into glasses in the kitchen.

Bethanne smiled lovingly at Sam. "Sounds like Maggie's on her way back. Is everything good here?"

Sam swiped her eyes with the backs of her hands and grinned. "Yeah. I think it is."

****

Ned, Elizabeth Mallory's trusted assistant sat at his desk on Wednesday morning. Frown lines created furrows in his bland face as he stared at his ultra-thin computer monitor.

Information about Jefferson Braden filled the widescreen. He'd begun his day bright and early, as was his habit, by going through his boss's email to help her prioritize her morning. He'd seen the one from Bernie Felder, which said he'd found Magda. He called Felder immediately for more details and was left dissatisfied with the meager information the detective would share with him.

Out of curiosity, he'd gone to the website for the Retreat at Rivers Bend, where Felder said Magda was staying. He shook his head as he looked at the photograph of the ruggedly handsome ex-football player at a charity event in Washington D.C.

He shook his head; he knew Mrs. Mallory wanted Magda to come back and resume her engagement to the

Allen twit, but seriously, what woman would choose Pierce over this Braden character?

Ned knew that no one would ever believe it, but he *liked* his boss. Sure, she had a megalomaniacal bent to her personality, but she'd always been good to him. Plus, she was a lonely old woman, and Ned knew a thing or two about loneliness.

He hadn't been in her employ when she drove her daughter away, but Ned heard the tale often enough—both Mrs. Mallory's version of events and what was probably a more fact-based account from her longtime servants. He knew enough to know she'd mismanaged the situation from beginning to tragic end, and she was going to make the same mistakes with Magda unless Ned could convince her to try another way this time.

He heard her sensible heels click on the floor and turned to watch Mrs. Mallory enter the office. While she was impeccably dressed and coiffed, she looked tired and older to Ned, who knew as no one else did, the toll this situation was taking on her.

"Good morning, ma'am." He rose and went to the coffee service to pour some into a delicate china cup. He prepared it the way she liked and carried it to her desk. "I have good news—Felder has found your granddaughter."

Her hawk-like eyes brightened, and she clasped her hands together. "Wonderful. Where is she?"

"She was in Rivers Bend, Virginia after all. He wouldn't tell me much—I called after reading his too brief email. He's traveling back to New York right now and will report here immediately upon his return."

"Fine. Make arrangements for us to travel to this Rivers Bend as soon as possible after my meeting with him. We can take the corporate jet and bring Elizabeth back with us. You can send a truck and driver to get her car and belongings." She squinted her eyes and frowned as she plotted. "I suppose we should bring Pierce with us."

Ned bowed his head and cleared his throat. "If I might make a suggestion, ma'am?"

She cocked her head like a bird and stared at him through unblinking eyes. "Of course, Ned, I have great respect for your ideas."

He smiled, pleased with the rare verbal praise. "Thank you, ma'am, your respect means so much to me."

She smiled; although, it didn't seem to be a natural expression for her, so she quickly stopped and waved her hand imperiously for Ned to continue.

"I believe your objectives might best be achieved by not going after your granddaughter with metaphorical guns blazing. Keeping in mind the endgame of having her back in the city, working with you at M.I., and engaged to Mr. Allen, perhaps waiting for *her* to come to *you* would be an effective course of action."

Mrs. Mallory snorted delicately. "Stubborn child is just like her mother—it would be better for me to go there and bring her home."

"With all due respect, Mrs. Mallory." A sheen of perspiration formed on Ned's forehead. "That method did not work with her mother, and if they are as much alike as you say, another method might be in order now."

She pursed her lips. "You may have a point," she conceded with reluctance.

"According to Mr. Felder, she's working at the town library and staying at a place called the Retreat at a Rivers Bend, which is owned by an attractive man, a former professional athlete, who is now very active in charitable works for children. I think it's safe to assume he's part of the attraction for her there."

Mrs. Mallory's eyes flashed. "Oh, no. She is *not* going to throw over an Allen for some nobody the way her mother did!"

"I suspect from the perspective of a young lady, Mr. Allen would pale in comparison to Jefferson Braden."

"Humph. We'll see about that."

"I think it might be best to let Mr. Allen pursue her and try to win her back. It would make him a most romantic figure to her and make her more inclined to resume their engagement. If you went there today to force her back, she'll just dig in her heels, if she's as stubborn as you say."

Mrs. Mallory leaned her ramrod straight spine back against her chair, something Ned had never seen her do before. Even that tiny sign of weakness seemed to Ned to be a sign of how fatigued this whole mess was making her.

"She is that stubborn and more, so you do make a good case. Fine. I'll hear what Mr. Felder has to say, and then I'll let Pierce find her and attempt to win her back. But if the young fool doesn't find her soon, I *will* be pointing him in the right direction."

Ned tried to keep the grin off his face; he really wanted Mrs. Mallory to have her granddaughter in her life, and her plan would have driven the young woman even further away.

"In the meantime, find out everything you can about this Braden person. We may need leverage with him at some point to get him away from Elizabeth. If there are any secrets to be learned about him, please do so, Ned."

Chapter 13

Magda stood in front of the bathroom mirror in her cabin; she almost didn't recognize the woman who looked back at her. Eyes sparkled with excitement, and a smidgeon of nervousness, at the prospect of her first date with Jeff. Her cheeks were pink, and she couldn't stop the smile that kept breaking out on her face. She leaned forward to fluff her unruly curls, which she'd let run wild since she got to Rivers Bend—no more headache-inducing tight French twists for her.

The cheerful knock on her front door—to the old "shave and a haircut" rhythm—made her jump back and her breath catch. It had to be Jeff. She smoothed the skirt of her white sundress with a print of large, red poppies splashed on it. She straightened the broad straps over her shoulders, which came up from a modest V-neckline and called out, "Coming!"

She practically skipped across the living room, excited as a teenage girl greeting her first-ever date. She felt her smile grow impossibly wider as she threw open the wooden door.

Jeff stood on the other side of the screen door with his eyes wide and his jaw dropped. The hum of the air conditioner was the only sound between them. Jeff had dressed up more than his usual baggy cargos and running shoes, but in his khaki shorts, sunny yellow polo shirt, and deck shoes with no socks, he was still decidedly more casual than she was.

In light of his frank appraisal of her, starting at her high-heeled wedge espadrilles, with the red ribbon that wound around her calves, to the top of her head, Magda felt her smile fade. She squirmed under his silent examination.

"I'm overdressed for tonight, aren't I? I can change really fast…"

"No!" He almost shouted, his voice deep and rough. "Don't you dare change—you look amazing. I don't care if every other woman there is in a burlap sack, you look beautiful, and I want to dance with you in that dress."

She smiled. "Okay." She opened the squeaky screen door. "C'mon in, I just need to grab my bag."

Jeff stepped in and looked at Petunia on her dog bed, next to the fireplace. Her tail thumped twice as she lifted her head with an effort, as though it was filled with concrete.

"You already gave the pooch her tranquilizer, I'm assuming. I've never seen her this mellow."

Magda called her response over her shoulder, as she rushed into the bedroom to grab her red straw bag, "I did. I wanted to make sure it kicked in before the fireworks start."

She came back in the room and squatted down to pet her beloved dog. "The vet said to give her a quarter of a pill, since she's so small, and good thing I did! Even that reduced portion has sent her into la-la land. I can't imagine what a full pill would do."

Jeff dropped to his haunches in front of the dog and rubbed one of her velvety ears between two fingers. "They set off the fireworks on the river; my house is farther away from it than your cabin, maybe we should move her over there."

"The farther away from the noise, the better. Are you sure you don't mind?"

"Of course not. I've gotten mighty attached to Petunia this week; I don't want her to be any more frightened than she has to be. It seems like the poor little pup had a rough road before she met you, so if there's anything I can do to make the next stage of her life a little easier, I'd like to do it."

Just when Magda thought Jeff couldn't get more perfect, he went and said something like that and brought her that much closer to falling for him like nine-pins. But the timing couldn't be worse. They were at different places in their lives and much as she loved the quirky little town of Rivers Bend, it was just a brief stopover for Petunia and her. She pushed those thoughts out of her mind—they had no place in tonight's fun. Magda was bound and determined to enjoy what time she had with this amazing man. She just had to guard her heart a little more carefully than she had been.

"Thanks, Jeff. Let me grab her dish and stuff."

His grin was sheepish as he stood up next to her. "No need. I bought stuff to keep at the house for her this week, since she's been hanging out there while you're at work."

Magda blinked. "You did?"

He ducked his head and brushed away the lock of hair that had fallen across his forehead. "Yeah. She's got a water bowl, food dish, food, a little bed, and one of those pull toy things she likes to play with—the big dog-sized one."

Magda chuckled. "She thinks she's a Rottweiler—

she scoffs at the little dog toys."

Jeff grinned. "I noticed."

"You notice a lot of things—you're really thoughtful." *And I am so not used to it.*

She glanced at Jeff and saw that her words brought a blush to his tan face. She smothered a grin, pleased she had the ability to flummox him a fraction of the way he could fluster her. She scooped up her sedated dog. "Okay. We're ready to roll."

****

Jeff eased the big pickup into a parallel spot on Main Street. They had to park a few blocks away from the gazebo; it seemed like the whole town had turned out for the evening's festivities.

As he shifted the truck into park, he smiled at Magda. "Wait right there, darlin', I'll come around to help you down."

He slid out of the truck and skimmed around the hood, whistling as he went. He always loved the concerts on the Green, but tonight he got to be here with a pretty girl in a summer dress and silly city shoes.

The only thing that cast a tiny shadow over the evening was this "friends with benefits" business. Most men would jump at the chance to have sex with an attractive woman and have none of the responsibilities of a relationship. Hell, it's what *he* usually wanted, but with Maggie he wanted more. And she sure deserved more. She was a woman in a million, not someone you treat like a paper napkin—use it up and toss it away. Nope, Maggie was a keeper. He just didn't know how to convince her to stay, or how to handle the situation with his daughter.

He opened the door and saw Maggie's bright,

expectant smile and felt his own grin spread in response. She seemed as excited about tonight as he was—that had to be a good sign, right?

He reached across her to unbuckle her seatbelt and with a devilish glint in his eye, he lifted her out of the truck bridal style and kept her in his arms on the sidewalk. He took his arm away from her back long enough to slam the passenger door shut.

A recorded patriotic tune played in the distance on a loudspeaker on the Green, as the live music hadn't started yet.

He adjusted Maggie into a more comfortable hold, and followed the sidewalk toward the music and smells of fried food and barbecue.

Magda squealed at the movement and tossed her arms around his neck.

"Don't worry, Maggie, I've got you."

A group of teenaged boys walked by, issuing catcalls. Jeff nodded at them pleasantly. "Hi guys. Good luck this season."

"Thanks, Mr. Braden!" They called back as they passed.

"Friends of Deidre's kids," he said casually by way of explanation, as if he weren't carrying her down a public street. "They play on the high school football team with Craig—Caitlin's twin."

"How nice," Maggie said with exaggerated politeness before pounding her little fists against him. "Jeff! What are you doing? Put me down!"

He stopped and kissed the tip of her nose before he grinned and said, "Those shoes looked like they'd be hard to walk in, so I thought I'd carry you."

She rolled her eyes. "Well, think again, Alley Oop,

I'm perfectly capable of walking in my shoes."

He laughed. "Alley Oop? Did you just call me a caveman?" He shook his head. "A caveman would club you and drag you off by your hair. *That's* my Plan B. I thought I'd try sweeping you off your feet first."

She tried to look stern, but couldn't quite keep the amusement out of her eyes. "If we're supposed to be "just friends," then carrying me onto the Green in front of the whole town might give things away."

He sighed, but put her down. "Fine. I might be a caveman, but you're a party pooper."

"Am not!"

"Are too."

They continued to bicker playfully as they walked to the park. The music got louder and was joined by a cacophony of happy voices and laughter. The aroma of food cooking made Jeff's mouth water almost as much as the woman by his side did.

They stopped at the edge of the green and Maggie vibrated with excitement; she bounced on those sexy, mile-high shoes. "Oh, Jeff, this is wonderful!"

He looked around with pride. Rivers Bend might be a tiny, little town, but it sure knew how to throw a big, old party. Red, white, and blue bunting hung off the railings around the gazebo, where the band was starting to tune up their instruments. Stalls selling food to benefit various local organizations and school clubs were off to the left. Blankets and folding chairs covered almost every inch of space in the park, except for the plywood dance floor at the bottom of the steps leading into the patriotically bedecked gazebo, as the whole town came out to celebrate the end of summer.

****

Magda stopped at the edge of the Green to take it all in—the noise, the smells and, oh my, the crowd! During the course of the week, she met a lot of them in the library and around town, but all together *en masse* like this, it was a little overwhelming.

Feeling suddenly bashful, she held back when Jeff stepped off the sidewalk onto the grass. He looked next to him, where she'd been a second ago and looked startled to see empty air. He flashed a knee-weakening grin over his shoulder.

"The offer to carry you still holds, if you're worried about getting your pretty shoes dirty."

A group of children waving glow sticks, little American flags, and giant poufs of pink cotton candy, darted between them and gave her time to get over her bout of nerves.

She rolled her eyes. "I'll still pass, but thanks."

She stepped up to his side and smiled up at him. "So many people, I was feeling a little overwhelmed for a minute there, but I'm back now."

Jeff gave a quizzical grin. "A big city girl like you afraid of a little crowd?"

She bit her bottom lip and hesitated before answering. "I've always been more on the outside of things. I never fit in entirely in either of the worlds I straddled." She squared her shoulders. "But that's too deep and dreary a topic for such a pretty, summer night."

A sharp whistle rent the air; Magda looked around to see the source and found a lanky man waving at them.

Jeff waved back and said, "There's Hank—Deidre's husband—that must be where the Braden clan has set up camp."

"He looks like a like a young Clint Eastwood," Magda observed as she waved shyly at Hank.

"Ya think?"

She nodded. "All tan, long, lean, and squinty-eyed. He looks like a cowboy."

Jeff threw back his head and laughed. "I can't wait to use that description to bust his ass."

She swatted his arm. "Jeff—don't!"

He shook his head once. "I'm not making any promises." He chuckled. "Our own Virginia cowboy."

"I know he's not a cowboy exactly; I'm just saying he looks like one."

"I'm sorry, I didn't mean to tease you," Jeff said but didn't look at all repentant. "You want to head over there and meet everyone?"

"Sure," she said with more confidence than she was feeling. Good golly, a first date—albeit a secret one—and now she had to meet his mother?

Jeff tucked one of his warm, strong hands under her elbow to help her over the uneven terrain. He leaned down to say, "Hank's on me all the time—busting my stones for being Mr. Celebrity-NFL star, so I'm looking forward to doing a little busting back at him."

As they made their way through the crowd, everyone had a smile and a greeting for Jeff, who smiled in return and inclined his head in acknowledgement. Magda felt like they were on a royal procession through the park. She lowered her eyes and smothered her smile. "I don't know where on Earth Hank would get an idea like that."

They reached where Hank stood next to a plaid

blanket spread on the ground. Deidre sat on it and smiled up at them. "Hi Jeff, hi Maggie. This is my husband, Hank, and our son, Craig." She gestured to the Clint Eastwood lookalike and the teenage boy next to him, who was every bit as tall as his dad, but well on his way to being as muscular as his Uncle Jeff. His sandy brown hair was longer in the front and flopped over his eyes; he smiled at Magda shyly.

"Nice to meet you, ma'am."

"Please—call me Magda, your sister does. Hi Cait." She smiled at Caitlin, who was sprawled next to her mother on the blanket. Magda noticed they were both wearing shorts; she smoothed the skirt of her sundress self-consciously.

Jeff brushed by her to lean down to kiss the cheek of an older woman sitting in a folding chair. She had smile lines around her eyes, and was tan and lean in a way that indicated she spent a lot of time outdoors. Her brown hair had a single streak of white in it on the right temple and was pulled back in a ponytail. Her long legs stretched out in front of her, and she wore denim Capri pants with a T-shirt with an American flag on it. From a distance, she could pass as one of Caitlin's friends, rather than her grandmother.

"Hi, Ma," Jeff said as he straightened up from kissing his mother and put his arm around Magda's waist. "This is Maggie Horvath. Maggie, this is my mom, Joyce Braden.

"Nice to meet you, Mrs. Braden."

"You too, sugar, but call me Joyce. I feel like we're old friends already, with the way my granddaughters have been going on about you."

Deidre shaded her eyes with her hand as she smiled

up into the sunlight at Magda. "Have a seat by me, Maggie. You're just in time for dinner. Hank and Craig were just going to get food."

Magda hesitated and glanced down at the blanket, where Joyce wanted her to sit. She didn't think there was any graceful way to get down on the green and black plaid throw in this dress. With a small sigh, she finally smoothed it taut against her bottom and tried to keep her legs together as she folded herself down to the ground.

She grimaced at Deidre, who was sitting lotus style on the blanket next to her. "I'm way overdressed. I love this sundress, and I never get to wear it, so I put it on for tonight, but shorts like yours would've been more practical."

Joyce leaned down from her chair to pat Magda's shoulder in a maternal fashion. "But not nearly so pretty."

"I like the dress." Jeff paused and added with an unabashed grin, "And the shoes."

As his mother looked between them with a speculative gleam in her eyes, Magda felt heat rise in her face.

Jeff's brother-in-law slapped Jeff on the back, but spoke to his son, "Now that Uncle Jeff is here, he can help me get the food and drinks. Why don't you go on and find your buddies."

"Okay—thanks, Dad!" Craig took off at a sprint toward a group of boys and girls at a picnic table closer to the river.

Hank looked at the rest of the group with a smile. "So—pit beef for everyone?"

"Pit beef?" Magda wrinkled her nose. She liked

beef, but the "pit" part had her a little nervous. "What's that?"

Hank raised an eyebrow. "You've never had pit beef?"

She shook her head. "Nope. I've never heard of it."

Jeff smiled at her. "You haven't lived until you've had a pit beef sandwich. C'mon, Hank, let's go get the ladies some dinner."

Deidre laughed at Magda's incredulous expression, while the two men walked toward the food stands. "It's way better than it sounds. Honest."

"You've been keeping me well fed all week at the Nosh Pit, so I trust you," Maggie replied with a shy smile; feeling nervous to suddenly find herself alone with Jeff's family at the beginning of their first date.

Jeff's sister, Heather, arrived at that moment, with a big canvas tote bag. "Hello all!" She called out cheerfully as she dropped the bag with a thump and flopped on the blanket.

Her olive shorts, white baby tee and Keds made the move easy for her, and Magda plucked a little at her skirt, to make sure it wasn't all bunched up and wished for about the thousandth time that she'd worn shorts, instead of trying to dazzle Jeff with her full-skirted dress with its tight bodice.

Heather brushed her artfully messy, layered brown hair off her face, where it fell while she leaned over the bag to paw around in it. She hoisted a huge thermos bottle and announced triumphantly, "Ta da!"

"Ooo," Deidre said with an interested grin. "What've you got in there, little sister?"

"I mixed up a batch of Lemon Drops for the grown-ups to enjoy." She produced plastic martini glasses with multi-colored polka dots on them from the tote and began to pour. "Where's my other niece?"

"Sam? She's at a party at Hadley Diemer's house," Magda explained as she took the cocktail Heather handed to her. "Her mother is having a big bash, and Hadley invited all the fifth grade girls for a parallel party."

Deidre took a sip of the drink Heather handed her, and closed her eye in bliss. "Yum. You are one fine mixologist, Heather." She passed a glass from her sister to her mother and said, "I heard about that party Sam's going to—lots of bigwigs coming from D.C. for it."

Magda took a dainty sip of her drink. "Oh my, this is good."

"But deceptive. It tastes like candy, but it hits you like a Mack truck," Joyce warned before taking a healthy gulp of her own cocktail.

****

"What are they doing?" Jeff squinted as he looked back at Magda.

"Looks like your sister showed up with some of those girly drinks she makes."

"They may taste girly, but most of them can knock you on your ass. I hope someone warns Maggie."

One side of Hank's mouth quirked up. "You've got it bad, Jefferson, whachya gonna do about it?"

They shuffled forward in the long line to place their order for pit beef.

"I don't know what you're talking about," Jeff tried to sound casual, but even he could tell he sounded stilted as he lied through his teeth.

"You get hit in the head a few too many times when you were playing ball? I'm talking about you and the cute little blonde in the pretty dress that you can't take your eyes off of," Hank drawled.

Jeff whipped his head around to face forward and away from Magda, in a vain attempt to disguise his interest.

"Too late, bro, I'm onto you," Hank teased. "Can't say as I blame you. I've been listening to Caitlin and Sam sing the woman's praises all week. She sounds real nice—a cutie-pie, too. And don't try to pretend you haven't noticed."

Jeff grinned sheepishly. "Nah, I've noticed. Not sure what to do about it, but I sure as hell have noticed."

Hanks eyes bulged. "Don't know what to do? Man, you really should've used a better helmet. Any fool would know what to do with a woman like Maggie."

Jeff looked back at Magda, took a deep breath, and exhaled. "I know what I'd like to do, but I have to think about Sam, and how things between Maggie and I would impact her life."

Hank shrugged. "Sam came out to the farm today with her friends to ride; she seemed pretty excited that y'all were going out on a date tonight."

Jeff's eyebrows shot up. "I told her we were riding here together—as friends. I never said it was a date."

Hank shook his head and emitted a sharp bark of laughter. "Your daughter is no dummy—and she's not a baby anymore, either. She *knows* you're on a date, and she seemed right happy about it."

Hope flared in Jeff's eyes, but just as quickly died. "But Maggie's leaving after Bethanne has the baby; I don't want Sam getting attached and used to her being in our lives and then losing all that."

"You worried about Sam or you?" Hank asked sagely.

"Got a point you're trying to make there, Yoda?"

"Yup. I think you're using Sam as an excuse not to get involved with Maggie."

"Oh yeah? Anything else?"

"No need to be all belligerent. And—yeah—I've got something else to say—I think you're an idiot."

"Don't hold back or anything, Hank, tell me what you *really* think," Jeff responded with a snort of laughter.

"Okay, I will. I know you wanted to protect Sam when she was little, but she's going to be a teenager before you know it, and it's important for her to have a good model of a healthy relationship. It's the best gift a parent can give to their child."

Jeff blinked several times and shook his head. "Where the hell did *that* come from?"

Hank shrugged. "When I was laid up with that torn meniscus, I watched a lot of *Dr. Phil*. That good ole boy knows his shit."

It was finally their turn, so Jeff had a little time to absorb Hank's words as his brother-in-law placed their order. They stepped aside to wait for their food.

"I'm gonna get us a couple of beers—you wait here for the food, okay?" Hank asked.

Jeff nodded; glad for a couple of minutes alone to keep thinking about the bomb Hank had just dropped on him. Had he been keeping women at arm's length emotionally to protect his daughter or to protect himself? He'd meant to protect Sam, but had he really been harming her by not showing her what a good relationship was like? Oh man, he *hated* analyzing his feelings—why did Hank have to plant these ideas in his head tonight?

Of course, until Maggie rolled into town there hadn't been a woman he'd consider having a deeper relationship with—one that would include his beloved child. If any woman was worth giving it a shot, it was Maggie, but she came complete with an expiration date. In a few short months, Maggie would be out of here to move on with her life somewhere else. Did he want to put Sam, or himself for that matter, through that kind of loss at the end of Maggie's time in Rivers Bend?

A smile teased up the corners of his mouth—in those few months, Maggie and he sure could have a lot of fun. Some of it naked fun, even.

"Do I want to know what's put that shit-eating grin on your face?" Hank asked as he shoved a red plastic cup of foamy beer, which dripped condensation on this steamy summer night, into Jeff's hand.

Jeff broke out a full-blown grin. "You might—it's pretty damn hot—but I think I'll keep it to myself."

Hank took a swig of his beer and swiped some suds off his mouth with the back of his hand. "Let me guess—it involves you, a hot, little, blonde librarian, and some extreme punishments for your overdue books? You naughty boy."

"Go to hell," Jeff said companionably as his eyes drifted to the librarian in question. His smile faded and the muscles in his jaw worked overtime. "What the fuck is he doing?"

Hank handed Jeff his beer to hold for him as their order was called. He took the tray of food with a smile at the kid who handed it to him then turned to see what Jeff was talking about. "Who? Jason?"

"Yeah. Jason." Jeff was afraid he was going to crack a tooth; he was clenching his jaw so tightly as he watched his baby brother, cozied up to Maggie on the blanket. Jason had his eyes locked on Maggie's as he took a sip of the cocktail she held out to him.

Hank said in an offhand manner. "Looks to me like he's doin' what he does best—hitting on a pretty woman."

"*My* pretty woman," Jeff growled as he stalked to the blanket, still carrying both of their beers.

****

Pierce's head lolled back as he listened to his father's voice drone on in yet another lecture on how he was letting down the family name. He sprawled in the desk chair in his elegantly appointed study. Magda hated the décor of this apartment—an opinion that betrayed her bourgeois roots, Pierce had always thought.

The decorator had captured exactly who he was and how he wanted to present himself to the world. Now that he thought about it, maybe the fact Magda didn't like it should have been his first indication that she didn't like *him*.

His father's voice snapped over the phone line. "Pierce, are you even listening to me?"

"Of course, Father," he lied easily.

"Then answer me—have you and Magda set a wedding date yet?"

"No, not yet."

Well, at least that wasn't a lie—although, if he were completely honest, he'd admit to his father that if Magda had her way, there never would *be* a wedding.

"What is the delay? You know how important this

marriage is to your grandfather."

Pierce sighed. He knew all too well how important this marriage was to his controlling grandfather. The man was willing to cut his own flesh-and-blood grandchild out of the family fold, if he didn't marry Elizabeth Mallory's granddaughter.

"All this pressure to unite our families wouldn't be falling on me now, if you had just been man enough to hold onto Magda's mother when you were in college. But you weren't, and instead, she left you for some immigrant factory worker."

A long silence met his drawled barb. Maybe it wasn't fair to blame his father, but Pierce did. When Magda's mother broke their family-arranged engagement and ran off with Tom Horvath, his grandfather and Magda's grandmother were both furious. Neither was used to having their will flouted, and it festered in both of them until now. They were both bound and determined that Pierce and Magda would correct the errors of the previous generation.

"I've heard that song from my father for my entire adult life; I don't need to hear it from my son also," his father finally said so wearily that Pierce felt a brief pang of guilt for poking at him.

His father continued, "And since he refuses to speak to you until you've achieved his obsessive goal of bringing a Mallory into the Allen family, *I'm* the one who has to listen to your grandfather's rants about your shortcomings."

"I'd think you'd enjoy that, Father, as you've always been so willing to discuss them with me."

"You can't deny you've been a disappointment, Pierce. The women, the gambling, the drugs, do you think we don't all know what you get up to? We're merely asking you to marry a perfectly attractive young woman, and it will all be overlooked. You'll be welcomed back into the family, and your grandfather will release his iron grip on your purse strings. Not to mention, *I* won't have to suffer through another tirade about your base ingratitude. Just set a date and marry the girl."

"And if the girl isn't in any hurry to marry me?"

"Then do whatever you have to do to make her hurry. I mean it, son. Your grandfather's already short patience is about to end, and when it does there will be no coming back for you. He'll cut you off completely and leave you destitute without a second thought, don't you doubt it for a minute."

Pierce slid open the top drawer of his desk, where a handgun nestled next to a crack pipe, both of which he'd purchased from his new dealer in Brooklyn. The man promised smoking crack would pack more of a punch than the cocaine Pierce had been snorting, and he'd been so right. He wished he'd left his effete, society dealer years ago. This street shit was powerful, and he felt invincible.

With cold eyes, he pulled the gun out of the drawer and said to his father as he played with it, "Fine, Father, I'll take your advice and do whatever it takes to get Magda to marry me."

His father breathed a sigh of relief. "That's fine, son, you won't regret it."

Maybe he would, maybe he wouldn't. Pierce felt backed into a corner, as a desperate plan took root in his drug-addled mind. "Thanks for the advice, Father, I intend to put it into effect just as soon as possible."

Chapter 14

As Jason leaned forward to take a sip of her cocktail with a teasing, flirtatious gleam in his eye, Magda's gaze was drawn to Jeff like a compass to magnetic north. He stalked toward them, ignoring all the cheerful greetings people called out as he passed. Hank trailed in his wake with a massive tray of sandwiches and fries; something seemed to have made him laugh, but Magda couldn't imagine what, since Jeff looked like a very non-funny storm cloud at the moment.

Jason sat back with a sigh. "Good drink, but I have to admit that I'm used to being able to hold a woman's attention a little better than this."

"Huh?" Magda murmured as Jeff stepped onto the blanket next to his brother.

Jason leaned back on his elbows to look up at Jeff. "Hey bro, is one of those beers for me?"

Jeff's posture indicated nothing but relaxed geniality, but the death grip he had on those two beer cups told another story.

"Nope. One is Hank's and the other is mine. Not everything you see and want is automatically yours, baby brother."

"That's right," Hank said, as he pried his cup out of Jeff's clutches. "Keep your dirty mitts off my beer, Jase."

Heather drained the last of her Lemon Drop, put the empty glass on the blanket, and stood. "This little pissing contest reminds me—I need to use the restroom, and I hate these portable ones. Maggie, can you let us into the library to use the ladies room?"

Magda dragged her eyes off the two Braden brothers and their mysterious tension to look at Heather. "Sure, I've got the key in my bag."

Joyce rose from her chair. "What a good idea! I'll come, too, but don't let on where we're going or we'll have every lady in town following us, and Maggie'll miss the whole concert."

Jeff smiled at her, and Magda was happy to see his familiar laugh lines make an appearance to crinkle at the corner of his eyes. "We don't want that to happen. Hurry back, Maggie, you still have to try your first pit beef sandwich."

Heather had already started to stroll toward Main Street, and Joyce and Magda fell in step behind her.

Magda smiled and called over her shoulder to Jeff, "We'll be back before you even know we're gone."

She continued to look over her shoulder just long enough to see Jeff's smile be replaced by thunder again as he glared down at his brother, who was sprawled on the blanket and inhaling one of their sandwiches.

Her brow furrowed in confusion as she asked Joyce, "What's with all the tension back there?" She jerked her thumb back at their group on the blanket.

"Brothers," Joyce chuckled. "As far as I can tell, they exist merely to torment each other. It's nothing for you to worry about. I usually just ignore them, unless furniture is being broken."

****

"What the hell, Jase?" Jeff growled.

Jason made his eyes wide with feigned innocence as he swallowed a huge mouthful of pit beef with a gulp. "What do you mean?"

"Cut the crap. You know what I mean." Jeff narrowed his eyes, and his voice was low and threatening.

Jason shrugged. "Hey—you said you weren't staking a claim, so Maggie's open game, right?"

Jeff's grip on his poor red cup got so tight that some foamy, amber liquid sloshed over the top onto his hand.

Deidre bit a fry and swallowed. "Oh leave him be, Jase. Don't you have enough sense not to poke the bear? Jeff's clearly gone on Maggie, and you're just flirting with her to get under his skin."

"Yep." Jason chortled. "And just look at him," he waved his hand at Jeff, "mission accomplished, dontcha think?"

Jeff ground his teeth together. What the hell was he thinking, taking Maggie on their first unofficial, official date with his entire family around? He should've taken her to a fancy restaurant for a romantic, candlelit dinner—not for pit beef sammies on the Green with his pain-in-the-ass younger brother coming on to her just to piss him off. Mission accomplished, indeed.

Deidre patted the blanket next to her. "Sit down and cool your jets before Maggie gets back. You don't want to scare her off with that scowl you've got on your face. Just relax, drink your beer—"

"And most important—ignore Jason," Hank interrupted his wife.

"What he said," Deidre agreed before taking a

dainty bite of her sandwich.

Jeff took their advice and sat on the blanket in a position that would put him squarely between Maggie and his horn-dog brother.

Jason looked pointedly at where he chose to sit and laughed. "Subtle. Man, you are so easy!"

****

Magda licked her fingers before wiping them on her paper napkin, crumpling it, and tossing it on the tray with the rest of their trash.

"Yum! The funnel cake was even better than the pit beef. It reminds me of the fried dough we used to get at the beach in Rhode Island when I was a kid."

She smiled at Jeff, who seemed mesmerized by the finger licking. It made her feel equal parts powerful and puzzled; she still didn't completely understand what it was Jeff saw in her. She'd looked him up online and seen lots of photographs of him with statuesque model types at charity events in D.C., but she tried to squelch those feelings of inadequacy and enjoy the ride—who was she to look such a big, hunk of a gift horse in the mouth?

The band launched into a lively number, and Jeff pushed to his feet and held out a hand to Magda. "May I have this dance, Ms. Horvath?" he asked in a formal tone, but with a twinkle in his eyes.

She took his hand and let him help her up. "Sure, but I've got to warn you—I'm not the best dancer."

He kept her hand in his as they strolled to the makeshift dance floor, where Jason was dancing with several women at once.

"It's like a harem." Magda chuckled.

She'd been relieved when she got back from the

ladies room earlier and a group of young, pretty women had swarmed around Jason at their picnic area. Their presence distracted him from needling Jeff by flirting with her.

"It would do the boy good to meet a woman with the ability to resist his charms," Jeff said with a grin.

She hesitated as they reached the edge of the plywood dance floor. "I wasn't kidding, Jeff; guard your feet, because I'm kind of a klutz and they are in imminent danger of being trounced."

He chuckled. "Do you expect me to believe you didn't have to take dance classes at that fancy boarding school you went to?"

"I did—and I could maybe muster a little box step action, but not much else." She gestured to the other dancers with her head. "Certainly not what everyone else is doing."

Jeff pulled her into his arms. "They're two-stepping; this is a good song for it. C'mon, I'll show you how."

As Jeff tucked her tight against his muscular body, Magda thought that a two-step with him had a lot more to recommend itself than an awkward box step in ninth grade dance class. She enjoyed the delicious sensation of his body pressed against hers and his warm hand spanning her back until it distracted her concentration, and she stumbled over his feet and knocked them both off balance.

"I'm so sorry! But you can't say I didn't warn you."

As they held onto each other and laughed, a flashbulb lit them up in the fading daylight. They both turned their heads sharply to locate the source and saw a young man, who didn't look to be much older than Caitlin and Craig, with camera equipment hanging from straps, and weighing down his pencil-thin neck.

"Evening, Sam," Jeff said genially.

"Hi, Mr. Braden. Ma'am." The young man smiled. "May I get another shot of you for the *Rivers Bend Gazette?*"

"Sure," Jeff agreed and twirled Magda until her back was against his front. Even in her high wedge sandals, Jeff was tall enough to rest his chin on top of her head. He wrapped his arms around her waist and she could feel his smile for the camera against the top of her skull. Relishing the multi-sensory experience of being surrounded by his scent, his strength, his radiating warmth, and his ever-present good humor, she flashed a bright smile at Jimmy Olsen.

He clicked a button on the camera, and she blinked against the sudden flare of light.

"Great! Thanks, folks. Our readers will love seeing our newest resident and our favorite son dancing together at the Labor Day concert."

He started to walk toward Jason and his women, when he snapped his fingers as he remembered something. "Oh—and I finally talked Mr. Johnson into letting me post some stories online, so check our new website and you'll see these pictures there, too."

****

Magda's palms felt sweaty in spite of the air-conditioning, which blasted blissfully cool air on her as Jeff and she rode through the summer night. Even after the sun went down, the air remained sultry and between the heat and dancing every dance with Jeff, she was more than happy to get into Jeff's truck with its powerful engine and cool air.

But it wasn't helping the sweaty palms, because they weren't the result of being warm. Nope. Nerves were to blame, because they were on their way home to put her "friends with benefits" plan into action.

The radio was tuned to a country music station, and its low music was the only sound in the cab of the truck. Magda swiped her palms surreptitiously on her skirt as she risked a nervous glance in Jeff's direction.

He was illuminated only by the glow of the dashboard lights—living in the city she'd forgotten how absolutely dark the nights are when you get away from the 24/7 glare of city lights, all to enable the residents their constant, frenetic activity. There was a peace to be found in a quiet, dark country night, which she might enjoy if she weren't about to pass out from anxiety and sexual tension.

Jeff's eyes were fixed on the bending road as he drove and revealed no clue to his mental state, but he tapped one finger on the steering wheel in time with the music. It looked to Magda to be a nervous movement, rather than a relaxed one, but she was probably just projecting her own fears.

Pierce had done a number on her self-esteem. Their sex life had never been what she would call fulfilling, and eventually it had dwindled altogether, so it hadn't been a complete shock when she overheard Taylor Brown talking about sleeping with him. However, his critique of her performance to the other woman was a hurtful surprise, and the idea that Jeff might end up thinking she was a dud in bed had her stomach doing flip-flops.

He cleared his throat, and when he spoke, his

words made her flip-flopping stomach freefall straight to her feet.

"I'm thinking this 'friends with benefits' business isn't going to work for me. Not with you."

She swallowed hard and looked out the side window so he wouldn't see the tears, which burned her eyes. Of course, she now stared into pitch-black nothingness, so she suspected she wasn't fooling him.

It didn't even take a roll in the hay for her to disappoint him evidently—guess their first date didn't measure up to the black-tie affairs she'd seen the online pictures of him attending—and she obviously didn't measure up to his usual beauty queen dates.

She finally trusted her voice not to quaver and betray her. "Okay. If that's how you feel—we can just be friends. No benefits."

He took his eyes off the road for a moment to gape at her in dismay. "What? No! That's not what I meant at all. Is that what *you* want?"

She looked at him with wide eyes and no small measure of relief. "No, it's most definitely *not* what I want."

"Phew! I think I might just about explode if we stayed platonic friends," Jeff admitted with a grin. "What I meant was that I don't like the whole clandestine aspect of our plan. It makes it feel like what we'd be doing was dirty—or bad—and it's not. It won't be."

He took a deep breath and gripped the steering wheel with both hands. "I guess what I'm trying to say is that you're a special woman, and I wouldn't feel right about sneaking around to sleep with you. You deserve more than that and I want to give you more than that—

so I'd like to be together out in the open for everyone to see."

Magda grinned and playfully fanned her face as she teased in a Scarlett O'Hara accent. "I do declare, Mr. Braden, I'm not into that kind of public display."

He chuckled and loosened his hold on the wheel. Her joke caused the mood in the truck to lighten. "You know that's not what I meant. I want people to know that we're dating."

In particular, his idiot brother and the streaking sheriff, both of whose attentions to Magda made Jeff crazy.

"Everyone? Even Sam?"

"Especially Sam," Jeff replied with certainty. "I'm going to talk to her tomorrow when she gets home from Hadley's sleepover. She doesn't need details about what we do together, but Hank said some stuff tonight that made me think I've been doing her a disservice by not letting her see me in a healthy relationship with a good woman."

Magda nibbled on her bottom lip as she considered his words. "I'm honored that I'm the woman you chose to bring into your life with your daughter, but I'm still leaving in a few months, Jeff. Six months is probably the longest I'll be here—depending on how long Bethanne can carry the baby and how much maternity leave she chooses to take after the birth."

"I know, and I understand that you need to make your own way in the world and that can't happen here in Rivers Bend. I'm going to explain it to Sam, so she'll understand, too and won't feel abandoned. It'll be good for her to see that not everyone who leaves is leaving *her*; that people come and go in our lives, and we learn to roll with it."

Magda nodded, but her throat was tight. She just hoped she'd be mature enough to remember that lesson when it was time to leave Rivers Bend—and Jeff—to start her life and career elsewhere.

They pulled up to the back of Jeff's house; he turned in his seat to face her. He rested one arm across the back of the seat and the other on the steering wheel. "We should get inside to Petunia before the fireworks start, but I want you to know there's no pressure. If you want to take time to think about what I said before we make love, I'll understand."

Magda licked her lips nervously and couldn't help but notice the hungry look in his eyes as they followed the motion of her tongue. "I don't need time to think— I'd like to date you during my time here in Rivers Bend. As long as you don't think it will hurt Sam in the end, because I really care about her and there *is* a definite end date to my time here."

His smile lit up the dark night more than the dim porch light next to the kitchen door. "Thanks for thinking of my daughter—we'll be okay when you go. I'll make sure of it." He exhaled loudly. "And thank God your answer was 'yes,' because I was trying to be a gentleman, but if you'd said 'thanks, but no thanks,' I was afraid I'd burst into flames and just leave a little pile of ashes here in the truck. I want you so much, Maggie."

He leaned over and pressed his warm firm lips to hers, and her eyes fluttered shut. Just as she was about to tangle her hands in his messy hair and pull him in for a more passionate kiss, he pulled away.

His voice was rough with desire. "Let's go inside."

****

"I think that was the grand finale of the fireworks show," Jeff said at the fading sound of a distant, prolonged boom. "And Miss Petunia slept through the whole thing thanks to the doggie downers."

He had been sorry to learn they'd have to miss the fireworks display tonight. He had visions of curling up on a blanket with Magda, sneaking kisses while the colorful lights exploded in the sky above them, but the reality had turned out to be even better than the fantasy. Instead of being surrounded by his family and the entire population of Rivers Bend, they were cuddled on the sofa in his comfortable family room, rather than on the hard ground. And said family room was in much closer proximity to his bedroom, where he fervently hoped the evening would end.

Those knockout pills of Petunia's were good stuff because the dog was able to sleep on his lap, where his current state of arousal—due to Magda snuggled into his side, with all her soft curves pressed into him and her head on his shoulder—couldn't be comfortable for the little pooch.

Magda reached toward his lap, and he held his breath in anticipation, but she stroked Petunia instead of him.

"I'm so glad the pill kept her calm. The last time there were fireworks in the city, she made herself sick with fear. She had to spend a night at the animal hospital. Of course, Pierce was no help—Petunia and he really hated each other."

Okay—enough talk about the ex. Jeff had better things in mind to do in his rarely childfree house tonight.

"Pierce sounds like a real tool." He ran his hand down Petunia's back and pressed a light kiss to the top of Magda's head. He nuzzled her there for a moment; her hair was so soft and her shampoo made it smell sweet and a little coconuty—it put him in mind of a Piña Colada. He took another sniff and continued. "But more importantly, he's your past—both Petunia's and your past—so what do you say we leave him back there where he belongs and make this a 'No Pierce' zone, at least for tonight."

****

Magda murmured her agreement and burrowed closer to Jeff's side. He had one arm wrapped tight around her and stroked little circles into her arm, while with the other he petted her dog in a soothing manner, as if with the movement he could erase the ugly memories of Pierce—and maybe he could.

She turned her head slightly so she could inhale Jeff's scent—it was absolutely delicious. In the crook of his neck, she could still smell hints of the soap he'd used in the shower and his piney, masculine aftershave. He smelled like what he was—all rugged, masculine man. Pierce always used expensive cologne, and when she caught a whiff of it—which wasn't hard to do, Pierce practically bathed in the stuff—she could always hear her father's voice saying the man smelled like a French whorehouse. Not that her dad had ever set foot in France, let alone one of their bordellos, but she knew that he would have said it about Pierce. He was not her father's kind of man, but her dad would have loved Jeff and been thrilled that she'd finally wised up and kicked Pierce to the curb.

Ugh. Enough about Pierce. Jeff was right—she'd

left Pierce behind in New York, now it was time to throw him out of her head as well. She kissed Jeff lightly where his neck met his broad shoulder and was rewarded by a quiet groan of pleasure.

She smiled against his skin. "You're absolutely right—there will be no more use of the 'P' word tonight. There's no room on this sofa for us and him, too."

Jeff smiled and gave her a squeeze. "It is a little snug here—what do you say we get Petunia settled for the night and move things upstairs to my big, comfortable bed?"

Magda gulped and feared Jeff would feel her heart racing where she was pressed against him. Now it was time for the real test—would she be able to keep the insecurities about her sexual performance that Pierce had so callously fostered out of Jeff's bed?

What if Pierce was right and she was a lousy lay? Would a man as masculine and virile as Jeff want a relationship with a woman who couldn't satisfy him between the sheets?

She felt his hard body tense beneath her as he pulled his arm away and put a hairsbreadth of distance between them. "Or I could bring you girls back to your cabin. I said 'no pressure' and I meant it, Maggie, if you don't want this, it doesn't happen."

God! He'd misinterpreted her hesitation and thought she didn't want him. Great—they weren't even off the sofa yet, and she was screwing it all up. "Oh, I want this, Jeff Braden! Don't try to back out now—unless *you* don't want to?"

He lifted Petunia off his lap and looked down, which drew her gaze to a most impressive bulge. "Does it *look* like I don't want to?"

She almost swallowed her tongue. "Um—no—all systems seem to be go on your end."

His voice was gentle as he slipped his arm back around her and shifted Petunia to the sofa on his other side. "So if *I* want to, and *you* want to, and we have the house to ourselves tonight, which doesn't happen often, what's holding you back, Maggie?"

"Nerves," she confessed in a whisper. "I don't want to be a disappointment to you."

"Based on the bonfire sized sparks between us, I don't think that's something you need to worry about, darlin'. Just snuggling with you in my family room has me hard enough to drive nails."

She giggled—*giggled*—she couldn't remember the last time she'd done that.

Jeff smiled in response. "Let's go upstairs, Maggie, and I'll show you just how desirable I think you are."

****

"None of this is going quite the why I imagined it," Jeff said with a rakish grin as they paused at the door to his bedroom. "For one thing, I thought I'd be carrying you up the stairs; not your doped up Shih Tzu."

Magda watched as he opened the door with the hand that wasn't holding her snoring dog and gestured for her to go in ahead of them. Nerves had her clutching the fleece dog bed and water dish, which Jeff had bought for Petunia, in a death grip.

She smiled over her shoulder as she crossed the threshold, striving to keep her tone lighter than she felt. "You're probably better off with Petunia—lugging me up a flight of stairs would've put your back out for sure, and that would have been a disappointing end to the evening for both of us."

"Nah," he scoffed. "You're just a little bit of a thing, Maggie, I could've carried you and Petunia both, but I didn't want to show off."

Maggie looked around the room in amazement—she was in Jeff's bedroom, about to make love. And what a bedroom! A huge king-sized cherry wood sleigh-bed dominated the room. It was covered with a fluffy, burgundy comforter and pillows in matching shams. Opposite the bed was a fireplace with a hearth composed of river rock. To the right were French doors, which she guessed led out to the balcony that ran the length of the front of the second floor of the house.

He gently pried the dog bed from her fingers and dropped it to the floor next to the wall between two doors opposite the balcony doors. He placed Petunia on it carefully and walked back to Magda; her heart threatened to pound through her chest, but he only took the aluminum water bowl from her hand.

"I'll fill this up and leave it in the bathroom for her—in case she wakes up thirsty."

He opened the door to the right of the dog bed and flicked on a switch, fluorescent light from the doorway seemed bright in the bedroom that was lit only by the moonlight coming through the French doors. Maggie heard water running and the clink of the bowl as he placed it on the marble floor she could see through the door.

He turned off the light as he exited the master bath and turned the bedside lamp on its dimmest setting. He walked past Magda to shut the bedroom door behind her with a soft click.

"Don't want Petunia waking up all dopey from her

meds and falling down the stairs," he explained. "Or have Mrs. Wilson seeing us in here in the morning when she gets here for work."

Magda was glad for the cover of the semi-darkness as she felt the heat of a blush creeping up her neck to cover her face. Curse her fair complexion and lack of sophistication—Jeff was probably used to a woman who wouldn't turn into a tomato at the mention of spending the night in his bed.

He stepped up beside her and rested his big, warm hands on her shoulders briefly, before they took a long, leisurely trip down her arms. She closed her eyes in bliss at the sensation, and her knees almost buckled as she felt him sweep her hair aside to kiss the side of her neck, just behind her ear.

His breath tickled her skin as he said with soft reverence, "You smell so good, Maggie; your skin is so soft right here." He punctuated his words with a nuzzle and another kiss to the sensitive spot on her neck. "Makes a man wonder if you're just as soft everywhere on your sweet body."

A breathless murmur was the only response she could muster as his hands slipped around her body to cup her breasts.

"I love this dress, but I've been imagining stripping you out of it all night," he murmured before moving one hand to her back.

She heard the rasp of the zipper that ran down the back of her dress as he slowly lowered it. She felt aroused beyond belief, but also bashful because she was one push of her dress from standing in front of Jeff wearing only a—thankfully—matching bra and panty set. It was just plain white and lace, but at least it wasn't a mismatched pair of granny panties and a practical cotton bra.

Jeff pushed on the shoulder straps of the sundress, and she felt the fabric as it brushed along her body to pool at her feet.

"Whoops, look what I did," he whispered with mock contrition, and she could hear the smile in his voice.

So far, Jeff was doing all the work, and Magda felt like she needed to step up her game. She stepped out of the dress and turned to face Jeff in one movement.

Desire darkened his eyes as they swept down her body from head to toe. "Have I mentioned how much I love those high shoes? Leave them on."

Magda stepped toward him and grasped the hem of his polo shirt. "You're awfully bossy," she teased. "And overdressed."

She pulled his shirt up and he helped her peel it over his head. He tossed it on the floor next to her dress and it was her turn to stare hungrily at him. She reached for the buckle of his braided leather belt.

"Still too many clothes." She popped the buckle and undid his shorts.

Jeff shoved them down impatiently and stood before her, clad only in a pair of navy boxer briefs.

She felt her mouth go dry, as a lower part of her body got correspondingly damp. She'd thought Jeff looked fine in his bathing suit, but lordy—the man in snug boxer briefs should be illegal.

He closed the hairsbreadth of distance between them and picked her up in a fireman's hold. Her face hung over his back and she had a glimpse of his tight buns, firmly encased in his briefs, before he tossed her gently on the bed.

She bounced a few times and laughed as she propped herself up on her elbows to watch Jeff's next move. He never took his eyes off her as he reached for the nightstand. He slid the drawer open and pulled out an unopened, economy-sized box of condoms.

She grinned and raised an eyebrow as she looked from the big box to Jeff's face. "Feeling optimistic?"

He shrugged and grinned back at her. "Nope—just confident," he tossed the box on the bed and placed his knees on either side of Magda's hips.

With a feather light touch, he traced an imaginary line from the top of her lacy panties to the bottom of her bra. She shivered at the contact.

He leaned down, which sandwiched her between his hard body and the soft bed, as he whispered, "And for the record, you should be thanking me—not busting on me—for the giant box of condoms. I drove all the way to the warehouse store in Leesburg to buy them, and this was the only size box they had—I thought there'd be too much gossip about us if I bought them at the pharmacy on Main Street." He smiled against her neck, before nipping at her earlobe.

Magda turned her head, so that his lips were against hers and kissed him lightly before her tongue darted out to tease his bottom lip. It seemed to be all the invitation he needed as he swept his own tongue into her mouth and kissed her passionately.

He took total control of the kiss and before she was completely lost to sensation, Magda found it interesting to observe that a man so laid-back in his day-to-day life could be so dominant and in control in the bedroom.

Then he rolled her just enough to reach the back

clasp of her bra, and as he threw it over his shoulder and she felt her breasts press into his rock-hard chest, all coherent thought was gone. She just *felt*—the silky fabric and cloud-like softness of the down comforter, where her back was pressed against it, and the tickle of Jeff's chest hair against her bare breasts in the front.

Her eyes drifted shut as she ran her hands over the strong planes of his back and reveled in the feel of his silky skin drawn taut against the hard muscles beneath it. Then suddenly she felt Jeff's weight pull off her and she rolled on the bed as he shifted position. Her eyes shot open—was Pierce right? Was she such a dud in the sack that Jeff didn't want to go any further with her?

Relief washed over her, when she saw Jeff reaching across the bed to reach the econo-box of condoms. He smiled and waved the box at her, "Safety first!"

He opened the box and pulled out a foil packet. He pushed his boxer briefs down in order to sheath himself and rejoined Maggie on the bed. She rolled on her side and covered her breasts with her arm. Jeff propped himself up next to her on one arm, and ran his hand gently, softly down the arm that she was using as a shield in her self-consciousness. She shivered as his had brushed against her breasts, too.

"None of this bashfulness, Maggie. I want to see every inch of you. Touch every inch of you."

When he moved her arm out of the way and stroked her nipples, Maggie couldn't hold back her moan. And when his hand slid across her belly and landed on parts farther south, she thought she might explode. Just from his touch. Guess she wasn't frigid after all.

"You are so ready," Jeff murmured as his hand found just the right spot and stroked.

"Mmm...I am. I don't think I've ever been so ready in my life." Magda reached out to touch Jeff, and found him hard and ready for her, too. He groaned as she gripped him.

"Seems like I'm not the only one."

"Nope. I wanted to go slow this first time, but I don't think that's going to happen, Maggie."

"Fast is okay with me," She said and refused to be embarrassed by the breathlessness in her voice. Any reasonable woman in her position with this man would be feeling breathless, too.

"There's so much I want to do with you, Maggie. I want to kiss you all over. To taste you." He rolled her gently onto her back. "But we have all night. Next time will be slow."

Jeff slid into her welcoming heat, and she cried out at the sensation. He moaned at the same time.

"Maggie...God...you feel so good."

As Jeff moved inside her, Magda felt pressure building in her body, and she twined her arms around Jeff's neck, wanting to be as close to him physically as she felt mentally. Jeff changed his angle, just a touch, but it was enough for her to feel the pressure release, and ripples of pleasure engulfed her. Jeff threw his head back at the sensation, and growled, as he lost himself in his own release.

There wasn't much room in her pleasure-addled brain for thinking, but one thought flashed into her mind, as she lay there clasped in Jeff's strong arms, both of them panting for breath.

Home. This feels like home.

Chapter 15

Jeff awoke to the sun pouring into his bedroom, as he did every morning. Even with his eyes still shut, he could tell the sun poured into the room through the windows and the French doors. He hated being wakened by an alarm clock, so he passed on shades in his bedroom so that the sun could be his wake-up call.

But something was different this morning—something warm and soft shared his bed. Not *something*, he corrected himself, *someone*. He opened his eyes and saw a riot of blonde curls spread out on the pillow next to his. He smiled as he watched Magda sleep. She was curled up on her side, facing him, and while she had the crisp, white sheet drawn up under her chin, he was all too aware she was gloriously naked underneath the covers.

He'd never had a woman spend the night at this house before—the logistics with a child made it near impossible, but he had to admit he hadn't wanted any woman to get this close to him until he met Maggie.

Last night had been amazing, and he sincerely hoped there'd be time for more before he had to leave to pick up Sam from her sleepover.

Maggie's eyes fluttered open, and she blinked her baby blues owlishly at him.

"Mornin'," he said with a gentle smile as he brushed a curl off her face.

"Morning," she whispered and shyly lowered her eyes.

At least he thought it was modesty, but as she slid the sheet off his body, he realized he wasn't the only one hoping for a repeat performance this morning.

She licked her lips as she looked at him. "I didn't get much of a chance to explore your body last night—you were too busy pleasing mine."

"Sorry about that darlin'," he winked. "I didn't mean to cramp your style—explore away!" He offered graciously, as he rolled over on his back, with his hands folded behind his head.

"Mmm, I will."

Her eyes devoured his body and then they paused at his hips. She shimmied down to be at eye level, and he suppressed a cry of triumph until he realized what caught her attention down there wasn't what he hoped it was, and he wasn't about to feel her mouth on him.

"I didn't notice you had a tattoo," she traced the swoopy red letter 'A' inked low on his hip. "What is it?"

"It's proof that eighteen year old boys shouldn't be left to their own devices with easy access to beer and tattoo parlors," he joked.

"I don't know—I like it, it's sexy. What does it mean?"

"It's the University of Alabama 'A'—where I went to college. Freshmen year, a bunch of guys from the football team decided we should all get one."

"I didn't know that about you—that you went to Alabama. The Crimson Tide," she said as she continued to run her finger around the curved lines of his tattoo.

He smiled quizzically. "You know about the

Crimson Tide? I didn't have you figured as a fan of college ball."

She looked up his body at him and grinned ruefully. "I'm not, but my dad was a huge Steely Dan fan; I know it from the song."

Clearing her throat, she sang a little off-key, "They call Alabama the Crimson Tide…"

He chuckled. "Ahh, mystery solved. That makes sense."

As her soft hand began to wander a little farther afield from his tat, a nearby part of his anatomy jerked and hardened in response. He noticed her gaze slide to the left at the movement and a slow, satisfied smile spread across her face. He propped himself up on his elbows so that he could better see the treat he was fairly certain was headed his way; her little pink tongue darted out to lick her lips. Before he knew it that little pink tongue was on his body and he could swear his eyes rolled back in his head.

"Oh darlin', that's the sort of exploration I can support most whole-heartedly," he managed to choke out.

She paused and looked up at him, her eyes dancing. "Glad to hear it, because I was about to take my exploration a little deeper." Her dimples peeked out before she took him in her mouth.

"My God, Maggie, that feels so good." He groaned, and this time there was no question that his eyes rolled back in his head as an unwanted thought flitted through it. He was falling for this woman. Hard. And he had no fucking idea how he was going to let her go in a few months when it was time for her to move on with her life.

****

"Okay ladies, here's a little snack for you." Francisco put a tray overflowing with grapes, cheese and crackers, and two wine glasses filled with sparkling water on the tray table within easy reach of Bethanne. "And now—I'm off to work."

"On the Sunday of Labor Day weekend?" Magda asked in surprise.

"No rest for the wicked." He winked. "Seriously though, it will be quiet in the office—no guests and no staff—so I'll be able to get a lot of paperwork done. Besides, I thought you two might want a chance to visit in private."

Bethanne plucked a grape from the bowl and popped it into her mouth. "Thanks, sweetie. I'll see you later."

Cisco pressed a soft, loving kiss to her forehead and ruffled Magda's hair as he walked past her, "Call if you need anything. See you later."

The women called their goodbyes, and Magda turned back to look at Bethanne and found her friend's eyes trained on her and alight with interest. "So…how did the big date with Jeff go?"

Magda felt her face heat up as she gulped down water from her glass and felt the bubbles tickle her nose.

Bethanne arched a brow. "That good, huh?"

Magda busied herself slicing a piece of cheese and positioning it just so on a water cracker.

Bethanne reached for another grape and munched it thoughtfully as she observed Magda's avoidance technique. "Wow. He must've rocked your world to have you so twitchy. Laid-back Jeff? I guess what they

224

say is true—still waters *do* run deep."

Magda held her hand under the cracker to catch any crumbs and bit it into with a crunch. She'd never been a kiss-and-tell kind of woman; what she felt for Jeff felt so personal—and scary—that she was hesitant to talk about it.

But Bethanne was her best friend, so she swallowed her cracker and admitted, "It was the best date I ever had. The best *night* I ever had, but…"

Bethanne froze in mid-reach for her water glass, her eyes wide. "Wait," she interrupted, "*Night*? You spent the *night* with Jeff? As in bedtime fun, spent the *night* with Jeff?"

Magda bobbed her head nervously. "Yep."

Bethanne picked up her glass and took a swig. "Man—I wish I had something a little stronger in here, I could use it. You? And Jeff? Doing the mattress mambo?"

Magda blushed and swatted gently at Bethanne's hand. "Is that what your Brazilian calls it?"

"Oh sweetie, you aren't ready for what my Brazilian calls it," Bethanne replied with a knowing laugh.

"The old Magda might not have been ready, but after last night—the new one is."

"My, my, my, my, my," Bethanne shook her head. "You and Jeff. So what does all of this mean for you two crazy kids?"

Magda shrugged and tried to look casual. "We're going to date and enjoy each other's company while I'm in Rivers Bend."

Bethanne's smile was kind and her voice gentle. "We were roommates for two years; I *know* you're not a casual sex kind of person—you never have been—how will you handle walking away in a few months?"

Magda took a deep breath and exhaled slowly before she answered. "Jeff and I both know there's an expiration date on this thing between us, and we're grown-ups, so we'll be fine, but we just want to be sure Sam understands I'll be leaving when you're ready to head back to work."

"Very mature." Bethanne sighed with relief. "Phew! I've got some news for you that I was really excited about, but the Jeff and you thing might have made it less good."

Magda curled her legs up underneath her and put her glass back on the tray with a clink. "What kind of news?"

"Okay—remember Sarah Fogelson from library school?"

Magda nodded. "Sure. She was nice," she took a green grape from the white bowl on the tray and ate it before continuing. "She moved back to Chicago after school, right? I've lost touch with her, well—with everybody, thanks to Pierce's manipulation."

Bethanne waved her index finger like a stern schoolmarm. "Now, now, there will be no mention of the 'P' word."

"Pierce?"

"I was thinking of 'prick,' but same difference."

Magda nodded. "When you're right, you're right. So, back to the news about Sarah Fogelson."

"Well," Bethanne bounced with excitement—well as much bouncing as her limited mobility would allow. "She's expecting a baby, too. A little before this one," she patted her baby bump, "is due to arrive. She got married to that guy she was long-distance dating when we were in school."

Magda smiled, but wrinkled her nose in confusion. "That's great for her—but why would Jeff and I dating impact the good newsiness of it?"

Bethanne grinned. "Here's the best part—she wants to stay home with the baby and asked if I knew anyone who might be interested in her job—which, fortuitously—will be available at the same time I'll be ready to go back to work. So I told her about you, and she wanted to know if you'd be interested in flying out to interview for it. When you told me about you and Jeff, I thought you might not want to move so far away from him, but now that I know you're both just going to have fun together for a few months, I'm excited all over again about this opportunity for you! It's a great job! It's a public library, which is what I know you want to do, and you've been a natural at it here in Rivers Bend…"

Magda's ears buzzed as Bethanne continued to talk about the job opening, but she didn't hear any of the details. She fumbled for her glass, and her hand slipped on the beads of condensation that coated it. She managed to bring the goblet to her lips and gulped some water down.

The notion of moving to Illinois brought the truth she'd been hiding from down on her like a ton of bricks. She was falling for Jeff, and leaving was going to be the hardest thing she'd ever done, but library jobs weren't growing on trees in this economy. She couldn't afford to miss out on the inside line to a plum opportunity like this one. Even more importantly, she couldn't—*wouldn't*—rearrange her whole life and put her professional dreams on hold to stay here with no job, just to hold onto a man. Even if he was the kind of man she'd always imagined meeting—imagined loving—since she was a little girl.

She swallowed hard and focused on Bethanne's words. Forcing her lips to curve up into what she hoped was an approximation of a smile, she said, "Slow down! I was kind of overwhelmed and didn't really hear what you were saying. Start over."

Bethanne laughed. "You're too funny; I'm so glad you're excited about this job! Sarah wanted me to be sure to tell you that she adores the neighborhood in Chicago where her branch is and said that you'll love living there…"

****

"Dad, I think it's great you're dating Maggie! Why were you so nervous about telling me?" Sam twisted under her seatbelt to turn and look at Jeff as he drove them home from Hadley's house.

He squirmed under her intent gaze, as if he was the child and she was the parent. No wonder he'd never told her about a woman before—this situation was damned uncomfortable.

He cleared his throat. "I just don't want you to feel like she's replacing you in my life. You'll always be my number one girl."

She blushed, but Jeff thought she looked pleased as well.

"Dad, you're so mushy." She bit her bottom lip. "But thanks for telling me that."

He gripped the wheel a little harder—this next bit was even more delicate. "I know you like Maggie…"

She interrupted him. "I do! If you were going to

date anyone, I'd pick her. I mean, if you were going to go out with someone like Hadley's mom..." she shuddered "...I wouldn't be so happy. But Maggie—"

Now it was his turn to interrupt. "Is going to be leaving Rivers Bend in a few months. It will be fun to hang out with her, but we have to remember she won't be here forever."

"She could be," Sam said stubbornly. "It's not like she has family or another job to get to or anything."

****

Pierce jiggled his leg like a jackhammer as he drummed his long fingers on the desk while he waited for his computer to boot up. Coming back to work after a long weekend was never easy for him, but today was even harder than normal.

Plus, Taylor and he had burned through his stash, and he had to find a way to sneak out of M.I. today and get to Brooklyn to score some more shit from his new dealer.

Speak of the devil and she shall appear—he heard Taylor's distinctive drawl from the other side of his door.

"I'll just show myself in, Myra."

Damn that woman! She *knew* they were supposed to play it cool at the office and what's the first thing she does? Waltz into his office like she has a right to do it.

He tried to glare as she entered and shut the door behind her with a soft click. Christ—she was every naughty fantasy secretary he'd ever had in that figure-hugging pencil skirt, and she knew it, too.

Her legs looked like they were ten miles long in it, and he remembered the feel of those long legs wrapped around him and couldn't quite hold on to his righteous indignation.

"Delectable as you look, my dear, we're supposed to stay the hell away from each other at M.I.," he grumbled.

She waved the manila file folder she held in the air. "I have a legitimate business reason to be here—I need your signature on these documents, Mr. Vice President."

"Fine." He glared. "But then you need to get the fuck out of here. It's bad enough we spent the weekend together in the Hamptons—old woman Mallory is sure to hear about it, she doesn't miss a trick, and I'm supposed to have ended our affair."

Taylor rolled her eyes. "Whatever. We were at the same house party—everyone who is anyone was there—a clever boy like you will be able to spin it with Mrs. Mallory if she confronts you."

She plopped the folder on his desk next to his computer and planted her tush next to it. She leaned back on her hands, which pressed her surgically-enhanced breasts forward; Pierce's mouth watered.

"God, Tay-Tay, I wish this whole thing was over so we could just be together!"

She lifted one leg and planted her platform stiletto on the seat between his legs. His body responded, and the triumphant gleam in her eyes showed him that she knew it.

"We're perfect for each other. I understand why your grandfather wants you to get married and settle down, but why can't it be with me? Why does it have to be with Miss Goody-Goody Horvath?"

He ran his had along her bare leg and bit back a groan. "Ancient family history—you know how that tired old song goes. But we'll be together in the end, I've got a plan."

She arched her back like a cat stretching while he stroked her leg. "It'd better be a foolproof plan, because I'm not going to wait forever."

He felt his heart stutter at her words. Taylor was *his* woman. He had to get married to Magda fast to fulfill his grandfather's demands, but the old bastard had never specified that they had to *stay* married. Once he was back in and had access to his family money, he'd transfer it to a secure off-shore account and divorce boring little Magda and marry his true mate: Taylor.

He never dreamed that Taylor wouldn't wait for his plan to play out. God—the thought of his wild beauty with another man's hands on her made him feel insane with rage. He couldn't let it happen. He needed to step up his plan and find Magda post haste.

His computer bonged to indicate it had downloaded email. He jumped, and his nervous gaze darted to the screen. In his excitement at what he saw there, he rolled his chair forward, which dislodged Taylor's foot from its perch.

"Gotcha!" he yelled as he clicked on an email with a flourish.

Taylor pushed off the desk to stand behind him to look at the screen. "Got whom? Magda?"

"Yes! I got an internet news alert with her name. Let's see where the little pain in the ass has been hiding."

Taylor leaned in closer, and he felt her straight hair tickle his cheek as she peered at the screen. "Rivers Bend Virginia? Where the hell is that?"

"And what is she doing there?" Pierce added as a picture filled the flat screen of his monitor. It was Magda all right, and she was wrapped in the arms of a giant of a man. Her hair was loose, and blonde curls tumbled around her beaming face. The man's lazy smile echoed her own, and he had his chin tucked possessively on the top of her head.

Taylor chuckled. "The correct question appears to be *who* is she doing? That man she's wearing like a pashmina is positively edible."

"That big, beefy redneck? Please!" Pierce scoffed.

"The big, beefy redneck is 'Jefferson Braden, former NFL great and Rivers Bend's favorite son,'" Taylor quoted from the caption under the photograph. "Mmm—I can see the attraction to Rivers Bend for Magda. Look at his arms! So manly."

Pierce felt jealous rage punch at his gut. "If that type of overly-muscled himbo is your type, then I guess he's okay."

Taylor licked her glossy lips before continuing to read the caption. "...and our newest resident, temporary librarian Magda Horvath, take a break from burning up the dance floor to pose for our photographer. Romance seems to be in the air for these two!' Huh. Sounds like the himbo *is* Magda's type."

"Not surprising—her middle-class roots will always show." Pierce sneered.

"Maybe," Taylor said as she stroked one perfectly manicured fingertip down Jeff's arm on the screen. "But if he is her type, you might want to rethink your plan. Fond as I am of you, darling, there's no way she'd willingly leave *him* for *you*."

Pierce's eyes narrowed as he stared at the photo of

Magda, who was glowing with happiness in a way she never had around him.

"The lady doesn't have to be willing. It would make things easier for me if she was, but it is by no means essential to my plan."

Chapter 16

"Okay, Sarah, I'll let you know when I've made my travel arrangements, but it's not going to be right away. I'm running the library for Bethanne with just one part-time assistant, so it's going to be a little tricky to leave."

A tap on the glass wall to the librarian's office made Magda look up to see Jeff. He held a bag from the Nosh Pit in one hand and her dog in the other. He smiled and used a finger to wave Petunia's paw at her.

Warmth suffused her. How was she supposed to keep things casual with a man secure enough in his masculinity to tote her frou-frou little dog all over town? And he brought her lunch. Her conflicted feelings about this conversation with Sarah Fogelson about the job in Chicago became clear. It was a great opportunity—no doubt about it—but she was falling in love, both with Jeff and with living in Rivers Bend, and when the time came, leaving them both would be hard.

She smiled at Jeff and held up her index finger to indicate she'd just be another moment.

"Sarah, I'm so sorry, but I'm on my own here, and a patron just came in, so I need to run." She hoped she'd be forgiven the little white lie, but technically Jeff was a library-card toting citizen of Rivers Bend, and he *might* check out a book while he was here. "Thanks again for the opportunity, Sarah, I'll be in touch."

She placed the receiver back in its cradle, without tearing her gaze from Jeff's. She waved him in with her other hand.

"Sorry to interrupt your call, but Petunia missed you something fierce, so we snuck away from the Retreat to bring you lunch."

"*Petunia* missed me?" Magda asked with amused skepticism.

"Yup," Jeff replied without shame as he put Petunia on the floor, where the dog promptly ran around the desk to her mistress. He put the bag on the desk and pulled out a stack of paper napkins.

Magda stooped to give Petunia a loving pet. "Well, I missed her, too."

He pulled out a sandwich wrapped in foil and handed it to her. "Turkey club on whole wheat toast—Deidre said it's your favorite."

"Yum! It *is* my favorite, thank you." She smiled at him.

"Hope I didn't rush you off the phone just now."

She felt reluctant to tell him about the job prospect in Chicago. She didn't want to spoil the time they had left together. She unwrapped her sandwich and took a bite. As she munched and stalled, it occurred to her there was no reason to say anything yet. When she made her plans to go out for the interview would be soon enough to bring it up—or when she had a firm offer. Why possibly ruin their good times about something that might never happen?

"Nope. You didn't cut it short, we were done."

****

"This photograph of your granddaughter surfaced on the internet yesterday."

Bernie stood up from the chair in Mrs. Mallory's home office to place his laptop on the desk in front of her.

She felt her mouth tighten in distaste as she beheld the picture of her granddaughter being groped by some massive Neanderthal. She forced her jaw to loosen; it wouldn't do to reveal her emotions to a subordinate like Bernie Felder. Although, it was no easy task as she looked at her granddaughter's mop of hair.

She thought she had finally seen the last of that unruly hairstyle, that she'd convinced Magda to wear her hair in a sophisticated French twist, which was much more suitable to her position in society.

And the man! He was so large and coarse looking. She felt her upper lip curl in disgust and willed it into a more benign position.

When she spoke, her voice was neutral and revealed none of her inner turmoil at the sight of this picture. "Who is this rather unsavory young man mauling my grandchild?"

****

Bernie struggled with his own facial expression, too. He didn't want to show a client how amused he was by her obvious attempts to conceal her anger, so he couldn't allow the grin that wanted to break out on his face.

He cleared his throat. "That's Jefferson Braden—I told you about him before—he's a retired football player who runs that corporate retreat with Miss Horvath's friend's husband."

"And this…" Her icy blue eyes searched the screen. "This *Rivers Bend Gazette* seems to believe he is romantically involved with Elizabeth?"

236

Internally, Bernie rolled his eyes at her persistent use of Magda's middle name—the old broad never gave up.

"Yes, ma'am, their relationship appears to have developed quickly after I came back to New York."

She sniffed. "What does she see in him? He looks overly developed."

With considerable effort, Bernie kept the humor out of his voice. "Some ladies like that in a man."

"No *lady* would, Mr. Felder," she corrected with condescension dripping from her mouth like icicles.

He didn't trust himself not to laugh if he opened his mouth, so Bernie remained silent.

After a few strained moments, Mrs. Mallory spoke. "You still have Pierce Allen under surveillance; do you know if he's seen this photography?"

"Yes, Mrs. M., we believe he saw it yesterday and is planning a trip to Rivers Bend."

She looked smug. "Good. Once she's seen a true gentleman rushing to her rescue, she'll come to her senses and come back to New York with him."

Rescue? Yeah—Magda needed rescuing from the big, handsome, rich, kind football player, who was clearly crazy about her. And who better to do said "rescuing" than some effete rich-boy junkie, who was only with her for her money and family name? Maybe it was time to give the iron maiden here a little reality check about her chosen "gentleman," so she'd see just how dangerous he could be to her granddaughter.

"My surveillance of Mr. Allen indicates his drug use is escalating. He's begun to use a dealer in Brooklyn and is exploring harder, street drugs."

There was a long pause before she said with

confidence, "Pierce is an Allen—a gentleman—and gentlemen can control such things."

"Control crack? Or heroin?" Bernie couldn't keep the derision out of his voice. "People from all walks of life become addicts. Social position is no magic bullet against it."

She raised an eyebrow as she waited for him to continue, clearly displeased to have someone she considered inferior contradict her views.

She held his gaze for a long time; when it became clear he wasn't going to lower his eyes like a submissive puppy, she spoke with a dismissive wave of her hand. "That has no bearing on his relationship with Elizabeth."

Bernie gritted his teeth and shook his head wearily, he couldn't wait to retire and be done with this kind of bullshit. "Let's hope not, but Mr. Allen is under a lot of pressure to revive their relationship, and he's not the most stable person in town. Highly strung people have been known to do crazy things in stressful situations."

"*People* maybe, but not *Allens*."

Her tone brooked no disagreement, and Bernie knew he'd done as much as he could to get her to listen to reason and she just wasn't having it. He gathered his things to leave but issued a silent prayer that he *was* wrong about Allen, even though he'd bet every dime in his retirement account that he wasn't.

****

"Heather's down by the pool to oversee the barbecue with the group of accountants from Cleveland, right?" Jeff asked as Cisco and he finished settling the horses for the night in the Retreat's barn. Since this group wanted another trail ride in the morning, Jason had decided it was easier to leave the horses here overnight, rather than toting them back and forth from the farm.

"Yes, but she has to leave by six, so I'm going to head over there in a bit to make sure everything is running smoothly," Cisco replied. "Although, I can't stay for long—I want to get home to Bethanne. She gets bored there all day by herself."

Jeff bent over to open a mini-fridge tucked under a shelf in the barn and pulled out a can of soda. "I imagine it would get pretty lonesome for her."

"It does, but having Maggie here helps—they had a nice long visit on Sunday. I came in to work for a while and gave them a chance to hash over that job opportunity in Chicago for Maggie."

Jeff froze with the red can at his lips—Maggie hadn't told him about any job opportunity, certainly not one that was half the country away from Rivers Bend.

"What's wrong, *meu amigo*? You look like a statue."

He brought the cool can to his lips and took a long drink before he answered. By the time he was finished, he managed to make his voice sound carefree. "It's nothing—I was just thinking about the logistics for tomorrow's ride."

He hoped a lightning bolt wouldn't shoot down and strike him right here in the barn. He had everything set for the accountants' ride—his real problem was the fact he'd spent the whole day before with Maggie. They lounged by the pool, ate dinner together with Sam—talked about anything and everything—except, apparently, this job opportunity in Chicago. Why wouldn't she have told him about it? Was she really

239

thinking about moving so far away?

He heard Cisco's booming voice from the yard—man, he hadn't even noticed his friend leave. "Hello, Maggie! Jeff's in the barn."

Jeff felt his stomach flip like a schoolboy's at the sound of her name—did he ever have it bad—and she might be a time zone away in a few months. He'd better remember that little factoid before he got too attached. He snorted—yeah right, like he wasn't already too attached.

He leaned one shoulder against the doorframe and squinted as his eyes adjusted from the dimness of the barn to the brightness of the late afternoon sun. The light formed a halo around Maggie's blonde hair as she approached the barn, still in her work clothes. How did she manage to make tailored gray slacks and a sleeveless pale pink silk blouse look so hot? Her face lit up when she saw him. She looked open and honest, not at all like a woman harboring a big secret.

****

Maggie saw Jeff silhouetted in the doorway to the barn and felt her heart race at the sight of him. He looked especially manly in his riding gear: well-worn jeans, boots, and a T-shirt with the Retreat's logo on it.

He pushed off the door jamb where he'd been leaning and moved toward her; she quickened her own pace in response, to close the distance between them even faster. They met in the middle and Magda rose up on her tiptoes to kiss him. Jeff responded, but with more reserve than normal and broke away to walk to a picnic table in the shade of an old oak tree by the barn. He sat on the table and planted his booted feet on the bench seat.

He smiled at her, but his eyes didn't crinkle at the corners like they usually did, and she realized the smile was purely on his lips—it didn't reach to his eyes.

She sat on the bench next to his right leg and squinted up at him. "Rough day?"

He shrugged and took a drink from his soda can. "Not especially—why do you ask?"

His offhand response irritated her. If he truly had a bad day, she would have been sympathetic, but it seemed like he was just in a pissy mood. She learned an important lesson with Pierce—she wasn't going to cater to any man's irrational bad moods again.

So she didn't even try to keep the snarkiness from her voice. "Gosh, I don't know, maybe because you're acting like a jerk?"

He raised his eyebrows. "You're right—I forgot to offer you one of these." He jiggled his soda. "My mama would never forgive me for not offering a beverage to a guest. Want a soda?"

"No, I don't want a soda. That's not what I meant, and you know it. What happened between lunch and now to put you in this foul mood?"

His gray eyes looked as cold as the Atlantic in January, as he regarded her for a long moment before answering. "I just had a very interesting conversation with Francisco about a certain job opening in Illinois."

She flushed and lowered her eyes. "Oh, that."

"Yeah. That. I know we're supposed to be keeping things casual, but I was wondering why you didn't tell me about it."

She pulled at a thread on her pants and didn't look him in the eyes. "There's nothing definite yet. I haven't even set up a time for an interview, so there really wasn't anything to say."

"Bullshit."

His response was so clipped and abrupt that her eyes grew wide, and she almost got whiplash as her head jerked up so fast to finally look at him.

His eyes softened a little. "My mama wouldn't be pleased with me using that kind of language in front of a lady either, but I have to call b.s., I'm sorry. You tell a friend about news that big, and I thought that we were friends, no matter what else is happening between us."

When she realized his sour mood was the result of hurt feelings, she felt a pang of remorse so sharp it was almost physical.

"I'm sorry, you're right. I should've told you, but it's not like they've even offered it to me yet, and I'm not sure what I'll say if they do."

He put his can on the table and leaned his forearms on his muscular thighs. "Now *that* surprises me."

She sighed. "Me, too. It's a great chance—it just seems so far away."

He nodded his agreement. "Half the country away from Rivers Bend, but we were just supposed to be a pit stop for you, right?"

Now it was her turn to shrug and be elusive. "That was the plan."

"It *was* the plan? It isn't anymore?"

She fiddled with his soda can, whose condensation left a dark ring on the wooden table, "I'm not sure. I really love it here—way more than I expected to."

A corner of Jeff's mouth quirked up, and this time his eyes crinkled and shone with their usual warmth. "That's a good thing, right?"

She inclined her head in agreement. "Right now it

is. I've got a job, a place to live, friends." She paused, lowered her eyes and blushed before adding, "And you." She lifted her gaze to his face. "But it's all just temporary and dependent upon my job, which will go away when Bethanne has the baby and is ready to go back to work."

"Out of all those things, only the job is temporary. If you wanted to stay, you'd still have a place to live, friends." He picked up his can and took a drink before finishing his sentence a little nervously, as if unsure of how it would be received. "And me."

Intense temptation burned inside her, and Magda felt a longing to stay in this town, where she felt at home for the first time since her dad's death, but she couldn't give in to it.

"I can't live in Cabin Five forever. Cisco and you refuse to let me pay for it, and you can't rent it to a paying guest while Petunia and I are planted there."

"You could move into Cisco and Bethanne's cottage when their new house is finished."

His offer came so quickly; she wondered if this wasn't the first time he thought about her staying in Rivers Bend. The idea made her breath catch—was Jeff interested in making their temporary fling into something more permanent?

"But Bethanne is looking forward to getting back to her work at the library, so I wouldn't have a job." She grinned. "Rivers Bend isn't exactly a hotbed of employment opportunities, you know. Although, Mr. Mancini has been griping about one of his nephews. Maybe I could get his job at the pizzeria."

"Not to discourage you from staying, but I can't see you working there. Do you speak Italian?" Jeff asked with a quick grin.

She sighed dramatically. "No, I don't, so I guess that's out. With no library job and no pizzeria job, what would I do here?"

Jeff's grin turned rakish and he winked. "You could always do me."

Magda laughed and swatted his leg, but before she could answer she heard the happy yip of her dog. She turned toward the house and saw Petunia straining at the leash held by a white-knuckled Sam.

"Hi Dad! Hi Maggie! Mrs. Wilson sent me out to tell you dinner's almost ready, so you should come in to clean up before. And, Maggie, she said there's plenty for you if you want to stay." The dog dragged her to the picnic table.

Petunia put her front paws on her beloved mistress's legs and wagged. Magda scratched her behind the ears and said, "Sounds good. I think I will stay—I'm too beat to even think about cooking something for myself. I don't know how Bethanne does it, running the library by herself. Now that Caitlin's back in school, I just have her for a few hours in the afternoon; the rest of the time, I'm on my own."

She gently moved Petunia off her legs, dusted the dirt off her trousers and stood. "Speaking of going back to school—how did your first day go? Was your new dress a hit?"

Sam glanced nervously at her father, before shifting her gaze back to Maggie. "It was great! Billy Perkins told me I looked real pretty in my dress."

Jeff hopped off the table and said with a glower. "Billy better be a girl's nickname."

Sam turned red as a geranium in July. "Daad!

Billy's a boy. I'm not a baby anymore, you know."

Jeff ruffled her hair. "Trust me—I know. But you're too young for dating, Peanut."

Sam wrapped the leash around her hand. "Sheesh, Dad, he just said I looked pretty—not that he wants to marry me or something."

The girl and dog turned to run back to the house. Magda and Jeff followed at a more leisurely pace.

He took Magda's hand in his. "You were smart to have a dog instead of a daughter. Petunia will never chase boys."

Magda sensed the concern for his daughter underneath his joking words and gave his hand a reassuring squeeze. "Nope. I only have to worry about her chasing squirrels, and she'll *never* catch one of them."

Jeff laughed and his large, warm hand squeezed back. "I don't think I'll have that same luck with Sam. I'm going to have to beat the boys off with a stick when she gets a little older."

"You're probably right, but she's a good kid. I don't think you have to worry too much. At least not yet, you can save the worry up for when she's a teenager."

As they approached the house, Jeff's eyes went from teasing to heated, and he pulled Magda away from the back porch and around the corner. "I wanted a minute more alone with you to thank you for helping me keep things in perspective about Sam and that boy. You're good for me, Maggie."

She felt the sharp edge of the shingles press into her back as he leaned his long, hard body into hers. Then a prickle ran up her spine and made the little hairs on the back of her neck stand at attention.

She peered over his broad shoulder into the woods. "I feel like someone's there—watching us—but I don't see anyone."

Jeff glanced over his shoulder, then focused his attention back on her. "No worries, city girl, it's probably just a critter—a deer or a fox. Who'd be watching us without saying anything? If it was Cisco or Heather, they wouldn't be shy about making their presence known."

She shivered. "I guess you're right, but I can't shake the feeling."

One side of his mouth quirked up. "I'll have to distract you then."

He bent his head and kissed her. It started out softly, but it quickly grew into a hard, stroking inferno of a kiss, as his tongue plunged into her welcoming mouth.

She twined her arms around his neck and pressed her body more firmly against his, until a piece of tissue paper wouldn't fit between them. She felt the hard ridge of his erection press into her belly and knew that Jeff was just as aroused as she was.

The screen door to the kitchen opened with a harsh squeak and Mrs. Wilson called out, "Soups on, you two! C'mon in."

Jeff broke their lip lock with a reluctant sigh and called around the corner, "Coming, Mrs. W!"

Magda's breathing was hard as she said, "Boy, do you ever know how to distract a girl!"

Jeff's breath was just as ragged as he leaned his forehead against hers. "What do you say I walk you home after dinner to distract you a little bit more? I hate to leave a woman before she's been fully distracted."

She smiled and licked her lips. "Sounds good to me—and maybe I'll be able to distract you to completion, too."

She felt his body shake against hers as he chuckled. "I can't stay the night, but on Friday, Sam's going to a slumber party at Madison's house. Maybe we can have a sleepover of our own that night."

"Mmm…count me in." Magda purred.

"But right now we'd better get inside before Mrs. W pops a gasket." Jeff used his hands on her shoulders to position Magda strategically in front of him. "Block me until I can get through the kitchen, otherwise there'll be no doubt about what we've been up to."

Magda laughed, but walked in front of him to serve as cover. "*Up* being the operative word here."

****

The small branch Pierce clutched as he peered from the woods snapped between his fingers as he watched Magda go inside with the man-mountain she'd been making out with on the side of the house. Who knew the cold little mackerel had it in her? Maybe their marriage had a shot after all. He shook his head—nah! Magda was too vanilla for his taste; Taylor was the spicy dish for him in the long term.

But in the short term, he needed Magda to get back in his grandfather's good graces, and that goal was greatly complicated by her involvement with the big lug who'd just had his tongue shoved down her throat.

He'd come to this Podunk town in the hopes of finding Magda bored out of her mind and inclined to be lured back to his side. Looked like that plan would be going nowhere fast. He'd been following her all afternoon, and the little twerp actually seemed to *like* it here in nowheresville.

When she walked down Main Street, everyone she passed—from the littlest toddler to the oldest senior citizen—had a cheery smile and greeting for her, and damned if Magda didn't blossom under all their attention.

And then he followed her home to this sprawling retreat on the river, which he supposed was beautiful if you liked this kind of thing. While he watched her interact with this Braden character, the last of his hopes for an easy resolution to his problems evaporated like water on a hot day.

Magda wouldn't leave this place and this man willingly. He patted the handgun stuffed in the pocket of his sports coat with a shaky hand, and then swiped the line of sweat that had formed on his upper lip. Good thing his Plan B didn't involve her coming willingly. And better still that he had the means at hand to put it into effect.

It looked like Magda would be with Braden tonight, so he'd have to wait until tomorrow to catch her alone.

He fingered the small, plastic bag in his other pocket—just as well, the delay gave him a chance to get back to his hotel room in Leesburg and take advantage of the kick-ass product his new dealer had supplied. It would steady his nerves, which he had to admit were a little on the shaky side at the moment.

He stumbled over a root and cursed under his breath. He *really* hated being in the sticks! Oh well, he'd put Plan B in action tomorrow and with any luck, he'd have Magda back in Manhattan with him, without having to spend a second night south of the Mason-Dixon line.

Chapter 17

Another thing to hate about small towns—it was impossible for a stranger to hide in them. In New York, Pierce would be able to stand on the street, out in the open, and no one would think a thing about it. Here in Mayberry, he had to crouch behind a shrub next to the library to wait for Magda to get to work.

He glanced down at his gold watch and saw that it was almost nine o'clock; she'd be here soon to open the library. He knew this because Magda was nothing if not disgustingly punctual and conscientious.

"Good morning, Magda!" the old Italian man across the street shouted out as he watered the flowers in the planters in front of his pizza parlor.

Pierce wiped the sweat off his clammy forehead. Why did the guy have to water his flowers anyway? Couldn't the flowers draw enough moisture out of the jungle-like humidity in the air? He felt like he was fully clothed in a sauna. Why anyone would choose to live here was beyond his comprehension.

Pierce heard the click of her heels on the sidewalk before he heard Magda's voice say to someone, "Thanks for buying my coffee, Dan, but it really wasn't necessary."

He ventured a peek through the dense foliage of the boxwood that shielded him and couldn't believe his rotten luck! Of all the people she could be with, stinking Magda had to be with the sheriff. And this lawman didn't look anything like Barney Fife—him, Pierce could've taken, but this guy? No chance. He wasn't as big as Magda's rube, but he was still a really large African-American man, who was muscular enough that he appeared ready to burst out of his tan uniform a la the Incredible Hulk.

And if Pierce wasn't mistaken—and he didn't think he was—this yokel was interested in Magda, too. His next words confirmed Pierce's suspicion.

"I guess I missed my chance and now it's Braden's job to buy your morning coffee," the sheriff said with a rueful grin.

Magda bristled—Pierce recognized the signs of that mood all too well, the poor bastard was about to be on the receiving end of some girl power speech.

"Actually, Dan, it's *my* job to keep myself in coffee." Her tone softened when she continued speaking and Pierce wasn't as familiar with that tone of voice from her. "But you're right that Jeff and I are dating now."

The sheriff drank from his paper cup and shrugged. "Figured as much—I am a crack detective after all—and you two looked pretty cozy at the dance on Saturday night."

Even from yards away, Pierce could see Magda turn red as a beet. Most of the girls in his social orbit blushed in a delicate way. Taylor, for example, would never allow herself to turn into a ripe tomato, but Magda had never cultivated that skill.

"I hope it won't affect our friendship, Dan."

The sheriff waved one ham-sized hand dismissively. "No worries, Magda, we're still friends."

He tipped his hat to her. "Have a good day. Maybe we could still have coffee together sometimes."

She smiled in obvious relief and said, "Of course, Dan, I'd like that."

Pierce heard the cop's heavy tread as he walked on to his neighboring office and then the click of Magda's heels as she walked the steps to the library door. Great—she was alone—it was time to put Plan B in action. He put one hand on the ground to push himself up, but froze when he heard a woman's voice blast like a foghorn through the quiet morning.

"Morning, Magda. Glad to see you opening the library in a punctual manner."

He could hear the smile in Magda's voice when she replied, "Good morning, Mrs. Warren. If you have a minute, I'm holding the new Rita Mae Brown mystery for you."

He heard the woman with the voice that could peel paint clump up the stairs. "Wonderful! That's why I came into town this morning."

The door to the library opened with a creak, and the two women entered the building. The door banged shut behind them. Damn it all to hell! Now he'd have to wait until the old bat left to catch Magda alone. He shifted so that he was sitting down in the shrubbery with his back against the library. He hoped the rough brick didn't do too much of a number on the fine fabric of his custom-made suit jacket, but he wasn't holding out too much hope on that score.

Unfortunately, by the time Mrs. Foghorn Leghorn got her book and left, a group of women with toddlers came in. By their happy chatter, he could tell it was story time at the library. He heaved a long-suffering sigh—no sense in sitting in the bushes for the next hour.

He waited until no one was in a position to see him and rose from his uncomfortable position with a stretch. He adjusted his sunglasses on his nose and walked quickly to the rental car he'd left parked on the street. As he unlocked it with the key fob, his hand shook violently. He climbed into the car and started up the engine—might as well go get a cup of coffee somewhere while story time was happening.

He glanced at his reflection in the rear-view mirror and started at his appearance. A clammy sheen of sweat formed on his forehead and upper lip. He wiped it off with his shaky hand.

One thing was certain, he had to get back to New York tonight—he'd used up his whole stash last night in his hotel room, and he definitely had the shakes today. A trip to Brooklyn was in order ASAP when he got Magda and himself back to civilization.

****

"The end." Magda closed the picture book decisively and smiled around the circle of moms and kids gathered around her on overstuffed cushions and beanbag chairs. "I hope to see you all next time."

She positioned her flowing skirt to allow her to get up with a modicum of grace and modesty and hurried to the circulation desk, where several people waited for her to check out their books. Story-time logistics were a lot easier when Caitlin had been on vacation—then her assistant could man the circulation desk while Magda read to the kids.

"I'm so sorry to keep you folks waiting," she apologized as she jammed the picture book on an already full book cart to be shelved. Shelving the books was normally Caitlin's job, but today was the girl's day off, so it looked like she'd be doing some shelving today, too.

She stood behind the circulation desk and reached across it for the first patron's stack of books. Her mind wandered as she exchanged pleasantries with the man and scanned the barcodes on the books to check them out to him. How did Bethanne manage to do her job with just one part-time assistant? She felt understaffed and overwhelmed—maybe it was her lack of experience in a public library. Maybe she didn't need to worry too much about the job in Chicago—she might not even be offered it. After their conversation last night, she knew it would make Jeff happy if she had to stay in Rivers Bend, but she had mixed feelings about it. She *was* happy here—happier than she'd been in a long time, but without useful work she didn't think she'd stay happy. Although, being with Jeff might be some compensation, but long-term it wouldn't be enough and she was afraid she'd start to resent him.

She tucked a complementary bookmark in the last book and handed the stack of volumes to the elderly man in front of her. "Enjoy!"

As she reached for the next person's book, she smiled at the woman and continued to think of Jeff. She'd been disappointed last night when he told her he didn't think he'd have time to come to the library to have lunch with her today. The accountants wanted him to lead a trail ride before they checked out and another group was checking in to the Retreat this afternoon. She tried to squelch the disappointment by reminding herself that it would make things easier for her if she didn't let herself get too used to his company.

The line to check out books grew as the story-time moms queued up with books for themselves and their little ones. She took a deep breath and exhaled before smiling at the next patron. At least Rivers Bend Public Library would keep her so busy, she wouldn't have time to worry about getting too close to Jeff.

****

"Get your head back in the game, *meu amigo*."

Cisco's words, called from the front porch, made Jeff realize with a start that he was still standing in the curved front drive of the Retreat, long after the van to the airport had pulled out with the Cleveland accountants in it.

He ran his hand through his hair. "Sorry man, I zoned out there for a minute."

Cisco bounded down the stairs and clapped him on the back. "You were a million miles away just now. What were you thinking about? Maybe a certain librarian?"

Jeff opened his eyes wide in feigned innocence. "I swear I was *not* thinking about your wife."

Cisco held his fists up and took a boxing stance, but his friendly smile belied the bellicose pose. "You better not be thinking about Bethanne with that big moondog expression on your face!" He dropped his fists. "Besides, you know I mean Maggie."

"I know—I just couldn't pass up the chance to break your stones a little."

"Do I even want to know what you were thinking about Maggie just now? Before you answer, keep in mind that I love her like a sister."

Jeff scowled. "Get your mind out of the gutter,

Cisco, I was just wishing I could have lunch with Maggie today. We've been kind of making a habit of it lately. I stop by the Nosh Pit and get lunch for us and bring it to the library, but with this group checking out and the new one checking in this afternoon, there's no time for it today."

"There should *always* be time for your special lady."

"In a perfect world, maybe, but in the real world, conflicting responsibilities get in the way."

Cisco raised his eyebrows. "Conflicting? You mean like that job in Chicago?"

Jeff rubbed his jaw line. "Yeah, that's a big one. It would suck to have her move so far away, but I don't want her to miss an opportunity for me, and I've got to stay here. My daughter is here, my family, my friends, my business—I can't pull up roots and follow her."

Cisco shrugged. "My mama always says 'don't borrow trouble' and that's good advice for you now. Worry about the job when—and if—the time comes. And it might never come—we don't know the future. In the meantime, I can cover the check-in when this group arrives from the airport. After you help your brother load the horses to go back to the farm, why don't you head into town and surprise Maggie with lunch?"

Jeff's eyes brightened. "Seriously man? You'd do that for me?"

"Sure. Plus, Heather will be here to help me get them settled in their rooms. If you could be back to take the 3:00 hike, then I could go home early to check on my own special lady."

Jeff stuck out his hand with a happy grin and Cisco shook it.

"That sounds like a good deal to me! I'll be back in plenty of time for the hike. Thanks, Cisco."

****

Magda shoved the heavy book cart out from behind the circulation desk and struggled to point it toward the stacks. It was so overloaded with books that it handled like an ornery grocery cart. She paused when she heard the front door creak open and shut with a thud.

She straightened up and adjusted her silk tank top to prepare to greet the incoming patron, but her smile faded when she saw the last person she hoped to see at the entrance of the library.

"Pierce!" she cried out in dismay. "What in the world are *you* doing here?"

His smile was so smarmy that she wondered how he'd been able to fool her for so long. She realized the lure of a family life with her grandmother and the man of her choice had put blinders on her eyes.

"Magda dearest, what else would I be doing in this one-horse town? I'm here to fetch my beloved fiancée and bring her back to our home, where she belongs."

****

Jeff hopped out of his truck on Main Street and looked at the closed door of the library with a furrowed brow. Who was the suit that just went inside? He literally knew everyone in Rivers Bend, but he didn't recognize this guy. Must be someone from D.C. who had a place up here.

He reached across the seat to pick up Petunia, "C'mon girl, we'll go to the back door of the Nosh Pit, so we won't break any health code violations by bringing you inside."

Friends and neighbors greeted both man and dog as

they made their way to the café. If anyone thought the incongruous sight of the big manly man walking the little dog on her Portland Pintos leash, they kept that opinion to themselves. The odd couple were fast becoming a common sight on the streets of Rivers Bend.

While some of the younger ladies might be sorry to have missed their chance with him, Jeff was so beloved by everyone that they were all glad to see him with someone as nice as Magda after so many years alone.

Jeff passed the front entrance to the Nosh Pit and turned up the alley. He rapped on the metal door in the back that was used mainly for deliveries and staff.

His sister opened the door with a puzzled expression, which eased into a smile when she saw Jeff and Petunia.

"Hey little bro, I was starting to think you wouldn't be in today."

He smiled and leaned down to give Deidre a peck on the cheek. "I didn't think I was going to be able to get away, but Cisco and I worked out a deal, so here I am! Maggie hasn't been in for lunch yet, has she? I was hoping to surprise her."

Deidre shook her head. "Haven't seen her yet for lunch. Today is story hour day, so I imagine it's a busy one for her."

She turned into the kitchen and called over her shoulder, "Wait there with Petunia; I'll get your usual order ready for you."

"Thanks, Dee."

"No problem, I like Maggie, and more importantly, I like Maggie *with* you."

She stood at the metal table to assemble their

sandwiches, her black Nosh Pit apron covering her jeans and white T-shirt. "Have you figured out a way to keep her in Rivers Bend? I've heard rumors there's a job in the Midwest that could take her away."

Jeff squatted to pick up Petunia, who strained at the end of her leash to get closer to Deidre and the food. He stood in the open doorway and leaned his left shoulder against the frame, while he cradled Petunia in his right arm. The dog seemed pacified by the extra attention, but her nose still twitched at the tantalizing aroma of roast beef.

"I'm trying my damndest, Dee, but that job would be a golden opportunity for her. What do I have to offer that could compare?"

Deidre frowned at him and waved the knife she'd been using to slice a tomato for their sandwiches. "If you've got to ask, you're a lot dumber than I always thought you were. You may not have a job to offer her, but you have a good heart to offer and a home—two things that woman has been sorely missing in her life."

****

Beloved fiancée? Home? Had Pierce gone completely round the bend? Looking at him more closely, Magda realized that he had. Sure, it was a hot day in Virginia, but he was sweating profusely—possibly because he was overdressed in a suit jacket and trousers, even if he had forgone his usual silk necktie. It was more than that, though, his skin was a combination of pasty gray and flushed. And the expression in his eyes, didn't match the smile on his lips. His eyes darted around in a squirrely manner, and he kept one hand in the pocket of his jacket—something he never did, as he swore it ruined the line of the suit.

Magda moved surreptitiously to place the book cart between them—it was foolish to feel frightened of Pierce, but his sudden, unhealthy appearance made her uneasy.

"Pierce, didn't you find my note? And the ring?"

He took a step toward her, but stopped when she took a corresponding step back. "I found them and you led me on a merry chase." He extended his left hand while the right remained firmly planted in his pocket. "But I found you now, and it's time for you to come home."

She shook her head. "New York isn't my home anymore, Pierce. I'm sorry, but you'll have to go back without me."

He looked around in disgust. "You'd pass up Manhattan society with me to stay here in Mayberry with that big, dumb jock?"

Her brain raced—Pierce must mean Jeff. Although, anyone who knew him knew Jeff was no dumb jock. How had Pierce found her? And why was he so anxious to have her back? There was not a doubt in her mind that she was looking at a desperate man, and what he appeared to be desperate for was her.

She strived to keep her voice level. "I've got commitments here in Rivers Bend; I'm not going back to New York. And frankly, I don't understand why you want me to."

His oily smile grew wider. "I'm sure everyone here would understand your desire to go home with me— your fiancé—and as to why? Why do you think? I miss you and I can't wait to go ahead with our marriage."

Magda wasn't sure how to handle Pierce's odd

behavior but thought maybe the best defense was a good offense, so she said, "I know all about Taylor Brown, and I think you'd be much happier married to her."

Pierce's scowled. "You're really not going to make this easy are you?"

Magda gripped the cart in front of her and sent out a fervent prayer that a patron would come in soon. It was almost noon; perhaps someone would come in on their lunch hour so that she wouldn't be alone with this frightening, wild-eyed Pierce.

It was just about the time Jeff usually came in for lunch, but since he was too busy with work today, it looked like she was on her own.

Instinct told her to keep Pierce talking to stall for time, but she didn't completely understand why she was so afraid. Pierce would never hurt her—would he? Maybe the Pierce she thought she knew wouldn't, but this Pierce was acting nothing like the sophisticated, cool man she'd been engaged to.

"Why do you really want me to come back to New York with you?"

"So we can be married—you know how much it means to our families."

"I'm sorry, but we are *not* getting married," She glanced down at her white knuckles on the wooden cart. "And I'm seeing someone else now, Pierce. I can't marry someone I don't love just to please our families. I'm sorry."

"Not as sorry as you will be."

His voice brought chills to her spine and Magda realized Pierce was even farther out on the edge of reason than she thought he was. She slowly raised her eyes and gasped.

In his wildly shaking hands, he gripped a gun that he was trying to keep steady as he aimed it directly at her.

Chapter 18

Jeff paused at the bottom of the library steps. He held Petunia's leash in one hand and the white paper Nosh Pit bag in the other. He leaned down to whisper to the dog, "Now be a good girl, Petunia. Remember this is a stealthy mission. We have to be really quiet going in so we can surprise your mistress."

The dog wagged in response, and he gave her an affectionate pat on the head before he straightened up and tiptoed up the marble stairs, glad he was wearing sneakers instead of his riding boots.

He heard a sound from the neighboring building and turned his head to find Dan coming out of the sheriff's office. He smiled a greeting at his old high school classmate and got a grim look in response. Uh oh. Looks like Magda told her admirer that she was unavailable and why.

He looped the red and white Pintos leash around his wrist and used that hand to carefully turn the handle. The library door had a wicked creak and he eased it open as slowly as possible so Maggie wouldn't be alerted to their arrival. He imagined her seated at her desk and the look of pleased surprise she'd have on her adorable face when she saw him there.

Of course, nothing in life ever happens the way you imagine it will, and this was no exception. When Jeff looked into the library he saw Maggie, her eyes wide with fear and a death grip on the book cart in front of her. The cart was the only barrier between her and the suit guy he'd seen going into the library a little while ago. And Jeff was fairly certain he was wrong about the guy being a weekend resident, because he was waving around a big ole handgun.

He could tell the man hadn't noticed him yet, but suspected Maggie had, by the way she pointedly avoided looking anywhere near his direction, so as not to alert the crazy gun guy to his presence.

Maggie started to talk to the guy, and she raised her voice in a way he suspected was designed to hide any sound Petunia and he might make. *Good girl.* Keep talking, at least long enough to buy him some time to figure out his next move—one that would disarm the crazy man without any bloodshed. At least not Maggie's blood. If the crazy man lost a little in the process, so be it.

"Pierce, I don't know what you're doing, but there's no need for a gun. We've known each other for a long time; we can talk about anything you want to, but please, put the gun down."

Her voice sounded pretty calm, given the situation, but a faint quaver on the "please" alerted Jeff to the fact that Maggie was much more frightened than she was showing.

He had to take out the guy with gun—evidently, he was her former fiancé, Pierce. What the hell was the lunatic doing?

****

Maggie's heart jumped when she glimpsed Jeff enter the library. She didn't dare even let her glance flicker in his direction since by some miracle Pierce hadn't seen him yet.

She mainly had talked to Pierce to keep his attention firmly focused on her and not her possible salvation in the form of one hunky man and a one-eyed Shih Tzu, but his response to her request to talk took her by complete and total surprise.

"The time for talking is over. I gave you the chance to just leave here with me—to come home and get married the way we're supposed to, the way we *have* to, but you wouldn't do it."

Pierce's voice shook almost as much as his gun hand, which was *so* not a good thing. An agitated Pierce waving a gun at her was pretty much the worst-case scenario. She had to keep him talking until Jeff or she could figure out a way to stop Pierce, without putting each other at risk.

"What do you mean by that—the way we 'have to?'"

"I mean that *I have to marry you*. You know what my grandfather is like, maybe better than anyone, because your grandmother is exactly the same way. And he is not going to turn my trust fund over to me until I'm married. To you. And I am in desperate need of that money—you might even say I'm in life or death need of that money. So you *are* going to marry me, whether you want to or not."

"What?"

"I'm sorry, Magda, but you're going to leave with me right now. Lucky for me, you decided to run away to Virginia. Did you know there is no mandatory waiting period in the commonwealth of Virginia to get married? We can get a license today and be married right away. We'll be able to be back in New York to give Grandfather the good news tonight."

Okay. Pierce hadn't just gone round the bend, he sprinted right off the cliff of sanity, and Magda had the definite impression that he was on some kind of hardcore drug right now, too. His behavior was totally irrational, and she couldn't afford to wait for Jeff to get an opening. She had to disable Pierce before he saw Jeff, as it was increasingly clear there was going to be no reasoning with the man.

The gears whirred so loudly in her head that she was surprised the two men couldn't hear them. As she saw it, she only had two things on her side in her current position—the element of surprise and the remarkably heavy book cart between Pierce and her.

Struggling to control any involuntary movement or sound that would give away her intention, Magda charged forward, using the book cart like a battering ram, and jammed it into Pierce's gut as hard as she could.

****

Jeff couldn't believe his eyes when Magda rushed forward like some sort of librarian-Amazon warrior hybrid and used the cart of books to knock over Pierce, who collapsed against the assault. The cart, already off balance with its heavy load of books, fell over and pinned him to the ground, under three shelves worth of spilled books.

The gun fell from his hand on impact, and Jeff dropped the bag and the leash to dive for the weapon before Pierce had a chance to recover and gain control of it again.

Pierce struggled to free his legs from the weight that pinned them down. He cursed loudly and recognizing the familiar voice, Petunia growled low in her throat. As brave as her mistress, the little dog darted forward with teeth bared and the fur raised on her back. She clamped her former tormentor's collar between her teeth, dug in her rear legs for leverage and pulled as hard as she could to prevent him from getting up off the ground.

Jeff stretched on the ground to shove the gun farther away from Pierce, and it skittered across the floor. He looked over his shoulder at Petunia as she incapacitated Pierce. He said with pride, "My two brave girls. Neither of you needed to wait for this knight in shining armor to rescue you, huh?"

****

Sheriff Monroe stood in the entrance to the library and took in the unbelievable scene in front of him. He'd heard a commotion when he was walking back to his office with his lunch and stopped in to see what was going on and what he saw was unprecedented in sleepy Rivers Bend.

A well-dressed stranger was sprawled on the floor, buried under a mountain of books. Magda's little dog was doing her best pit bull impersonation as she held on to his expensive collar with her sharp little teeth to help keep the man on the ground. Jeff Braden was on the ground next to a bag, from which had spilled sandwiches and soda cans, and Maggie stood in the middle of the room, hugging herself in a vain attempt to stop the shivering that made her look like she was at the North Pole in January without a coat. And at Dan's feet was a handgun, which based on their positions on the floor he deduced that Jeff had dived to shove away from the stranger's outstretched hand.

"And I thought being a small town sheriff would be dull. Does anyone want to tell me what in the hell is going on here?"

****

Jeff looked at Pierce, still being held down by a toy dog and a pile of books. The man whimpered quietly to himself.

"I came to have lunch with Maggie and found this lunatic holding a gun on her, rambling on about kidnapping her, and forcing her to marry him this afternoon."

He heard Maggie giggle in a shaky way that indicated shock and hysteria might be setting in, so he hurried over to pull her into his arms as Dan knelt next to Pierce in order to read him his rights and snap on some handcuffs.

Seeing someone else take charge of her nemesis, Petunia released Pierce's collar and trotted over to Jeff and Magda, her tail held high over her back, waving like a banner.

"It's over now, Maggie, you're safe." Jeff used the same soft, soothing croon that he would with a skittish horse on his mother's farm.

"I know," she replied, but the chattering of her teeth diminished the confident tone for which she strove.

Jeff knew his heart was in his eyes when he smiled down at her, but she was so brave, strong, and beautiful that he couldn't help it.

He heard Dan hoist the book cart off Pierce and the thumping clatter of the books as they tumbled off him when the sheriff pulled him to his feet.

"I'm going to take him next door to lock-up. My

268

deputy will be back in a minute for the gun. Until he gets here, secure the crime scene; don't let anyone in here." He spoke to Jeff and jerked his head at Magda before he continued. "And when she's feeling up to it, I'm going to need to talk to Magda."

Jeff nodded. "Got it. Thanks Dan. It's good you came by when you did—I appreciate it."

Pierce hung his head and muttered to himself as Dan stood behind him, a firm grip on his cuffed hands, and walked him out of the library.

Magda pulled out of his arms and began to pick up the books from the floor to put them back on the cart. She needed to do something normal—routine—Jeff got that, he really did, but Dan wouldn't want her to straighten up the crime scene just yet. He squatted next to her and stilled her hand with one of his own.

"I don't think you can do that until you get the go-ahead from Dan."

She nodded. "Right." Her voice sounded a little more normal, but he could tell she was still in shock. Petunia bumped her little head against Magda's shin and finally he saw her dimples come out in full force as she smiled at her pet. She dropped a book and scooped the dog up in her arms and hugged her close. "You were such a brave girl—holding Pierce down like that—you always did hate him, didn't you? Did he used to hurt you, baby? I'm so sorry. I didn't know how crazy he was."

Tears fell from her blue eyes to roll down her now dimple-free cheeks.

Jeff reached over and gently brushed a tear away. "Hey, hey, hey, none of that—you don't know if he hurt her or not. And if you had known, you would've kicked his crazy ass to the curb a long time ago—right?"

She squeezed her eyes shut and nodded fervently. "I would have been gone so fast his head still would be spinning."

Jeff rubbed one of Petunia's velvety ears between his thumb and forefinger. "Of course you would have, so no guilt trip now. Place the blame firmly where it belongs—on Pierce's strung-out head."

She opened her eyes, which were grave. "He *was* strung-out on something, wasn't he? When I realized it, that's when I got really scared. Normal Pierce couldn't be bothered to bestir himself to hurt me, but high-as-a-kite Pierce? I had no clue what he was capable of doing."

Jeff sat on the floor and pulled both woman and dog onto his lap. Magda held onto Petunia, but snuggled her head under his chin. He rubbed his cheek against her silky curls before resting his chin on top of her head.

He smiled as he said, "It does seem like he snapped like a twig, but *you* were amazing! You kept him talking and when you charged him with that book cart? I'm confident enough in my masculinity to admit it was a real turn on."

She chuckled. "I *did* feel like 'Buffy The Trust-Fund-Baby Slayer.'"

Jeff leaned his head back and laughed. He gave her a squeeze and said, "Well, he's the sheriff's problem now."

Her smile faded and she pulled her head back and blinked up at him. "What do you think is going to happen to him?"

"I don't know and after seeing him point that gun at you—I don't much care."

They heard the front door open, and Jeff took a breath to call out that the library was closed, but he saw that it was Dan's deputy. Maybe it was a sign that he was getting older, but the lawman didn't look old enough to shave to Jeff.

"Hi Mr. Braden, Ms. Horvath. I need to close up the library to conduct our investigation now. Sheriff Monroe wanted me to tell you that you can take Ms. Horvath home for now, but you need to come back as soon as she's able to this afternoon to answer some questions."

Magda slid out of his arms, and they had never felt so empty to Jeff before. She put Petunia down on the floor and stood.

Jeff did the same. "Sounds good—Maggie, why don't you get your stuff, and I'll drive you home. We can get your car when we come back to talk to Dan."

A flush spread from the collar of the deputy's tan uniform up to his broad-brimmed hat. "I'm sorry, sir, but Sheriff Monroe also told me to tell you not to dawdle."

Magda came out of her office with her purse over her shoulder and a briefcase in her hand. She switched the light off and shut the door. "Okay, I'm ready to go."

"We'll lock up when we're done, ma'am."

****

Whisked away by the motherly Mrs. Wilson as soon as they got to the Retreat, Magda was upstairs being coddled at the moment. Jeff felt the separation from her like a physical wound, and he really didn't know how he was going to handle it when she moved.

Maybe his sister was right—maybe he could convince her to stay here with him. He shook his head—it would be too selfish to keep her from her dreams just because he would be too lonely without her by his side.

He heaved a deep sigh and propped his feet up on the desk. He wove his fingers together behind his head and dropped his head into them.

The door flew open and Cisco charged in, "What the hell is this I hear about some maniac trying to kidnap Maggie?"

"News does spread fast in a small town," Jeff observed with a wry smile.

"When the sheriff takes a handcuffed stranger on a perp walk down Main Street and the library is closed off with yellow caution tape, there's gonna be talk. I want the whole story, so I can get home and tell my high-risk pregnancy wife that her best friend is safe before someone else calls her."

That snapped Jeff to attention. "I didn't think of that, sorry! Maggie is fine—no thanks to her insane ex-fiancé. We don't have the whole story yet, but Maggie was incredible! He was waving a gun at her and talking about forcing her to marry him, and she took him down with a book cart. Hottest damn thing I ever saw. He's in custody now, and she's upstairs getting the full pampering treatment from Mrs. Wilson. Now get home and tell Bethanne before someone else does."

"Thanks, *meu amigo*. I'll hurry back to lead the hike since the sheriff wants you back in town for a command performance. Take care of our girl Maggie, okay?"

Jeff's face was solemn. "For always—if she'd let me."

Chapter 19

"I can't believe his family was able to get Pierce whisked away to a rehab facility. That miserable s.o.b. should be in jail!"

Jeff leaned his back against his truck, which was parked in front of the sheriff's office where Dan had delivered the news. Pierce's father and a team of lawyers had swept in, and with the help of some highly-placed judges, they had gotten Pierce relocated to a rehabilitation center in California. The family jet had already flown him away from Rivers Bend by the time Jeff and Magda got to the sheriff's office to make their statements.

Magda shrugged in a resigned manner. "Power, privilege, and money can buy you anything. The Allens have all that and friends in high places, too."

"The man held a gun at you," Jeff said through gritted teeth.

"Yeah. I remember." Magda chuckled as she leaned against the truck next to him and bumped his arm with her shoulder. "It's kind of hard to forget, but he didn't hurt me. I'm okay."

Jeff put his arm around her shoulders and pulled her into his side. "So, he should just get off scot-free? You're all right with that kind of deal?"

"I'm not thrilled about it, but I've learned what people like my grandmother and the Allens can do.

They're powerful people. He may not end up going to jail, but I think he'll pay in his own way."

"How?" Jeff's skepticism was clear.

"In his world, pride is everything, and he'll be completely humiliated if word of this gets out—and it always does! Plus, I'm pretty sure even my grandmother will give up on fixing us up now, and he'll lose his job at M.I."

Jeff twisted his head to look down at her with a quizzical expression. "He must have meant a lot to you for you to be this forgiving about what he did to you. Do you still have feelings for him?"

"No," she replied emphatically. "I don't think I ever really had strong feelings for him. I left myself drift into our engagement to please our families, but anything I might have thought I felt for him was gone long before he pointed that gun at me. I know that's probably hard for you to understand."

"Why wouldn't I understand?"

She looked down at her feet and scuffed the toe of her left Ked on the sidewalk. "You had your great love—you married your college sweetheart and had a beautiful daughter with her. And then you lost her tragically; you've never remarried, so it's obvious your feelings for her still run deep."

Jeff's jaw dropped. "Is that really how you see it?"

His obvious shock caused her to look up at him with surprise. "Well, yes. Bethanne hinted to me once that things weren't all roses in your marriage, but I thought she was wrong. Otherwise, you wouldn't still be holding on to her memory."

Jeff looked around; then lowered his voice, very conscious of discussing such a private topic in such a public location. "I am *not* holding on to her memory. I think we need to have a talk and clear up some misconceptions, but this isn't the place for it. Can we relocate to your cabin?"

****

Magda came out of Cabin Five with two glasses of iced tea. "Sorry, it's not sweet tea," she apologized as she set the glasses down on the small table between the two Adirondack chairs.

Jeff sat in one, with his long legs stretched out in front of him and crossed at the ankles. He looked away from the river, where he'd been gazing, to smile up at her. "Unsweetened tea is fine. There's no law that says you have to serve sweet tea in Virginia."

She returned his smile and sat in the other chair. "That's one misconception corrected—any others you want to clear up while you're at it?"

He picked up his glass, but didn't drink from it. It seemed to Magda like he was just using it to keep his hands busy. She couldn't imagine what he was going to say that would have his normally unflappable demeanor flapped.

Finally, he spoke, "You're wrong about my marriage. I want you to know the truth, but Sam doesn't know any of this, and I have to ask you not to say anything to her about what I'm going to tell you."

"Cross my heart," Magda said as she put her words into action, and made an "X" over her left breast.

He cleared his throat and took a sip of his tea. "Crystal—that was Sam's mother's name—and I were college sweethearts, that much of what you said was accurate, but I don't think our relationship would've lasted past Tuscaloosa if she hadn't been pregnant.

That's the reason we got married."

"That's the reason lots of people get married." Magda's voice and smile were both gentle. "When she's a little older, I'm sure Sam would understand."

Jeff slammed his glass down on the table and ran his hand through his hair. "Maybe she would—if that were the whole story, but it's not. There's more."

Magda waved her hand in encouragement. "Go on then, I didn't mean to interrupt."

He took a deep breath. "I learned after we were married that Crystal had gotten pregnant on purpose. She suspected that I was going to break up with her, but I'd just signed my first deal with the Portland Pintos, and she liked the idea of being a pro ball player's wife. She knew I was kind of old-fashioned and that family meant everything to me, so she was pretty certain I'd want to get married if she was pregnant—and she was right. No thought about the child or what I wanted, just that she wanted the lifestyle that she thought would come with my job."

"I'm sure it seemed very glamorous to her."

Jeff raised one shoulder in a shrug. "The reality was less so. She had a newborn baby, was far away from family and friends, and I was on the road a lot. Even when I was home, I just wanted to stay in with the baby and chill. Crystal would get angry that I didn't want to leave the baby with a sitter and hit the clubs. But that life didn't hold any appeal for me. I worked hard for the Pintos, and when I was home, that's where I wanted to be—home, not out on the town partying, but that's all Crystal wanted to do."

"That's a big difference of priorities—how did you resolve it?"

"She found a creative solution. I stayed home with the baby, and she went out on the town with another man: one of my teammates."

"Oh Jeff, I'm so sorry. That must have been tough," she said as she reached across the small table to squeeze his hand.

He turned his hand over to clasp hers and smiled at her. "It was a long time ago, and if I'm going to be completely honest with you, Crystal and I didn't love each other. My ego took a hit, but not my heart."

Magda nodded her understanding. "That's how I felt about Pierce's cheating."

They sat in silence for a few minutes, holding hands and watching the Potomac flow by; above them, a hawk caught an air current and wheeled high above the river.

Jeff watched it and said with his eyes still on the sky, "There's a little bit more if you want to hear it, and this is the part I've always tried to protect Sam from knowing."

"I'd like to hear it, if you don't mind telling me."

Jeff shook his head. "No, I don't mind. I want to be completely upfront with you—no secrets." He took a deep breath before continuing, "You know that Crystal died in a car wreck?"

Magda nodded.

"She wasn't alone; she was with her boyfriend. It was a rainy night and they'd had a little too much to drink..." He paused and traced circles on Magda's palm while he continued, "I came home from practice to find she'd left Sam with a sitter, and the girl had a note for me. Crystal didn't even wait to be sure that Sam was safe with me before she left—she just left her baby forever, with a teenaged girl." He shook his head in disbelief.

"What did the note say?"

"That she wanted more out of life than she had with Sam and me. She didn't want to be a housewife and stay-at-home mom, but she didn't want a career either. She wanted to party 24/7, and since her boyfriend felt the same way, he'd be able to provide her with the lifestyle she craved. She said that she was leaving Sam with me because a child would cramp her style, and that it was obvious Sam meant more to me than she did to Crystal."

He locked serious eyes with Magda. "That's why I never want Sam to know the truth—no child should have to feel like her mother didn't want her."

Magda understood Jeff completely, but also feared that no secret could be kept forever—especially in this computer age. As a librarian, she knew better than Jeff how easily accessible information was on the internet, and in this case it worried her.

"I can't even imagine how hurtful it would be for Sam, but you might want to consider telling her at some point."

Jeff's eyes widened. "I'm surprised to hear you say that."

She sighed. "You know I would never see Sam hurt for anything in the world, but I'm just thinking that if she hears about it from someone else—someone who doesn't love her as much as you do—it would hurt even more. And a simple online search of her mother's name would probably yield old articles about the accident."

Jeff exhaled and conceded, "That's true. I'll give it some serious thought."

Magda squeezed his hand. "Thank you for trusting me with the truth."

Jeff's voice was rough. "I didn't want you thinking you were competing with a ghost, because the truth is there is no competition. Crystal gave me Sam, and I'll be forever grateful to her for that gift, but my feelings for you are so much stronger than anything I ever felt for Crystal."

"And I want you to know that my feelings for you are more real than what I thought I felt for Pierce..."

Jeff flashed a quick grin. "Considering he just tried to kidnap you at gunpoint, I certainly hope so!"

Magda rolled her eyes in mock exasperation, but her dimples peeked out to reveal her true emotion. "You know what I mean. Sheesh! Try to pay the man a compliment..."

Jeff chuckled. "I sensed a 'but' coming, so I tried to divert you."

Magda's expression grew serious. "You're right, there was a 'but' coming—I was going to say, *but* we have to remember that I'll be leaving soon."

"Leaving, right. I know that's the plan, but plans can change. And even if they don't, I want to enjoy every minute we spend together now." He paused and waggled his eyebrows at her. "And speaking of enjoying our time together—Sam went to the farm to ride horses, and have dinner with my mom. She won't be home for hours—what do you say we head into the cabin and get to some enjoying of each other?"

****

Elizabeth Mallory hung up the phone with a thoughtful air. Her secretary, Ned, sat opposite her desk with a stack of file folders neatly stacked on his lap. His face expressed genuine concern for his employer.

"A disturbing call, ma'am?"

She sighed and turned her head to look at him. "Since you no doubt heard my side of the entire conversation, you know that it was not pleasant."

He'd worked with her long enough to not be intimidated by her squelching response. "You're correct, of course, I did hear, and I wanted to be sure that you're all right."

The ghost of a smile played at the corners of her tight lips. "Thank you for your concern, Ned. I'm fine—just stunned by Pierce's behavior. I'm not sure how to salvage this situation with my granddaughter."

My. God. The old lady never gave up.

"Are you sure you want to salvage it? If Mr. Allen is so unstable and drug addicted that he would try to kidnap Miss Horvath at gunpoint, I have to express some surprise that you'd find the situation to be salvageable."

"Pierce is getting help for his issues; when he's well again, perhaps…."

Ned cleared his throat. "It is my understanding that Miss Horvath is seeing another gentleman now."

"Gentleman?" If Elizabeth Mallory wasn't such a perfect lady, one might describe the sound she made as a snort. "You mean the footballer? I'm sure her infatuation with him will wane."

Knowing what an independent young woman Magda was, Ned was not nearly so sure that she'd toss over a good man for Pierce Allen—certainly not after the attempted kidnapping.

He knew the old lady was lonely without her granddaughter in Manhattan, but she seemed incapable of understanding the most basic things about the young woman's character, and thus unable to facilitate a future relationship with her.

Sometimes, Ned thought he was the only real friend Mrs. Mallory had, and so he strove to smooth the way to her continued relationship with her granddaughter. Left to her own devices, Mrs. Mallory would surely blow it sky high.

"I've taken the liberty of doing some research on Jefferson Braden. He seems to be a decent young man—he does a lot of charity work and runs a successful business."

Mrs. Mallory tapped her chin with her forefinger. "And this decent young man—who are his people?"

Here was the rub, at least as far as his ultra-snobbish employer was concerned. He decided to stretch the truth—or at least lead her to a conclusion that he knew to be erroneous. "They are horse people in Virginia."

Mrs. Mallory pressed her lips together. "No, Ned, they are horse *farmers* in Virginia. Not at all the same thing, as you well know, and not at all a suitable match for a Mallory."

Good thing Magda was a Horvath, was Ned's thought, but he knew better than to say more at this point.

"Would you like me to get the telephone number where Miss Horvath is staying?"

"Why?"

"So you can call her to see how she is doing after her ordeal?"

"No. Elizabeth made it clear that she doesn't wish to speak to me, but perhaps the address, Ned, please.

I'll write her a note."

****

A week after Pierce's attack, as had become her habit, Magda went straight from work to the main house at the Retreat. This way she could get her mail, pick up Petunia, and have dinner with Jeff and Sam. Aside from the drama with Pierce, her life here in Rivers Bend was falling into a happy pattern.

As she stood at the check-in desk in the lobby and looked through today's mail, Magda realized this was the happiest she'd been in her whole adult life.

The door to the front porch opened and she turned her head to see who was there. Silhouetted by the bright sun behind him was the man who was a huge part of her current happiness. Although, he was not its only source: here in Rivers Bend she'd found satisfying work, good friends, and a real sense of community. Oh yeah—and a smoking relationship with the super-hot man at the front door.

"Hi beautiful," Jeff said with a grin as he strode over to her and planted a steamy kiss on her smiling lips.

He looked down at the thick expensive looking cream-colored envelope in her hand. "Fancy! What is it? A wedding invitation? I clean up real good if you're looking for a date."

She screwed up her mouth. "No need to dust off your tuxedo, it's nothing fun. It's a note from my grandmother—I guess the incident with Pierce led her to discover where I've been."

Jeff's brows drew together. "And she *wrote* to you? Snail mail? Doesn't she think what happened to you should rate at least a telephone call from your only blood relation?"

Magda felt embarrassed by her messed up family situation, especially when she thought about how Jeff's family had rallied around her following the Pierce debacle. "I guess I'm not worth the long-distance charges." She shrugged as if that thought didn't cut her to the quick, and joked, "But you think she could've texted me—Omg. R u ok?"

Jeff seemed to see through her show of bravado, as he pulled her into his arms and tucked her head under his chin. "Oh baby, I'm so sorry. She doesn't know what she's missing by not having a relationship with you. What does she say in her note?"

She reluctantly pulled away and looked at the envelope. "I don't know. I haven't opened it yet."

And she wasn't sure she wanted to open it in front of Jeff—he of the well-adjusted Braden clan. He'd never understand if, as she suspected, her grandmother would stay true to form and have written a too-formal note that observed all the social niceties without any real sense of warmth or familial feeling.

She sighed and slit the envelope flap with the letter opener that was on the reception desk. She pulled out her grandmother's elegant note card and read. Jeff rubbed soothing circles on her back; there was no way he missed the tension the note caused in her body.

"She hopes I'm well after the 'recent unpleasantness,' and she's heard Pierce is doing well in treatment…"

She paused, shook her head and chuckled humorlessly before continuing to paraphrase her grandmother's note, "And she's sure that he and I will be able to work through whatever problems we have when he's released."

"*What?*" Jeff yelled. "Is she insane? She still wants you to marry the man after he threatened you with a gun?"

Magda nodded. "And that's my Grandmommy Dearest, ladies and gentleman."

Jeff whistled softly. "The rich really *are* different, huh?"

"I can't speak for all of them, but my grandmother certainly is. You know, I've always held out the hope that someday she'd love me and want me in her life—just because of *me*." She tapped her chest over her heart. "Because of who I am in here. Guess that's never going to happen."

"Maybe not with your grandmother, but *I* want you in my life because of who you are in here." He rested one hand over her heart. "And so does my family, Bethanne, Cisco, Ty—hell, darlin'—the whole town of Rivers Bend. You've even charmed that old battleax, Mrs. Warren."

She smiled wistfully. "Then I'm really lucky to have ended up here at this point in my life."

If only her time here didn't have to end, but Magda was very aware that she'd be leaving her idyllic life in this small town in the not too distant future. Oh well. There was no guarantee that she would stay happy here. With no job, she wouldn't feel good about herself if she just hung out and sponged off of Jeff.

And Jeff's feelings for her might not last. It hadn't escaped her notice that while she'd expressed the hope that she could be loved and wanted for herself, Jeff had ignored the loved part and just talked about *wanting* her in his life. And in her experience, *wanting* tended to not last nearly so long as *loving*.

Jeff tapped a business-sized envelope in her hand that she had already opened. "What's this?"

"It's from that library in Illinois—details about my job interview."

She saw Jeff's eyes dim and his Adam's apple bob as he swallowed hard. She felt a little hope flare in her heart—he might not love her, but he was going to miss her.

"Oh." His voice was all forced casualness. "And when is that happening?"

"In a couple of weeks."

He bobbed his head. "Okay. Great. Well. Good luck with that. I know it means a lot to you."

She felt tears sting at the back of her eyes, and her throat burned with the effort to keep them from falling. His support for her, in spite of the fact he didn't want her to move to Illinois, touched her deeply, and it tempted her to tear up the letter from the library and throw it in the trash bin behind the desk. But she knew that unemployment loomed on her horizon, and she couldn't pass up such a good opportunity for a man who couldn't even bring himself to say the "L" word. Not that she was ready to say the "L" word either. She was so confused!

"Thank you, Jeff, your support means the world to me." Her voice sounded hoarse, and she was relieved to hear Sam's voice yell from the living quarters.

"Dad! Magda! It's time to eat!"

Phew—saved by the dinner bell.

Chapter 20

Exhausted, Magda dragged her small suitcase behind her through Dulles International Airport. Storms in Chicago had delayed her flight, and she hoped that the rental car places would still be open at this hour because she certainly couldn't call anyone in Rivers Bend to ask them to pick her up—it was past midnight.

She sighed with envy as she saw the small cluster of people waiting to pick up their loved ones just outside the secured gate area. Oh well—worst-case scenario, she'd just have to stay at one of the airport hotels and get up early to rent a car and drive home in time to open the library. And then one figure caught her attention. He was taller than all the other people, and his brown hair was in its familiar tousled state. Her heart leaped at the sight: Jeff had come to get her, and he'd waited all this time for her much delayed flight to arrive!

She noticed a mischievous glint in his eyes and then noticed the hand-lettered sign he held up, as if he were a hired driver waiting for his fare:

Lucky Librarian Limousine Service
Are you feeling lucky?
Magda Horvath

With a laugh and renewed energy in her step, Magda rushed toward Jeff.

"I certainly *am* feeling lucky! I was just worrying

that all the car rental places would be closed for the night, and I was trying to figure out what to do to get home, and then there you are!"

"I aim to please," he said with a wink, before he stooped to plant a resounding kiss to her lips.

Ignoring the crowd around them, Magda let the handle fall from her fingers; the suitcase landed with a thump as she twined her arms around Jeff's neck and returned his kiss with fervor.

As a low moan escaped her, Jeff pulled back with great reluctance. "Did I ever miss you, Maggie! How long have you been gone—six or seven years?"

She smiled. "Um, not quite, it's only been two days."

Jeff picked up her suitcase. "Felt like longer to me. Do we need to go to baggage claim or is this it?"

"Nope, this carry-on is it."

"Great, we can go straight to the truck then."

"My flight was so delayed—you must've been waiting here for hours."

He led her through the lit parking lot to his truck and helped her in and snuck another kiss in the process. "I pretty much exhausted the entertainment opportunities at the airport, but I didn't mind."

He walked around the back of the truck and got in on the driver's side. As he backed out of the parking space, he said, "I guess we can't ignore the elephant in the room any longer. How did your interview go?"

Magda knew that Jeff didn't want her to leave—and truth be told, she wasn't all that hot on moving so far away either, but it was too good an opportunity to pass up.

She stared straight out the windshield at the

parking lot that looked orange in the glowing lights and shrugged. "It was all right."

Jeff stopped at a booth to pay for their parking and pulled out as the attendant triggered the gate to lift to let them pass. "Did they offer you the job?"

"No, not yet. There are a couple of other qualified candidates, but Sarah has recommended me, so there's a good chance that they will offer it to me."

"You don't sound as happy about it as I thought you would. Didn't you like it there?"

"It was really cold there already, so I'm a little worried about what the winter will be like."

He glanced off the road to smile at her. "Not many people move to Chicago for the balmy climate."

She looked down at her hands, which were clasped in her lap and smiled sadly. "No, I don't suppose they do, but it *is* a nice city—lots to see and do there."

Jeff's smile faded. "It's a big city; there must be a lot more to do there than there is in sleepy, little Rivers Bend."

"Maybe, but you have to know if I didn't need the job, I wouldn't leave Rivers Bend." *Wouldn't leave you* was the unspoken end of her sentence.

After that, they drove in silence, with only the country music playing on the radio providing sound inside the truck. Magda didn't know what Jeff's silence meant, but she was feeling too tired and raw to ask him what he was thinking and to have the conversation that question would start.

The traffic thinned as they got farther away from the Washington D.C. metro area and closer to the tranquility of Rivers Bend.

Jeff cleared his throat and asked the question she

had really hoped he wouldn't because she didn't know the answer to it.

"So, if they offer you this job, will you take it?"

She inhaled through her nose and breathed out in a whoosh through her mouth. "I don't want to, but I don't really see a choice. I'm hoping they take a good long time to make their decision."

"Maybe something closer to Rivers Bend will come up in the meantime," Jeff suggested hopefully.

"I've been looking, and nothing has yet. This job is the only nibble I've gotten."

Jeff turned onto the driveway to the Retreat. "We're home," he announced.

His words hit Magda like a sledgehammer—*home*. She was home. A home she loved, full of great people and satisfying work, but it wasn't really *her* work—it was Bethanne's, and she'd have to give it back soon. So actually, this *wasn't* her home—she felt like a cuckoo bird, taking over another bird's nest. She loved another woman's daughter, worked at another woman's job. But boy-oh-boy did she want this to be her home and for Jeff to be her man forever.

He pulled up to her cabin; the headlights swept over the porch and illuminated it briefly, before he turned off the engine and plunged them into darkness.

Maybe she should start pulling away from Jeff now, so it wouldn't hurt as much when it was time for her to move on, but the idea sat in the pit of her stomach like a bunch of ice cubes.

****

"There's no need to see me in."

Ignoring her words, Jeff threw open his door and hopped out. He smiled into the cab, now illuminated by the dim overheard light. "No good Virginia boy would let a lady carry her own luggage—or walk to her door alone in the dark."

He shut the door and trotted to her side of the truck to open her door. He placed one hand on the doorframe and the other on the roof of the truck; he leaned in to lay a sizzling kiss on her.

He ran his lips to her ear and whispered, "Besides, when they announced your flight was delayed, I called Heather and she's spending the night at the house with Sam and Petunia. I thought we could take advantage of a little time alone here—so I could show you just how much I missed you, and I've got *a lot* of missing you stored up."

He slid his lips back to hers and teased them with his tongue to get her to open to him.

With a breathy moan, she opened her lips to allow his tongue to tangle with hers. She fumbled with her seat belt, but had trouble due to her trembling hands. She felt Jeff smile against her lips, as he reached down without breaking the kiss to smoothly unlatch her restraint.

As soon as she was free, Magda turned in her seat and Jeff stepped back enough to allow her to swing her legs out of the cab and wrap them around his waist. The skirt of her conservative interview suit slid up to reveal an expanse of shapely leg encased in sheer hose.

He thought he felt her pulling away from him emotionally on the ride home, but he must have misinterpreted her silence because she felt just as desperate for him as he was for her.

He ran his hands up her silky thighs, to cup her bottom. He slid her out of the truck with her legs still wrapped around his waist and her arms wrapped around his neck. Their mouths fused together with a desperate hunger, brought on by their brief separation.

Jeff took one hand off her luscious ass just long enough to reach behind her and slam the truck door closed.

"I'll get your suitcase later," he said roughly.

"Later is good," she replied with a breathless laugh as Jeff carried her up the stairs of her porch.

"Keys?" He prompted.

Her head thumped against his, disappointment in her voice. "In my purse, in the truck."

"Damn." Jeff slid her slowly down his body, which he knew would leave her with no doubt as to how very much he wanted her. "Don't move an inch. I'll be right back."

He sprinted to the truck, jerked the door open, and bent to grab her purse from the floor of the passenger side. He got back to her in record time, and she grabbed for the bag to root around in it for the key. She found it and raised it with a triumphant smile as Jeff took it from her hand to open the cabin door. He held the screen door open with his backside as he swung the other door in.

He grinned at Magda. "Now, where were we?"

Without waiting for a response, he effortlessly lifted her up and she wriggled against him as she wrapped her legs back around him. He moaned and rotated his hips against her.

She pressed against him and said with a catch in her voice, "I think we were here."

"Here is good."

He stepped into the cabin and shut the door behind

them with his hip. "Know where's better?"

He strode through the small living room and into the bedroom. He laid her down on the rustic, four-poster bed and covered her soft body with his hard one. "*Here* is better."

She murmured her agreement as he captured her mouth in another senses-shorting kiss.

Jeff slid his hands along her white silk blouse to tease her breasts. God, he hadn't felt this hungry from a woman since he was a teenager. He just hoped he wouldn't embarrass himself by exploding the second he was inside her.

He shuddered as he felt her eager, little hand brush against the hardest part of him as it tugged at his belt buckle. He gently steered her hand away and said with regret, "Much as I want your hands on me, darlin', I won't last a minute if you touch me right now."

She twisted a little beneath him to reach again for his pants and he bit back a groan.

"Sometimes fast is okay," she said with encouragement.

He pulled away from her questing fingers. "Not *this* fast." His voice dropped and became seductive. "I don't want to be the only one having a good time here."

He pulled her blouse out of her skirt and slid his hands along the bared flesh of her feminine, slightly rounded belly, before running them over her ribs to cup the full breasts contained by her silky white bra. He flicked the front clasp open and all her arguments fled as her eyes drifted shut and she sighed softly. She appeared lost to sensation, which was just where Jeff wanted her. It was a win-win situation really. It bought him some time to get his explosive physical reaction to her under control, so things wouldn't be over before they started, and it put Maggie on the receiving end of as much pleasure as he could give her—and he intended to give her a lot of pleasure.

The blue light of the digital clock on the nightstand caught his eye and it was much later than he thought, due to the delayed arrival of her flight. "Unfortunately, I can't stay all night, since Sam is home—so I can't take as much time as I'd like."

Magda again reached for his pants. "I've already told you, I missed you, and I'm totally onboard for fast."

Jeff grinned and took his hand off hers, where he'd been trying to stop her attempts to undo his jeans, and held it up away from his fly. "Tut, tut, tut. You've had a long day, tonight's all about you."

He pulled her close, and took a deep breath as it brought her soft body up against him. Slow wouldn't be easy, but he missed Maggie so much the last couple of days, and since he was better at showing his feelings than speaking them, he wanted to show her just what she meant to him. He slid his hand around her side and unfastened her skirt and pushed it down. Damn. Pantyhose. They were clearly an invention created to torment the person trying to get them off a woman.

He felt Maggie's smile against his chest, before she said, "Let me help with these."

She shimmied out of her stockings, and when she straightened up, he took them out of her hands and tossed them over his shoulder. She laughed, but stopped when he pushed her panties down, and touched her where they'd been, and discovered she'd been telling the truth; she was ready. Knowing he caused this reaction in her body made him puff up with pride. Her breath caught, and he moved them backwards to the bed, where he lowered her to the fluffy comforter.

He let out a breath of admiration, and Maggie flushed all over at the sound. She scooted over to make room for him on the bed. He climbed up next to her. "You are so beautiful, darlin.'"

She got even pinker. "Am not."

"I hate to disagree with a lady, but…yeah…you really are."

Jeff kissed her mouth, and then her throat, which elicited a quiet moan. "Every. Damn. Inch of you. Beautiful." He continued his kiss tour of her soft, curvy body and didn't stop until he got to her center. He smiled up at her, and found her watching him with anticipation.

"Welcome home, Maggie." He said before he pressed a fervent, intimate kiss against her core, designed to show just how very missed she had been.

****

"Knock, knock." Magda called out from the door of Bethanne's bedroom.

"Maggie! You're home! Come on in and tell me all about your interview," Bethanne's face was wreathed in smiles when she heard her friend.

Magda laughed as she planted herself on the bed next to Bethanne.

"I'd be flattered that you sound so happy to see me, if I didn't suspect you're going stir crazy and would welcome a burglar with the same degree of happiness."

Bethanne swatted at her friend's hand and then clasped it with affection. "I'm way happier to see you than a thief, which isn't to say I wouldn't try to engage one in conversation. Cisco pops in and out during the day, and Sam stops by most afternoons; sometimes Ty comes for lunch, so I don't mean to sound too 'poor me,' but the days are kind of long and lonely," she patted her belly. "And this one isn't much of a conversationalist yet. He mostly just kicks me."

Magda chuckled. "Can I get you anything?"

Bethanne shook her head. "No thanks. You just missed Cisco; he got me all settled and then had to go back to work. Enough small talk—how did the interview go? Did they offer you the job? God, it's such a good opportunity for you!"

Bethanne was so enthusiastic that Magda didn't know how to answer her. What could she say? That, no thank you, she didn't want to move from Rivers Bend? To say to her best friend in the whole world—someone who'd always been there for her, through thick and thin—that she'd prefer to stay here and keep doing Bethanne's job. To tell her how her whole life, she'd straddled two worlds—her father's and her grandmother's—and never felt like she belonged in either. That she never fit in anywhere until she came to Rivers Bend? So, yes please, let me take *your* job and someone else can have the job a thousand miles away from the only place she'd ever felt at home.

She'd never actually hidden anything from Bethanne before, and Magda toyed with the idea of telling her the truth.

Before she could find the right words, Bethanne heaved a deep sigh and said, "I can't tell you how much I want to get back to my work at the library. I didn't realize how much I'd miss it; how much it defines me. I can't wait to be a mom—you know what a long road it's been to get here and how much this baby means to me—but it doesn't change the fact that I'm also the Rivers Bend librarian, and I love it! I even miss the crankiest of patrons and the musty, dusty smell of the place."

Magda took a deep breath—after that speech, she couldn't very well tell Bethanne how she really felt and that in her secret heart of hearts, she'd hoped that Bethanne didn't feel the way she did and would be willing to turn over the job to Magda and stay home with her baby. Clearly, that wasn't an option, so now was not the time for the unvarnished truth.

"I think the interview went well, but no offer yet. They have other interviews lined up; I guess since they have a few months before they need to fill the position, they're taking their time and are trying to find the right person."

Bethanne waved her arm in Magda's direction with a flourish, like an old-time magician's assistant might do. "Ta da! They've found the perfect person! Who could do better than you? They can call off the search right now."

Magda smiled, but it felt faint and false, even to her.

Bethanne narrowed her eyes. "What's up? Don't you want the job? I thought it was perfect for you—just what you always said you wanted to do."

"It is…"

"But…" Bethanne prompted. "You can't fool your best friend—I can tell you're not into this job, so I repeat—what's up?"

"It's a great chance. I just wish it were a little closer to Rivers Bend—like in D.C. or Baltimore.

Chicago is so far away."

"Far from Rivers Bend? Or from Jeff?"

"From both," Magda admitted. "But in this economy, jobs—especially public library jobs—aren't growing on trees. So, if they offer it to me, I'll probably accept."

Bethanne's eyes were as warm as the whisky their color resembled. "Oh, sweetie, you've gone and fallen in love with Jeff, haven't you?"

****

Jeez! And Magda told him Chicago was cold! It had nothing on the icy glare his sister pierced Jeff with, as she sat on the opposite side of his desk from him.

She spoke through tight lips, "It's not enough that you're bringing that cretin to work here—"

Jeff held up his hands. "Hold on—Mick is not a cretin. He's a good guy; I don't know what you have against him, but unless he's physically hurt you—in which case tell me, and I'll kill him—I want you to cowboy up and get along with him here at work. He has a great head for business, and Cisco and I think he'll be good for the Retreat. Which, need I remind you, benefits all of us."

Heather crossed her legs and turned her head to glare at the wall. "He never physically hurt me—where do you get this stuff? I just don't like him, and it will be uncomfortable for me to work with him. But, you're the boss, right?"

Jeff took a breath to defend himself, but Heather cut him off and continued, "Anyway, don't distract me from my main point, which is—it's bad enough I have to work with Mick, but how can you let Maggie leave Rivers Bend and move all the way to hell-and-gone?"

Jeff's jaw dropped. "I'm not *letting* her move! Nobody wants her to stay more than me—"

Heather slapped her hand on the desk. "Then *do* something about it, Jeff!"

"I've tried!" he yelled back, and then lowered his voice to continue, "I've asked her to stay—even offered her a free place to live. She. Turned. Me. Down. Okay? She turned me down. Happy now?"

The tight lines around Heather's mouth eased in sympathy for her brother's obvious pain and frustration. "Of course I'm not happy! What kind of bitch do you think I am?"

Jeff ran his hands through his already messy hair. "I don't think you're any kind of bitch. I'm sorry I yelled. It's just kind of a sore subject for me."

Heather furrowed her brow and asked, "Why won't she stay? I thought she liked it here. She's made tons of friends, and she's doing a great job at the library, she fits in like a native, even Mrs. Warren has stopped referring to her as 'that Yankee girl.' Well…sometimes she still calls her that, but now it sounds like an endearment. And I thought you two were in a good place."

Jeff leaned back as far as his leather desk chair would allow. "She does like it here, and we are in a good place. But her career and independence are important to Maggie; she doesn't want to stay here if she's not doing useful work."

"So give her a job," Heather said with clear exasperation. "You made up a job to give to stinking Mick, why can't you do the same for Maggie? Who, by the way, is a person I actually *like* and *want* to have around."

Jeff shook his head once. "She's a librarian—we don't exactly need one at the Retreat."

"I'm sure you could think of something else for her to do and convince her to stay. For reasons a mere sister can't understand, women seem willing to do things for you when you turn on that old Jeff Braden charm."

Jeff rolled his eyes. "Making her stay here to do a job she doesn't want or care about, just to keep her close to me for my own selfish reason, how would that make me any better than her grandmother? Mrs. Mallory did exactly the same thing to keep Maggie in New York, and look how well that turned out."

Heather slouched in her chair and folded her arms across her chest. "Point taken. I guess it might not be the best idea I've ever had, but this is a different situation."

Jeff raised his eyebrows. "Oh yeah? Tell me how it's different, 'cause I don't see it."

"Well, duh, because Pierce wanted Maggie there for her social connections and money. You want her here because you love her."

Chapter 21

"Me? In love with Jeff?" Magda gasped in astonishment.

Bethanne inclined her head. "That's the situation as I see it."

With a vigorous shake of her head Magda said, "No, no, no, no, no, no, no! It's too soon to love Jeff. I take longer than this to decide if I want to buy a new coat."

Bethanne laughed. "I know you're not a rash person by nature, but love has a way of tossing all the rules out the window. Are you *honestly* trying to tell me that you don't love Jeff? Don't kid a kidder, Maggie," her eyes narrowed. "Or maybe you're not trying to fool *me*—you're trying to fool *yourself* into believing that you're not in love with Jeff."

Magda flopped on her back to avoid Bethanne's all-too-knowing gaze. She stared at the ceiling fan as it swirled slowly over the bed causing a welcome breeze on the warm autumn day in Virginia.

"Maybe you're right—you know me too well, I guess better than I know myself. I love Jeff," she said the three words as if she were trying them on for size. Then repeated with more emphasis, "I am in love with Jeff."

She heaved a sigh before continuing. "But it doesn't change anything. I knew all along that I was only in Rivers Bend temporarily, and since I haven't found anything closer, if they offer me the job in Chicago, I'll take it and things with Jeff will end."

"Why?"

"Why what?"

"Why do things with Jeff have to end if you take the job?"

Magda turned her head on the pillow, so she faced Bethanne. "There's that little matter of the thousand miles that will be separating us. Makes for a tricky dinner date."

"Maybe you can't grab a pizza and watch *Jeopardy* together on a Tuesday night, but that doesn't mean things have to end if you move."

"*When*," Magda corrected. "Not if. *When* I move."

"Fine. *When* you move, it doesn't have to be all or nothing. Y'all can keep seeing each other long distance."

"That *never* works out. And I'd just fall more in love with Jeff—cause he's…well, he's Jeff. Who wouldn't fall deeper in love with him? So, I'll get more attached and then when it ends, I'll be even more hurt. It's better to pull the bandage off quickly and stop seeing each other when I leave Rivers Bend. A nice clean break."

"You're mixing your medical metaphors—good thing you're a librarian and not a doctor, Maggie." Bethanne teased with a wink. Then, she asked seriously, "Why do you keep saying things have to end?"

"I told you, long distance relationships never work."

Bethanne laughed shortly and patted her pregnant

tummy. "Baby Francisco begs to differ. He says his Mommy and Daddy dated long distance almost their entire relationship, and they worked things out—he's proof of it."

Magda cocked her head and pursed her lips. "Tell my soon-to-be godson that his parents were the exception to the rule. They were the one in a million couple who could make a long distance relationship work."

"I don't think that's true at all." Bethanne's eyes twinkled, and her thoughtful frown turned into a devilish smile. "Although Cisco *did* make it easier. Honestly! The things that man could do to me over the phone were unbelievable."

Maggie screwed up her face. "I was your roommate at the time—trust me—I know all about the things he could with you over the phone."

Bethanne grinned unabashedly. "It was such a tiny apartment. Sorry if we used to disturb you."

A reluctant grin tugged at the corners of Magda's mouth. "It's okay. I was mostly just envious."

"And now you have a good thing like that going with Jeff, and you're not willing to take a chance on it."

"But there's so much risk. If it doesn't work, I'd be hurt or Jeff would be hurt—probably both of us will end up hurt. Most importantly, Sam would be hurt, and if there's anything I can do to keep that from happening, I'll do it."

Bethanne slapped her hand on the bed and raised her voice, "But if it *does* work out, think about how happy all three of you would be! Honest to God, if I didn't have to stay in this position, I would so get up and shake you!"

Magda sat up with her legs curled underneath her and her hand on top of the one Bethanne had just smacked on the bed. She furrowed her brow with concern. "Don't get upset—that can't be good for little Francisco. I promise that I'll think about what you said," she smiled in what she hoped was a reassuring manner. "Okay?"

"I'd rather you say that you'll just keep seeing Jeff instead of 'thinking about it,'" Bethanne used air quotes to punctuate her last words; then added grudgingly, "But if it's the best you can do right now—I'll take it. Just, please, don't be so willing to throw love away just because you're chicken."

Magda frowned and put her hands on her hips. "Hey! I am *not* a chicken!"

Bethanne shrugged. "If the feathers fit..." She grinned as she bent the arm that was on top and flapped it like a wing before launching into her best chicken impersonation, "Bwaaack, bwaaack, bwaaaack!"

****

"Love her?" Jeff sputtered. "You think I love Maggie?"

"Yep," Heather smirked.

"Love?"

"Yes. L.O.V.E.—love. You looove her." His sister taunted him like they were back in the schoolyard.

Jeff leaned back in his desk chair so hard that it squeaked. He rubbed his hand over his chin. "Well, damn. You're right. I *do* love her."

Heather leaned back and crossed her long legs; she made no attempt not to look smug. "Of course I am." She cupped her ear with one hand. "But I'm not sure I heard you—would you mind saying it again?"

Jeff scowled. "Gloating is not a becoming activity, young lady."

Heather's laughter pealed through the room. "I know it's not, but it just feels so darned good! I don't believe you've ever acknowledged that I was right about anything before. I call it B.B.S.—Big Brother Syndrome—you still think of me as being a kid, so you never see that I've become a woman of dazzling intelligence," she breathed on her knuckles and rubbed them on an imaginary lapel.

Jeff leaned forward to grab a piece of paper from the desk, which he crumpled and threw at Heather.

She laughed as it bounced harmlessly off her head. "So. You finally admit that you love Maggie."

Jeff nodded and exhaled. "Yeah. Yeah, I do, but it's all the more reason to let her go."

Heather narrowed her eyes and blew her bangs off her forehead with a huff. "I've never put much stock in that whole 'if you love someone, set them free' line of bull. If you love someone—thank your lucky stars and hold on with both hands! It's such a rare gift, you can't let it get away."

Jeff considered her words, and then said with a slow shake of his head. "No. I won't use my feelings for her to trap Maggie here. I think she could be happy in Rivers Bend—with me—but unless she decides that for herself, I won't pressure her to stay."

****

Jeff trotted down the front steps of the Retreat and mulled over the unexpected turn his meeting with Heather had taken. He'd expected to get to the bottom of her mysterious animosity toward Mick before he arrived and work conditions became unbearable. It certainly would be an unusual marketing strategy for a corporate retreat, designed for team-building, to have its own staff fighting like cats and dogs in front of the visitors.

But his baby sister had turned the tables on him, and somehow gotten him to admit his love for Maggie—love he'd been doing his damndest to ignore.

He wondered how he should act with Maggie now that he realized he loved her. He needed a little time to think it over before he faced her, and whenever he needed to think, he ran. Hence, his running shorts, long-sleeved T-shirt and running shoes. He stretched and mulled and then spotted a stick on the driveway. He bent down to pick it up and tossed it onto the lawn.

A happy yip indicated that Petunia was near, and sure enough, she bounded by to retrieve the stick, her Portland Pintos leash trailing behind with no person attached.

Jeff put his hands on his narrow hips and took a deep breath. So much for his "Jog and Brood." He knew that if Petunia was here, her owner wouldn't be far behind.

Maggie's cheerful voice called out behind him, "Hiya, Jeff! Going for a run before dinner?"

He pasted a smile on his face and turned around. He still didn't know how he wanted to handle things with Maggie, but he decided to use his old standby when he didn't know what to say: casual good humor.

"I was thinking about a run—what gave me away?"

He managed to smile and wink in a playful way, even though his heart stuttered at the sight of Maggie looking completely adorable in snug jeans and his

Pintos jersey. She toed the ground with her tennis shoes, which gave him pause—she seemed to be as nervous as he felt, but what did she have to be nervous about? Was his newly-discovered love for her showing in his eyes and freaking her out? He quickly looked down, too.

"Well, there was the stretching and the athletic shorts," Maggie teased, but her voice sounded a little strained to his ears.

He was spared having to keep the banter going by his daughter's voice from the porch. Oblivious to whatever strange emotional undercurrents were happening between Maggie and him on the driveway, Sam called out, "Maggie—I'm so glad to see you! Could you come quiz me on my vocab words?"

Jeff grabbed at the out like a drowning man at a straw. "All righty then. I'll just head out for my run. See y'all at dinner."

****

Maggie watched Jeff jog down the trail into the woods with a frown on her face. Sure, she needed some time to process the feelings she had for him, just recently unearthed during her conversation with Bethanne. She'd been planning to buy some time by telling Mrs. Wilson that she'd make dinner for herself in her cabin tonight. But those plans went awry when she rounded the corner and saw the wondrous sight of Jeff's tight buns on display in running shorts as he bent over to pick up a stick. It was a sight so splendid, it made a woman certain of the existence of a merciful God.

And then Jeff acted as awkward as she felt, which completely puzzled her. Was her love for him so transparent that he could see it and didn't know how to let her down easy?

Sam called out again, a little impatient this time, "Helloooo! Maggie did you hear me? Vocab?"

Magda tore her gaze off the spot where Jeff had been swallowed up by the woods and gave her head a shake. "Sorry, Sam—I heard you, and I'd be happy to help you. Do you have your flash cards?"

"They're in the kitchen where I was doing my homework."

Maggie climbed the steps with one last longing look over her shoulder toward Jeff. "Okay then—to the kitchen!"

She patted Sam on the back in an affectionate, but distracted, way as she passed by on her way into the house.

She heard Petunia follow her up the stairs and drop her stick onto the wooden porch with a thump.

Sam's puzzled voice followed her into the house, "What's up with Dad and Maggie? I'll tell you what I think Petunia—grown-ups are weird!"

****

Maggie dried the dishes as Mrs. Wilson washed, and handed them to Jeff to put away; sadly, it was the most interaction they'd had since he came back from his run. She knew why she needed a little temporary space—she was still reeling from the realization that she loved him—but she didn't know what his deal was, and it made her a little anxious. Her hand shook slightly as she handed him the last plate with a nervous smile.

"I should head home—thank you for dinner, Mrs. Wilson."

The matronly housekeeper beamed at her fondly as

she reached through the soapy water in the sink to pull the plug and drain it. "Thank you for helping with the cleanup, dear. The dishwasher repairman is coming in the morning, so this should be the only night we have to do the dishes by hand. Thank heavens there are no guests here tonight. I sure do appreciate both of you helping me."

"No problem," Jeff said.

"Least I could do, since you've been feeding me five nights a week," Maggie said at the same time.

She strolled to the back door and pulled Petunia's leash off the coat hook. She snapped her fingers to call the dog, who yawned and stretched before leaving her cozy spot under the kitchen table.

Magda bent down to snap the leash onto the collar and said, "Night all."

"Night," Jeff replied.

Mrs. Wilson whirled around with her soapy hands on her ample hips. "Jefferson Braden, what do you mean "Night!" Do I have to tell your momma that you seem to have lost the manners that I *know* she taught you? How could you let a lady walk home alone? At night. In the dark."

Jeff hung his head. "No, ma'am, you don't have to tell on me to Mom. I'll walk Maggie home."

Mrs. Wilson stared at him for a long moment and then gave her a sharp nod. "Good. I'll stay here with Sam until you get back."

"Thanks, Mrs. W. She's finished her homework, so she can watch the TV for an hour."

He reached around Maggie to turn the knob of the back door to shove it open as Mrs. Wilson ambled down the hallway to the family room to join Sam in front of the TV.

Magda glared at him. "How touched I am that you'd rather walk me home than be ratted out to your mother." She snorted. "Don't do me any favors, I can see myself home."

Jeff grinned sheepishly as he shut the door behind them, which left them in the dark on the back porch, except for the square of light in the window of the door. "I'm sorry, Maggie, I've been a real jerk tonight. Please let me walk you home."

Magda drew her brows together. "I've been a little off tonight, too, so, okay, it would be nice to have you walk me home."

They walked down the stairs and followed the back drive around the house to the front yard and to the path through the woods to Magda's cabin.

They were silent as they strolled along. There was an autumnal nip in the evening air, and the leaves had begun to fall. Maggie scuffed her feet through the dried leaves on the path and enjoyed the crinkly sound they made.

Petunia happily strained at the end of her lead and sniffed at all the tantalizing smells in the leaves.

"Nice night," Jeff observed.

"It is—it's nice that it's still so pleasant here—in New England it's probably pretty cold already," Magda kicked herself internally, even as she spoke the words. Great—weather chitchat! Is this what they'd been reduced to—what the hell was going on between them?

The path opened up to her cabin perched high above the river. Jeff followed her up the steps and leaned against the post at the top with his hands shoved into the pockets of his jeans.

"We've never had to resort to talking about the weather before—that's one of the things I enjoy most about being with you. We never run out of things to talk about. I've never had that experience with a woman before."

Magda leaned on the post opposite him and let go of Petunia's leash before crossing her arms across her chest. "Then why are we suddenly talking to each other like we're strangers?"

"I had an illuminating talk with my sister, Heather, this afternoon, and I realized that I don't want to turn into your grandmother."

Magda allowed herself a long, lingering look up Jeff's body, from his denim clad legs to the forest green, waffle knit Henley, both of which clung to his very strong, very male body in all the right places.

She raised her gaze to meet his own and said with a teasing smile, "Trust me, Jeff Braden, *no one* is going to mistake you for Elizabeth Mallory."

He chuckled. "Maybe not physically, but Heather seemed to be of the mind that I should do whatever it takes to talk you into staying here, but I'm thinking that if I use whatever it is that's going on between us to convince you to stay in Rivers Bend, then I'm no better than your grandmother. I'd be doing the exact same thing she did when she manipulated your emotions to get you to move to New York."

Magda's eyes opened wide. "It's not the same thing at all—you would never be so Machiavellian. You're one of the straightest shooters I've ever met; although, I do appreciate you not trying to change my mind."

She paused and grinned. "And for the record," she

gestured between them, "here in America, I believe they call 'whatever this is between us' dating."

He nodded. "Right—dating—I've heard talk about this dating thing."

Magda laughed, relieved that the awkwardness between them seemed to be passing.

He scrunched down so they were eye-to-eye. "But I don't want our dating to keep you from doing what you need to do with your life."

Magda returned his serious gaze. "I don't want to move so far away—you have to know that, and if anything closer opens up, trust me, I'll take the job, but I had an interesting conversation this afternoon too, and it made me think."

Jeff raised an eyebrow and straightened up to his full height. "Really? What about?"

"You. Me. Us. And I realized that if I let the fear of being hurt when I leave here stop me from enjoying our time together now, then I'm just a big chicken." She frowned. "And I am *no* chicken."

One side of Jeff's mouth turned up. "No, you're not a chicken—you're one of the bravest people I know. The way you moved to New York because it was the best way you could take care of your dad, and then the way you left it all behind to come here and start over: totally brave. And don't even get me started on the way you took Pierce down with that book cart!"

She felt her cheeks heat up and looked down at her feet. "Thanks."

She could feel Jeff's intent stare and peeked up at him through her lashes. "What?"

"I'm about to admit something that's going to make me sound like a caveman—or a teenage boy, or worse, a teenage caveman—but I like seeing you in my football jersey. It's sexy as hell."

Magda bit her bottom lip and said, "It probably makes me sounds like a silly teenage girl, but I like wearing your jersey. I was always envious of the girls in high school who wore their boyfriend's letterman jackets to class, but I wasn't the kind of girl that boys gave their jackets to."

"I would've given you my jacket."

"Then it's too bad you didn't go to my prep school," she joked.

Jeff's ferocious tone startled her. "Were all the boys blind at your school?"

She rolled her eyes. "Not blind, just snobs. Because my dad was a 'nobody,'" she made air quotes with her fingers around the word. "None of them would give me the time of day. I was a total social outcast."

"What a pack of idiots you went to school with—a girl as cute, funny, and sweet as you. I wouldn't have cared if your father was Charles Manson."

Magda scrunched up her nose and asked with skepticism, "Really? Charles Manson?"

"Okay, maybe Manson would've given me pause, but you know what I mean."

"I do—and thanks for saying it."

Jeff pulled her to him and tucked her head under his chin. "I mean it, and I wish I could stay and show you just how *much* I mean it, but Mrs. Wilson is waiting for me before she can go home for the night."

She nuzzled his chest and inhaled the uniquely masculine scent that was all Jeff. "I understand. Thanks for walking me home. Good night."

He used his thumb and forefinger to gently tilt her

chin up and pressed a tender kiss to her lips, and it felt like a vow.

"See you for lunch tomorrow," he said before he trotted down the steps and loped up the path to his house.

Magda pressed her fingers to her still burning lips as she watched him go and whispered to Petunia, "Oh my, girl, I am so over my head with that man."

Chapter 22

Magda sped up the road to her cabin. The November trees had dropped all their leaves, and their bare branches were silhouetted against the bright blue sky of the clear, crisp day. She stopped the car with a jolt and grabbed her bag from the passenger seat.

The whole town of Rivers Bend closed up shop at noon today so that everyone could attend the high school's last game of the season against their archrivals, and the library was no exception. But she still needed to change out of her work clothes and get over to the main house to meet up with Jeff and Sam. The coach had asked Jeff to do the coin toss at the start of the game, so they had to be there a little early.

She fumbled around in her big purse for her key and stumbled over the big gift-wrapped box at her front door.

"What the heck?" she asked out loud as she squatted next to the box. There was a note tucked in to the giant gold ribbon, and she slid it out with a puzzled frown. Her name was written on the envelope in Jeff's now-familiar block print.

She pulled the flap out and took out a piece of the Retreat's notepaper.

Dearest Maggie,

A few weeks ago, you told me something about your high school years, and I wanted to correct a terrible wrong. I'd be honored if you'd wear what's in this box to the game this afternoon.

> *—Jeff*

She felt the burn of unshed tears behind her eyes and blinked them back.

"Oh no he didn't," she whispered as she lifted the top of the box.

She looked down at her gift nestled in the white tissue paper in the box and smiled through her happy tears. "Oh yes, he did."

****

Jeff clicked "send" on an email confirming a big booking for the Retreat with a satisfied smile. The tentative knock on his office door followed by Maggie's quiet, "May I come in?" replaced his already happy expression with what he knew was a shit-eating grin. He sure hoped she was wearing his present.

"You're always welcome here, darlin', come on in."

The knob of the door turned ever so slowly before the door swung open to reveal Maggie, who was wearing those snug jeans he loved, boots and a fuzzy green sweater that made him ache to touch her. A gold scarf was knotted around her neck. Green and gold—the Rivers Bend High colors—nice touch. Whether she wanted to admit it or not, Maggie was turning into a local.

But in his opinion, the best part of her outfit was his present, which was so big she was swimming in it.

"You're wearing your present—do you like it?"

She tugged at the rolled up cuffs of his old high school letterman jacket and beamed at him. "Like it? No. I *love* it!"

She launched herself at him, and Jeff caught her with ease and swung her around before putting her down and stepping back to inspect her from head to toe.

"It looks great on you—way better than it ever did on me."

"I find that to be highly doubtful—it's huge on me, but I couldn't love it more. I can't believe you thought of it."

"I remembered what you said about never having a boy give you one in high school—I still think your classmates were a pack of blind assholes, by the way—so I dug this out of my mom's attic, and had it dry-cleaned so I could give it to the prettiest girl in town."

He loved the way his words brought a flush to her cheeks.

"It's the best present I ever got—thank you. You made a former lonely high school geek's dream come true."

He pulled her close to him and slipped his hands under the jacket to feel her in the fluffy sweater, which was even softer than it looked and warm from her body heat.

"Sam has a slumber party after the game tonight, so we have the house to ourselves—maybe I can knock a couple of other dreams out of the park for you," he said with a teasing smile. "Or maybe some of my dreams."

He loved seeing his banter bring out her dimples as she said, "I'm willing to try it, but maybe you should tell me one of your dreams, so I can plan ahead."

He ran his hands under the bottom of her sweater, and her skin was even softer than the angora. He pulled her tight against him, so she'd feel exactly how aroused she made him. He leaned down to whisper one of his many fantasies about her in her ear and heard a loud thud from the doorway.

"Oh gross! Can't you two do that stuff in private?"

His daughter stood in the doorway, her overnight bag being dropped to the floor had supplied the thump. Her words were harsh, and typical for a kid finding her parent in a romantic situation, but he saw the pleasure in her eyes and knew Sam wanted Maggie to be a part of their lives as much as he did.

"Not that I'm not always happy to see you, Peanut, because I am, but we *were* in private until you busted in here," Jeff said with a loving smile.

Maggie gently disengaged from Jeff's embrace and smiled sheepishly at Sam. "Sorry you had to see that."

Sam grinned and shrugged. "I'll live. You look great in Dad's jacket! Were you surprised?"

"Thanks—and I was totally surprised! I'm psyched that I get to wear it to the big game tonight."

"If we ever get out of here," Sam replied with a huff.

Jeff picked up her overnight bag and ruffled her hair. "You're as subtle as a sledgehammer, kiddo. Maggie and I are ready to roll, so let's get going."

****

When they got to the high school, Jeff was whisked away to prepare for the pre-game ceremonies, and Sam ran off to sit with her friends.

Even though they'd arrived early, the stands were packed, and Magda was surprised to realize she recognized almost every face in the crowd. A feeling of warmth suffused her as she realized that she could sit anywhere in this stadium and be with a friend. This

317

sense of belonging was new to her, and she liked it. She *really* liked it. When it was time to leave Rivers Bend, she would miss everyone else almost as much as she'd miss Jeff.

She took a deep breath and craned her neck to look for an open seat, when the air was pierced with a shrill whistle and Ty's voice hollered, "Maggie! Over here!"

She looked around to find him, and saw him waving frantically from a prime spot in the front row.

He grinned when he saw her notice him and cupped his hands to his mouth to yell, "I saved you a seat."

She wended her way through the crowd, exchanging greetings as she went. When she finally got to Ty, he lifted up the leather jacket from the seat next to him and patted the spot where it had been in invitation.

"I was saving space for you and Jeff—when he's done with his 'favorite son' duties. I had to fight off hordes of people, so you may express suitable gratitude now." He waved his hand imperiously before shrugging into his bomber jacket.

She smiled as she sat in the seat next to his, "Thank you."

He bumped her shoulder with his. "Nice jacket. Jeff's?" His tone was incredulous.

She turned to look at him with a puzzled smile. "Yes, it's Jeff's jacket from high school. Why do you sound so surprised?"

"Back in high school, we were pretty much the only two guys on the team who never gave their jacket to a girl: me, for obvious reasons, and Jeff because he was afraid it would give a girl ideas."

"Ideas?"

"He thought she'd read too much into it."

"Really?"

"Yeah—Jeff was a hot ticket back in the day. All the girls wanted him, and he dated his fair share of them, but he was always really focused on getting into college and playing football, so he never let things get too serious, and at Rivers Bend High, nothing was more serious than giving a girl your jacket."

"Wow. Lucky for me he got over that phobia," she joked.

Ty turned to her, his eyes serious. "Maybe he just finally met the girl he thought was worthy of it."

The crackle of the loudspeaker interrupted their conversation as the team was announced and took the field.

Magda rose with everyone else and put her hand over her heart for the singing of the National Anthem. She recognized the girl who was at the microphone singing. She was a regular library patron and was always shy, serious, and sweet in her interactions with Magda, so she was stunned by the girl's full, rich voice. The hair on Magda's arms rose at the beauty of the sound. All too soon, the song was over and the coaches and captains of the two teams joined Jeff at center field for the coin toss.

Magda stood on tiptoes to get a better look and heard Ty chuckle beside her.

"I'm glad to see that you have it just as bad for Jeff as he has it for you, Jacket-worthy Girl."

She felt her face heat up. "What? I was interested in the toss. I really want Rivers Bend to win it."

"Oh, you really want something all right, but it's

not the coin toss," Ty smirked.

The crowd fell silent as Jeff flipped the coin and then roared as Jeff's voice announced over the P.A. system, "Heads! Rivers Bend wins the toss and will receive."

Magda jumped up and down and hooted with everyone else on the Rivers Bend side of the field, as Jeff shook hands with the coaches and fist bumped his nephew, before Craig snapped on his helmet.

Jeff waved to the crowd, who responded with an affectionate and enthusiastic cheer as he jogged over to Ty and Magda.

He called out when he got close enough for them to hear, "Y'all save a seat for me?"

"We can squeeze you in," Ty responded.

"I can think of a way to make space," Jeff grinned as he sat down and pulled Magda onto his lap and pressed a noisy kiss to her cheek.

"Woo…."A group of high school kids sitting behind them called out, before they dissolved into laughter and smoochy noises.

Magda felt herself blush again, but the kickoff distracted everyone, and Jeff set her on her feet and stood to cheer on his old team.

****

Magda slouched against Jeff's big truck as she waited for him to finish speaking with the team in the locker room. Now that the sun had set, it was darned chilly in the high school parking lot, and she wished she had thought to ask for the keys, so she could have been sitting in the toasty warm cab of the truck. She shivered and wrapped Jeff's jacket even tighter around her— luckily it was big enough on her that it functioned like a blanket.

She exhaled and saw a puff of air, like smoke, in front of her face. She smiled as it brought back the happy memory of waiting at the bus stop with the other neighborhood kids on winter mornings and attempting to make smoke rings with their breath. She made her mouth into a perfect "O" and breathed out, pleased beyond measure as a ring floated out toward the orange fluorescent lights, which illuminated the parking lot with their eerie glow. She'd always been the best smoke ring breather at the bus stop, and apparently, she still had it. She'd enjoyed elementary school—she'd been a little bashful, so she wasn't part of the popular crowd, but she had friends and the other kids hadn't clued into the fact yet that her grandmother was richer than Croesus. Once that realization came—when she was just about Sam's age—the other kids started to treat her differently. Some pulled away, intimidated by her grandmother's wealth, while others started to cozy up to her in the hopes that she'd share the wealth.

She was jerked back into the present by the click of heels on the pavement and peered into the night to see who was approaching. She took a deep, fortifying breath when she realized it was Hadley's mother, Gloria Peterson. Ugh! The one person in Rivers Bend that she didn't like—and boy would Gloria be disappointed that Jeff wasn't the one by his truck.

"Halloo!" Gloria trilled.

"Hi Gloria," Magda replied without enthusiasm.

"Has Jeff abandoned you, you poor thing?" Gloria asked with a sympathetic moue, but hope flared in her eyes.

"The coach asked him to speak to the boys—

congratulate them on their big win. He should be out soon. It was an exciting game, wasn't it?"

Gloria shrugged, without Jeff here to impress, she apparently wouldn't even feign interest in the game. "I guess. I didn't come to watch the game. I came to watch Jeff, but he only had eyes for you."

Magda didn't know whether to feel annoyed with, or sorry for Gloria, until the woman spoke again and swung her firmly into the annoyed with camp.

"I couldn't figure out what he saw in *you*," she squinted at Magda as if she were regarding an especially unpleasant specimen under a microscope. "And then the whole hostage-taking thing happened to you."

Magda wrinkled her brow in confusion. "Do you mean when my ex-fiancé…"

Gloria interrupted avidly, "Your ex-fiancé—*Pierce Allen*!"

"Yes, that's his name, but I don't know that I was exactly a hostage…"

Gloria interrupted again as she waved her hand in a graceful, but clearly dismissive gesture. "Potato, potahto—hostage or not—my point is that you were engaged to *Pierce Allen*. It was the talk of the last cocktail party I went to in D.C., and I learned that your grandmother is Elizabeth Mallory!"

Magda lifted one shoulder. "Yes, she is my grandmother, but I don't understand what any of this has to do with Jeff and me."

"It made me understand your appeal to him, and it made me realize that you and I can be such *dear* friends."

Magda sighed, it was just like junior high all over

again—one of the social-climbing popular girls wanted to be her "friend" and hitch her wagon to the Mallory star.

"My grandmother is *so* not the reason Jeff is dating me, Gloria, if anything, I'd say he's dating me in *spite* of her. And as far as you and I being friends, I don't think so, but thanks."

Gloria clasped her hands to her bosom, her beautiful face crumpled as she pleaded in dismay, "Why ever not? We must have so much in common."

One side of Magda's mouth quirked up, "Let's see if you feel the same way after I tell you something that isn't common knowledge right now."

Gloria reached out to grip Magda's arms. "Of course dear, you can tell me anything at all—that's what I mean—you and I are so simpatico."

"My grandmother and I are estranged—we have been most of my life, but this time I don't see us reconciling. I tried the whole New York society thing to please her, and I learned it's not for me. So anyone who wants to be friends with me as a way to get "in" with my grandmother's set is doomed to disappointment. And I'm thinking of following Jeff's example and devoting a good portion of my trust fund to charitable causes."

Gloria frowned, and it marred her lovely features almost as much as her ugly words, "What a stupid girl you are—to throw all that away to be a small town librarian. You're right—I don't think we can be friends."

Magda rolled her eyes and Gloria was spared her response by Jeff's voice as it boomed across the almost empty parking lot, "Hey Maggie, darlin', are you still here or did you give up on me and run off with Ty?"

"I'm still here," Magda called out.

"And so am I!" Gloria chirped, once again full of false cheer now that Jeff was here.

"Oh. Hi Gloria. What's up? Where are the girls? I thought they were with you. Sam said you'd be giving them a ride back to your house after the game," Jeff said with a frown, as he stepped up between the two women.

Gloria ran one scarlet talon up his arm and purred. "They're waiting in my car. I offered to find you to get Sam's overnight bag."

Magda smothered a snort, she'd just bet that Gloria offered to find Jeff—jumped at the chance was more like it.

Jeff twisted subtly away from Gloria's clutches and pulled a chilly Magda into the warmth of his side. He reached in the pocket of his jeans with his free hand and pulled out his car keys and then unlocked the truck with a click of the fob.

"We don't want to hold you up, then. Let me get Sam's bag and you can get back to the girls."

He bent over to reach across the back seat for the duffle bag, and Magda clenched her fists in the long sleeves of the letterman jacket to keep from popping Gloria in the kisser when the woman actually licked her lips as she stared transfixed at Jeff's ass.

Jeff handed her the Hello Kitty overnight bag. "Here you go, Gloria," he hugged Magda's back to his front and presented them as a team to the other woman, who bristled at the sight. He continued, "We'll pick Sam up tomorrow morning at ten."

A glimpse of what Magda knew to be Gloria's true

face flickered in orange glow of the parking lot lights, before she schooled her features back into their normal flirtatious mode. "How lovely, Jeff, you know you're welcome in my home whenever you want to come."

She winked—actually *winked*—as she tossed the last word over her shoulder and sashayed to her car, which was parked on the other side of the lot.

"Subtle," Maggie observed in a sarcastic tone.

"Subtlety is *not* Glo's strong suit." Jeff chuckled.

The gentle amusement in his chuckle chilled Magda more than the November night. It put a horrible thought in her head, and she twisted in his arms to face him, her face solemn. "Promise me something?"

"Anything, darlin', I'd give you the world in a box if I could." Jeff's smile was quizzical.

She took a deep breath and blurted out, "When I leave Rivers Bend, *please* do not date that woman. She's a grasping piranha, and you can do so much better than Gloria."

Jeff pulled her tight against him, and it felt warm and safe. Home. She turned her head to rub her cheek against his broad chest. He rested his chin on top of her curly head.

"I don't know if I deserve better, but I've already got the best woman in Virginia right here in my arms— why would I trade down for Gloria?"

"Because when I leave, there's not a doubt in my mind that Gloria is going to put the full court press on you. And she's so beautiful on the outside, and when she's with you she hides the ugliness underneath…"

"I see it, Maggie, don't worry. I see the real Gloria, and I wasn't interested in her before you came to town, and I won't be interested in her if—when—you leave.

No pressure, I understand and respect your need to work and not be a lady of leisure, but I'm not going to get over you like that," he snapped his fingers behind her back, before rubbing her neck under her hair with surprising gentleness in his strong hands. "I don't see myself being in a relationship with anyone but you. Especially not with a man-eater like Gloria."

Magda felt torn and a little ashamed of herself for feeling that way. She knew that Jeff didn't want her to leave, and she wanted him to be happy, but a huge part of her loathed the idea of Jeff with another woman. The rational part of her brain understood that she was the one choosing to leave to pursue her career, and it wasn't fair to expect him to never, ever date another woman, but the idea of it made her shiver, and it had nothing to do with the cold.

Jeff misinterpreted her tremble and said, "We need to get you somewhere warm. You're chilled through, and we've got a big, cozy house all to ourselves for the whole night. Come to think of it—why are we wasting time in the high school parking lot?" He waggled his eyebrows and grinned. "Unless you have another secret high school fantasy I can fulfill—maybe involving making out in my truck after the big game? It's a little too cold to go under the bleachers, which was the spot of choice for canoodling when I went to school here."

His words made Maggie smile. "Canoodling? What are you ninety years old?"

"Hey—I'm not that much older than you!" He kept his arms around her and steered her toward the passenger side of his truck.

"Central heating wins out—I choose indoor canoodling tonight," she decided with a brisk nod.

Jeff opened the door and lifted her in. She turned her head and was now at eye level with Jeff as he leaned in, which made it easy to see the heat in his eyes. His teasing tone of voice and casual stance belied the passion she saw there. One thing she'd learned about Jeff was that he had a lot more depth than the world-at-large gave him credit for possessing. He always seemed laid back, but he was extremely intelligent and was always aware of everything going on around him.

And at the moment, all that concentrated focus was aimed at her. Lucky, lucky her. She trembled a bit at the delicious promise of a whole night alone with Jeff in the house, with her as the focus of all that sensual attention.

His lips tilted up, "You're really cold—let's get you home."

He ducked his head in to kiss her, and cold was the last thing she was feeling as the heat of his lips met hers, and his big hands framed her face.

They were both breathing hard, the puffs of air drifting into the night, when he pulled back with a show of great reluctance and cleared his throat. "Like I said, let me get you home and warm you up. We can save the outdoor canoodling for baseball season, when the weather's a little more cooperative."

He shut the door and skimmed around the front of the truck.

Magda stared straight ahead and felt her chest tighten. It all sounded good—except she wouldn't be in Rivers Bend for baseball season canoodling. Heck, she wouldn't even be here for all of *hockey* season canoodling.

Jeff opened his door and got in. He cupped his

hands over his mouth and breathed into them, before rubbing them briskly together. He started up the truck and fiddled with the controls on the dashboard to get the heater cranked up and then aimed all the vents at Magda.

He grinned at her in that sexy way that always stopped her heart, and Magda decided to give in to the fantasy that something miraculous would happen and she'd be able to stay in Rivers Bend with things just the way they were right now. Canoodling with Jeff through all the sports seasons.

She snapped her seat belt into place. "Sounds good to me. Let's head home."

Chapter 23

The delicious aroma of roasting turkey filled Jeff's kitchen. Already overflowing with casually dressed Bradens, Magda heard a cheerful voice call, "Knock! Knock!"

Heather kicked the back door open with one of her Ugg clad feet, as her arms were otherwise occupied with lugging a case of champagne.

"I can't cook for beans, but here's my contribution to the Thanksgiving dinner," she announced cheerfully as she plopped the cardboard carton on the counter and hugged Magda.

The kitchen was hot from the cooking and the body heat of all the people who refused to vacate it for the comfort of the family room and possibly miss some fun, so Heather's cheek, cold from the outdoors, felt heavenly against Maggie's warm one.

Cheerful greetings flew from every corner of the kitchen and Jason pulled a bottle from the case. "Pre-chilled! Good work, sis. Who's in?"

He popped the cork to delighted squeals and a babble of voices clamoring for glasses of the bubbly.

Jeff stepped up behind Magda and wrapped his arms around her middle. He leaned down to whisper in her ear, which tickled and caused a heat completely unrelated to the hot kitchen. "You're looking a little shell-shocked—is the Braden clan too much for you?"

She snuggled back into his embrace with a delighted smile. "No way—I'm loving it! I've never had a Thanksgiving like this one before. Most of my life it was just Dad and me, so it was really quiet. And the couple of times I spent the day with my grandmother it was way more…"

"Dignified?" he suggested with a chuckle.

"Cold," she corrected. "Not so full of noise, people, food—love."

Jason handed her a juice glass full of champagne. "Sorry, Mags, we ran out of the fancy glasses."

"Thanks—this is perfect," she twisted her neck to smile up at Jeff. "This is *all* perfect. Thanks for including me in your family's celebration."

"Where else would you be, darlin'?"

She cocked her head as she pondered his question. Nowhere. There was nowhere else she would rather be and no one else she would rather be with than Jeff and his boisterous family. She took a sip of her champagne and the bubbles tickled her nose.

She hadn't screwed up her courage yet to tell Jeff that she'd heard from Illinois yesterday and they'd offered her the job. She asked them for the long holiday weekend to consider their offer, but nothing else had come up, and Bethanne's due date was drawing near, so it was her only employment option. Barring a miracle this weekend, she'd be saying "yes"—reluctantly—to their offer on Monday.

"You've gone all quiet. Is the champagne that bad?" Jeff asked.

"No, it's yummy, I was just taking it all in."

"Hey Maggie," Jeff's mother yelled to be heard over all the conversations taking place at once. "How are you at peeling potatoes?"

"I'm a pro." Maggie laughed.

"Then come on over here and give me a hand. I think Mrs. Wilson bought every potato in Idaho for this meal!"

She twisted out of Jeff's embrace, when he jokingly acted like he wouldn't let her go. She squeezed between talking and laughing Bradens, until she got to the sink where Joyce was elbows deep in potatoes.

"That's a lot of spuds," she observed with a laugh in her voice.

"It's a lot of Bradens," Joyce joked as she handed her a peeler. "I'm so happy you're with us this year, Maggie, you fit right in with my crazy brood."

Jason squeezed in behind her to plunk a glass of champagne on the granite counter next to his mother. "I'm not sure that's a compliment, Mags," he winked and moved on to give Mrs. Wilson an old jelly jar filled to the brim with champagne.

Joyce bumped hips companionably with her as they peeled. "I'm uncommonly proud of all my kids, and I love having you with us—I meant it as a compliment."

Magda wished they were chopping onions instead of peeling potatoes, so she could explain away the tears that stung her eyes at Joyce's kind words.

Her voice was thick, "Thanks, Joyce, I love being here. It's the best Thanksgiving I've had since my dad passed away."

"The Pintos game's on in five minutes!" Hank hollered from the hall.

A rush of Bradens grabbed snacks and drinks and poured toward him.

Ty's voice sounded from behind Hank, as if he had

come in the front door instead of the back, "Hey everyone, make way—we've got a visitor. I found her out front when I pulled in. Y'all must have been making too much of a ruckus to hear her knock."

The Bradens parted like the Red Sea to let Ty and the mysterious visitor in the kitchen.

Magda and Joyce both looked over their shoulders with open curiosity to see who it might be. When Magda saw who it was, she dropped both the potato and the peeler, which landed in the sink with a thump and a clatter.

"Hello, Elizabeth," her grandmother said.

****

Jeff looked between the petite, elegant lady and Maggie as if he were watching a match at Wimbledon.

"Grandmother. What are you doing here?"

Maggie's voice sounded small and dull, and Jeff felt his heart wrench in his chest for her. He couldn't believe his warm, wonderful Maggie was related to this ice queen. And the way Mrs. Mallory's lips curled in distaste, as she looked Maggie up and down made him want to kick the immaculately dressed old biddy the hell out of his house. He thought Maggie looked perfect in her tight jeans and his Pintos jersey, which she wore to honor his old team during their big Thanksgiving Day game today.

He realized that the rest of the room had fallen silent as everyone stared at Mrs. Mallory as if she'd just landed from Mars and said "take me to your leader."

His mom recovered first and dried her hands briskly on a towel, which she then tossed on the counter. She advanced with a smile on her face and her hand extended. "You're Maggie's grandmother—how lovely you could join us for the holiday—I'm Joyce Braden."

You could barely call what Mrs. Mallory's lips did a smile, as she hesitated before offering Joyce a quick, limp handshake. "Hello, Mrs. Braden. Thank you for your kind welcome, since my *Elizabeth*," She emphasized the name to correct Joyce, "seems to have lost her manners."

Joyce frowned; it went against all Virginia protocol to be rude to a guest, but Jeff could tell his mom didn't like Mrs. Mallory picking on Maggie.

"Well, I don't know that I agree with you, ma'am, I think Maggie is a lovely girl."

Her defense seemed to unfreeze Maggie, who stepped up next to Joyce and linked arms with her. "Thank you, Joyce. I appreciate your kindness and acceptance more than I could say."

Joyce kissed her cheek and he saw Maggie's grip on his mom's tighten. Seeing her nerves finally unstuck his feet, and he planted himself firmly at Maggie's other side. He took her hand, which felt like ice, and offered his other to Mrs. Mallory. "Hi there. I'm Jefferson Braden. Welcome to my home. Happy Thanksgiving."

Jeff received the same disdainful shake his mother had.

"You still haven't answered me, Grandmother, what are you doing here? And please don't make another crack about my manners because in my opinion, showing up uninvited on Thanksgiving is a far worse offense."

Her voice was still quiet, but it sounded like steel and Jeff gave her hand an approving squeeze.

Jason barked out a laugh at her reprimand, which he covered up by pretending to cough when Elizabeth Mallory turned her icy gaze to him.

"Champagne, ma'am?" Jason held up the bottle with a disarming smile.

"Sparkling wine," Mrs. Mallory corrected with an imperious sniff.

Okay. Jeff had just about reached his limit with this woman. "Pardon me?" he asked with a coldness to rival the old lady's.

She pivoted her head and Jeff felt like a poor little field mouse that a hawk had just gotten in her sights.

"It's sparkling wine. Champagne comes only from France—and that is *not* French."

As her words fell like stones into the silent kitchen, Mrs. Mallory turned her attention back to Magda. "To answer your repeated question, Elizabeth, about why I am here. I'm here to bring you home."

Jeff had become very attuned to Maggie's body in the last few months, and right now it vibrated with anger and barely suppressed tension. He rubbed a soothing circle on her soft palm, with his work-calloused thumb.

The response to Mrs. Mallory's declaration came from a most unexpected source—his normally taciturn brother-in-law, who leaned against the counter. Hank's weathered face looked even more stoic than it usually did, and in his plaid flannel shirt, jeans, and cowboy boots, he looked like a gunslinger about to have a showdown. Jeff squinted as he peered at Hank—did he even have a toothpick clenched between his teeth?

Hank's voice was a deep rumble as he stated, "It looks very much to me—*ma'am*—that Maggie is already home. Here. With the people who love her."

Direct hit. Mrs. Mallory actually took a step back as if he had struck her before quickly regaining her composure.

Jeff felt Maggie's neatly trimmed fingernails dig into his palm as she clenched his hand and turned her head to flash Hank a grateful smile.

She kept smiling at Hank, not bothering to turn her head when she spoke to Mrs. Mallory. "Hank's right, Grandmother, I *am* already home. So, if that's the only reason you came to Rivers Bend, I'm afraid you wasted the trip."

****

Maggie realized the rest of the Braden clan had taken their cue from Hank, when they closed ranks around her, both literally and figuratively. As they surrounded her, she realized they were making a point of including her in their family unit and their support helped put even more steel in her spine.

Sam scooted in front of her and Jeff and they each put a protective hand on the child's shoulders. It occurred to her that they looked like they were both Sam's parents in this position, and her grandmother's eyes widened fractionally at the sight. From Elizabeth Mallory that small gesture was the equivalent of a normal person shouting in outrage.

"Elizabeth, I would like to speak to you in private."

As Magda took a breath to respond, a loud electronic bloop filled the silence.

"That's me," Ty said apologetically as he fumbled in the pocket of his jeans to pull out his phone. "Oh my God! It's a text from Cisco. Looks like my little nephew decided he wants to join us for Thanksgiving!

Bethanne's just been admitted to the hospital. I've got to get there. Sorry, Maggie, wish I could stay for you."

"No worries, I understand—of course you have to go."

"I'll take you," Heather said with alacrity.

"My car's here," Ty responded.

Heather grabbed one of his shaking hands and held it up, with a wry smile as she said, "You're too flipped out to drive. Consider me your personal chauffeur for the day."

Mrs. Wilson's voice rose above the ensuing babble, "All of you—go! I'll keep an eye on dinner. When the little one is safely here, y'all come back for a true Thanksgiving celebration."

As everyone grabbed their coats and keys and ran for the door, Mrs. Mallory asked in a perplexed voice, "She's not the first woman to give birth, why do you all have to go?"

Sam looked at the older woman for a beat, like one might at an exotic animal at a zoo, before answering solemnly, "Because that's what family does."

****

Way to put the old bat in her place, Jeff thought with an unholy glee that would certainly not be a Dr. Spock-approved child-rearing technique.

Mrs. Wilson stepped onto the back porch with Petunia to wave everyone off, which left only Jeff, Magda, Mrs. Mallory, and Sam in the kitchen.

He felt a shiver of unease dance up his spine at the way the old lady was looking at his daughter.

Evidently, Maggie wasn't all that crazy about it either because her voice was sharper than he'd ever heard it sound, "Sam is one-hundred percent correct,

Grandmother. We all have something we need to do that cannot wait. You, on the other hand, *can* wait. You may call me when you get back to New York, and we'll discuss whatever it is you came here to say at that time."

Mrs. Mallory's eyes flashed, but her voice remained in control—freakishly calm. She was one scary son of a bitch and Jeff admired Maggie even more than usual, for her bravery in facing down the dragon.

"Sam? Would that be Samantha Braden—daughter of Jefferson and Crystal Braden?"

Jeff felt a wave of coldness wash down his body from the top of his head to the tips of his toes when Mrs. Mallory brought up Crystal. Why hadn't he taken Maggie's advice and spoken to Sam about it before now? She wouldn't—*couldn't*—reveal the truth about her mother's death to Sam before he had the opportunity to do so—could she?

"That's me," Sam jutted her little chin out and tugged at Maggie's hand in an effort to get her moving toward the door. "And if you'll excuse us please, ma'am, we need to get to the hospital."

Mrs. Mallory's icy gaze raked over the child. "As your own mother chose to abandon you to run off with another man when you were an infant, I can see where you would want to turn *my* granddaughter into a mother-figure, but I'm afraid that Elizabeth is coming back to New York with me. So, you'll just have to look elsewhere for your surrogate mother."

Jeff felt all the blood drain from his face, and the champagne churned in his stomach as he looked at his beloved child's stricken face. Brave little Peanut, her face crumpled, but she struggled valiantly not to cry in front of this vicious monster.

"You're lying," the little girl said in a small voice. "Tell her, Daddy."

Jeff's eyes felt like cocktail onions as he fought back tears of sorrow for Sam and rage at Old Woman Mallory. "Oh Peanut, I'm so sorry…" His voice broke as he saw his daughter deflate like a punctured balloon before turning heel and running up the back stairs to the second floor.

Maggie's voice shook with so much fury that Jeff was surprised steam wasn't rising off her head. "You horrible, *horrible* old woman! How could you do that to an innocent child?

If Mrs. Mallory was cowed by her granddaughter's anger, she gave no sign of it. She lifted one shoulder with casual disregard. "*I* needed to speak with you alone, and *she* was sticking to you like a limpet. What else could I do to get her to leave?"

Maggie's face drained of all color except for two circles of red on her cheeks. Her hands were clenched into fists, and Jeff realized if she was aiming to punch Mrs. M., he would do nothing to stop her.

"Oh, I don't know." Her tight voice was brittle and laced with sarcasm. "Maybe you could say 'I need to speak to my granddaughter in private—would you mind giving us a few moments alone?' Something— *anything*—other than bringing a little girl's world crashing down around her ears? And now—*now*—you expect me to have a civil conversation with you? I'm going upstairs to try to comfort a child I love like she's my own, and when I come back downstairs you better be the hell out of our house and well on your way back to New York."

Our house. Jeff liked the sound of that a lot—even in the midst of his current state of emotional turmoil. Maggie thought of it as *their* house.

"Elizabeth," her grandmother implored, seeming to finally appreciate the gravity of her miscalculation.

"Magda!" she screamed. "My name is *Magda*! I realize it's too ethnic for your taste, but stop calling me by my mother's name—by your name! I'm not you! I'll never be you."

And with that heartfelt declaration, she ran up the stairs calling his daughter's name.

"I've got to second her feelings on you getting the hell out of our home. You'll have to excuse my bad manners, but I save the good ones for human beings."

Her eyes narrowed. "Aren't you at all curious as to *how* I knew about your late wife? Didn't it occur to you that my granddaughter told me—that she shared with me information you had given her in confidence?"

"No, because I know your granddaughter a helluva lot better than you do. And the woman has more honor in her little toe than you have in your entire body—she would never betray a confidence. Now. Get. Out. Of. My. House. Before I call my good friend, Sheriff Monroe, to forcibly remove you."

Mrs. Mallory gasped. "I will leave, but don't think this is over young man, because it most certainly is not."

Jeff actually laughed, although it was a harsh and humorless rasp. "If you think you've left yourself with any hope of a relationship with Maggie, you're as crazy as you are nasty. I hate to be the one to tell you this, Mrs. Mallory—oh wait, no I don't, I kind of *love* being the one to tell you this—it most certainly is over for you. I'll never let you hurt my daughter or Maggie again. Are we perfectly clear?"

Chapter 24

Magda ran straight to Sam's room but stopped dead in the open doorway at the sight of the completely empty room. She raised her voice, which sounded more than a little desperate even to her own ears. "Sam, honey, where are you?"

A brief, muffled yip answered from behind the closed closet door. If Petunia was in there, it was a safe bet that Sam was too. She crossed the room and tapped lightly on the door for admittance.

"Is *he* with you?" Sam's tear-choked voice asked.

"Your dad? No, I'm alone."

"Then you can come in."

Magda turned the handle to the walk-in closet and felt her heart squeeze in her chest at the sight of Sam's tear-stained face as the child huddled on the floor with Petunia clutched in her arms.

"Oh honey, I'm so sorry!" Magda dropped to the ground and pulled the girl and dog both into a tight embrace.

She rocked them gently and made soothing sounds as Sam's body wrenched with sobs. Sam hiccupped as she swallowed a sob. "Did you know?"

"I did."

"Tell me," the child demanded.

"I don't know a lot of details. I think you should talk to your dad about it." Magda's voice was soft and gentle.

"I don't wanna talk to him. He lied to me my whole life. He told me that my mom loved me."

"Oh baby, I'm sure she *did* love you. And I know for a fact that your dad loves you more than anything in the whole world."

Sam snorted. "Sure, that's why he never told me the truth."

"I may not know a lot about your mom, but I know your dad pretty well, and he didn't keep things from you to hurt you. He did it out of his love for you. He was trying to protect you."

"Yeah—that worked out great," Sam scoffed, but the tough attitude was betrayed by a watery sniffle.

"I'll agree—it didn't turn out great, but that doesn't change the fact that he did it because he loves you."

Sam shrugged and buried her face in Magda's shoulder, which muffled her voice, "I could hear you telling your grandmother off just now."

Magda smoothed the child's hair. "You could?"

"Well—yeah—you were really hollering."

"I was majorly angry with her—I still am."

"Did you mean what you said to her?" Sam's voice trembled.

Maggie creased her brow. "About her getting out and going back to New York without me? You better believe I meant it!"

"Not that—the part about…y'know…loving me like I was your own child."

Understanding dawned and Magda wrapped her arms a little tighter around the girl. "I never meant anything more. I love you Sam, and it's breaking my heart that you're sad, and it's all my fault."

"Actually, I believe it's all *my* fault," Jeff's deep voice rumbled from the door to the closet.

****

When Jeff saw them snuggled together on the closet floor, it was like the gears of his heart locked into place, and he was whole. These three females—Maggie, Sam, and Petunia—were his life. His family. His home. And somehow, he had to make things right for all of them.

"Maggie's right, Sam. I made a mistake—a *huge* one—by not telling you about your mom, but I thought I was doing right by you. I was trying to protect you because Peanut, you're my whole world. Please forgive me."

He detected a hint of softening in his daughter's mulish expression and tear-reddened eyes, but just the barest hint.

She sniffed loudly and said, "Will you answer all my questions?"

Jeff held up his hands in total acquiescence. "Absolutely. I'll tell you whatever you want to know. May I come in the closet with you? Because if I can't hug y'all soon, I'm gonna bust."

He saw a hint of Maggie's dimples for the first time since her grandmother had shown up, and his daughter nodded mutely as fresh tears leaked from her eyes.

He dropped to his knees beside them, and pulled his three best girls into his arms.

****

Elizabeth Mallory walked down the steps of Jeff Braden's home with her spine ramrod straight. She would not give in to the urge to slump her shoulders in dejection and rush to her limousine with her tail between her legs.

Ned Bellingham leapt out of the back and searched her face as if for some hint as to how her summit meeting had gone.

She gave the barest shake of her head to her chauffeur who had emerged from the front of the black limousine. The man slid back behind the wheel.

Ned also picked up on her non-verbal command and held the car door open for her. He followed her into the vehicle and sat in the seat facing her.

She pressed the intercom button to speak with the driver. "We'll be going back to New York now, Lewis."

"Yes ma'am," his voice replied through the speaker before the long car drove smoothly and noiselessly out of the driveway and away from her only link to the daughter she had lost in such similar circumstances thirty years before.

Ned didn't speak, for which she was grateful, but she knew they couldn't spend the entire trip back to Manhattan in silence.

Not entirely sure she could trust her voice not to betray the tears a lady would never shed in public, she delicately cleared her throat. "It did not go well, Ned. It appears Mr. Churchill—and you—were correct. Those who fail to learn from history are doomed to repeat it."

She watched Ned's expectant face fall and marveled at how the man seemed to genuinely like her. He might be the only person who did.

"Oh ma'am, I'm so terribly sorry."

She raised her chin a fraction. "I'm fine, Ned, but as you can see, my granddaughter has elected to remain in Virginia."

Ned appeared to be occupied with brushing non-existent lint from his immaculate trousers, but Elizabeth had known him long enough to know that he was avoiding meeting her eyes. Probably because he was about to ask a question he feared would overstep his bounds.

"If I might presume to ask—what happened?"

Ned's eyes widened as she recounted events and he reached for the crystal decanter of Scotch, and he poured a good measure into one of the matching glasses when she got to the part of the story where she revealed to Sam that her mother had abandoned her.

Her already guilty conscience stung at her secretary's unspoken disapproval of her actions. "How was I supposed to know her father had never told her? I assumed he had, because if he had done so the child would have turned her back on her mother's memory and bonded with her father. She would have been completely his."

Her voice held a note of wonder. Jeff could have had everything with his daughter that she'd wanted with her own. Yet he'd chosen a different path—why?

They hit a bump in the road and even the smooth-riding limousine jolted. Amber liquid sloshed in Ned's glass, and he hurriedly took a sip, so it wouldn't spill on the buttery-soft tan leather upholstery.

He swallowed with a gulp before he said, "He didn't have to do so—the child already adores him."

Mrs. Mallory blinked twice. "But why does she?"

Ned tilted his head to one side as if surprised by the need to explain Sam's affection for her father. "Because he loves her. In all the reports we've read from Mr.

345

Felder and all I've read online, there is every indication that he's devoted his entire life to the child. That sort of unconditional love and devotion inspired the girl to reciprocate."

Mrs. Mallory frowned. "Really? I'd never have thought that would work."

She turned her head to look out the window at the passing scenery. She preferred the city, but this was an attractive part of the world. And her granddaughter had never been comfortable living in the city. She could see why Elizab—*Magda*—might want to settle here. And if this Braden fellow did such a fine job loving his daughter, maybe he would love Magda with the same intensity.

Mrs. Mallory sighed. No one had ever loved her with that degree of passion. Her parents thought of her as an object to be displayed, and as she matured, a pawn to make an appropriate matrimonial alliance. There was nothing wrong with it—that's what happened with all the girls in her social circle at the time. And then her husband, chosen for her by her parents, treated in her in much the same way as her parents had. Mr. Mallory had been much older than she, and he wanted his wife to be a charming hostess for him. In truth, she was as much a showpiece as was their country home in Greenwich. Again, all the women she knew had the same sort of marriage, so if a tiny, secret part of her yearned for more, she squashed it.

When her daughter arrived, Mrs. Mallory raised her in the same way her parents had reared her—after all, she'd had the perfect life, by their standards. Didn't she? But, her daughter threw it all away for that son of immigrants: Tom Horvath. And now their child was doing the same thing. Why did no one take the same obedient, practical approach to life that she had at their age?

Ned's voice broke her out of her reverie, "What are you going to do now, ma'am?"

"To be frank, Ned, I don't have any idea what to do next."

And she realized it was the first time in her long life that she had ever uttered those words.

****

Maggie was the first to break the embrace. "I'm going to see if Mrs. Wilson needs help getting the food in order, and then I'm going to head over to the hospital."

"Do you know where it is?" Jeff asked with an amused tilt of his lips.

"Well…no…but I was trying to give you two a chance to talk in private."

A shrill ring sounded from the pocket of his jeans. It sounded like an old-fashioned telephone bell.

"Why do you have that obnoxious ringtone?" Sam asked with a dramatic eye roll.

Funny, but that typical tween impatience with her old man was what convinced Jeff that everything was going to be all right between them.

"What? It's old-school. I like it," he replied before answering his phone. "Hello. Oh, hi, Mom. What's happening? No, we're not in a ditch somewhere. Maggie, Sam and I are all fine. We're still at home. She is? Okay, we'll be there as soon as possible. Bye Mom—love you too."

Maggie looked at him, her eyes as wide as saucers. "Is Bethanne all right?"

He reached out to clasp her hand. "She's fine, but…"

"See, I don't like 'but,'" Maggie said.

"There is an issue with her blood pressure, so they want to do a C-section right away."

He felt Maggie's hand shake, and then his daughter snuggled closer and he realized she was scared for their friends too. "But they'll be okay, right Dad? The baby and Bethanne?"

He wasn't sure how to answer that question. Even his unflappable mother had sounded a little—well— *flapped* on the phone, but given what had just happened between them he didn't want to tell his daughter even the smallest untruth right now. "She's getting the best possible care; everyone at the hospital is going to do everything they can to keep them both safe and well."

Maggie jumped to her feet. "I'm going to get my shoes and go to the hospital. Mrs. Wilson can give me directions. You two—talk."

She bent down to kiss the tops of both their heads and then rushed out. Petunia squirmed out of Sam's arms and followed, her little nails tapping out a staccato beat on the oak floors.

"We should probably go too," Jeff said apologetically. "But I want to talk to you about your mom—answer any questions you have."

Sam bit her bottom lip. "I want to be at the hospital with everyone, so it's okay with me if we talk later. I'm too worried about Bethanne now to think of all the questions I have."

"Fair enough."

She looked up at him, her eyes troubled, which was like a punch in the gut to Jeff, knowing his actions had caused it.

"Would you tell me one thing before we go?"

"Of course, Peanut."

"Did my mom leave because of me?"

Jeff's lips formed a straight line and he shook his head. "No. She left because of me."

Sam knitted her brow and frowned at him. Disapproval radiated from her every pore. "Did you have a girlfriend?"

Jeff felt like she'd thrown a bucket of ice water on him. "What? No! Why would you think I had a girlfriend when I was married to your mom?"

She shrugged and screwed up her mouth. "That's why Hadley's mom left her dad."

Jeff scowled. "Well, it was most definitely not why your mom left me. Our life together just wasn't what she wanted. *I* couldn't give her everything she wanted, so she felt like she had to go somewhere else to find it. She had the accident on the night she left, Sam. There is no indication that she was leaving you forever—just me. She was still going to live in Portland, just not with us." He searched her face, "Do you understand the difference?"

Sam leaned back and stared at the ceiling as she thought. "I think so. You're saying she didn't 'abandon' me, like that awful woman said. You probably would've had custody of me, but I still would have visited her, like Hadley and her parents in reverse."

Jeff nodded. "That's what I think would have happened, but your mom passed away before anything could be worked out."

He sent up a silent prayer that God would forgive him that slight stretching of the truth. Crystal had given no sign about would happen next, but Jeff had always wanted to believe that she wouldn't have been able to leave her daughter without a backwards glance. Leaving him was another matter, and oddly, it hurt him less that she could leave him so cavalierly than the thought she could leave Sam.

Her next words showed Jeff that his daughter had been thinking about things just as hard as he had been—just different things.

"And that's why you don't want to pressure Maggie to stay with us. You're afraid she'll decide there's something more she wants in life and leave us like Mom did."

The phrase "out of the mouths of babes" had never been more apt. Jeff felt his jaw drop. Shut it with a click of his teeth and then felt it drop again.

"I hadn't thought of it that way before, Peanut, but you're absolutely right."

Chapter 25

Jeff and Sam skidded into the maternity waiting room at the hospital. He searched the familiar and well-loved faces of his family and friends until he located the one he was looking for: Maggie. She was wedged between his mother and Ty on one of those uncomfortable little sofas they always seemed to have in hospitals.

She held one of Ty's hands between both of hers and rubbed it as if she was trying to warm him up.

All heads jerked to stare at the door when they entered; clearly they were still waiting for word from the doctor.

He ran his hand through his hair. "Sorry, it's just us. No word yet?"

"No, man, and I'm going crazy! She's my baby sister, and there's nothing I can do to help her, and no one is telling us what the hell is going on back there..."

Maggie increased the pace of her rubbing as if it would somehow make everything all right, and Sam ran to Ty and threw her arms around his neck.

"She'll be okay. Daddy says the doctors are going to take the best care of her."

Jeff felt a lump in his throat that his daughter's faith in him had remained intact.

Ty hugged her back and a half-smile formed at his lips as he looked at Jeff over Sam's head. "If your dad says so, then it must be okay."

Maggie released his hand and came to Jeff's side. He hugged her to him with one arm as he asked, "Do your parents know what's going on? Do you want me to call them?"

Ty shook his head. "I already did. They were staying in South Carolina for Thanksgiving, since we thought there would be a little more time before the baby came, but they're on their way now. I don't even want to think about how many speeding tickets they're going to get today."

Sam sat on the seat Maggie had vacated and rested her head on Joyce's shoulder. "Where's Cisco?"

"He's in with Bethanne," Ty answered. "They'll let us know as soon as they can, but this waiting is killing me!"

Jason stood up and shook his legs to straighten the bottoms of his jeans over his boots. "I'm going to the cafeteria to get coffee for everyone. Peanut, wanna come with to help me carry it back? I'll get you a hot chocolate for your troubles."

Sam stood. "Sure, Uncle Jason."

Joyce moved into the chair Jason had left and indicated with her head for Jeff and Maggie to take the two places now open next to Ty.

It seemed like an eternity while they waited. Jason brought back enough coffee to give an entire army regiment the caffeine jitters, and they all drank down every drop, grateful to have an activity to occupy their time and attention.

Sam dozed off between Deidre and Hank, but everyone else was wide awake when the weary-looking doctor entered in his scrubs. A little cap covered his head and protective booties were stretched over his shoes to indicate he'd come right from the delivery room to them.

"It's a boy." He smiled. "But y'all knew that already. He's a little small, and he'll have to stay with us for a while, but he's a good, healthy boy."

A collective sigh of relief went around the room.

"And my sister?" Ty asked anxiously as he clutched Maggie's hand.

"She's fine, Ty, just fine," the doctor assured him. "A little weak, but we have her blood pressure stabilized, and she'll be right as rain and chasing your new little nephew around the house before you know it. But don't take my word for it, you can go in and see for yourself."

As they all rose, the doctor held up his hands to stop them. "Sorry folks, immediate family only right now. Y'all have to wait a little bit longer."

He clapped Ty on the back, and the two men left the waiting room.

Joyce stretched. "I'm going outside to call Bethanne's folks—they have to be out of their minds with worry—and Mrs. Wilson."

Jeff sat back down and pulled Maggie into his lap. "Looks like we're godparents."

She beamed. "That's right! We are! I never thought I'd be anyone's godmother, since I don't have much family."

Jeff gave her a quick kiss. "You do now, darlin'."

"God help you." Heather laughed. "You're part of Clan Braden now."

Maggie snuggled up to Jeff, and her curls felt like satin against his neck.

"That's fine by me," she said.

Except it wasn't, Jeff knew, not really. For now, she might think it was, but she wouldn't be happy long-term without useful work to occupy her time and energy. And if she realized that and left him the way Crystal had done, it would break his heart in a way Crystal's departure never did.

****

Magda inhaled the wonderful fresh air scent that was all man and all Jeff as she nuzzled his neck. She was so thankful that Bethanne and the baby were both fine. With the warm, solid comfort of sitting in Jeff's lap, his strong arms wrapped around her, she could ignore the speculative stares they got from his family as they waited until they could see Bethanne and baby Francisco.

While the birth was wonderful, blessed news, it also brought her one step closer to leaving Rivers Bend, which wasn't nearly as happy to contemplate as was the new little life that lay in his incubator down the hall.

Now that leaving seemed more real, Magda wasn't sure she'd be strong enough to do it. She tried to take a long, honest look at herself—would she be able to stay here, draining her savings and sponging off Jeff while she waited for her trust fund to kick in?

Perhaps, at first she could. She'd be so blissed out to be with Jeff, Sam, and all her new friends here in Rivers Bend that it would be fine. At first. But she didn't want to turn into a woman like Hadley's mother. And she'd seen plenty of them during her time in New York—women who were content to be provided for and serve as arm candy for their men, but that wasn't her.

Ty came back into the waiting room, evidence of

tears clung to his lashes. "He's beautiful."

Magda raised her head, but stayed cozy in Jeff's lap. "How's Bethanne?"

"She's asleep now, and I still can't tear Cisco away from her side. The doc says y'all can come back in the morning to see them. I'm going to stay until my folks get here, but y'all go home and have your Thanksgiving dinner. Thank you so much for being here for me."

Jeff nodded. "No problem, Ty. Jason and I will get your car back to the hospital for you."

He made the offer without hesitation. Magda loved the way he was always thinking of others.

"Thanks. I forgot that I left it at your house." Ty laughed.

Jeff grinned as he traced a slow circle on Magda's back and the warmth of his hand burned through the Pintos jersey she put on that morning in honor of the game. It seemed like a lifetime ago.

"You've had other things on your mind, Ty. Jason and I will bring it back after we eat—right, bro?"

Jason nodded. "No problemo, Ty. Just get some rest, man. You look like hell."

Magda left Jeff's lap with great reluctance. It had been really scary waiting for news of Bethanne and the baby, but the comfort of being surrounded by loved ones during times of stress was new to her, and it filled her with warmth.

She remembered the long hours she'd sat, alone, in hospital waiting rooms, anxiously awaiting news of her father and thought about how hard it would be to go back to that kind of solitude now that she knew something better existed.

But would Jeff and his family be worth the

sacrifice of her self-reliance and independence? Those two character traits had gotten her through some dark days, but would they still be enough in the future now that she'd experienced more?

She wrapped an arm around Sam, who had eased up beside her and rubbed the sleep from her eyes. She didn't know the answers to her questions right now and decided that while she was in the South to take a page out of Scarlett O'Hara's book and "think about it tomorrow."

****

Magda peeked around the massive balloon bouquet she carried into the hospital room.

"C'mon in," Bethanne's voice called. "I'm awake."

"I was afraid you'd still be asleep, it's so early, but I really wanted to see you and the baby before I open the library."

"He's in the nursery right now."

"I know—I stopped to look at him on my way to your room. I might be a little prejudiced, but I think my godson is the most beautiful baby ever born."

Bethanne laughed. "I don't think that's prejudiced at all. It sounds like a very informed opinion to me— one which I happen to share."

Magda tied the pastel balloons to the bottom frame of Bethanne's hospital bed and perched next to them at the foot of the bed, so that she faced her friend. "How are you feeling?"

"Sore, but happy. So unbelievably, amazingly, over-the-moon happy! And just between us, kind of scared. He's so tiny, and he needs Cisco and I so much—what if I mess up?"

Magda shook her head with an affectionate smile.

"There is no way you're going to mess up. You've been waiting to be a mom for such a long time—you're ready for it. I have every confidence in you."

Bethanne adjusted the thin blanket at her waist. "Have you heard from Illinois yet?"

Magda's brows drew together then she shrugged. "Kind of an abrupt change of subject, but okay. They called on Wednesday to offer me the job."

Bethanne's tired, but happy, face fell and she said in a half-hearted way. "Congratulations."

"Thanks, but I haven't accepted it yet."

Hope flared in Bethanne's eyes, which Magda didn't understand at all. Her friend had been the biggest cheerleader about this new job.

"You haven't? Why not?"

"I don't know. I think I'm just putting off the inevitable because I really don't want to leave Rivers Bend."

"Or Jeff."

"Or Jeff," Magda conceded as she fiddled with the strings on the balloons making them bob in the air. "But I don't have any other offers."

Bethanne took a deep breath. "You do now."

Her fidgeting hands stilled, and she slowly turned her head toward Bethanne. "I do? What do you mean?"

"We need to confirm it with the Mayor, but I had a great idea—if you're game, but why wouldn't you be game? I think it's brilliant, if I do say so myself; the solution to all our problems…"

Magda held up her hands. "Slow down. What are you talking about? The solution to all *our* problems? I know what mine are, but what problems are you having, and what can I do to help you?"

"Funny you should ask because you can help with my problem if you're willing, but if you want to go to Illinois…"

"I don't want to go anywhere. I want to stay in Rivers Bend, so if the plan that has you all nervous and rambling can keep me here, I'm all in, so calm down and explain."

Bethanne's eyes softened. "The minute—*the second*—I saw baby Francisco, I didn't see how I could leave him all day, every day, when my maternity leave is over. I know other people do it, but I love him so much, and he's so small and needs so much care. And running the library single-handedly requires a lot of time and energy…"

"Tell me about it! I've been whining to anyone who'll listen that I have no idea how you do it!"

"I love my work, and I don't want to leave it completely, which is how I came up with my plan: you and I run the library together."

"Like a job share?"

Bethanne nodded eagerly. "Exactly! We'd be co-directors. Each of us working part-time to provide one full-time librarian. And it wouldn't cost the town any more money than it pays right now. I can get my health benefits through Cisco and the Retreat, so you can get the benefits that go with the position. And our new house is almost ready, so you can move into our cottage on the Retreat grounds—it's perfect!"

Magda felt a lot like she had the time in second grade when she'd gotten the wind knocked out of her playing Red Rover during recess. Having all the answers to her prayers presented to her in this way, made her feel the same way she did back then, but this time it was pure joy that made it hard for her to catch her breath.

"You're too quiet—what are you thinking?" Bethanne prompted.

"I'm thinking that you're freaking brilliant! I'm in!"

****

Magda checked her watch for about the millionth time that morning. Jeff should be at the library soon for their daily lunch visit. She'd picked up the phone to call him to tell him about Bethanne's plan almost as many times as she'd looked at her watch, but she wanted to see his face when she told him.

Her head jerked up when the door opened with its familiar loud creak, but disappointment filled her heart when Mrs. Warren strode in. She forced a smile to her face. "Hello, Mrs. Warren."

The elderly woman smiled knowingly. "Hello Magda. Were you expecting someone else?"

Magda felt the blush creep from her neck up to cover her face and Mrs. Warren brayed, "Don't be embarrassed, child. If I were waiting on a fine-looking man like that Jefferson Braden to bring me my lunch, I'd be disappointed to see an old lady like me, too."

The door creaked open again, and this time it was Jeff, with a plain brown paper bag in his hand.

He walked right to the circulation desk, which he leaned across to kiss her soundly.

Mrs. Warren chuckled and called over her shoulder as she went to the New Fiction display, "That's what I'm talking about—of course, *I'd* be a disappointment."

Jeff smiled his crooked smile with a question in his eyes. "What is Mrs. Warren talking about?"

"Just an inside joke."

"You've won over the hearts of this entire town—you do know that don't you?"

Embarrassed, she reached for their lunch bag and ignored his question. "What did you bring today? It's not from the Nosh Pit."

"Nope. We have a special treat today: Mrs. Wilson's homemade Thanksgiving leftover sandwiches. They're like Thanksgiving dinner on a roll: turkey, cranberry, stuffing…" He smacked his lips.

Magda's stomach grumbled. It had been a long time since the cup of coffee and yogurt that she'd gulped down at the crack of dawn so that she'd have time to visit Bethanne before work.

"Sounds amazing—but I wanted to talk to you before we ate."

"Uh oh. Sounds serious."

"It is. I was offered the job in Illinois."

The bag crinkled as Jeff's hand tightened involuntarily on it. "Well, that's great, darlin', I'm really proud of you. When do you have to leave?"

She smiled at him. "I don't."

His intense gaze locked on to hers. "You don't? You turned it down?"

"I did."

"But I know how important it is for you to work, and I want you to be happy."

She licked her lips nervously. "I'll still be working. An offer came up much closer to home."

His eyes flashed with an almost desperate hope. "It did? Where is it?"

She patted the seat of the chair, next to her thigh. "Right here."

"What about Bethanne?"

"She wants to be able to spend more time with the baby, so we're going to be co-directors of the Rivers Bend Public Library. We talked to the Mayor about us sharing the job this morning, and he's all for it."

Jeff threw back his head and whooped, which drew the interested stares of all the library patrons. Oblivious to anything but her he asked, "You're staying?"

She nodded.

"Here in Rivers Bend?" he asked for clarification.

She laughed and nodded again.

He shoved through the swinging gate to get behind the circulation desk, where he picked her up and swung her in a circle. "Did y'all hear the news? Maggie's staying here in Rivers Bend!"

A cheer went up in the library, and Maggie was filled with a happiness and sense of belonging that she'd never dreamed she'd find when she got to town a few months ago.

Since Jeff held her up, she was eye level with him for a change, and in his eyes she saw all of her own emotions mirrored back at her: joy, surprise and a fair degree of desire.

"Okay, folks," Jeff called out without ever looking away from her eyes. "The library's closed for lunch. Now."

As the townsfolk chuckled and shuffled past them, Jeff added in a husky voice, "And we need a lot of time for lunch today. I'm feeling very hungry, like I want to really savor a long, slow lunch. Over and over again."

Mrs. Warren laughed. "It's been years—no, *decades*—since I enjoyed a long, slow lunch over and over again. Have fun, children."

Jeff grinned devilishly. "Oh we will, Mrs. Warren. Lock the door on your way out, will you, please?"

"Sure thing, Jefferson."

He waited until they heard Mrs. Warren pull the creaky door shut and the door lock click into place.

Jeff set her bottom on the circulation desk, and stepped between her thighs with intent.

"Jeff, we can't! Not here. Anyone could see through the front window—and you know Mrs. Warren is going straight to the Nosh Pit to spread the word about me staying in town."

He exhaled loudly. "You're right. Wait! I have an idea."

Magda squirmed. "It always makes me a little nervous when you get that gleam in your eye."

"Oh, you'll like this idea. When I was in high school, there was a spot right here in this library that was almost as popular for canoodling as under the bleachers."

"Really?"

"Uh huh," he turned and squatted down a bit. "Hop on."

"Like a piggyback ride? You're crazy!" She laughed, but scooted forward and hopped on nonetheless.

He locked his arms under her knees at his waist and said contemplatively as he walked by the non-fiction stacks and perused the signs, which indicated what Dewey Decimal classification numbers were down each row. When he got to the one labeled 400-499, he stopped.

"This is it."

"Yeah?" She asked skeptically as he walked to the

end of the aisle.

"Yep. These books never seemed to be real popular and this row ends in a wall, so you were almost always guaranteed privacy."

He released Magda and dropped her gently to her feet, before turning around and picking her up again so they were face to face. He sank down to the floor until he sat and Magda straddled his lap.

"Okay, that maneuver was a lot easier to do when I was seventeen."

She laughed and peered behind him with a frown. "Wow! You weren't kidding about these books not getting much use—look at how dusty they are! I need to ask Caitlin to come down this row to dust them off."

"If you're thinking about dusting, I'm doing this all wrong," Jeff said before he pressed his lips to that oh-so-sensitive spot where her neck met her shoulders.

Magda bit her bottom lip to keep from moaning out loud but threw back her head and arched her back in delight. The position pressed her core firmly against his hard body, and this time she couldn't hold back the low moan, which escaped her lips right before Jeff captured them in a passionate kiss.

After what could have been mere moments or hours—Jeff's drugging kiss caused Magda to lose all track of time—Jeff pulled away reluctantly. His head fell back against the books with a thud.

"Why are you stopping?"

"Because there's something I need to say before this goes any further. It's something I've been wanting to say for some time now, but I didn't want you to feel pressured by it."

He took a deep breath and continued, "I love you,

Magda Elizabeth Horvath. I love your intelligence, your innate honor, your wacky sense of humor. I love how you love my daughter. I love every last thing about you."

Her heart raced like a hummingbird's wings—no man had ever said those words to her before and meant them—and this wasn't just any man. It was Jeff. The man she'd fallen a little in love with the first time she saw him and she'd fallen deeper and deeper the more she got to know him.

She felt like her happiness must be surrounding her like a halo of light that all the world could see.

Home. She was home.

In a place she loved, with work she loved and did well, and a man she adored, who adored her right back.

"I love you, too, Jefferson Lee Braden, so very much! I'm actually a little frightened by how happy I am right now."

He kissed the tip of her nose gently. "Don't be scared, Maggie, none of it's going anywhere. Certainly not me. You're stuck with me for as long as you can stand having me around."

He flexed his hips to press the evidence of his love into her body, where she sat on his lap. "Now can I show you how much I love you?"

She looked around, as if to be sure no one was there. "I really want to—it just feels so odd to be doing this here in the 400 section. You are most definitely expanding my horizons, Mr. Braden."

He ground against her and said with a rakish grin, "Just you wait, Ms. Horvath, stick with me and I'll give you the whole world—right here in Rivers Bend."

A word from the author...

After years working in the business world, my love of reading led me to get my MLS, and I currently work part-time in a school library, a job which allows me lots of time to explore my other love—writing romance! I live in Maryland, with my husband, who is my real-life romance hero. We both enjoy traveling to visit our far-flung family and friends, and spending time on the beach with an umbrella drink and a good book.